W9-CYU-052

ISBN 978-1-4278-0632-1

9 781427 806321

50999

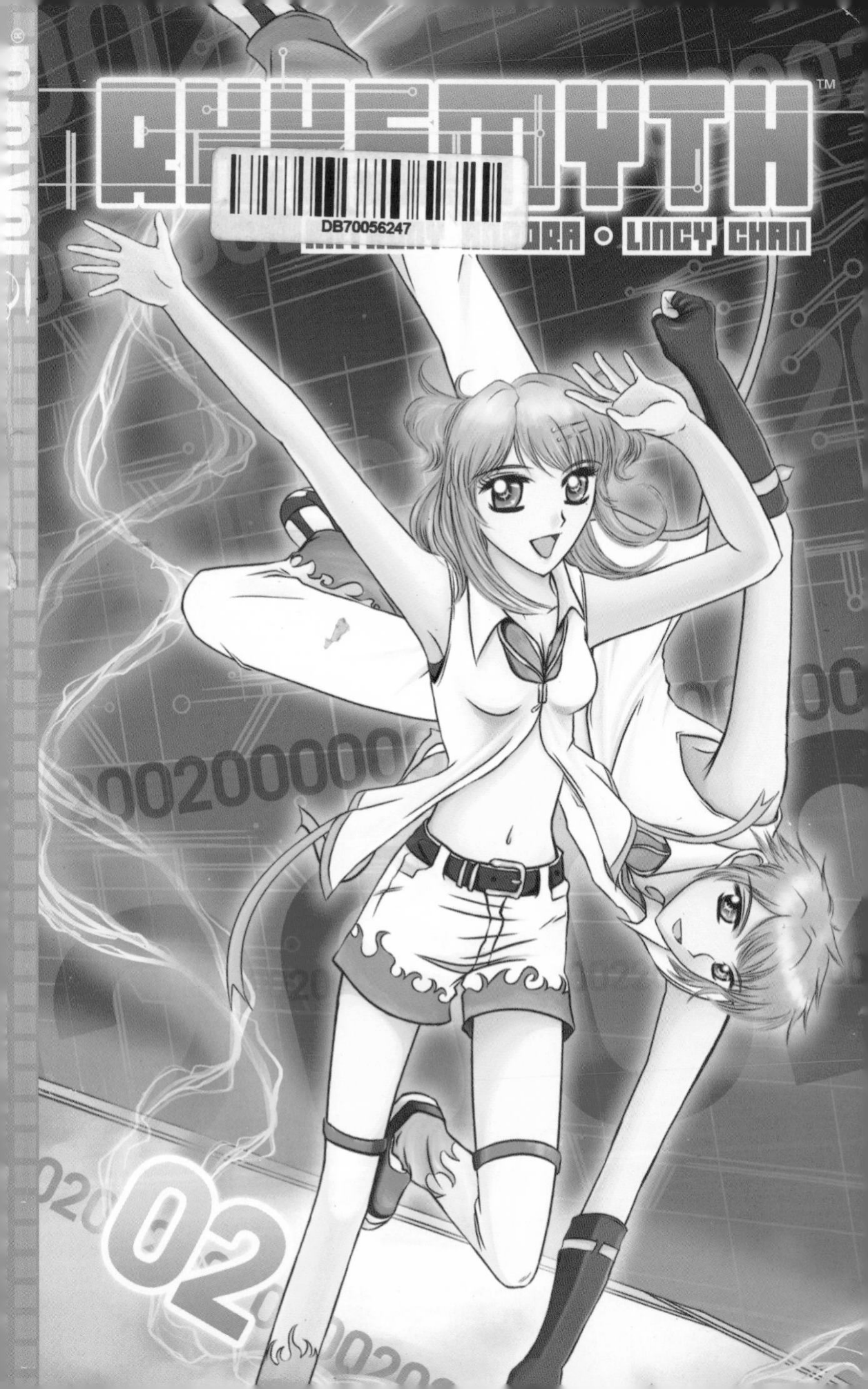
LINCY CHAN
02

Volume 2

Story by Anthony Andora
Art by Lincy Chan

HAMBURG // LONDON // LOS ANGELES // TOKYO

Rhysmyth Volume 2
Story by Anthony Andora
Art by Lincy Chan

Lettering - Lucas Rivera
Cover Design - Jose Macasocol, Jr.

Editor - Alexis Kirsch
Digital Imaging Manager - Chris Buford
Pre-Production Supervisor - Erika Terriquez
Production Manager - Elisabeth Brizzi
Managing Editor - Vy Nguyen
Creative Director - Anne Marie Horne
Editor-in-Chief - Rob Tokar
Publisher - Mike Kiley
President and C.O.O. - John Parker
C.E.O. and Chief Creative Officer - Stu Levy

A  Manga

TOKYOPOP and ⟡ are trademarks or registered trademarks of TOKYOPOP Inc.

TOKYOPOP Inc.
5900 Wilshire Blvd. Suite 2000
Los Angeles, CA 90036

E-mail: info@TOKYOPOP.com
Come visit us online at www.TOKYOPOP.com

© 2008 Anthony Andora, Lincy Chan and TOKYOPOP Inc.
All Rights Reserved.
"Rhysmyth" is a trademark of TOKYOPOP Inc.

All rights reserved. No portion of this book may be reproduced or transmitted in any form or by any means without written permission from the copyright holders. This manga is a work of fiction. Any resemblance to actual events or locales or persons, living or dead, is entirely coincidental.

ISBN: 978-1-4278-0632-1

First TOKYOPOP printing: May 2008
10 9 8 7 6 5 4 3 2 1
Printed in the USA

CONTENTS

LOADING>>>>>

RhysMyTh

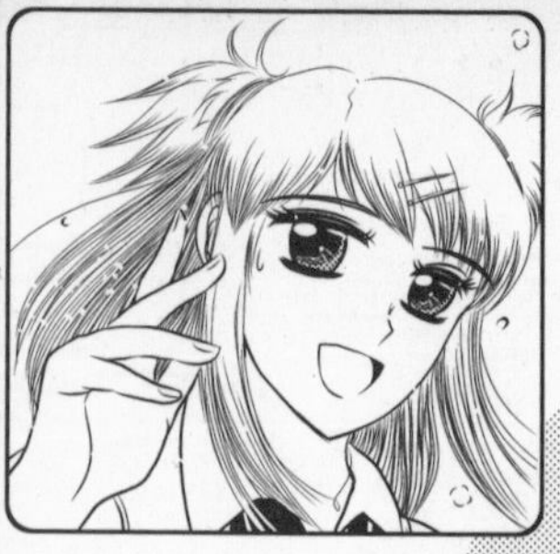

ELENA BOHDANA
Sophomore
Hair: Pink / Eye color: Blue / Height: 5'2"

Elena stumbled into the world of Rhysmyth looking for an extracurricular activity to call her own. Bumbling, kindhearted yet gutsy, she is starting to show signs of newfound self-confidence. Aided by Wahzee's training, Elena battles Taylor to determine who competes in the upcoming tournament.

WAHZEE ZAMEEL
Junior
Hair: Silver and Black / Eye color: Reddish Brown
Height: 5'10"

Unrivaled in his skill and passion for Rhysmyth, Wahzee was encouraged by the coach to take a chance on Elena. Training her in secret after an unintentional encounter, Wahzee now sees a hidden, unpolished gem that ultimately might help him accomplish his goal.

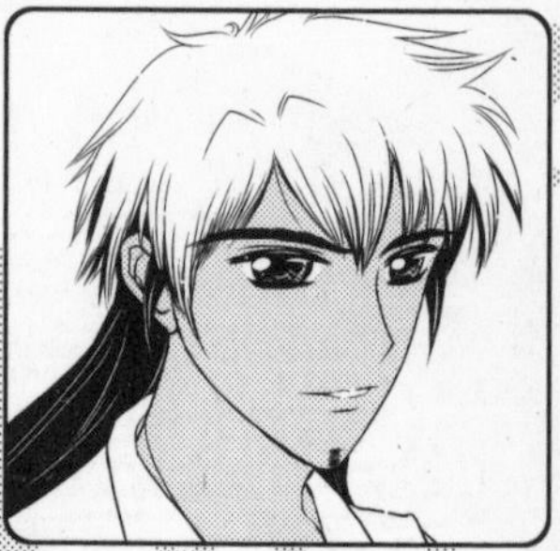

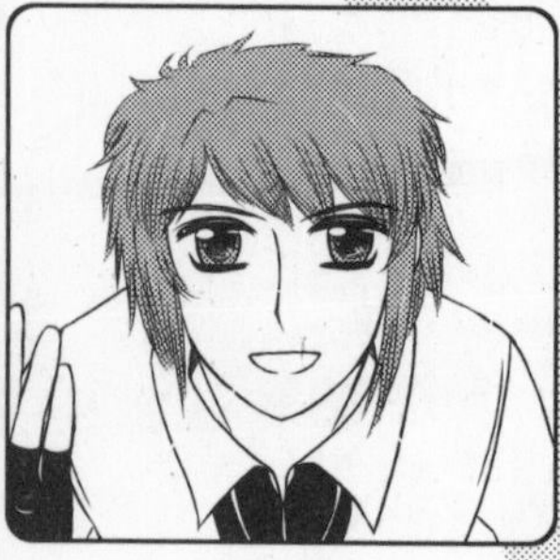

DIOCEL MANIBUSAN
Junior
Hair: Orange-Brown / Eye color: Brown / Height: 5'8"

Friendly and competitive, Diocel is eager to offer encouragement to Elena and quick to anger in battle against Wahzee. His hidden feelings for Elena add a new dynamic to his self-acknowledged rivalry with Wahzee.

TAYLOR HAMILTON
Sophomore
Hair: Blonde / Eye color: Blue / Height: 5'5"

Confident and sassy, Taylor has always viewed herself as the only girl who belongs on the Rhysmyth team. Elena's surprising tenacity forces her to go all out in their ongoing battle from volume 1.

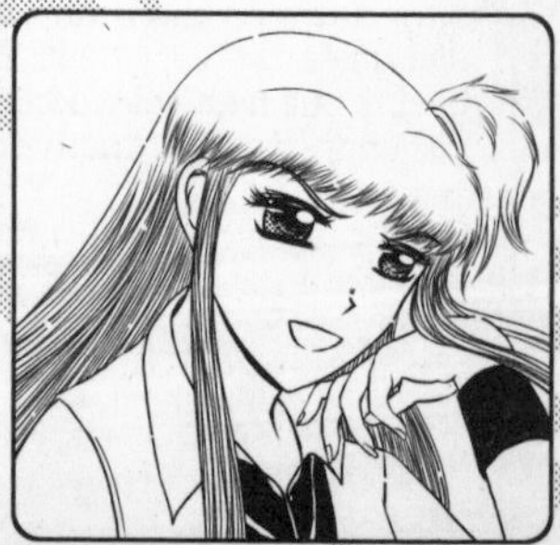

ANDREW LIU
Junior
Hair: Black / Eye color: Black / Height: 5'7"

Sweet and shy, Andrew helped Elena learn the ropes of Rhysmyth by dutifully performing his job as official team manager. He finds it easy to see the best in others, so the list of people he admires never stops growing.

TINA JOHNSON
Sophomore
Hair: Black / Eye color: Dark Brown / Height: 5'7"

Smart, witty and extremely loyal, Tina has been Elena's best friend for years and helps to balance Elena's extreme naivety.

COACH SHAKESPEARE WILLIAMS
Age: 30s
Hair: Purple / Eye color: Purple / Height: 5'9"

Affectionately known as Coach Shakes, he never fails to bring an attitude of joyful exuberance to all Rhysmyth team practices and functions. His emotional outbursts always garner a reaction of some sort.

Story so Far...

Clumsy high school student Elena tumbled down a flight of stairs...into the action-packed world of Rhysmyth!

Now she's on the team–to her surprise–and competing alongside the very best: the beautiful and confident Taylor, the brainy but free-spirited Diocel and the most hardcore of them all, unpredictable team captain Wahzee.

With the District Tournament coming up, Highwall High School is primed for a revenge rematch showdown with archrival Mountain Ridge Prep. Now Elena must find out where she really belongs. Can she contribute against an uber-talented opponent? And will Diocel's attraction to her affect the team's performance?

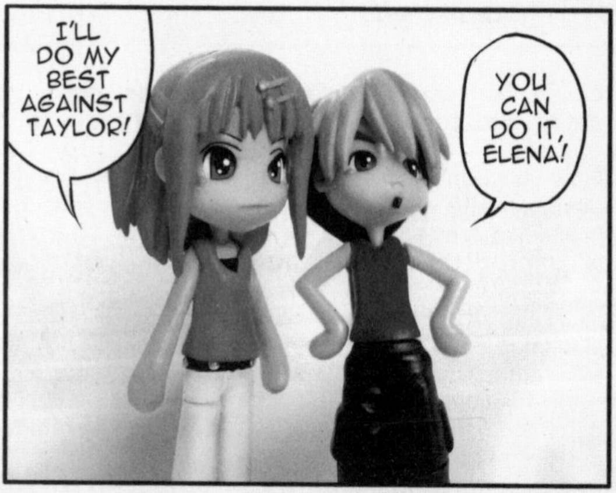
I'LL DO MY BEST AGAINST TAYLOR!
YOU CAN DO IT, ELENA!

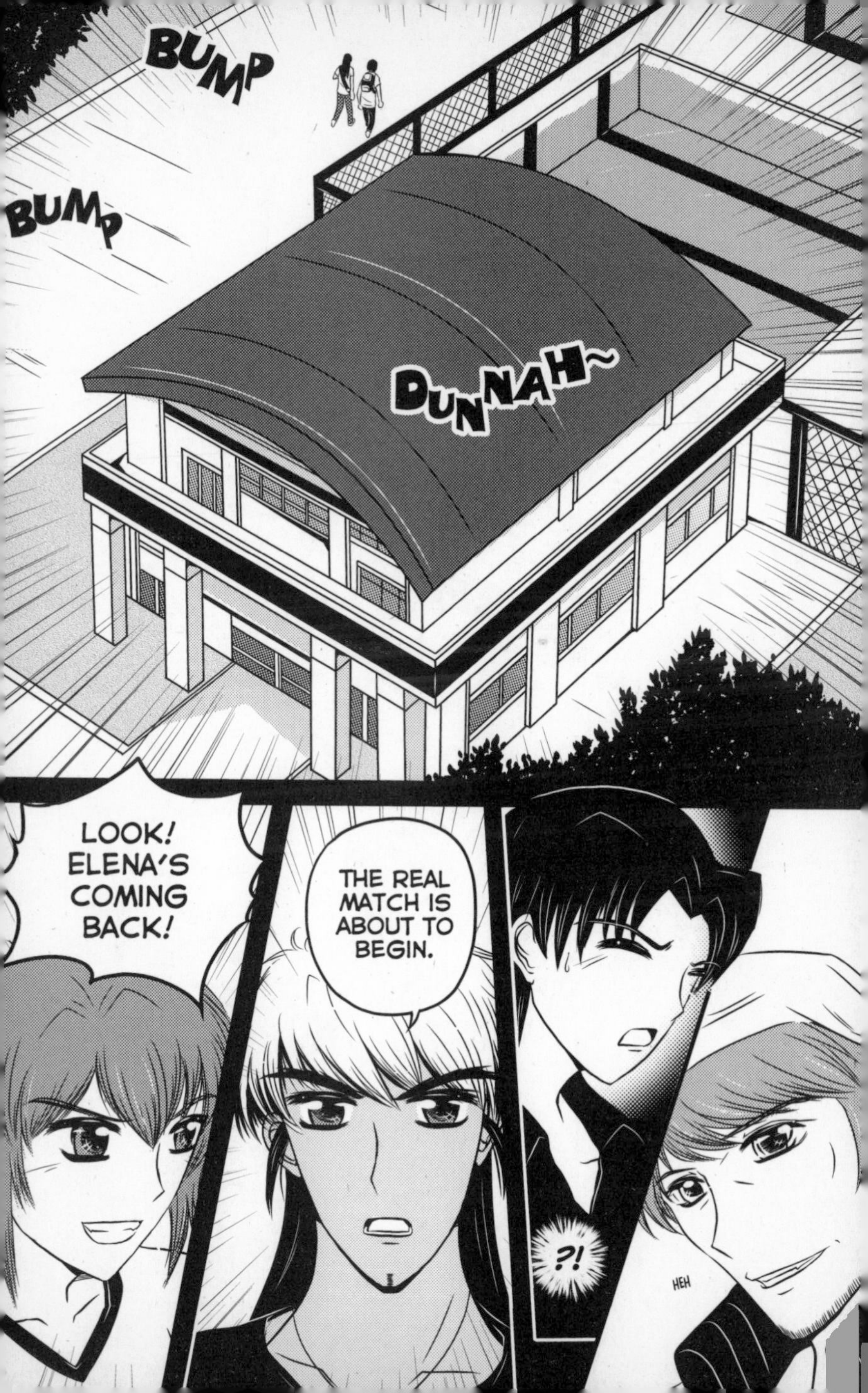
BUMP
BUMP
DUNNAH~
LOOK! ELENA'S COMING BACK!
THE REAL MATCH IS ABOUT TO BEGIN.
?!
HEH

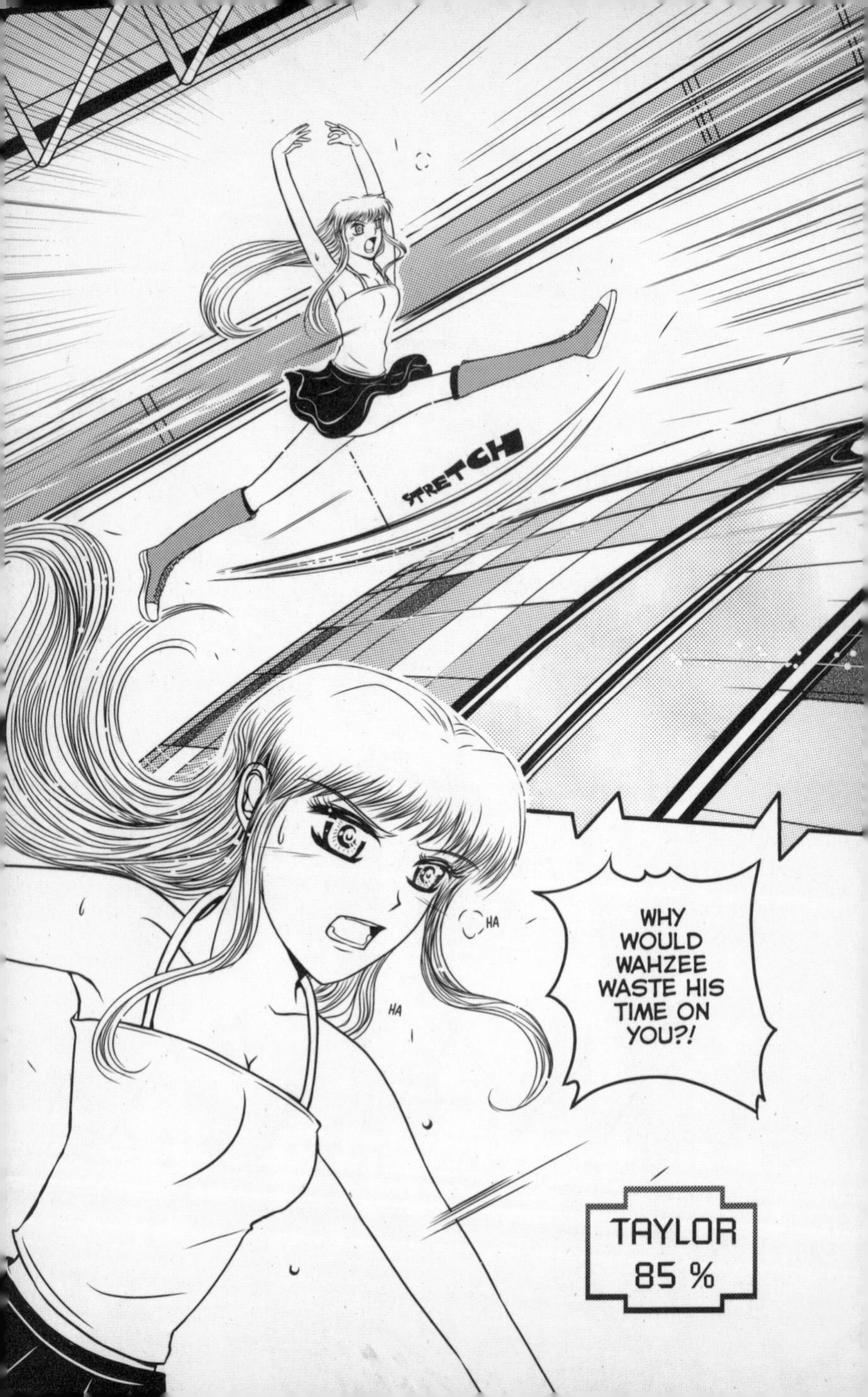
STRETCH
HA
HA
WHY WOULD WAHZEE WASTE HIS TIME ON YOU?!
TAYLOR 85 %

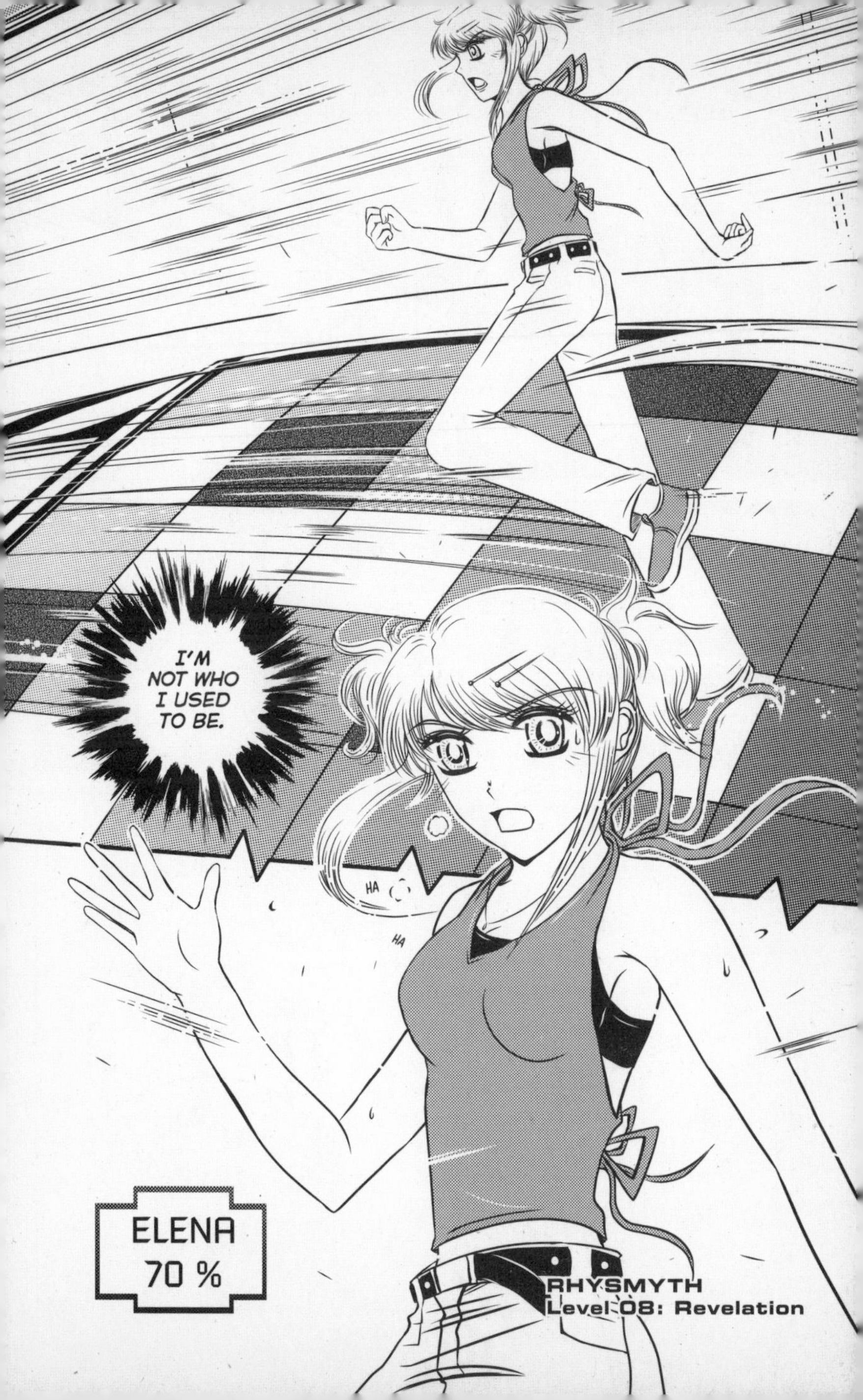
I'M NOT WHO I USED TO BE.
HA
HA
ELENA 70 %
RHYSMYTH
Level 08: Revelation

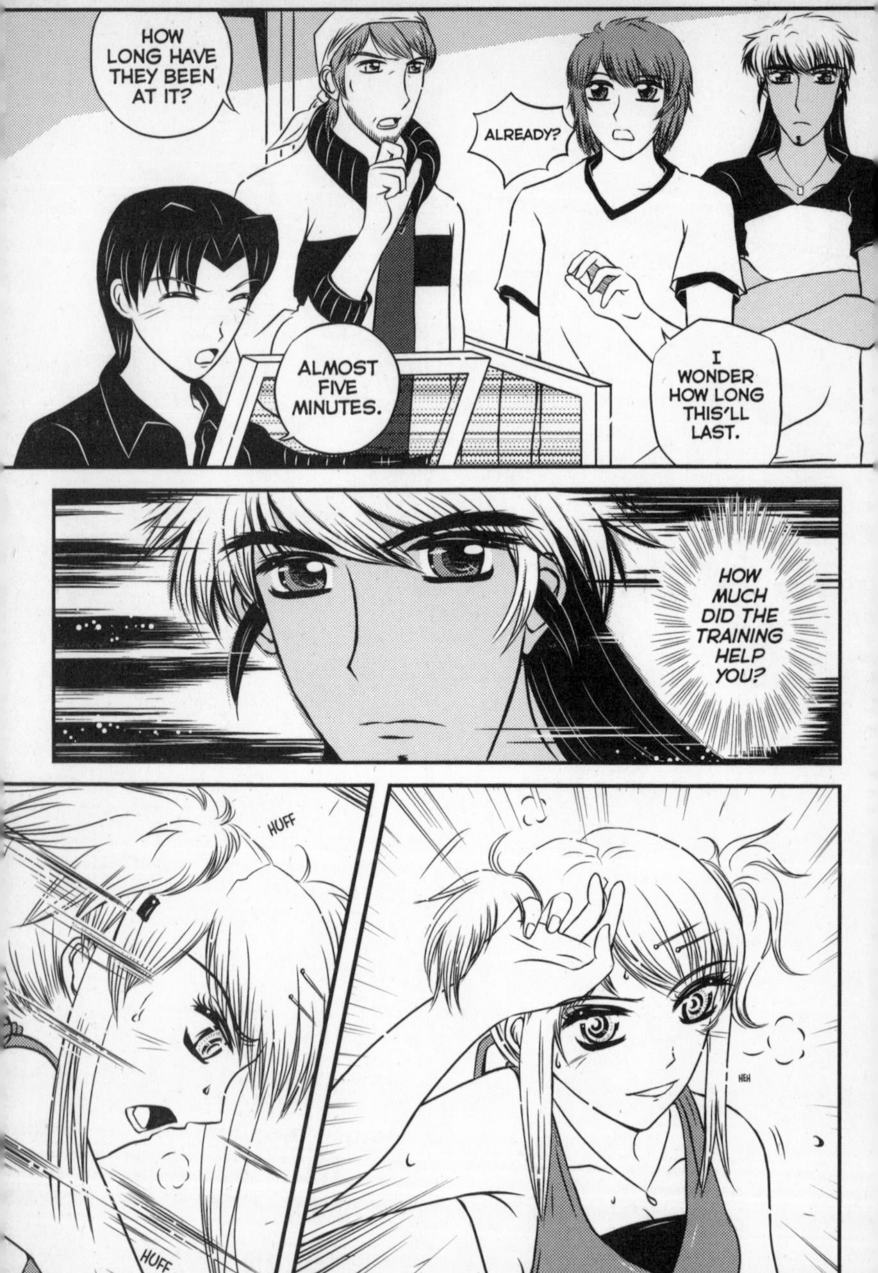
HOW LONG HAVE THEY BEEN AT IT?
ALREADY?
ALMOST FIVE MINUTES.
I WONDER HOW LONG THIS'LL LAST.
HOW MUCH DID THE TRAINING HELP YOU?
HUFF
HUFF
HEH

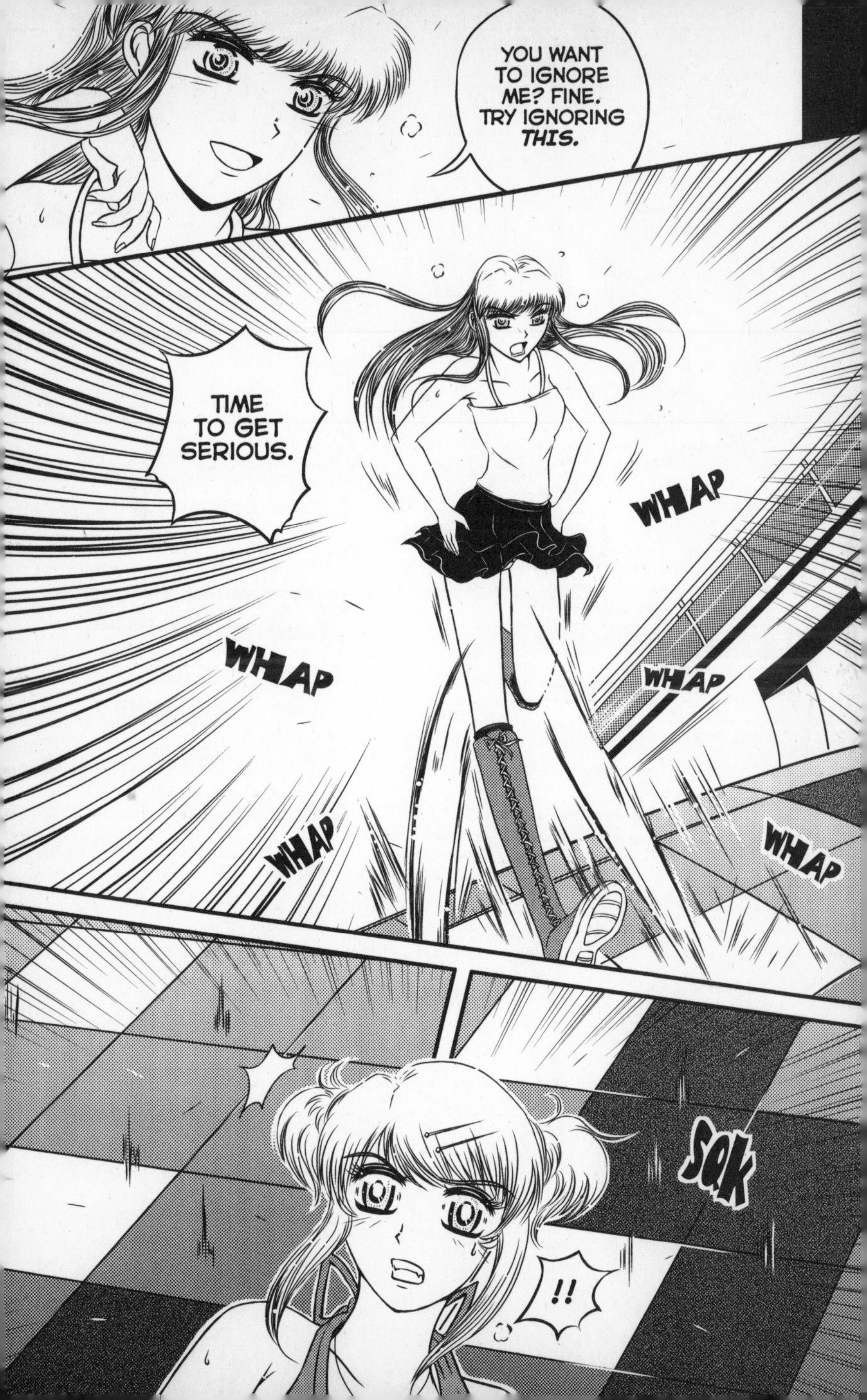
YOU WANT TO IGNORE ME? FINE. TRY IGNORING THIS.
TIME TO GET SERIOUS.
WHAP
WHAP
WHAP
WHAP
WHAP
SQK
!!

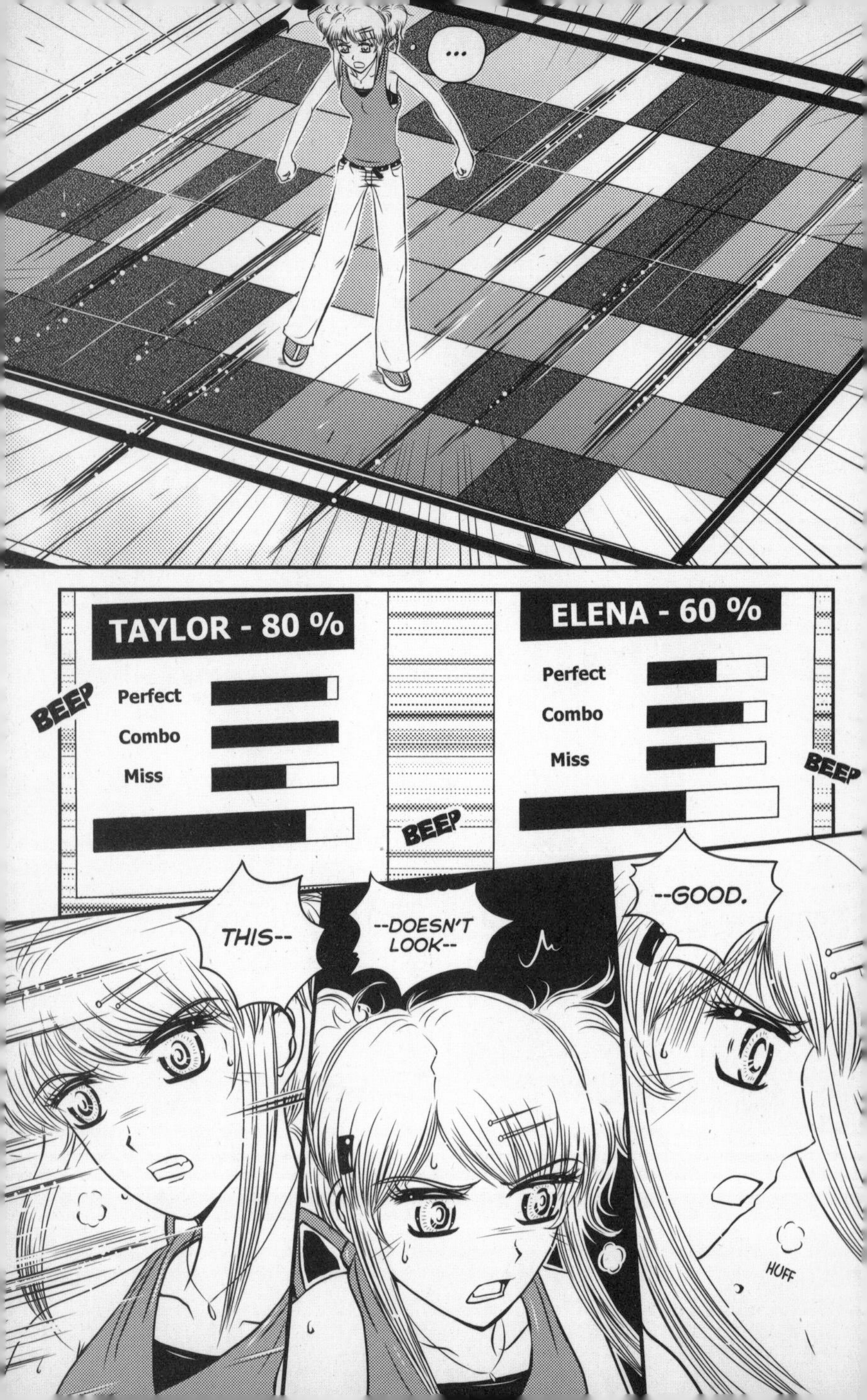
...
TAYLOR - 80 %
Perfect
Combo
Miss
BEEP
BEEP
ELENA - 60 %
Perfect
Combo
Miss
BEEP
THIS--
--DOESN'T LOOK--
--GOOD.
HUFF

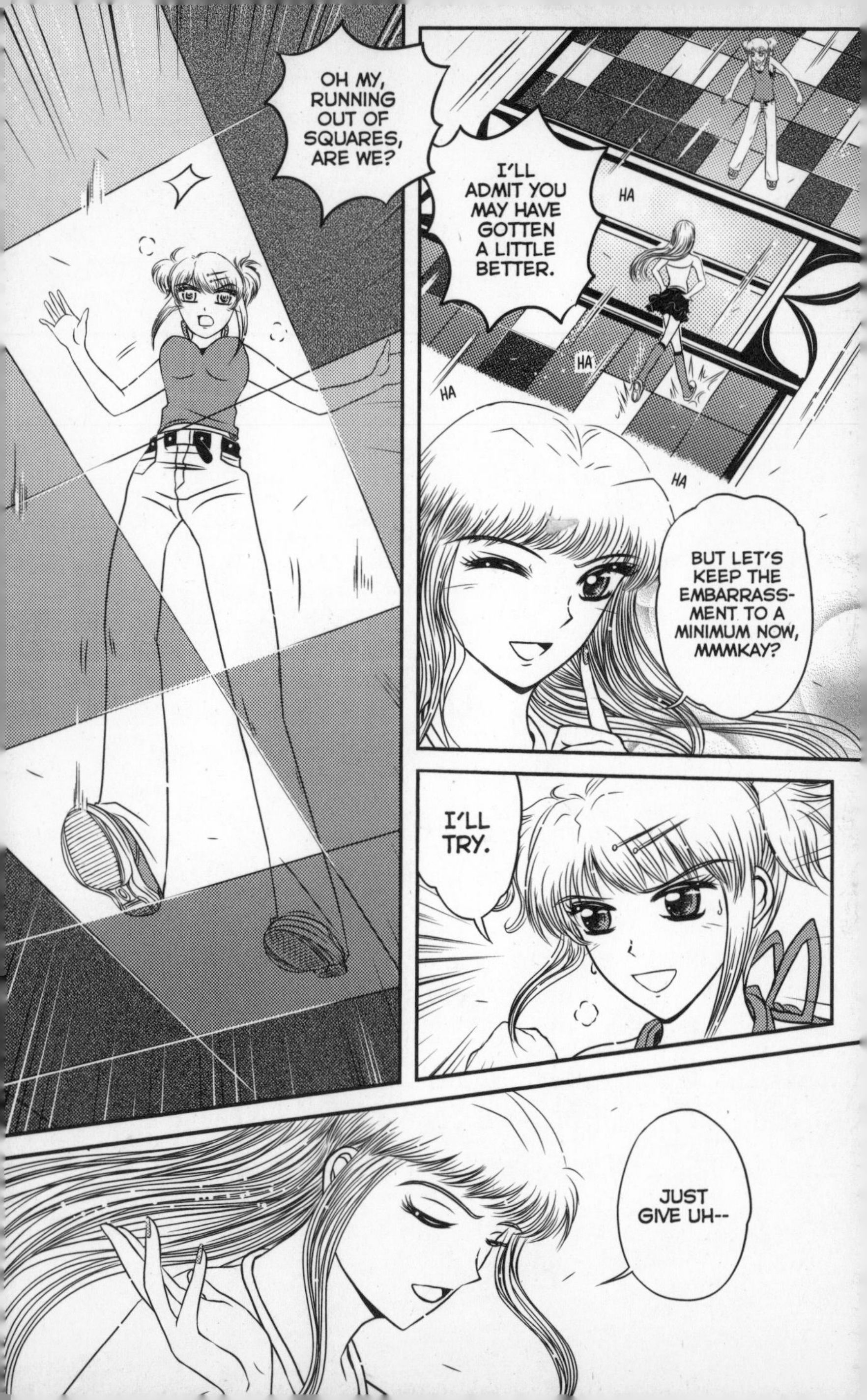
OH MY, RUNNING OUT OF SQUARES, ARE WE?
I'LL ADMIT YOU MAY HAVE GOTTEN A LITTLE BETTER.
HA
HA
HA
HA
BUT LET'S KEEP THE EMBARRASS-MENT TO A MINIMUM NOW, MMMKAY?
I'LL TRY.
JUST GIVE UH--

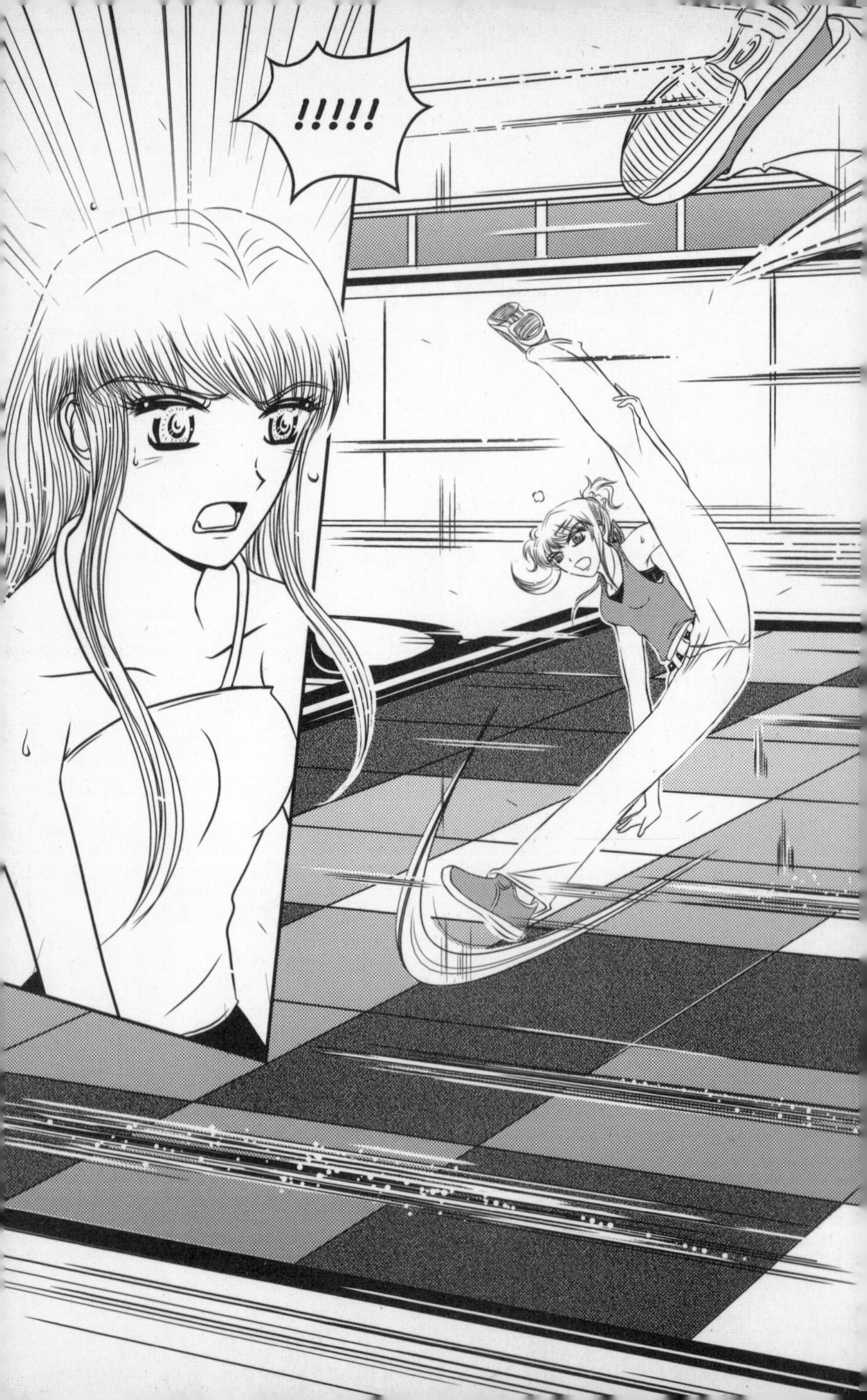
!!!!!

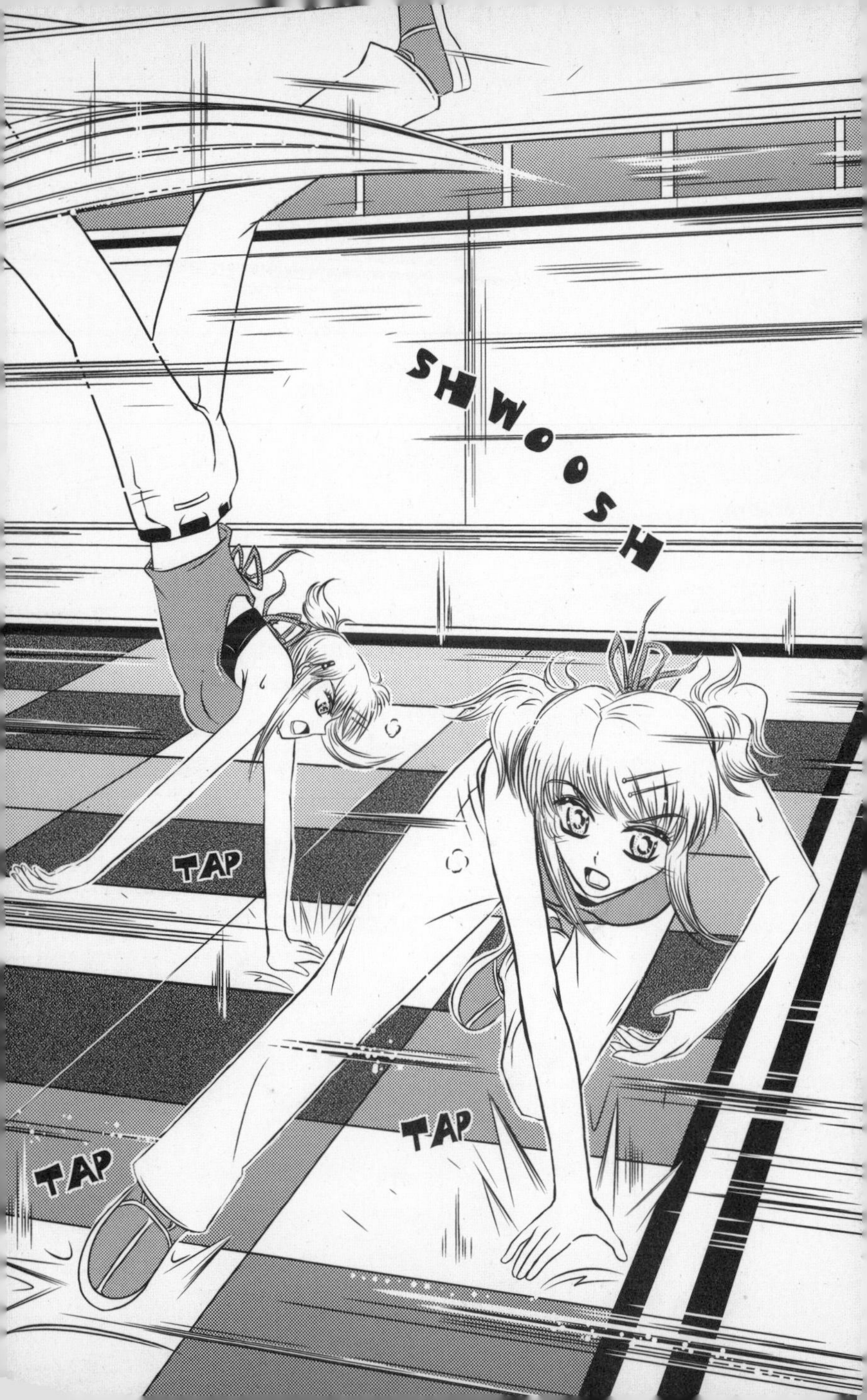
SHWOOSH
TAP
TAP
TAP

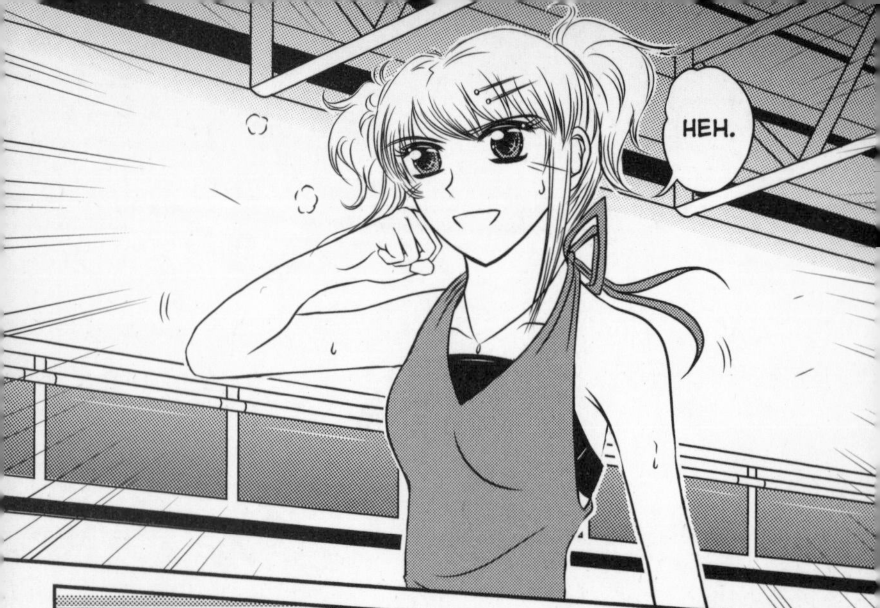
HEH.
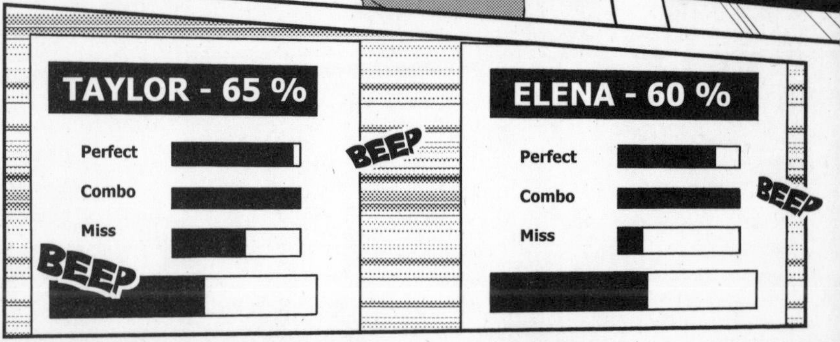
TAYLOR - 65 %
Perfect
Combo
Miss
BEEP
BEEP
ELENA - 60 %
Perfect
Combo
Miss
BEEP
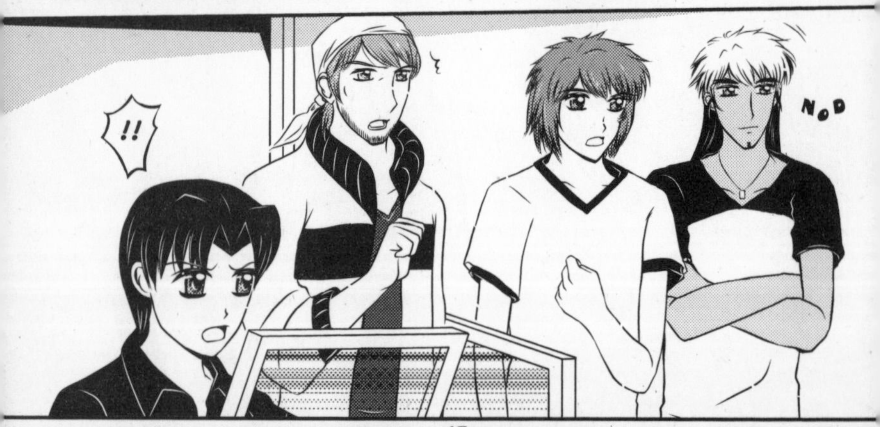
!!
NOD

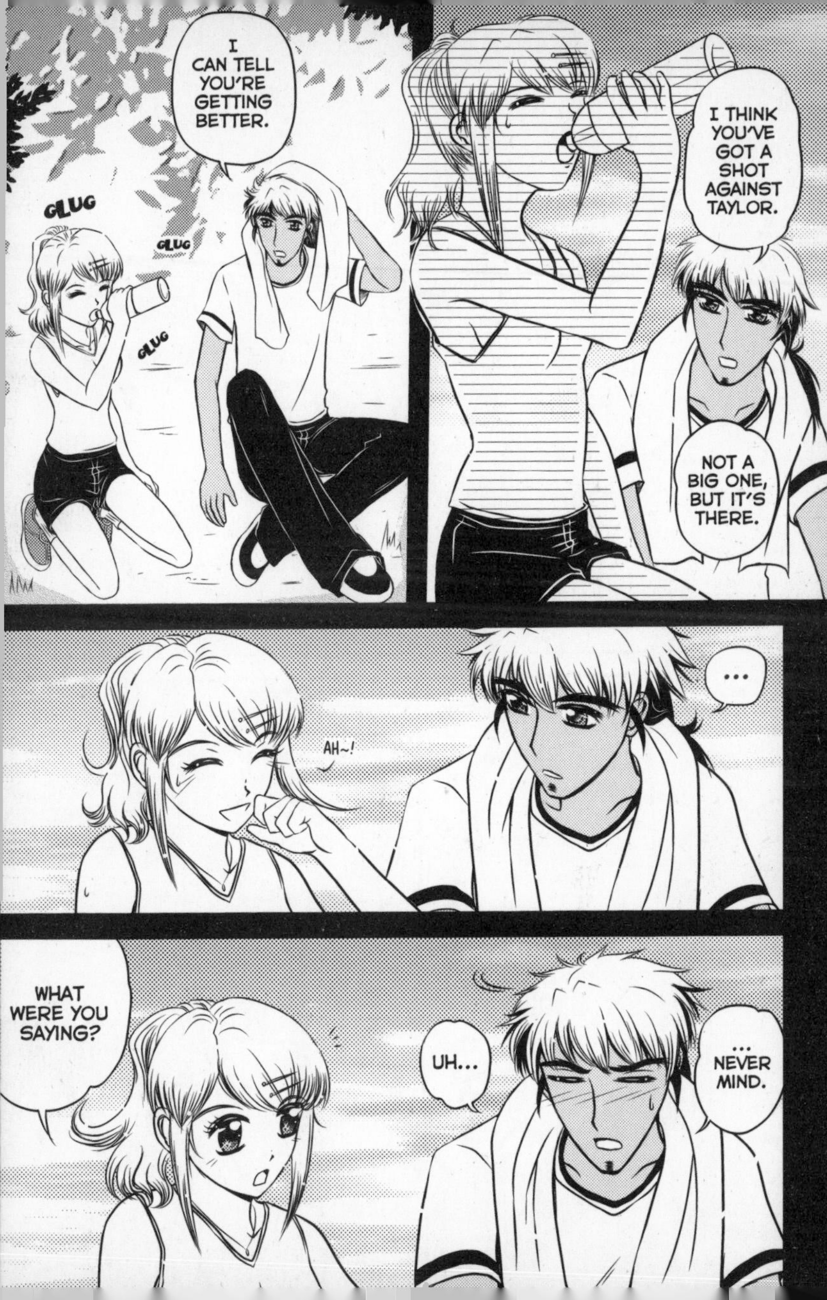
I CAN TELL YOU'RE GETTING BETTER.
GLUG
GLUG
GLUG
I THINK YOU'VE GOT A SHOT AGAINST TAYLOR.
NOT A BIG ONE, BUT IT'S THERE.
AH~!
...
WHAT WERE YOU SAYING?
UH...
...NEVER MIND.

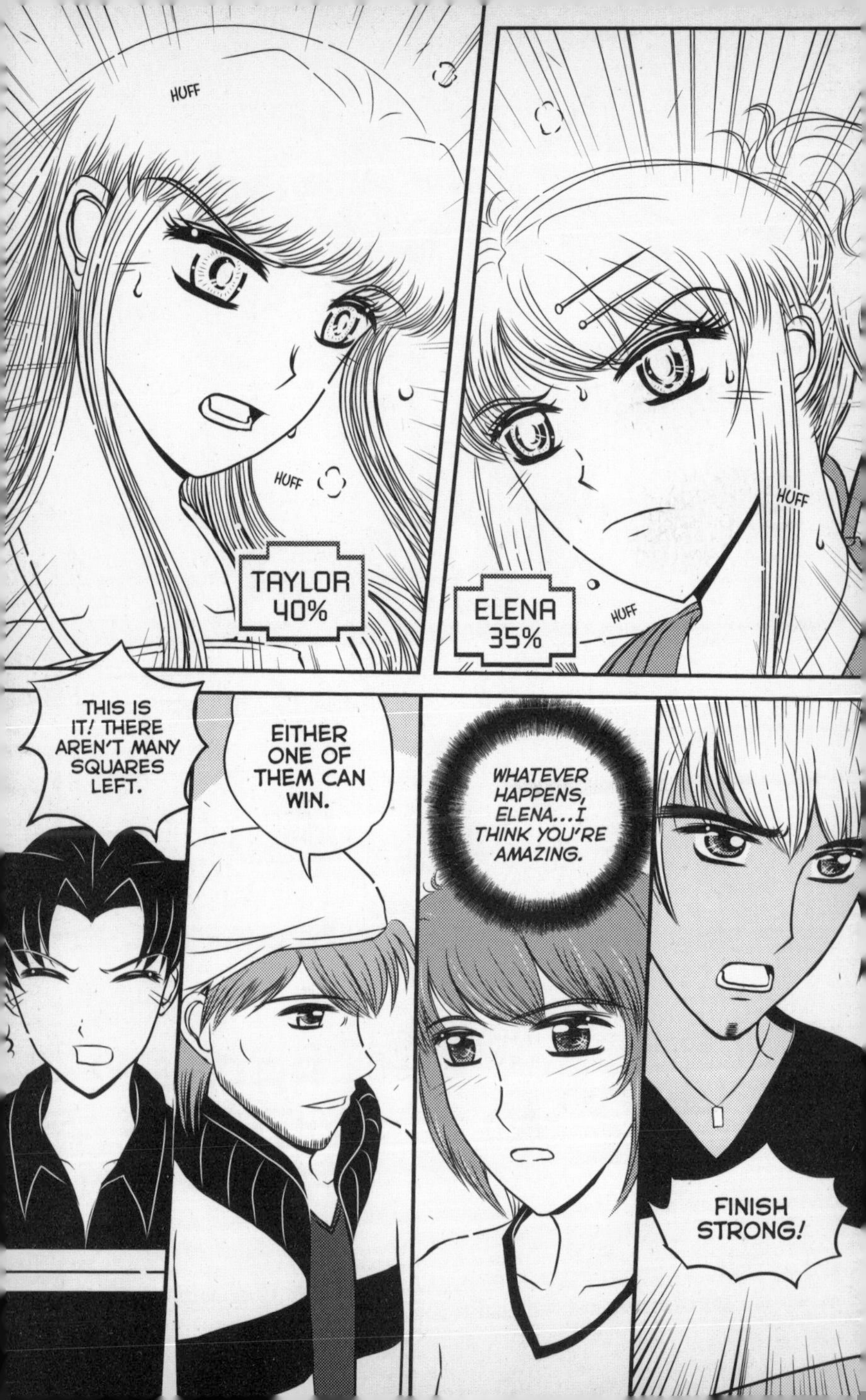
HUFF
HUFF
TAYLOR 40%
HUFF
HUFF
ELENA 35%
THIS IS IT! THERE AREN'T MANY SQUARES LEFT.
EITHER ONE OF THEM CAN WIN.
WHATEVER HAPPENS, ELENA...I THINK YOU'RE AMAZING.
FINISH STRONG!

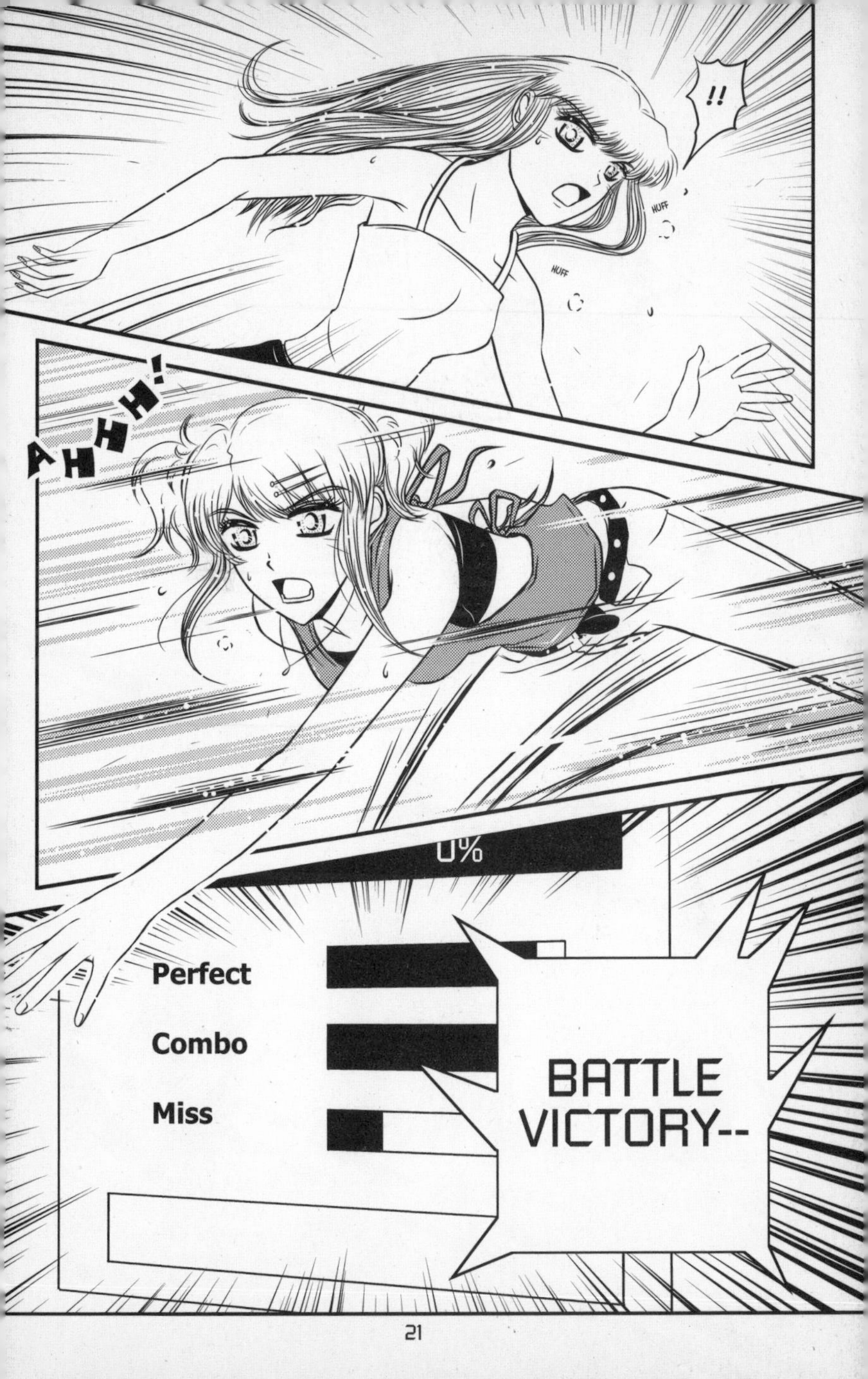
!!
HUFF
HUFF
AHHHH!
0%
Perfect
Combo
Miss
BATTLE VICTORY--

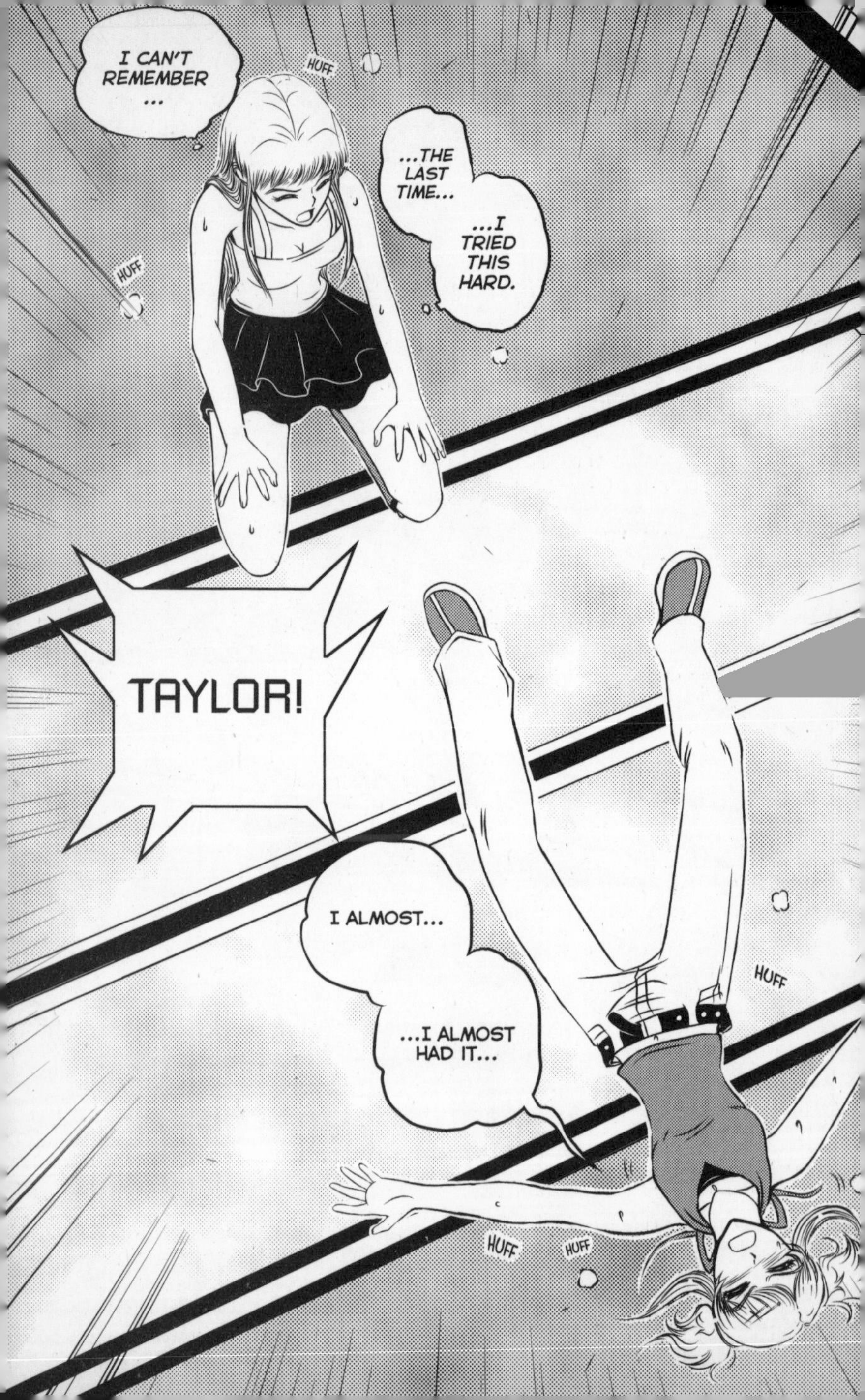
I CAN'T REMEMBER ...
HUFF
...THE LAST TIME...
...I TRIED THIS HARD.
HUFF
TAYLOR!
I ALMOST...
...I ALMOST HAD IT...
HUFF
HUFF
HUFF

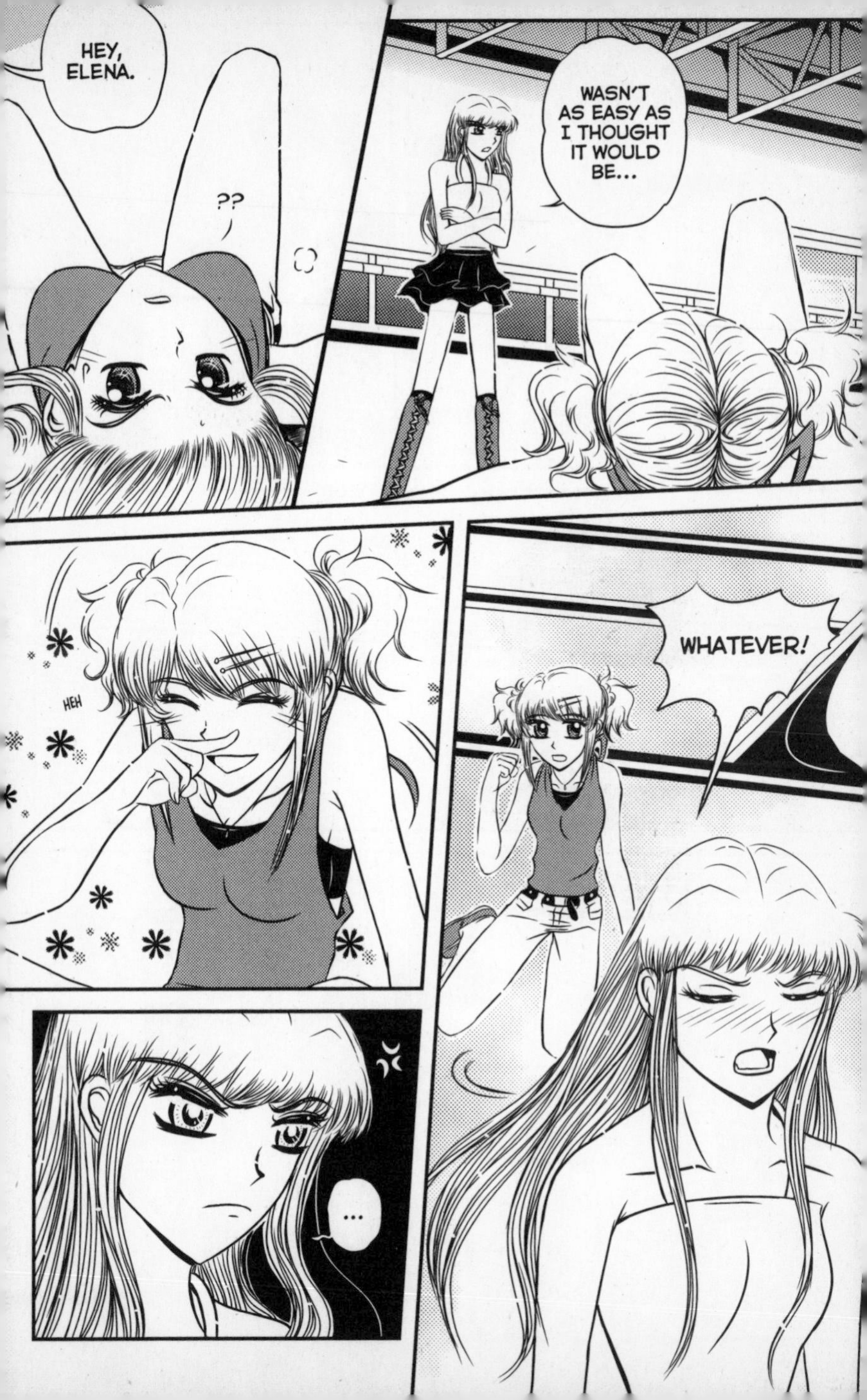
HEY, ELENA.
??
WASN'T AS EASY AS I THOUGHT IT WOULD BE...
HEH
WHATEVER!
...

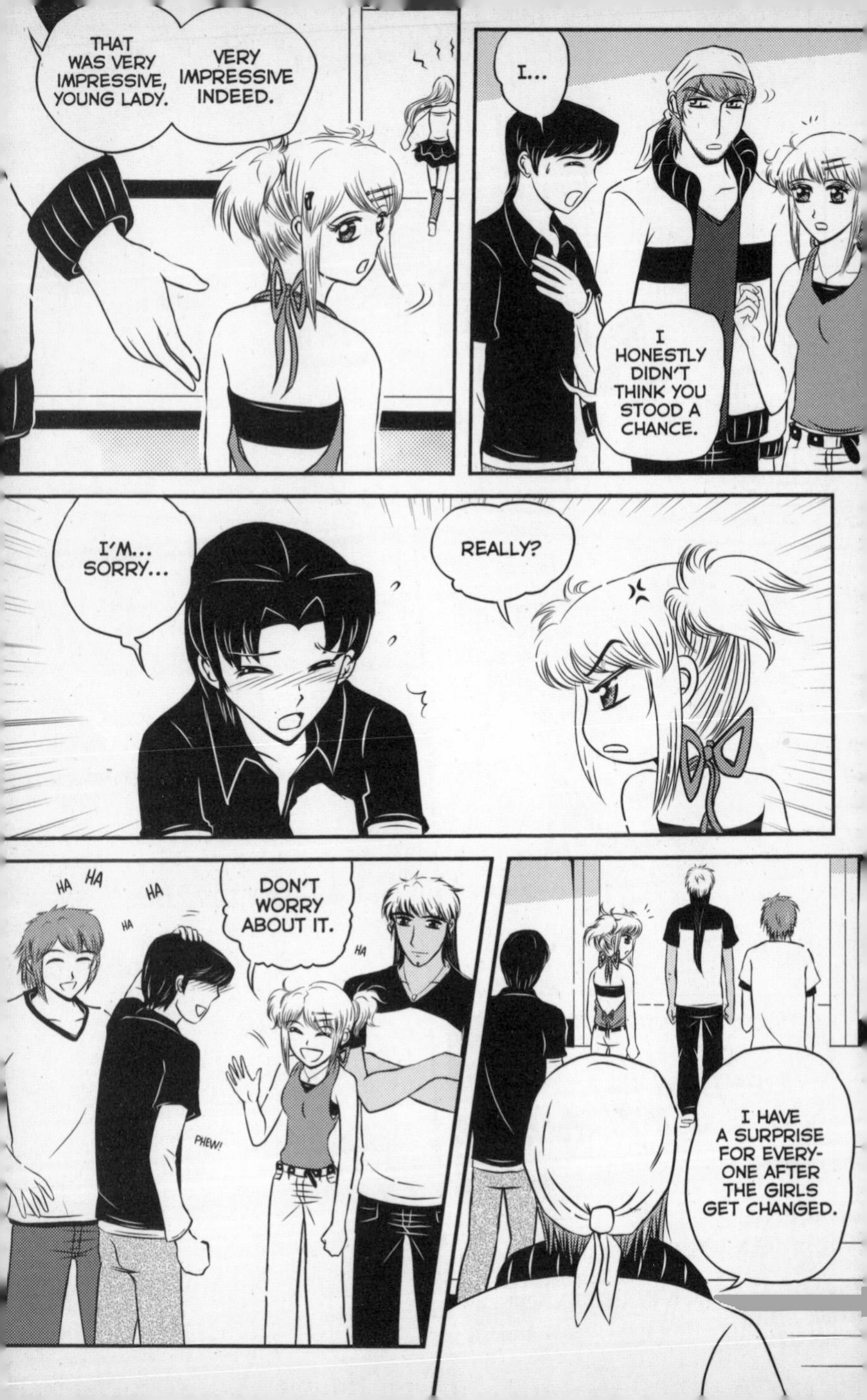

THAT WAS VERY IMPRESSIVE, YOUNG LADY.
VERY IMPRESSIVE INDEED.
I...
I HONESTLY DIDN'T THINK YOU STOOD A CHANCE.
I'M... SORRY...
REALLY?
HA HA HA HA
DON'T WORRY ABOUT IT.
HA
PHEW!
I HAVE A SURPRISE FOR EVERY-ONE AFTER THE GIRLS GET CHANGED.

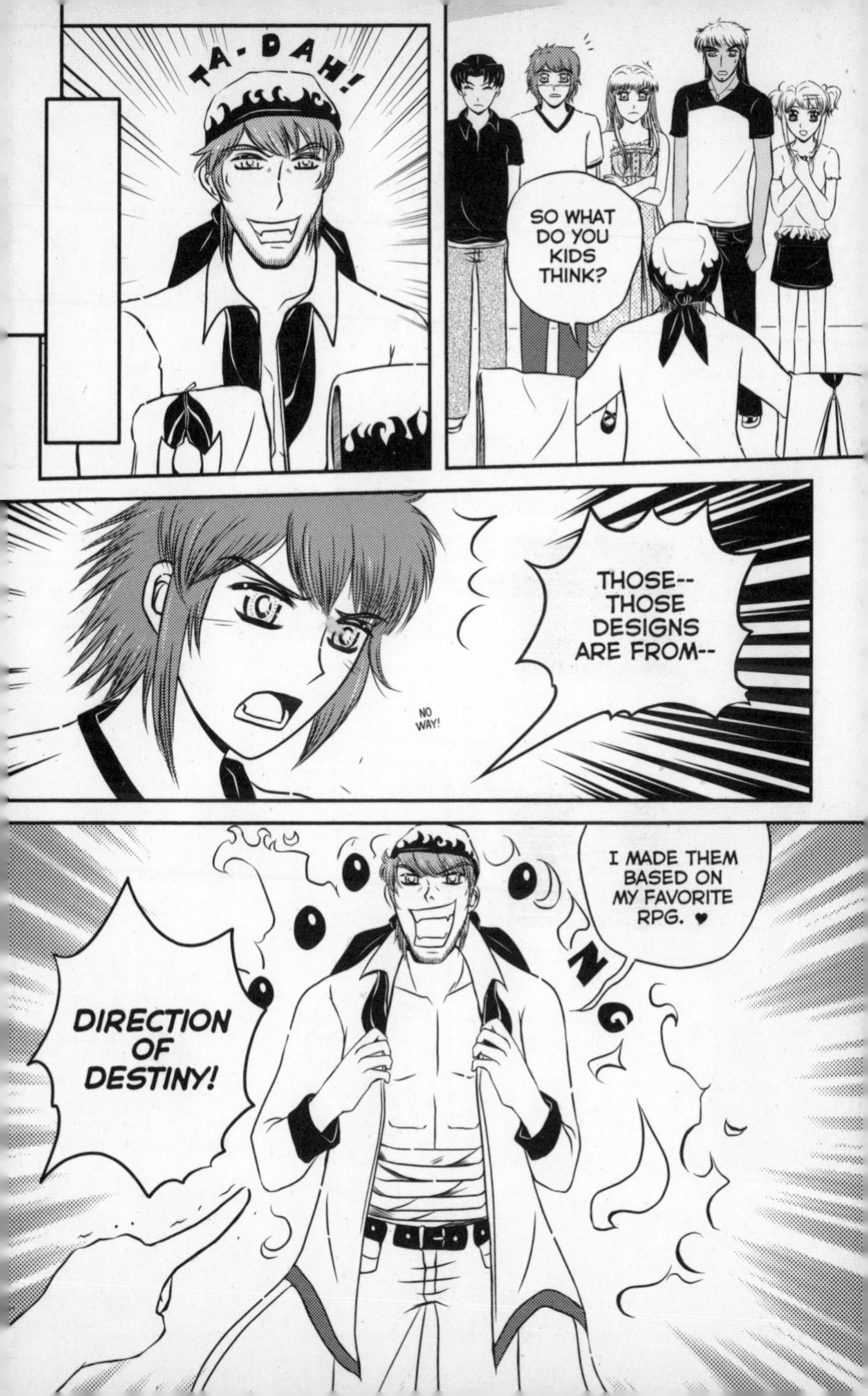
TA-DAH!
SO WHAT DO YOU KIDS THINK?
THOSE-- THOSE DESIGNS ARE FROM--
NO WAY!
DIRECTION OF DESTINY!
OOOONG
I MADE THEM BASED ON MY FAVORITE RPG. ♥

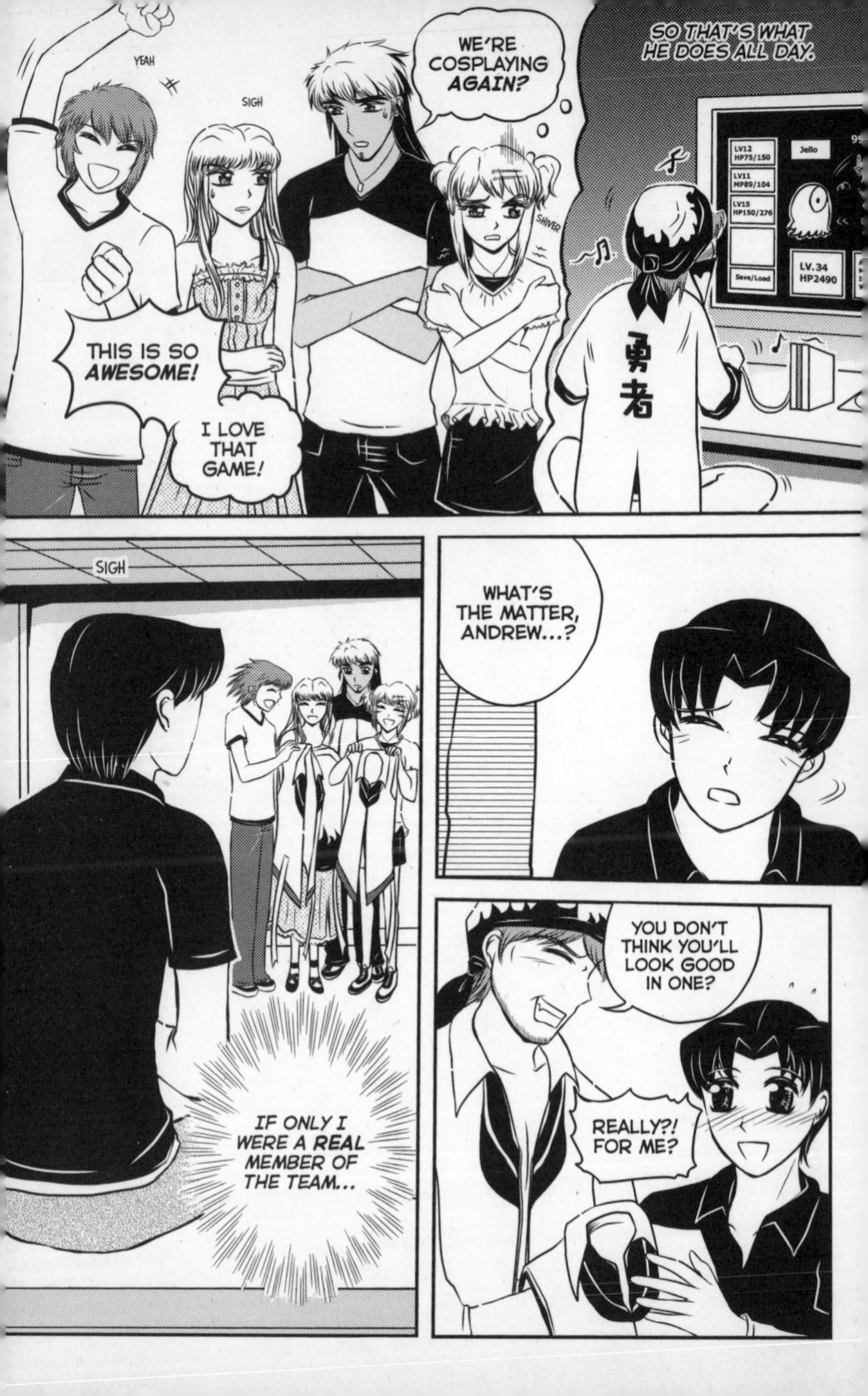
YEAH
SIGH
WE'RE COSPLAYING AGAIN?
SO THAT'S WHAT HE DOES ALL DAY.
LV12 HP75/150
LV11 MP89/104
LV15 HP150/276
Jello
LV.34 HP2490
Save/Load
SHIVER
THIS IS SO AWESOME!
I LOVE THAT GAME!
勇者
SIGH
IF ONLY I WERE A REAL MEMBER OF THE TEAM...
WHAT'S THE MATTER, ANDREW...?
YOU DON'T THINK YOU'LL LOOK GOOD IN ONE?
REALLY?! FOR ME?

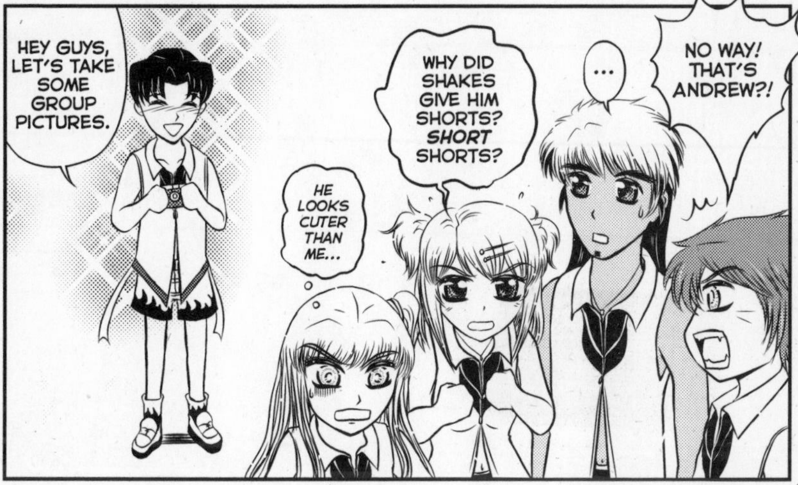
HEY GUYS, LET'S TAKE SOME GROUP PICTURES.
HE LOOKS CUTER THAN ME...
WHY DID SHAKES GIVE HIM SHORTS? SHORT SHORTS?
...
NO WAY! THAT'S ANDREW?!

SURPRISE

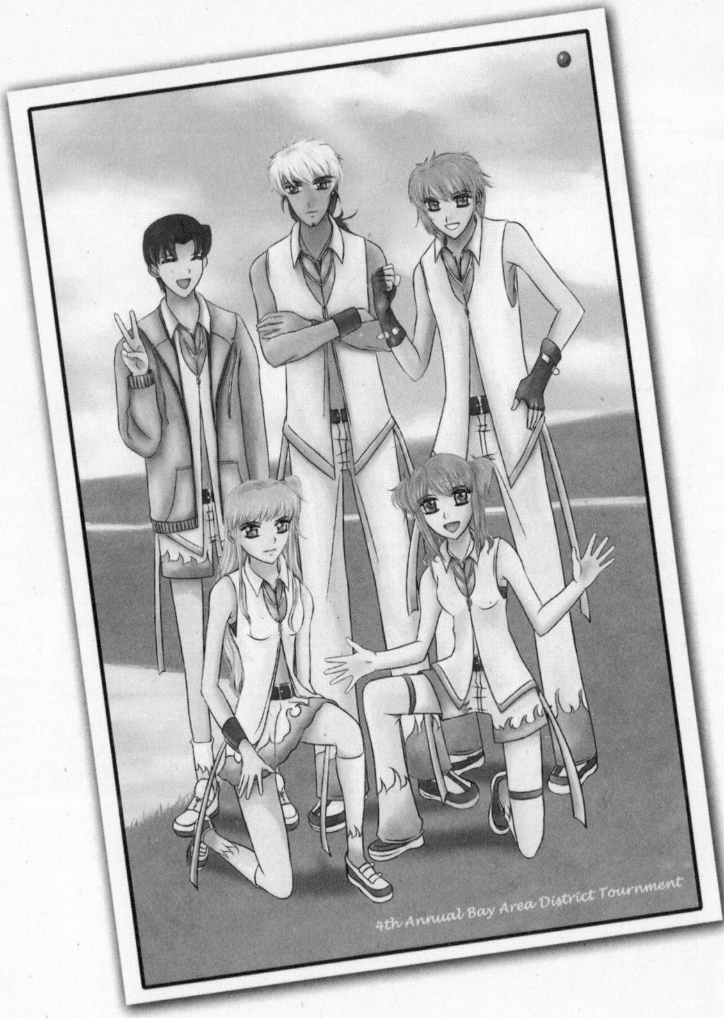
4th Annual Bay Area District Tournment

RHYSMYTH
Level 09: Synergy

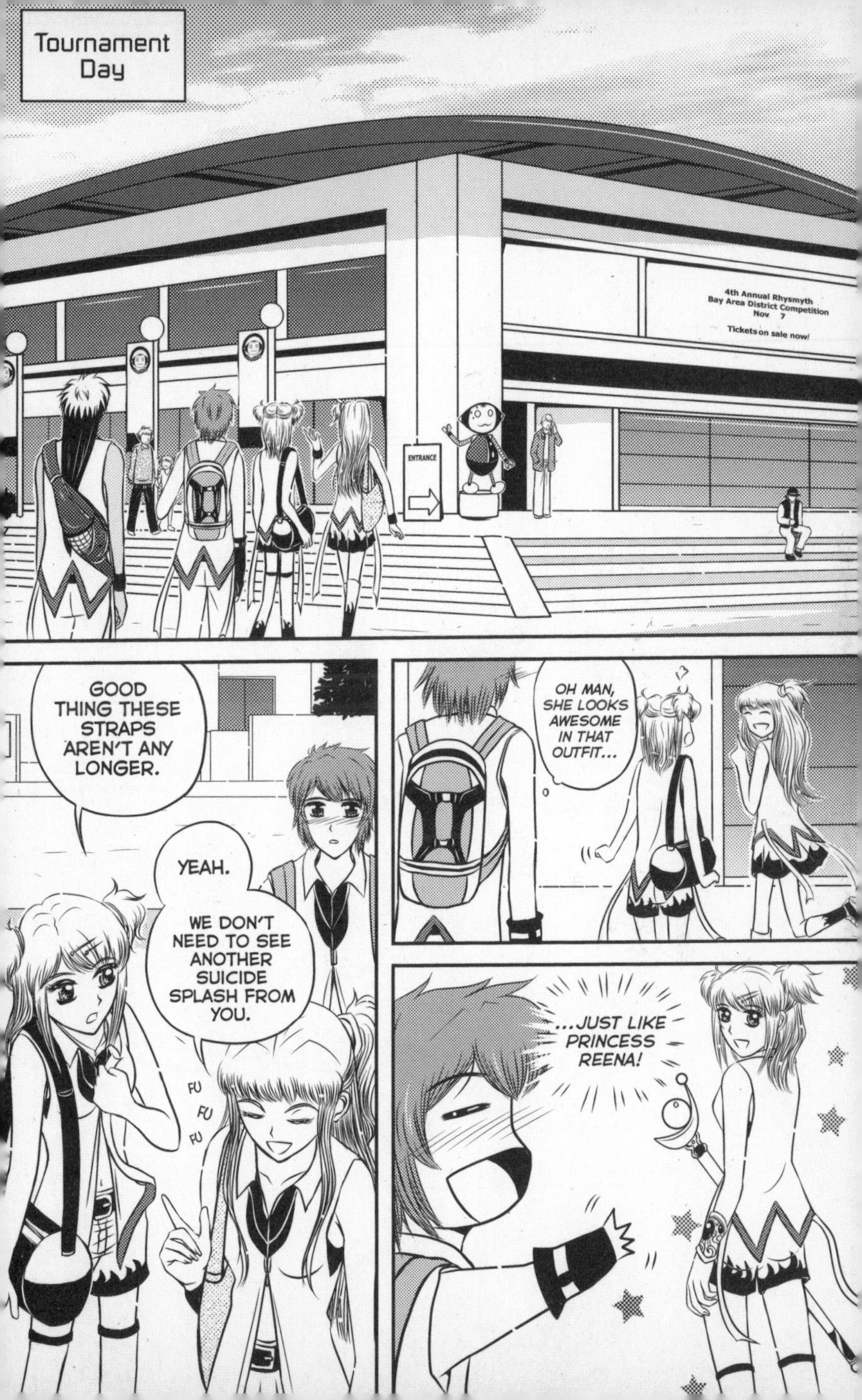
Tournament Day
4th Annual Rhysmyth Bay Area District Competition Nov 7
Tickets on sale now!
ENTRANCE
GOOD THING THESE STRAPS AREN'T ANY LONGER.
YEAH.
WE DON'T NEED TO SEE ANOTHER SUICIDE SPLASH FROM YOU.
FU FU FU
OH MAN, SHE LOOKS AWESOME IN THAT OUTFIT...
...JUST LIKE PRINCESS REENA!

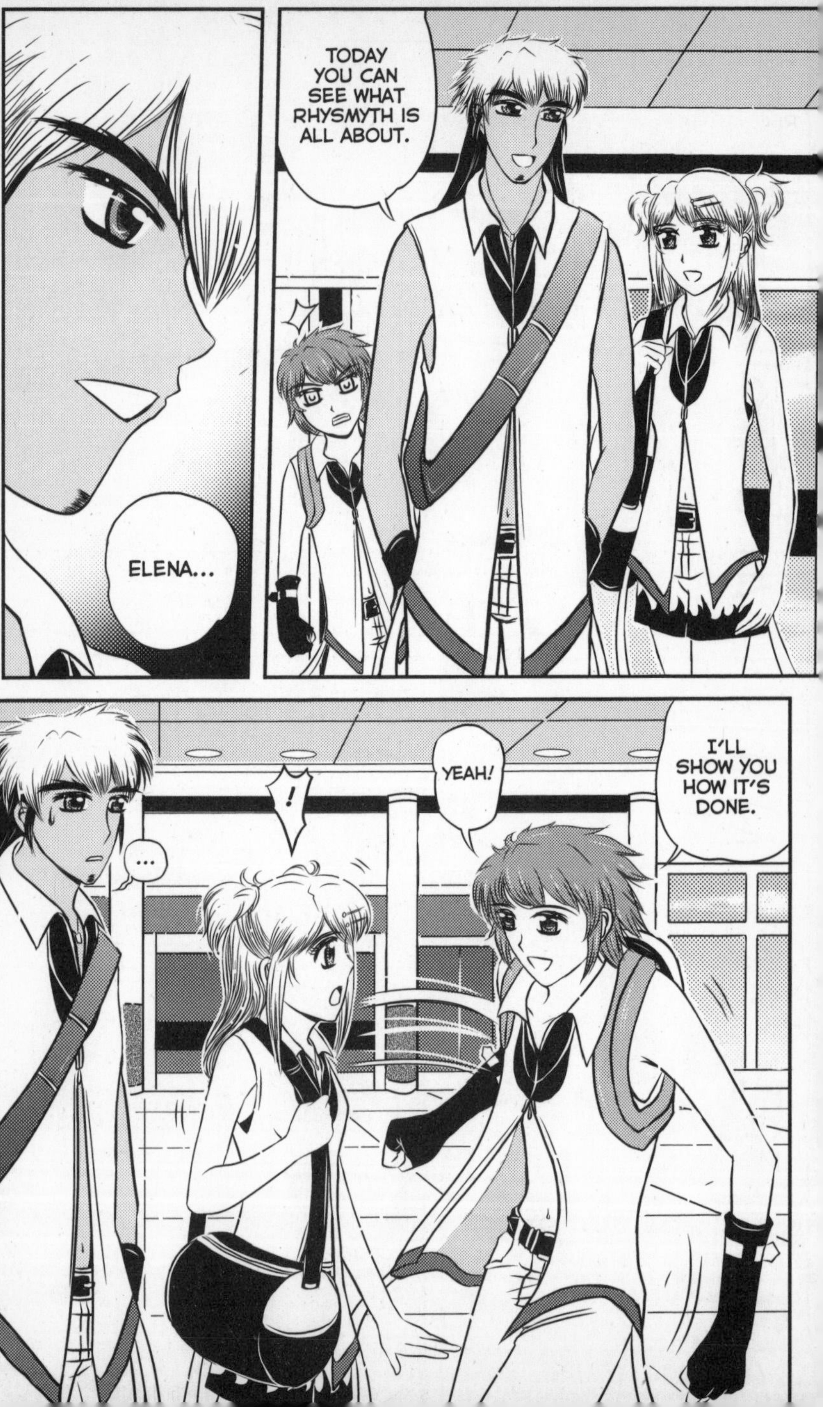
ELENA...
TODAY YOU CAN SEE WHAT RHYSMYTH IS ALL ABOUT.
...
!
YEAH!
I'LL SHOW YOU HOW IT'S DONE.

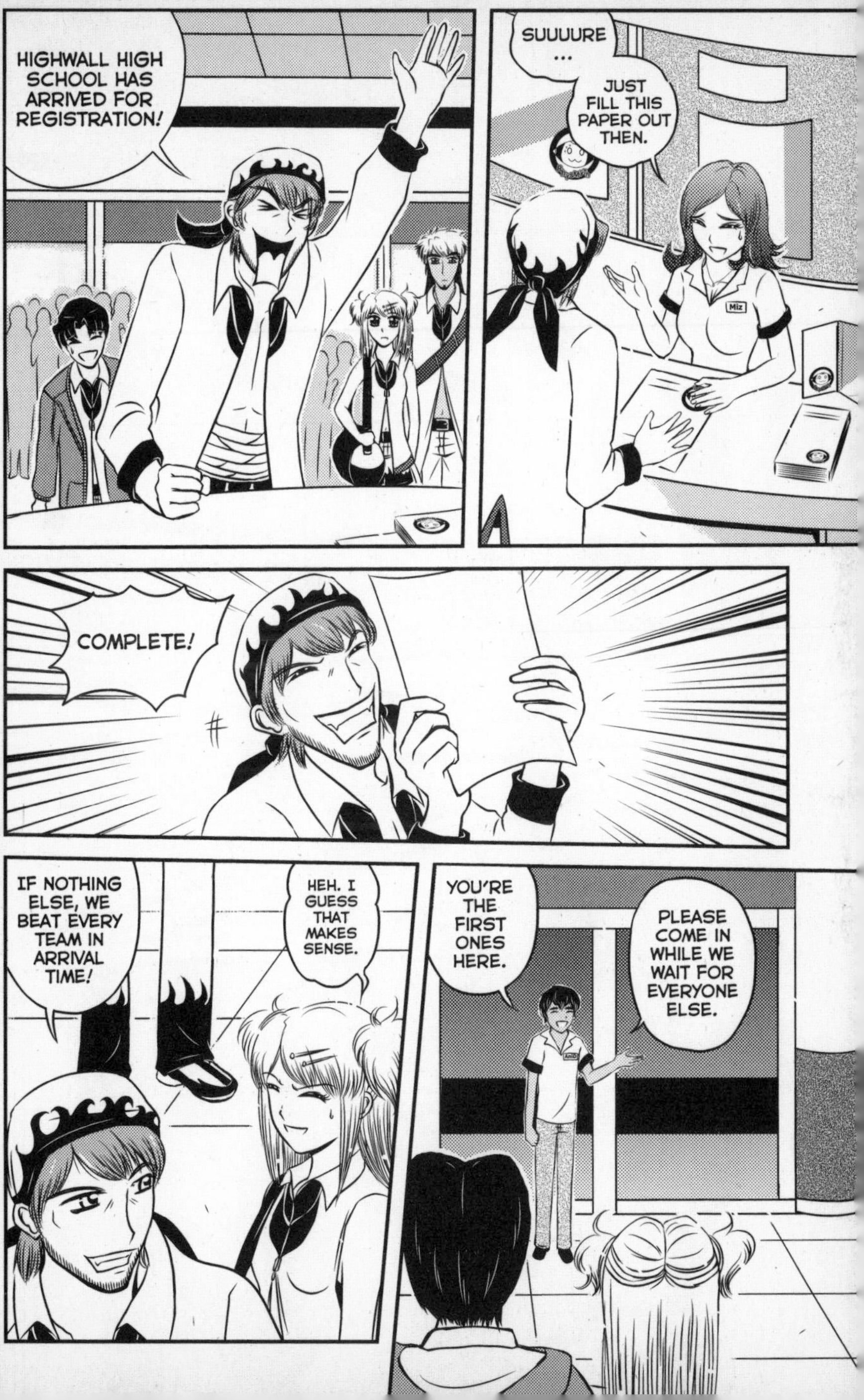
HIGHWALL HIGH SCHOOL HAS ARRIVED FOR REGISTRATION!
SUUUURE ...
JUST FILL THIS PAPER OUT THEN.
Miz
COMPLETE!
IF NOTHING ELSE, WE BEAT EVERY TEAM IN ARRIVAL TIME!
HEH. I GUESS THAT MAKES SENSE.
YOU'RE THE FIRST ONES HERE.
PLEASE COME IN WHILE WE WAIT FOR EVERYONE ELSE.

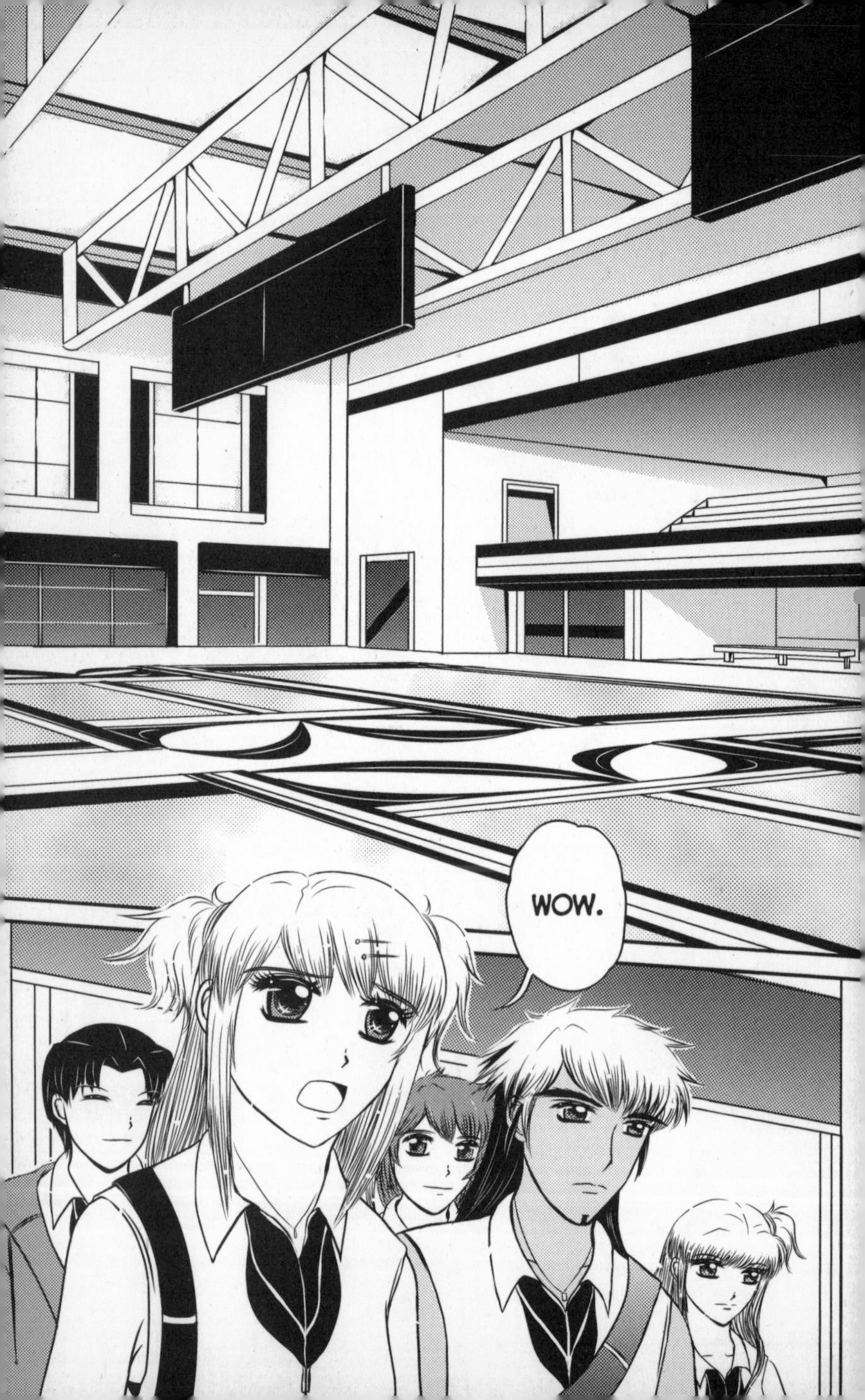
WOW.

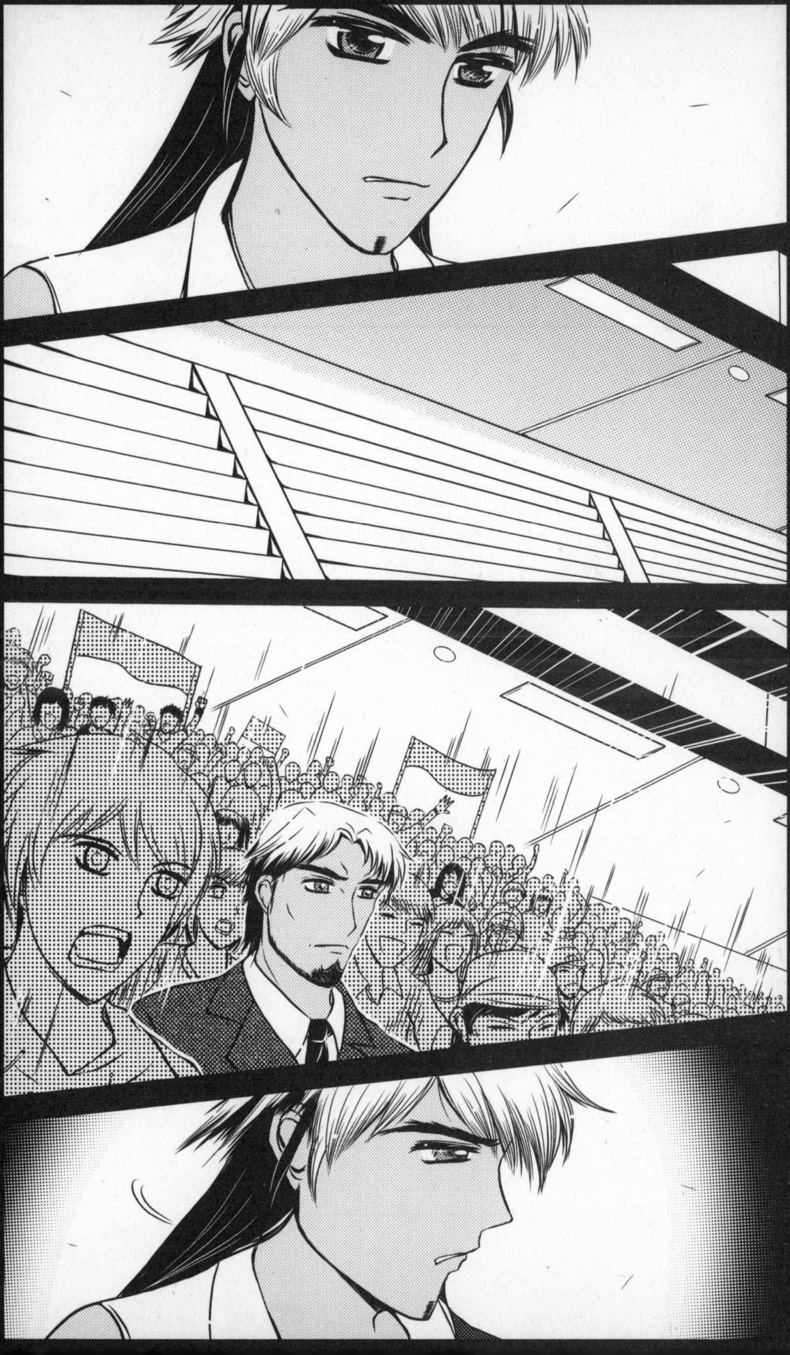

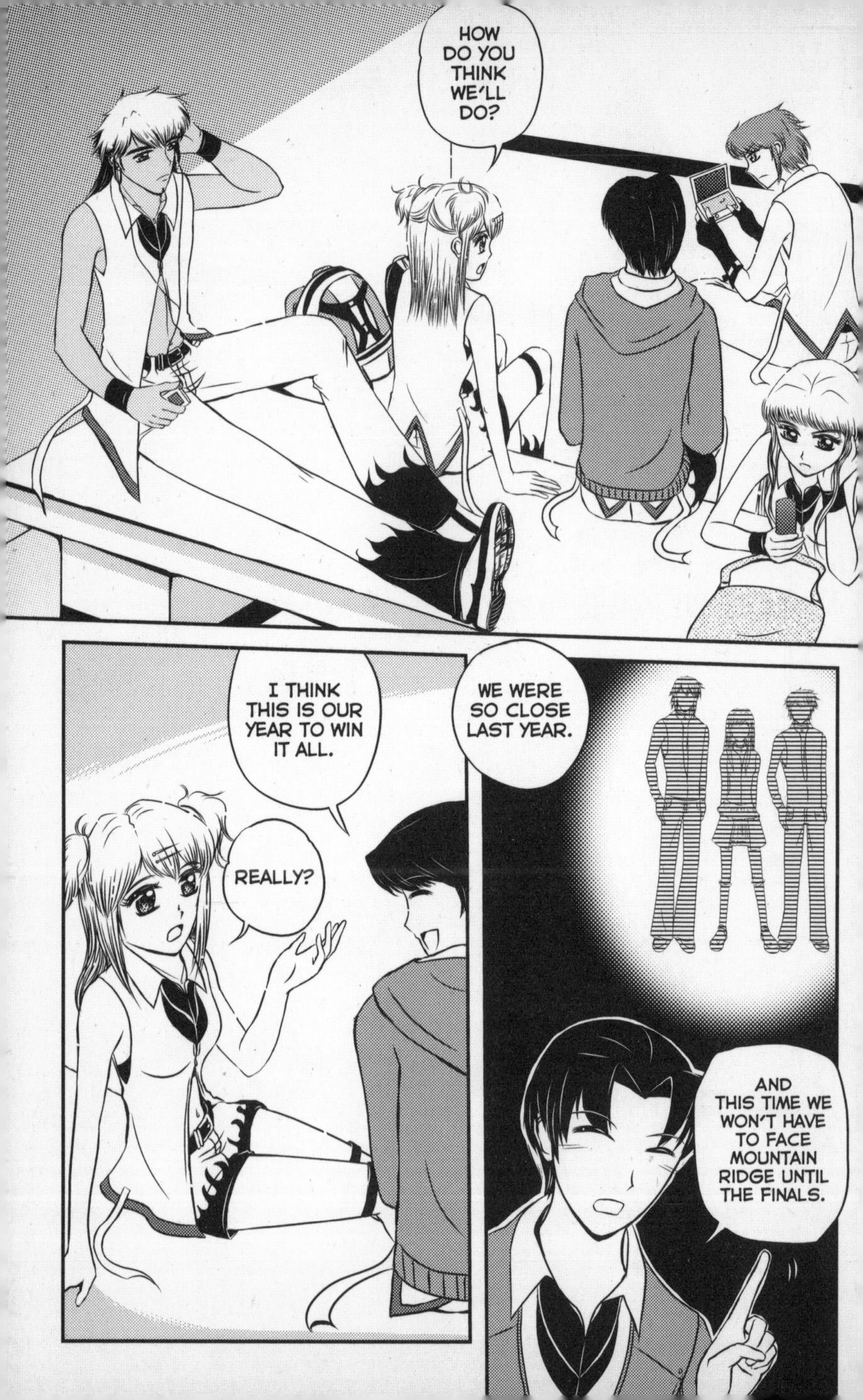
HOW DO YOU THINK WE'LL DO?
I THINK THIS IS OUR YEAR TO WIN IT ALL.
REALLY?
WE WERE SO CLOSE LAST YEAR.
AND THIS TIME WE WON'T HAVE TO FACE MOUNTAIN RIDGE UNTIL THE FINALS.

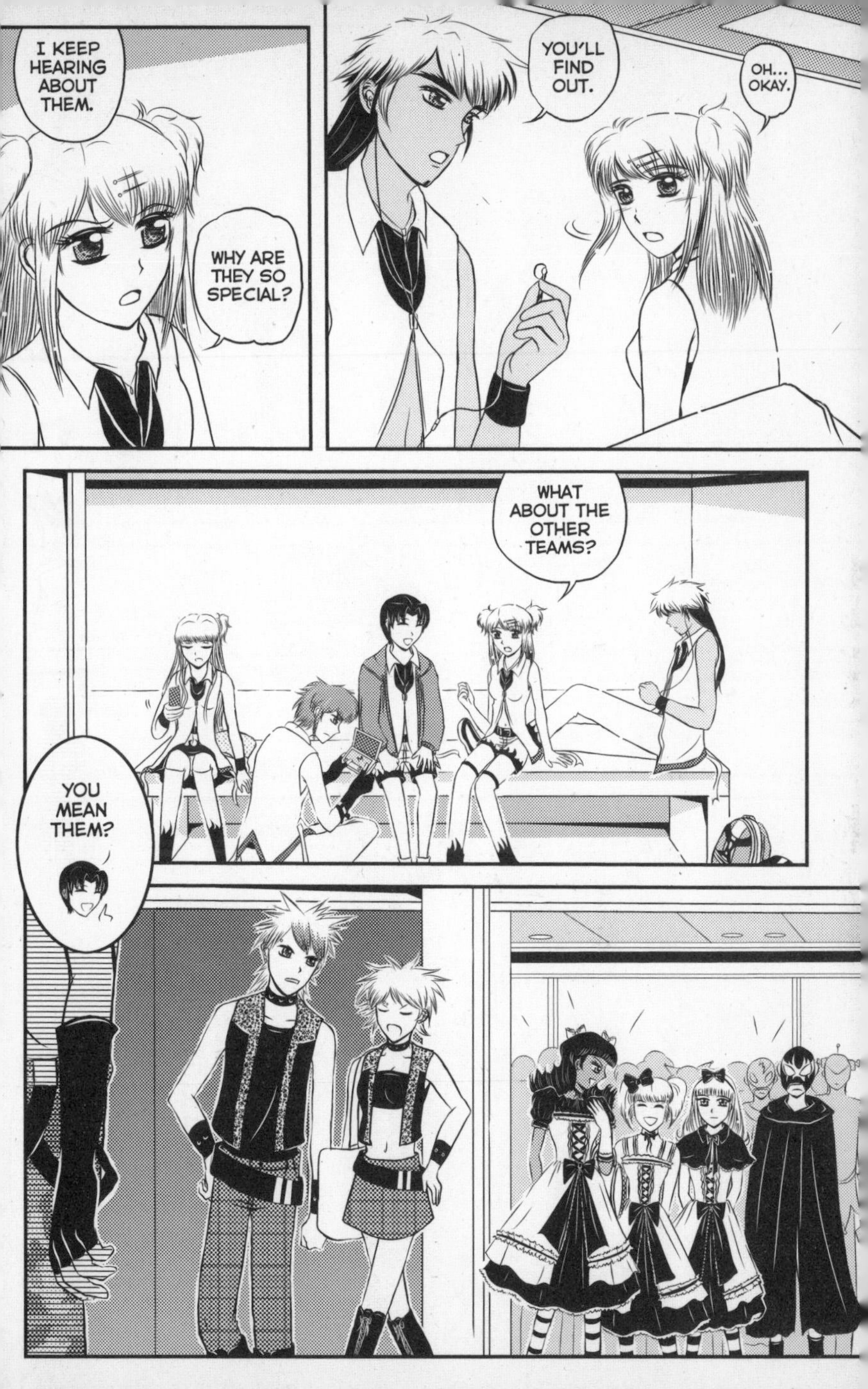
I KEEP HEARING ABOUT THEM.
WHY ARE THEY SO SPECIAL?
YOU'LL FIND OUT.
OH... OKAY.
WHAT ABOUT THE OTHER TEAMS?
YOU MEAN THEM?

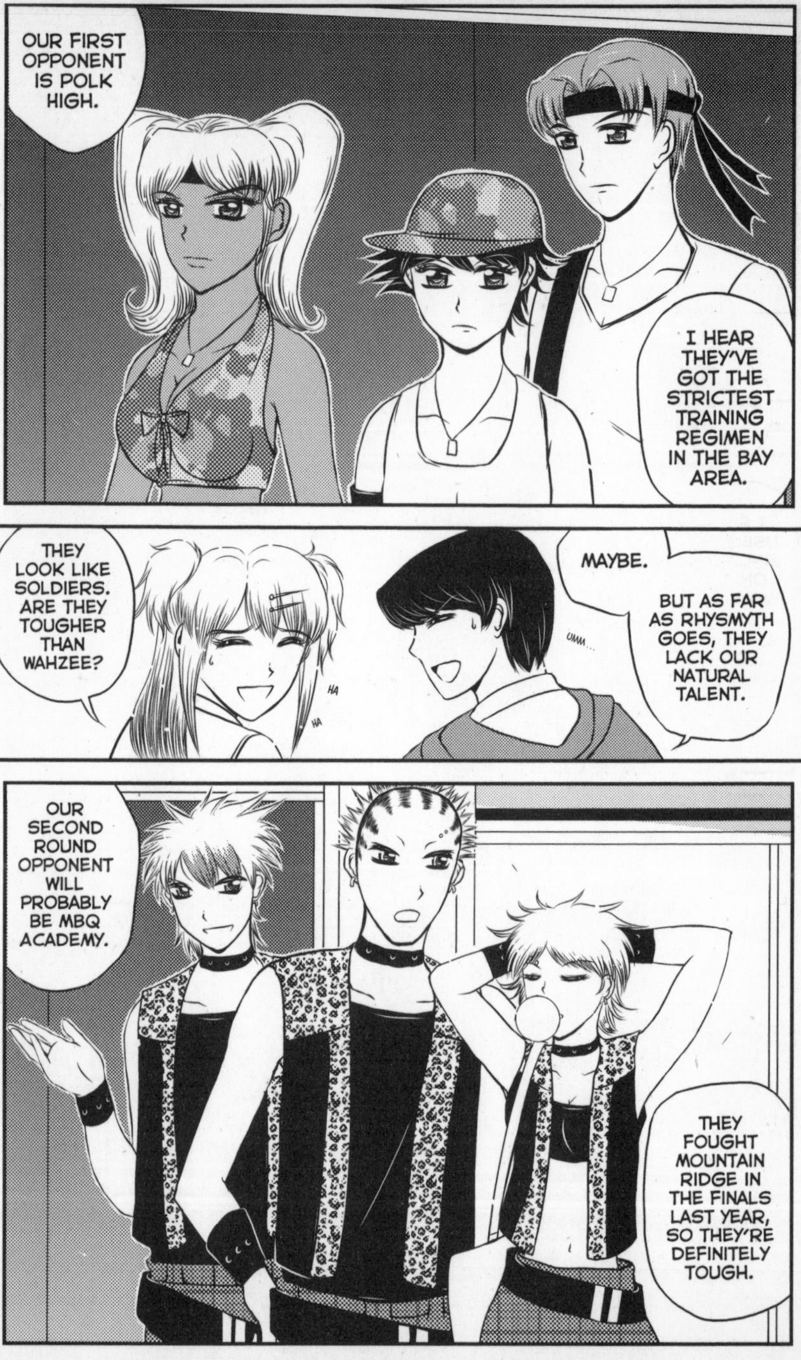
OUR FIRST OPPONENT IS POLK HIGH.
I HEAR THEY'VE GOT THE STRICTEST TRAINING REGIMEN IN THE BAY AREA.
THEY LOOK LIKE SOLDIERS. ARE THEY TOUGHER THAN WAHZEE?
HA
HA
UMM...
MAYBE.
BUT AS FAR AS RHYSMYTH GOES, THEY LACK OUR NATURAL TALENT.
OUR SECOND ROUND OPPONENT WILL PROBABLY BE MBQ ACADEMY.
THEY FOUGHT MOUNTAIN RIDGE IN THE FINALS LAST YEAR, SO THEY'RE DEFINITELY TOUGH.

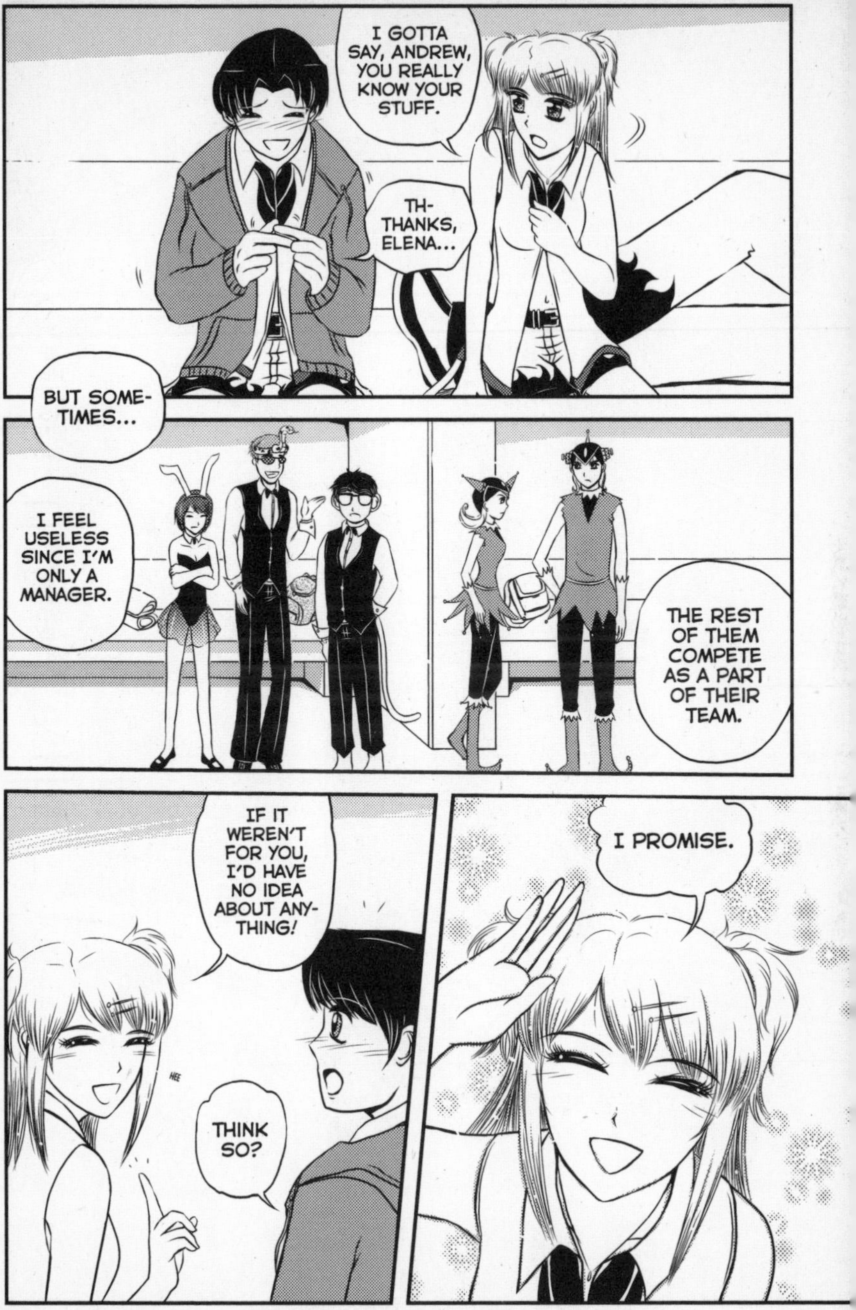
I GOTTA SAY, ANDREW, YOU REALLY KNOW YOUR STUFF.
TH- THANKS, ELENA...
BUT SOME- TIMES...
I FEEL USELESS SINCE I'M ONLY A MANAGER.
THE REST OF THEM COMPETE AS A PART OF THEIR TEAM.
IF IT WEREN'T FOR YOU, I'D HAVE NO IDEA ABOUT ANY- THING!
HEE
THINK SO?
I PROMISE.

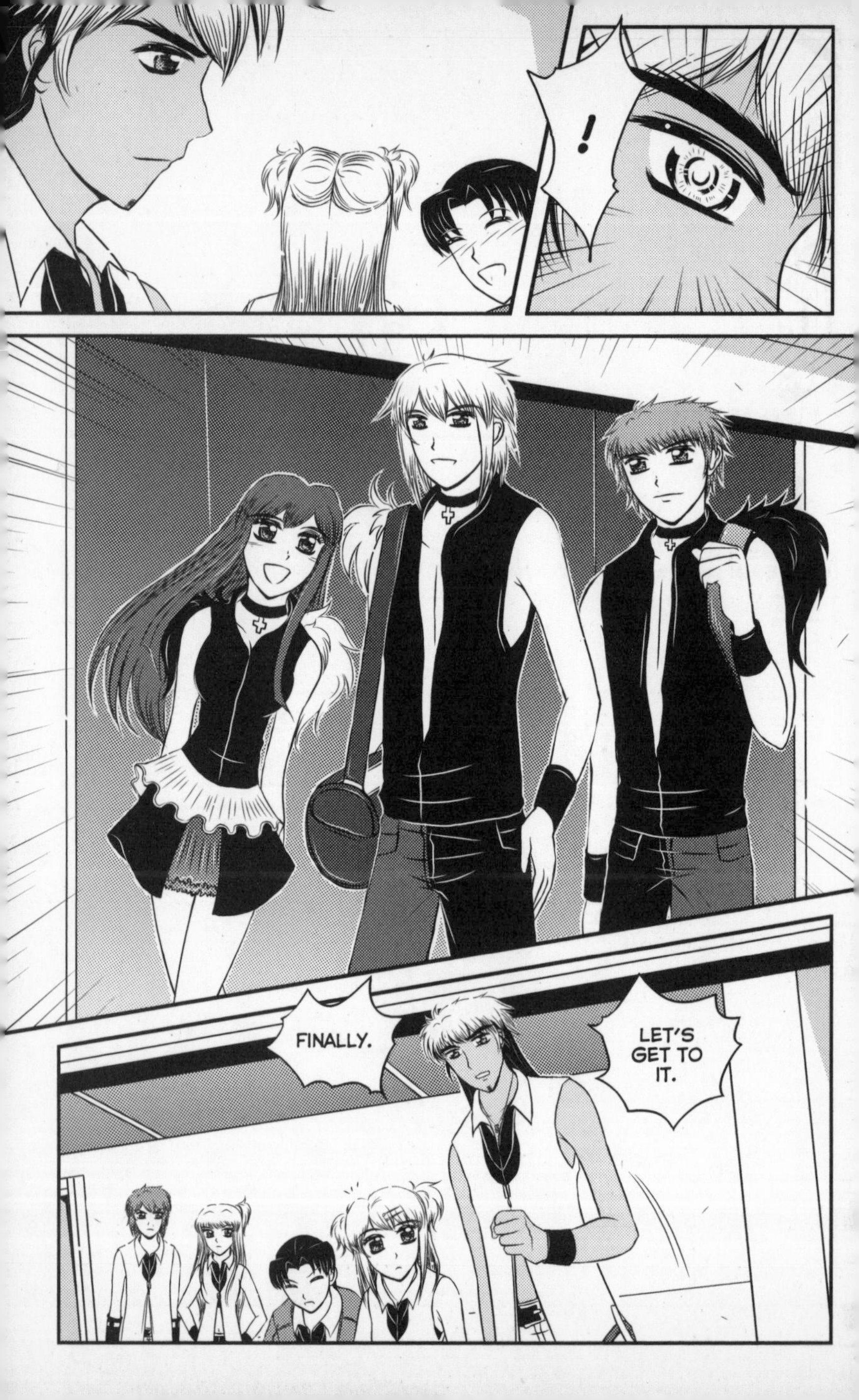
!
FINALLY.
LET'S GET TO IT.

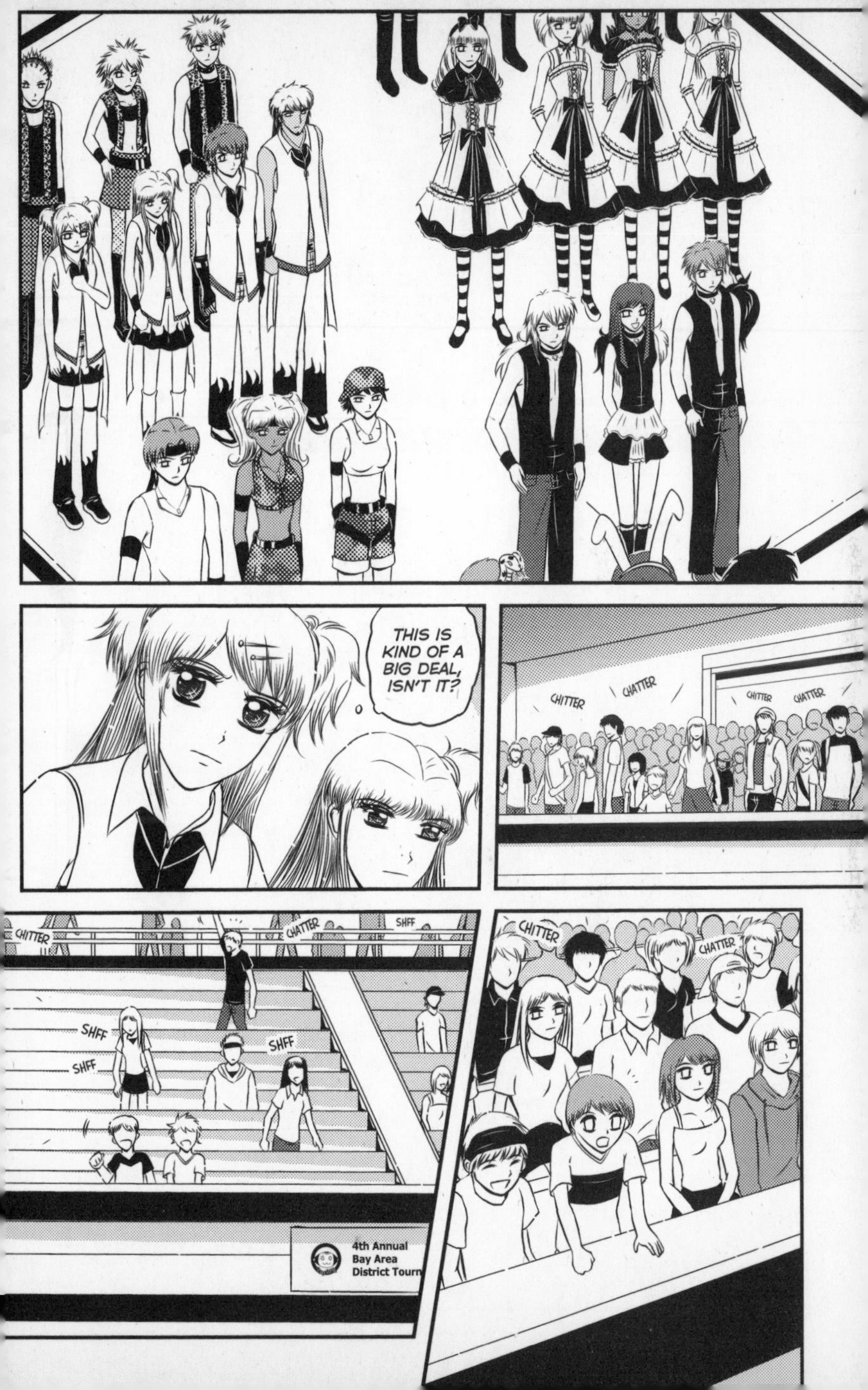
THIS IS KIND OF A BIG DEAL, ISN'T IT?
CHITTER
CHATTER
CHITTER
CHATTER
CHITTER
CHATTER
SHFF
SHFF
SHFF
SHFF
4th Annual
Bay Area
District Tourn
CHITTER
CHATTER

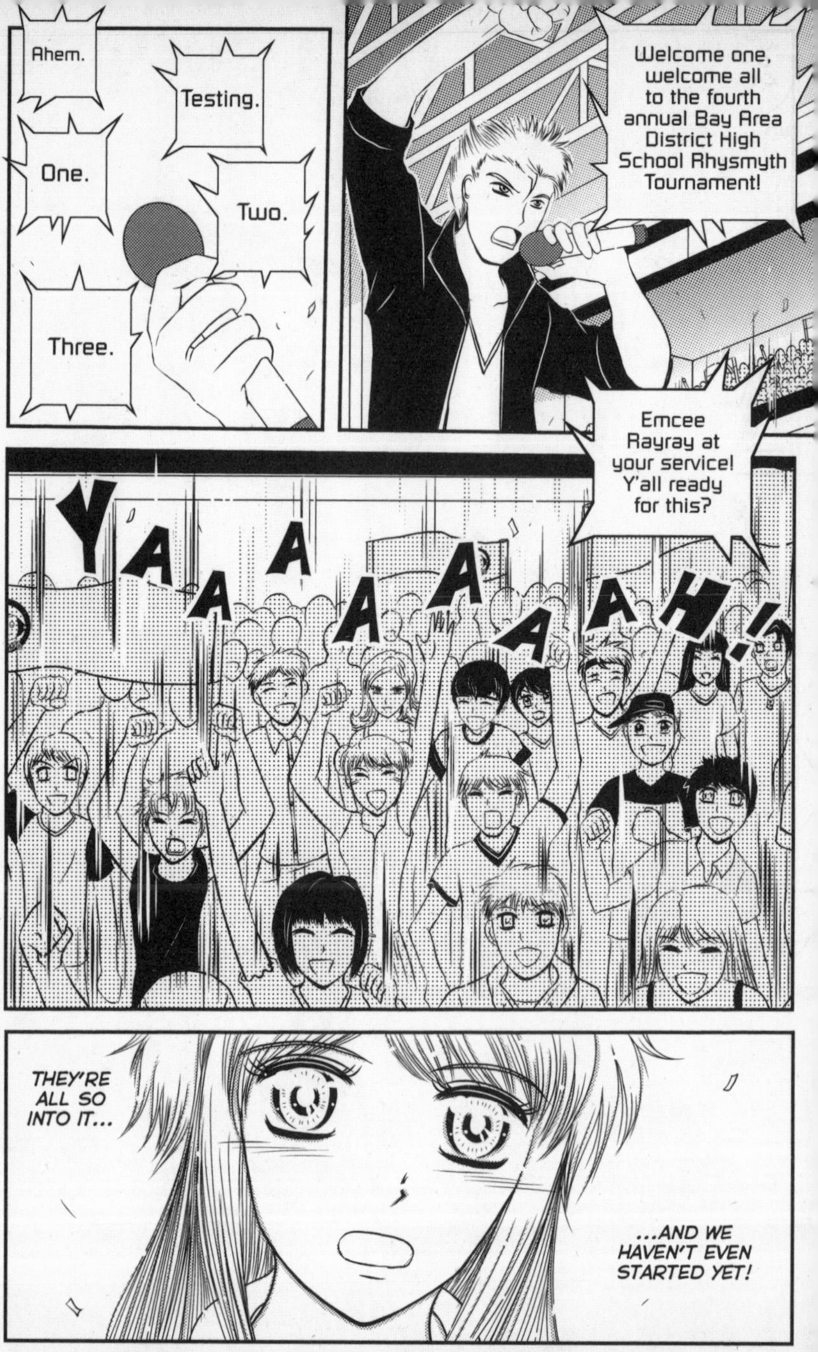
Ahem.
Testing.
One.
Two.
Three.
Welcome one, welcome all to the fourth annual Bay Area District High School Rhysmyth Tournament!
Emcee Rayray at your service! Y'all ready for this?
YAAAAAAAAH!!
THEY'RE ALL SO INTO IT...
...AND WE HAVEN'T EVEN STARTED YET!

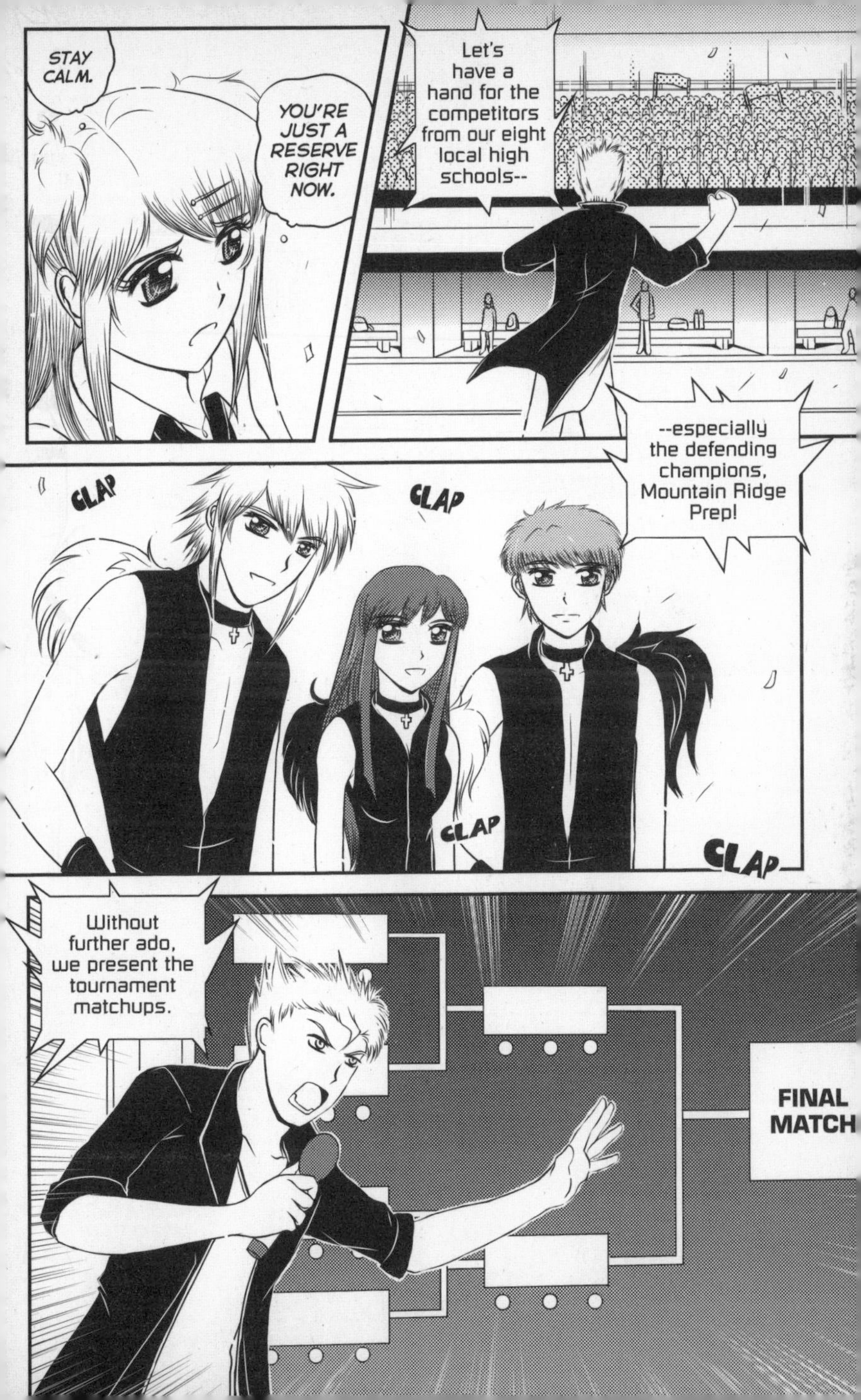
STAY CALM.
YOU'RE JUST A RESERVE RIGHT NOW.
Let's have a hand for the competitors from our eight local high schools--
--especially the defending champions, Mountain Ridge Prep!
CLAP
CLAP
CLAP
CLAP
Without further ado, we present the tournament matchups.
FINAL MATCH

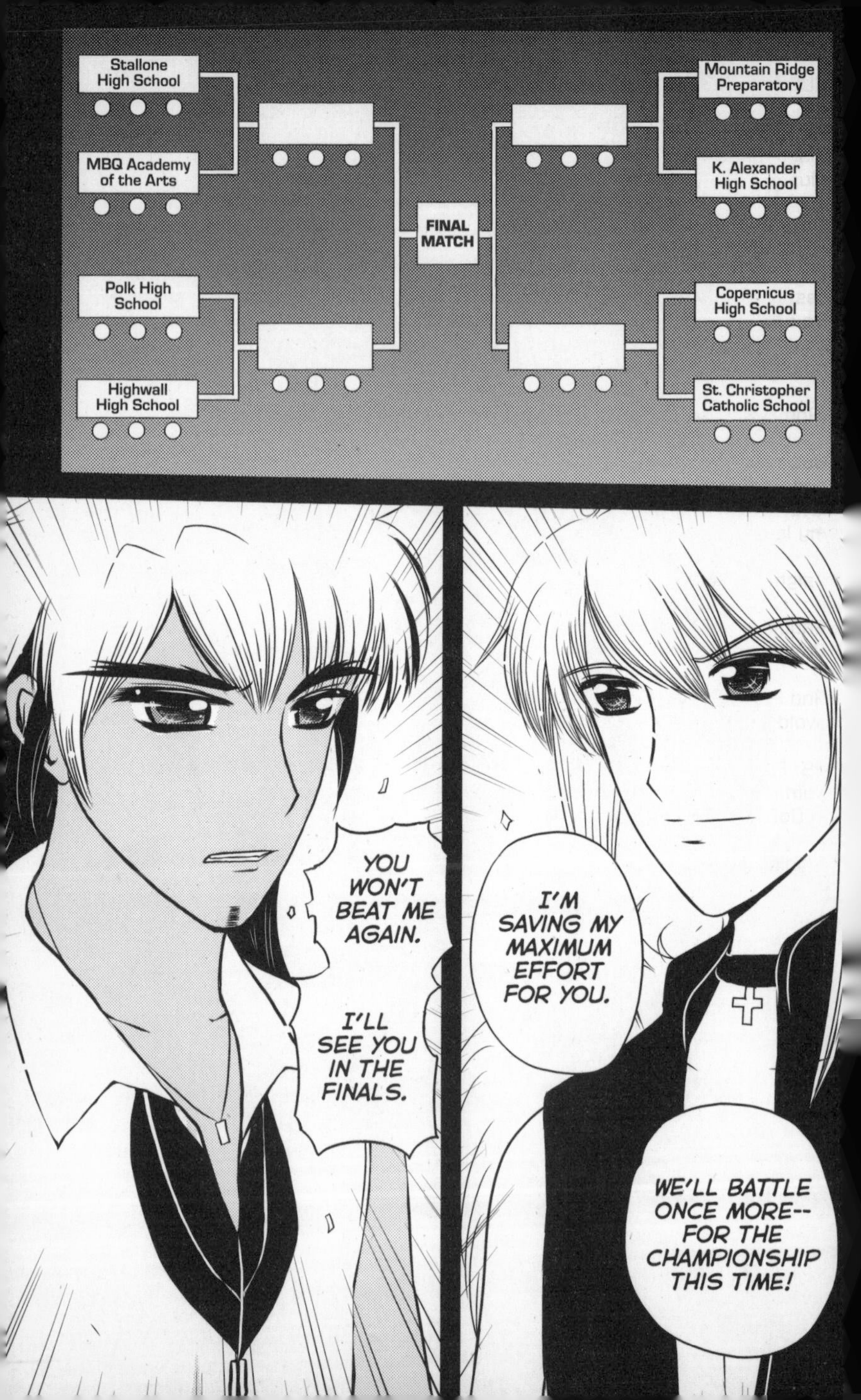
Stallone High School
MBQ Academy of the Arts
Polk High School
Highwall High School
FINAL MATCH
Mountain Ridge Preparatory
K. Alexander High School
Copernicus High School
St. Christopher Catholic School
YOU WON'T BEAT ME AGAIN.
I'LL SEE YOU IN THE FINALS.
I'M SAVING MY MAXIMUM EFFORT FOR YOU.
WE'LL BATTLE ONCE MORE-- FOR THE CHAMPIONSHIP THIS TIME!

SUBJECT: dun dun dun dunnnnnn!

Location: el roomo
Mood: Flustered
Music: DoD Sndtrk "Cosmic Roma"

Direction of Destiny Excelsior Edition for the GameStation720 is kinda taking over my life. But I'm not complaining!!

Last time I played I had to NOT save because I totally destroyed my storyline. So earlier today I tried again from the original save point--climactic battle time against the Dark Phantom "Wah-Zee" atop Mount Pinotubo! There's no way I could let him run off with Princess Reena TWICE, was there?

(And don't you just LOVE the renaming ability on this game?!)

But, of course, I didn't follow through with my combo light attack in time and...BLECH! That traitorous Dark Phantom runs off with my beautiful level 36 power mage and I'm stuck in some dirty-ass cave all by my lonesome...

: sigh :

Should I just move on and save from there and see what happens? Or should I try it again one more time from that save point?

And PLEASE, no spoilers if you comment! I'm doing my best as it is to avoid looking at FAQs and such and such.

PS: For all you hardcore Rhysmyth fans out there, catch me and my team from Highwall High competing at the Center this weekend-- in DoD cosplay, no less!!

Signing off--Diocel   0 Comments.

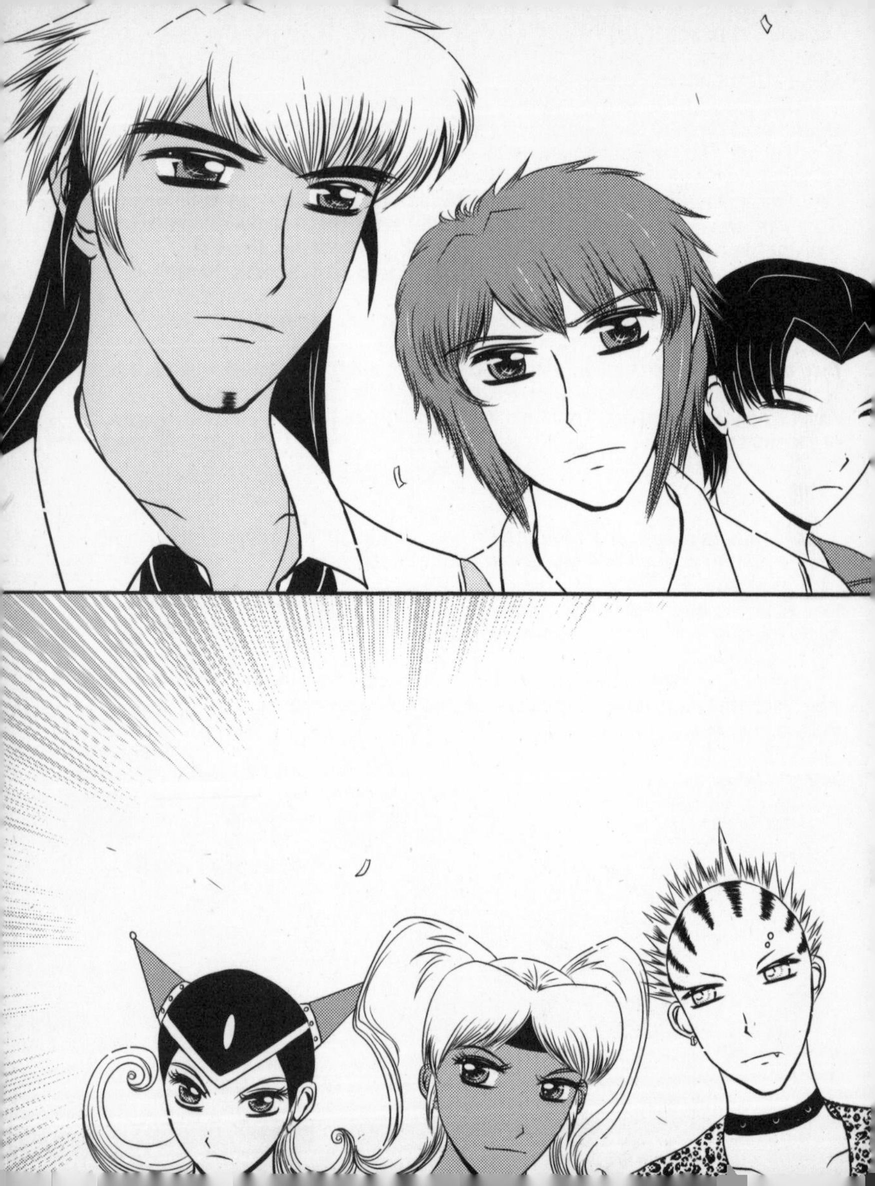

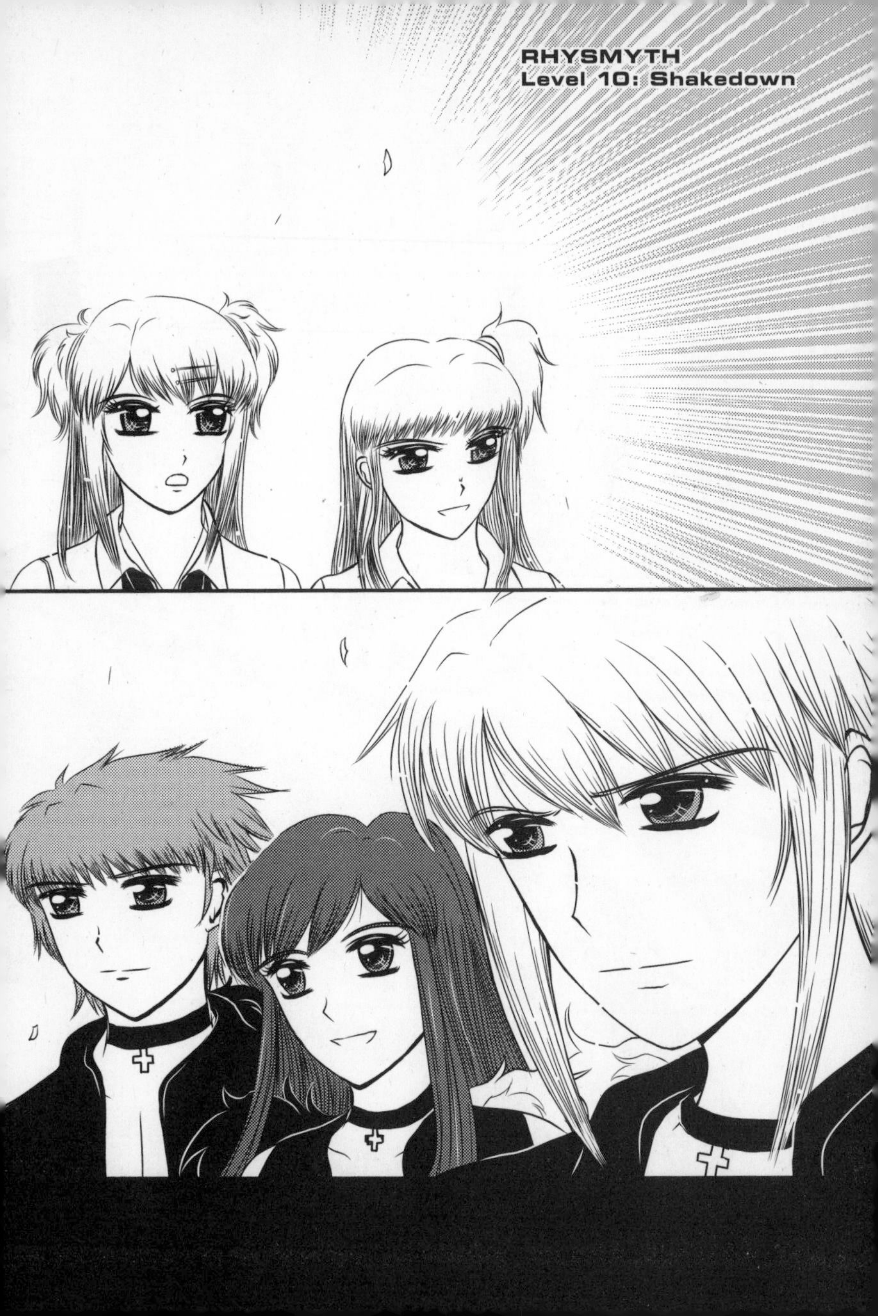
RHYSMYTH
Level 10: Shakedown

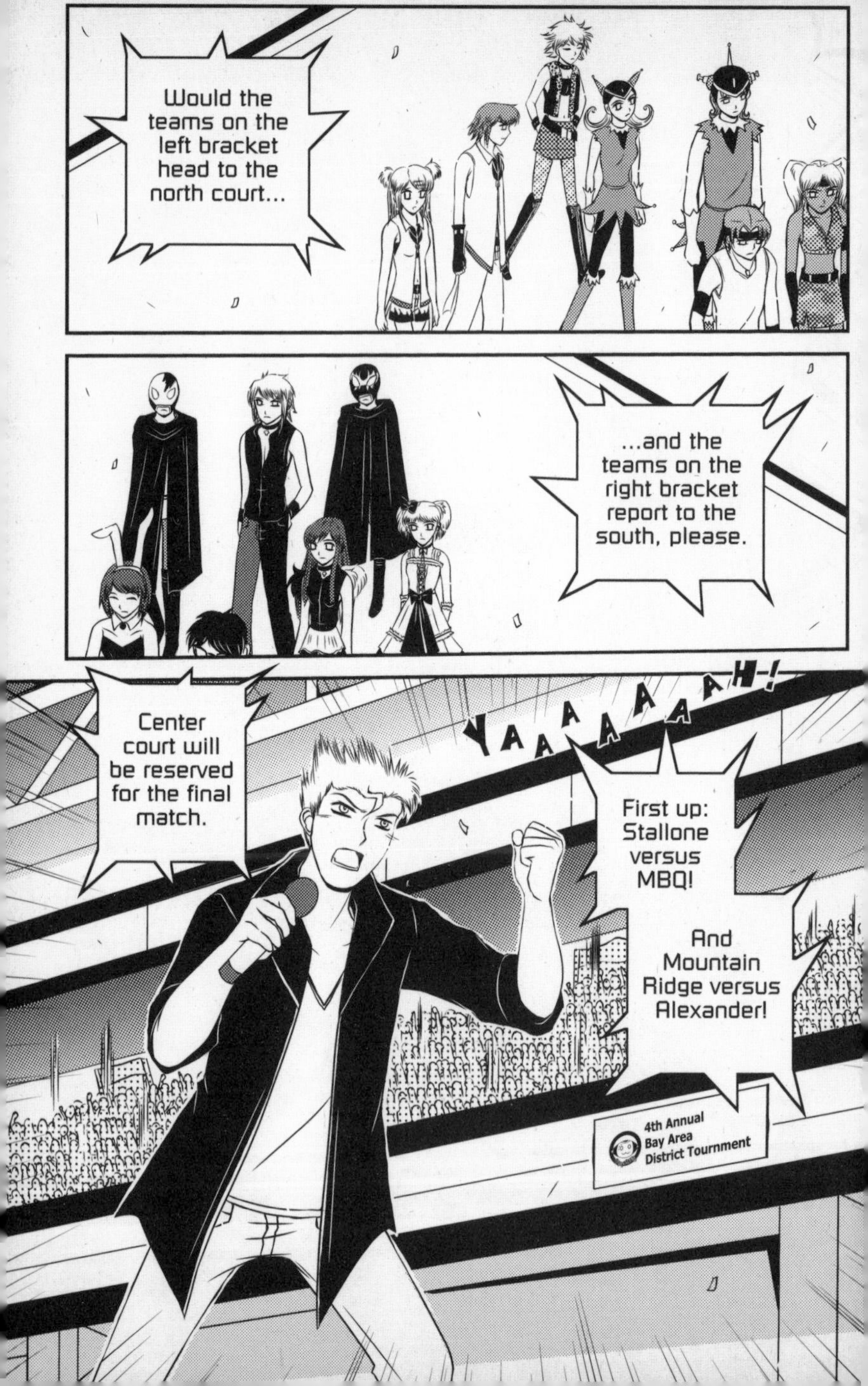
Would the teams on the left bracket head to the north court...
...and the teams on the right bracket report to the south, please.
Center court will be reserved for the final match.
YAAAAAAAAH!
First up: Stallone versus MBQ!
And Mountain Ridge versus Alexander!
4th Annual Bay Area District Tournment

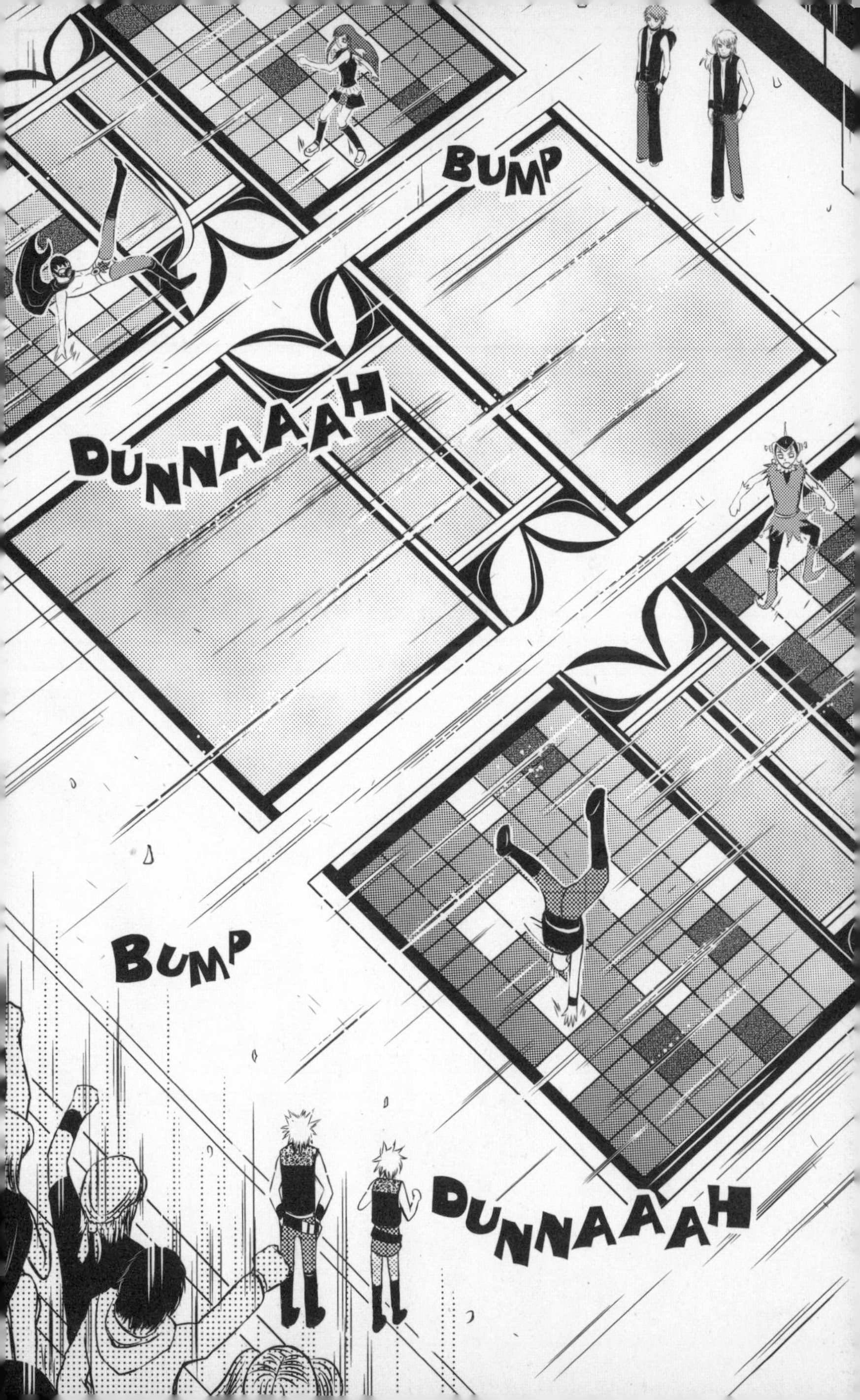
BUMP
DUNNAAAH
BUMP
DUNNAAAH

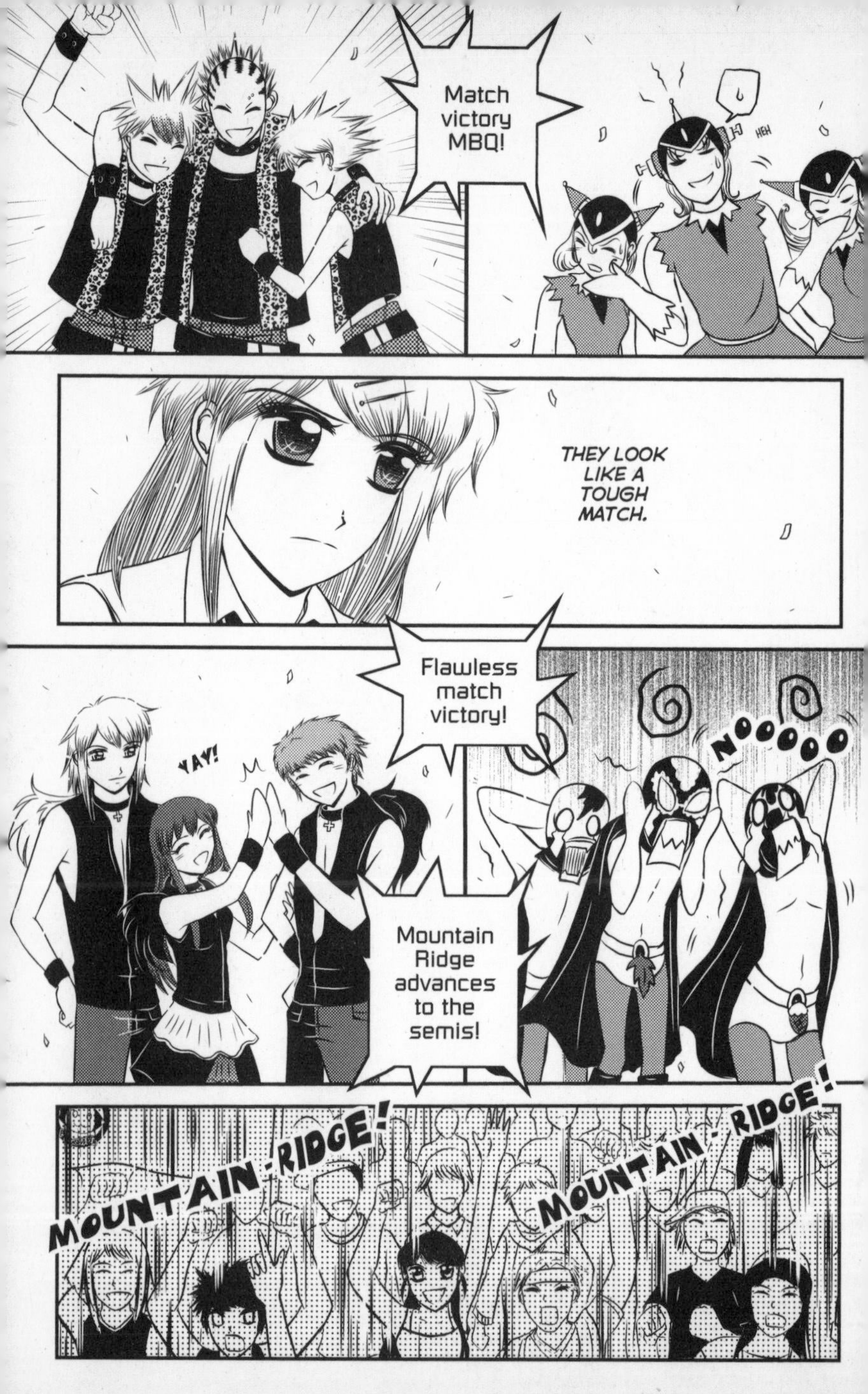
Match victory MBQ!
HEH
THEY LOOK LIKE A TOUGH MATCH.
Flawless match victory!
YAY!
Mountain Ridge advances to the semis!
NOOOOO
MOUNTAIN-RIDGE!
MOUNTAIN-RIDGE!

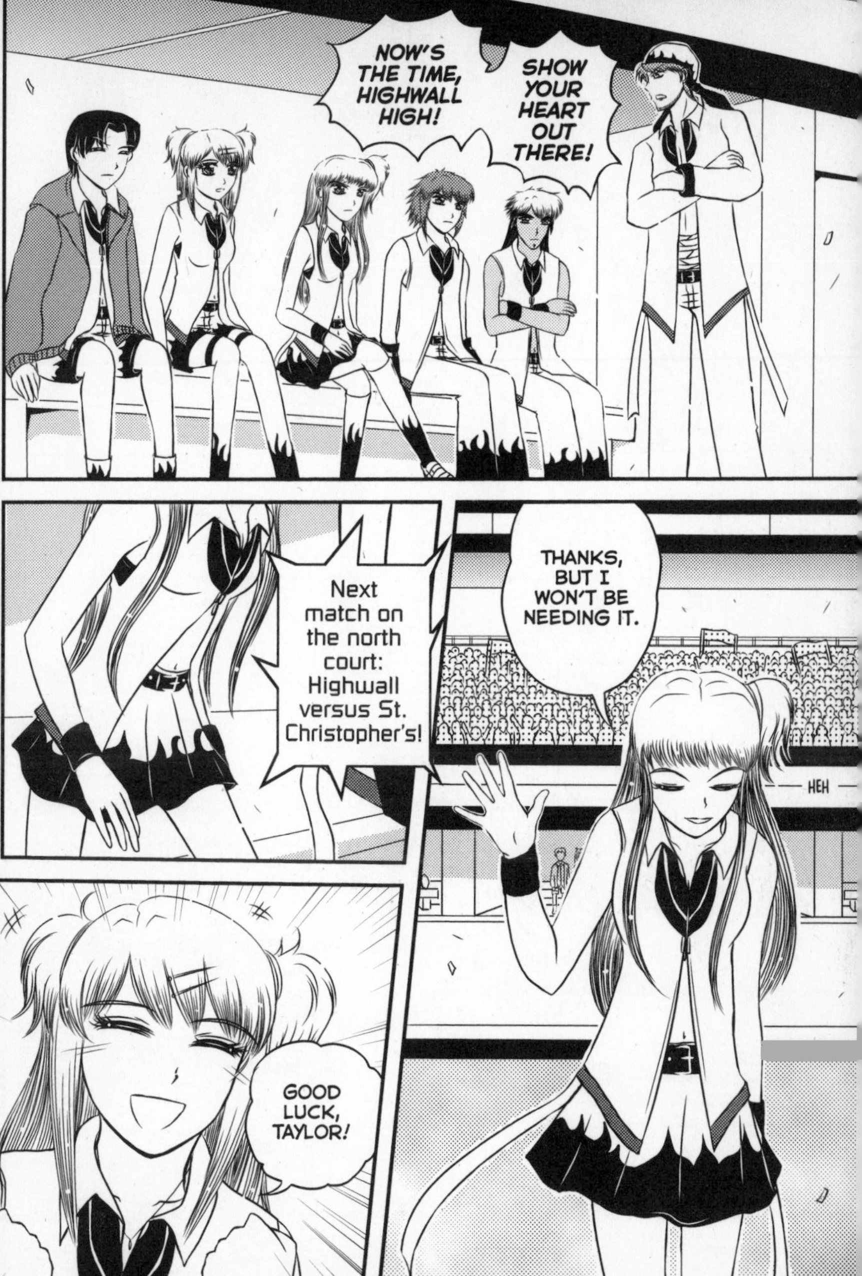
NOW'S THE TIME, HIGHWALL HIGH!
SHOW YOUR HEART OUT THERE!
Next match on the north court: Highwall versus St. Christopher's!
THANKS, BUT I WON'T BE NEEDING IT.
HEH
GOOD LUCK, TAYLOR!

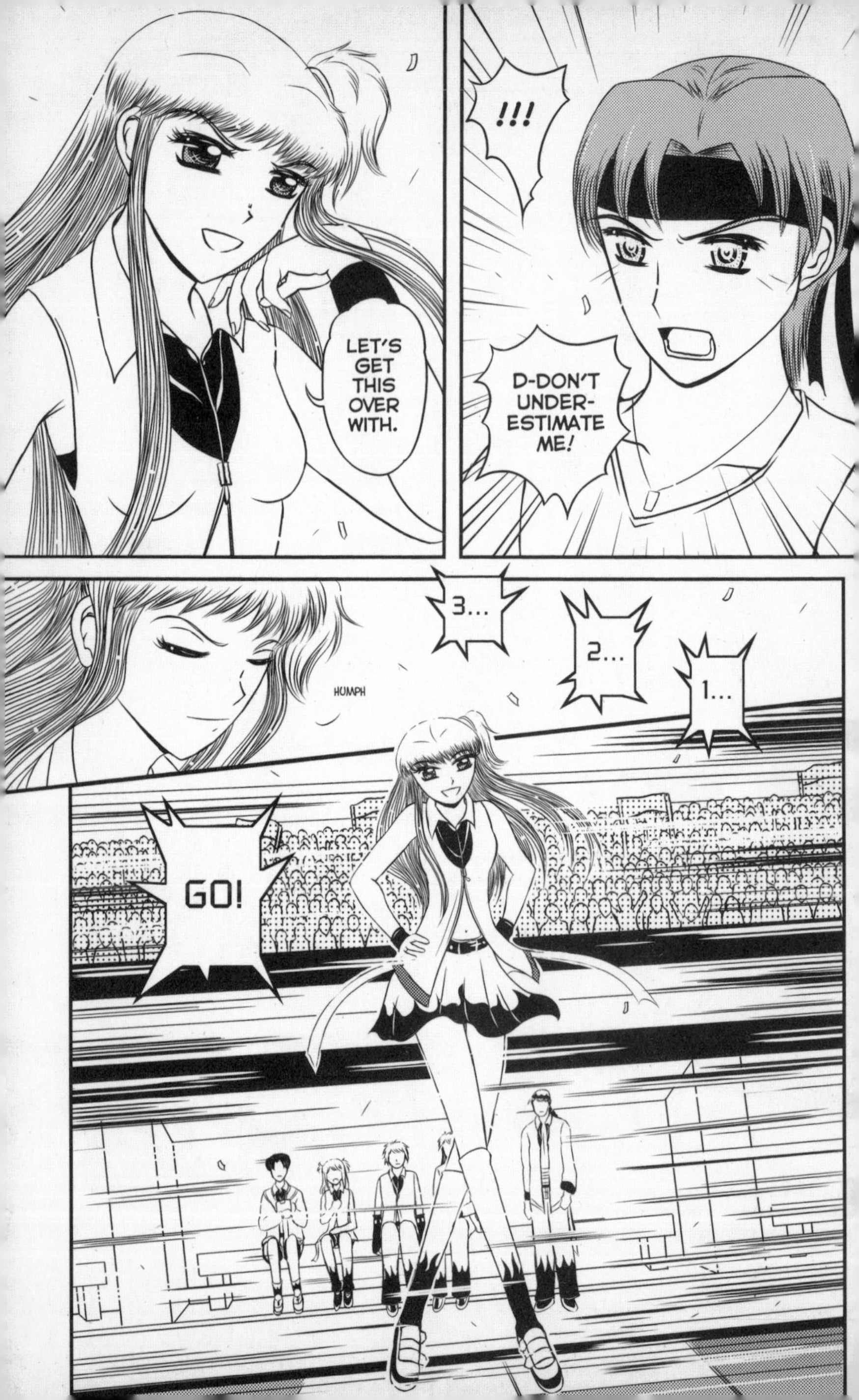
LET'S GET THIS OVER WITH.
!!!
D-DON'T UNDER-ESTIMATE ME!
HUMPH
3...
2...
1...
GO!

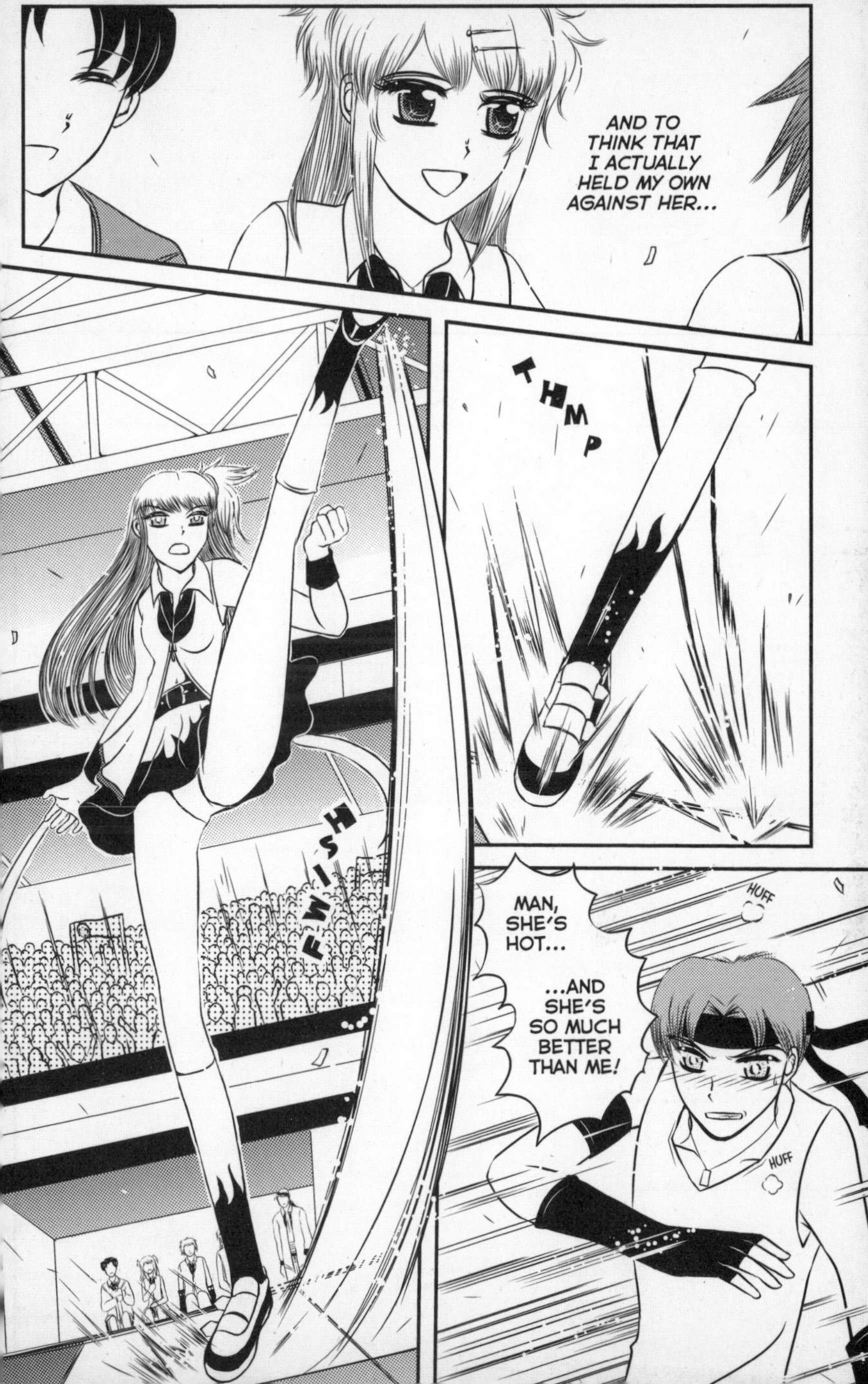
AND TO THINK THAT I ACTUALLY HELD MY OWN AGAINST HER...
FWISH
KHMP
MAN, SHE'S HOT...
...AND SHE'S SO MUCH BETTER THAN ME!
HUFF
HUFF

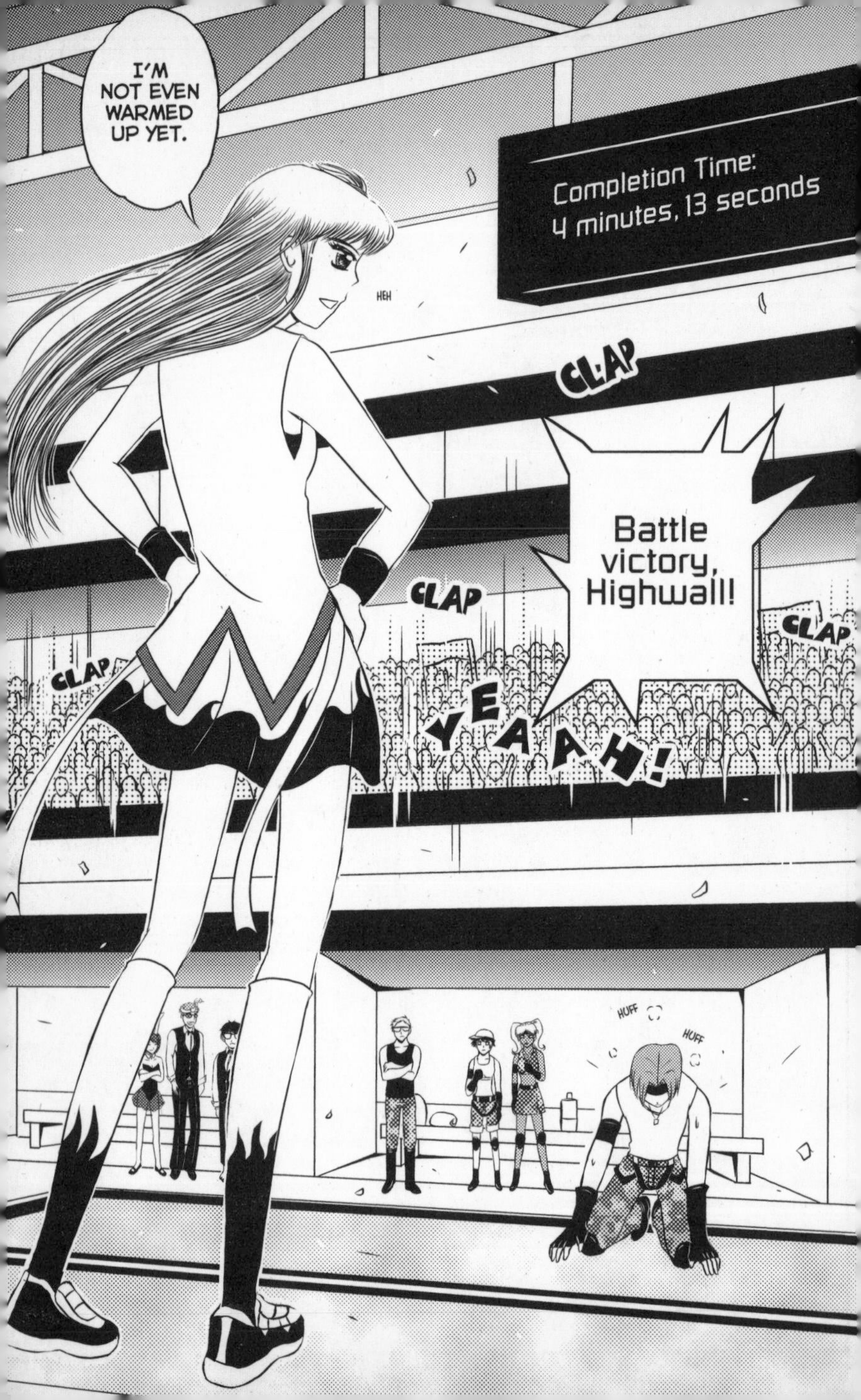
I'M NOT EVEN WARMED UP YET.
Completion Time: 4 minutes, 13 seconds
HEH
CLAP
Battle victory, Highwall!
CLAP
CLAP
CLAP
YEAAH!
HUFF
HUFF

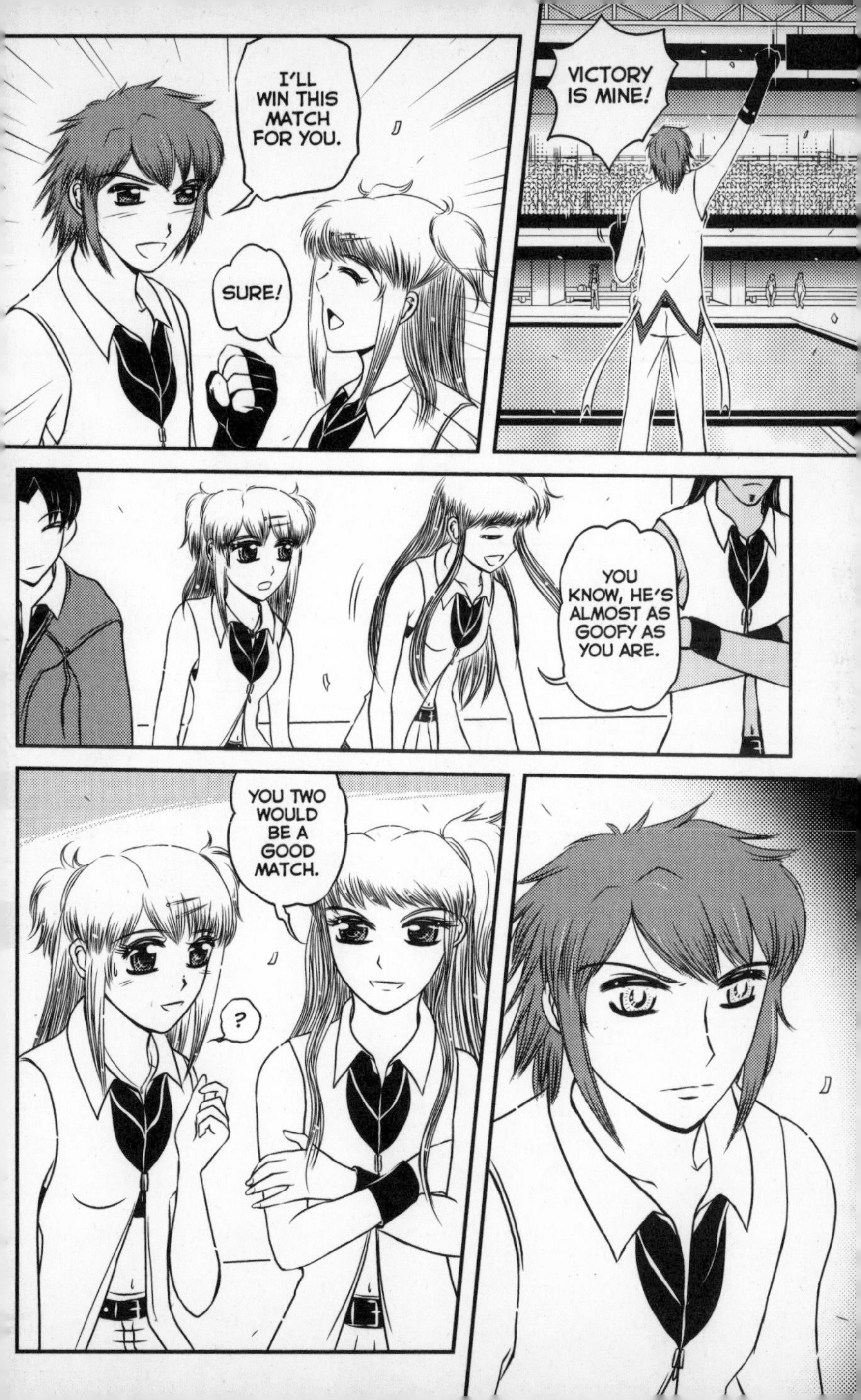
I'LL WIN THIS MATCH FOR YOU.
SURE!
VICTORY IS MINE!
YOU KNOW, HE'S ALMOST AS GOOFY AS YOU ARE.
YOU TWO WOULD BE A GOOD MATCH.
?

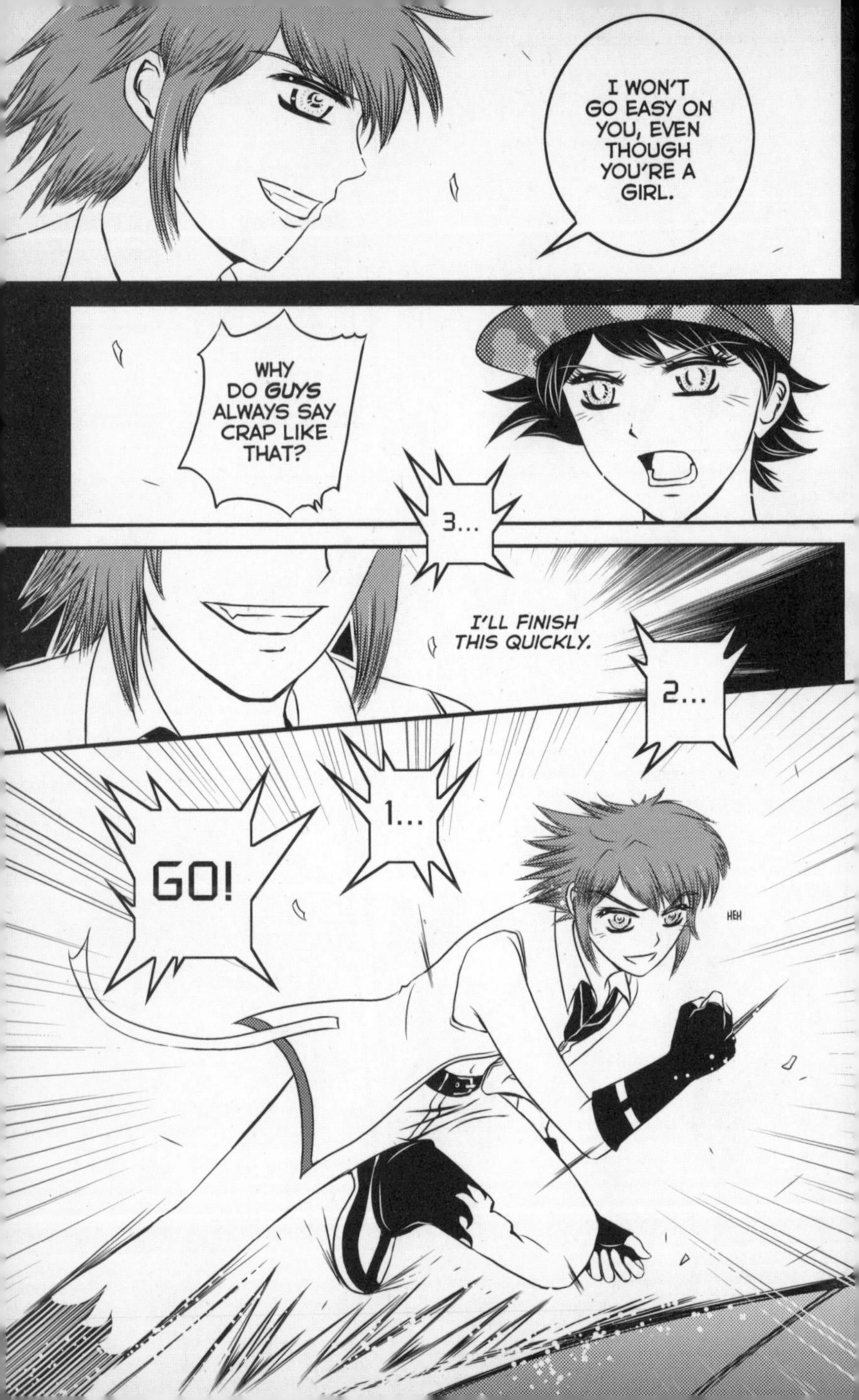
I WON'T GO EASY ON YOU, EVEN THOUGH YOU'RE A GIRL.
WHY DO GUYS ALWAYS SAY CRAP LIKE THAT?
3...
I'LL FINISH THIS QUICKLY.
2...
GO!
1...
HEH

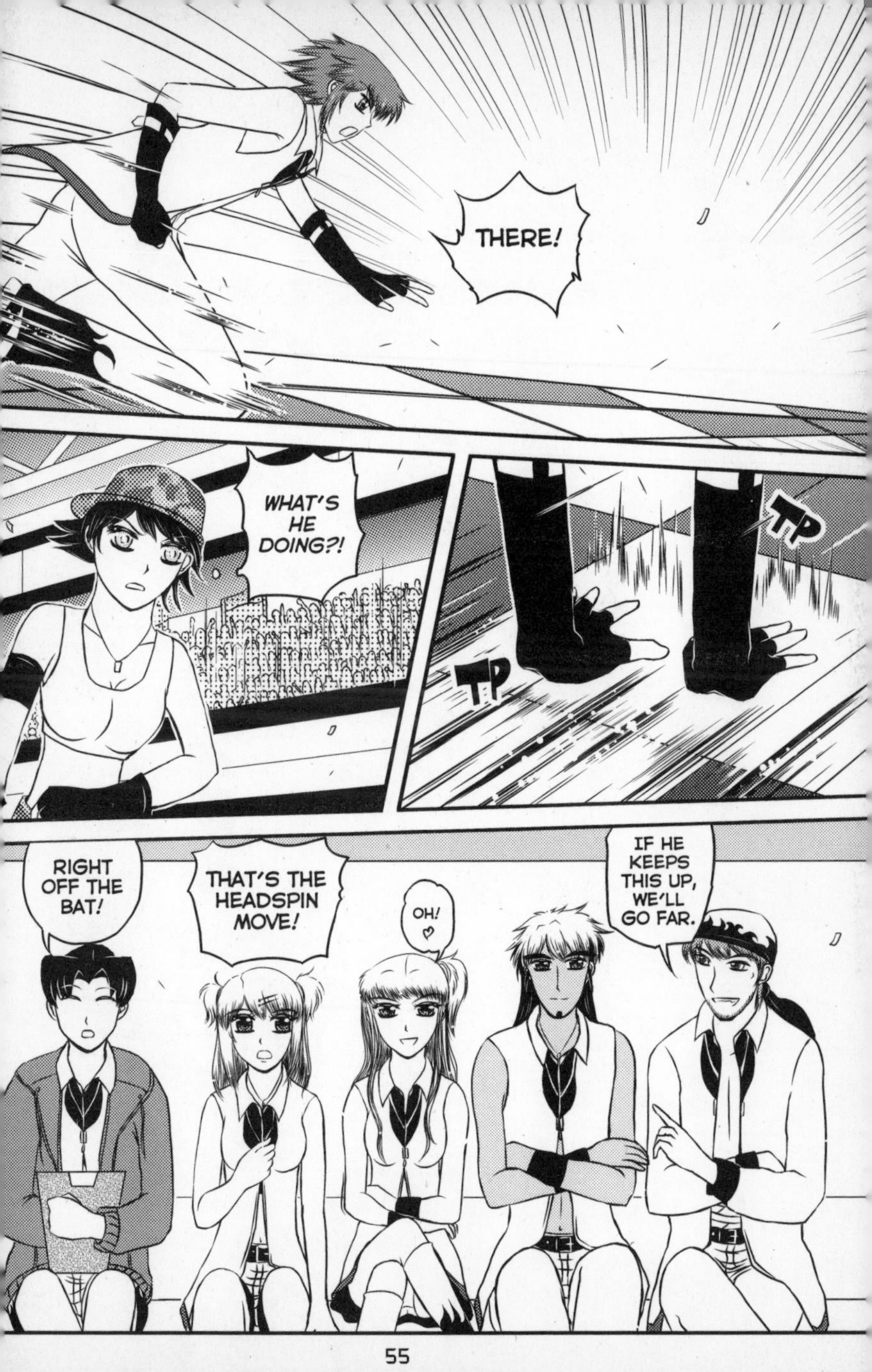
THERE!
WHAT'S HE DOING?!
TP
TP
RIGHT OFF THE BAT!
THAT'S THE HEADSPIN MOVE!
OH! ♡
IF HE KEEPS THIS UP, WE'LL GO FAR.

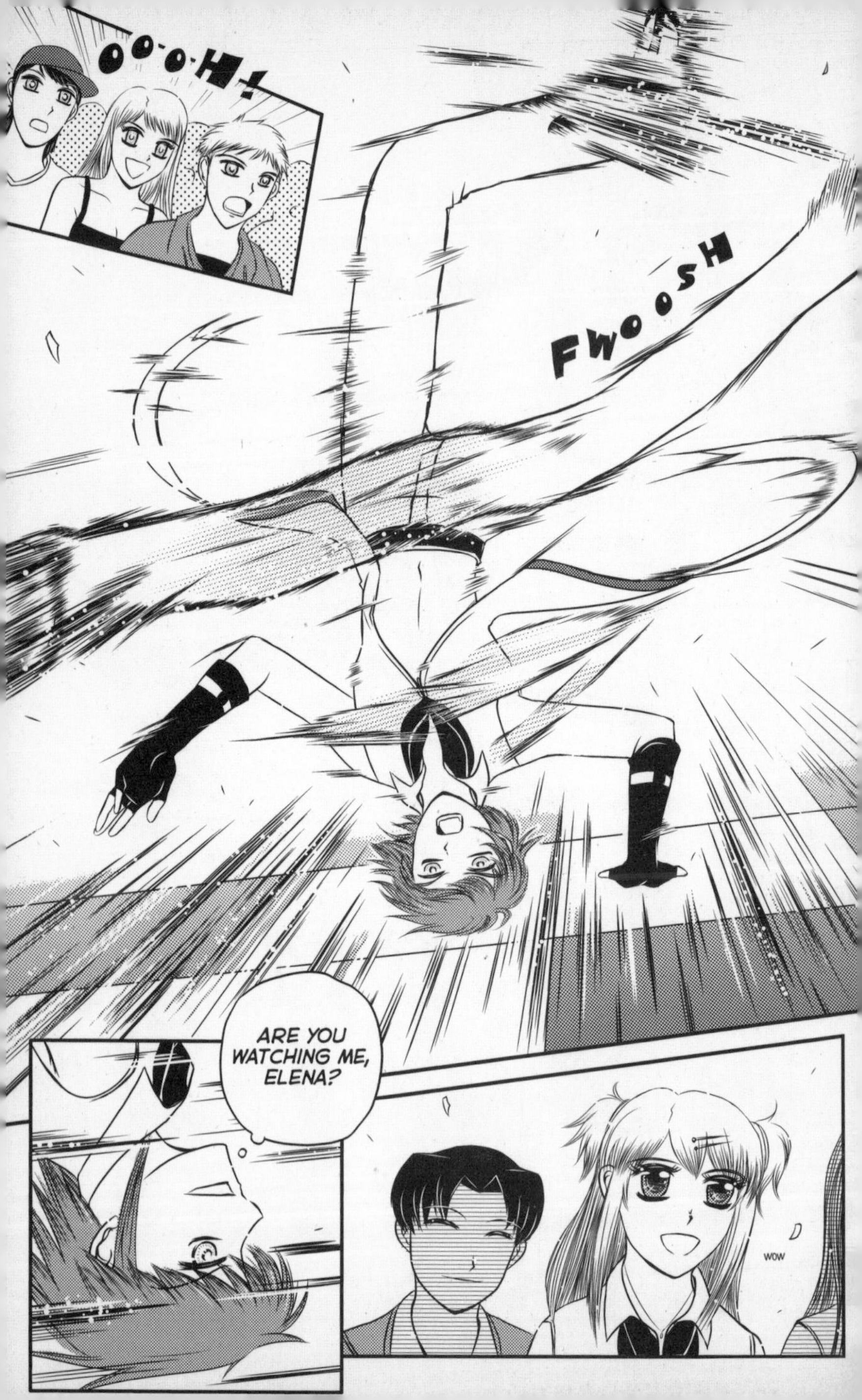
OO-O-H!
FWOOSH
ARE YOU WATCHING ME, ELENA?
WOW

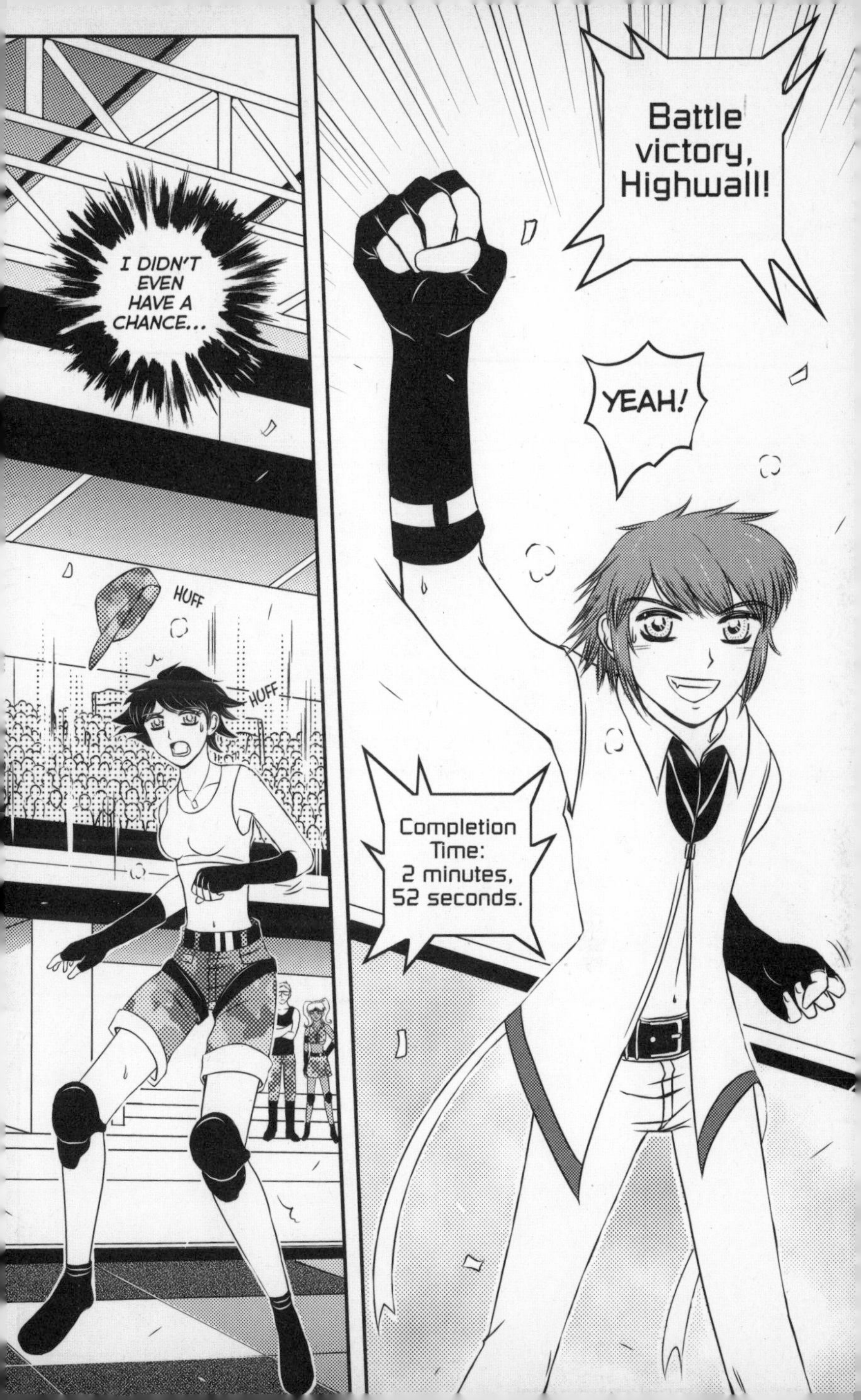
I DIDN'T EVEN HAVE A CHANCE...
HUFF
HUFF
Battle victory, Highwall!
YEAH!
Completion Time: 2 minutes, 52 seconds.

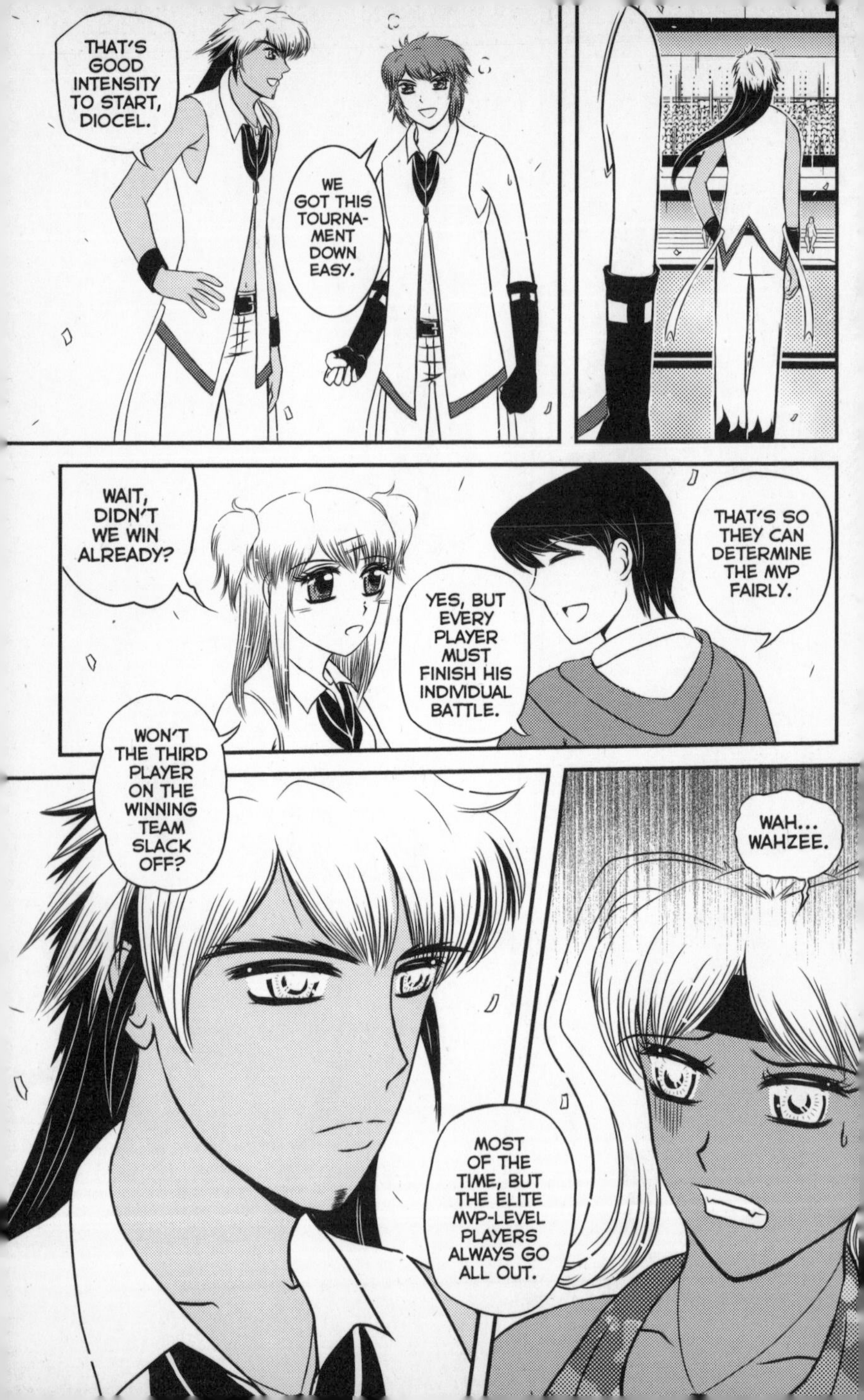
THAT'S GOOD INTENSITY TO START, DIOCEL.
WE GOT THIS TOURNA-MENT DOWN EASY.
WAIT, DIDN'T WE WIN ALREADY?
YES, BUT EVERY PLAYER MUST FINISH HIS INDIVIDUAL BATTLE.
THAT'S SO THEY CAN DETERMINE THE MVP FAIRLY.
WON'T THE THIRD PLAYER ON THE WINNING TEAM SLACK OFF?
MOST OF THE TIME, BUT THE ELITE MVP-LEVEL PLAYERS ALWAYS GO ALL OUT.
WAH... WAHZEE.

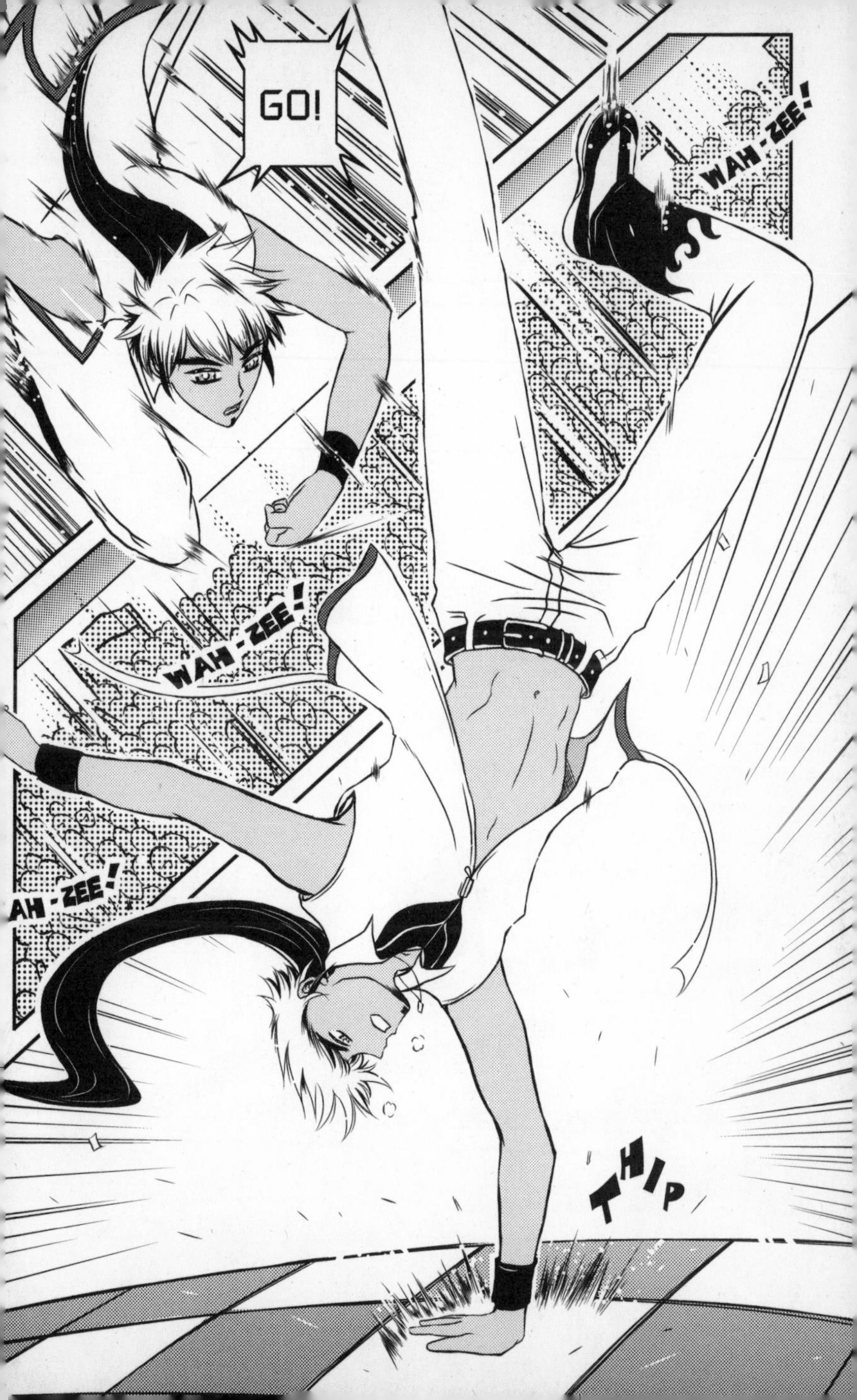
GO!
WAH-ZEE!
WAH-ZEE!
AH-ZEE!
THIP

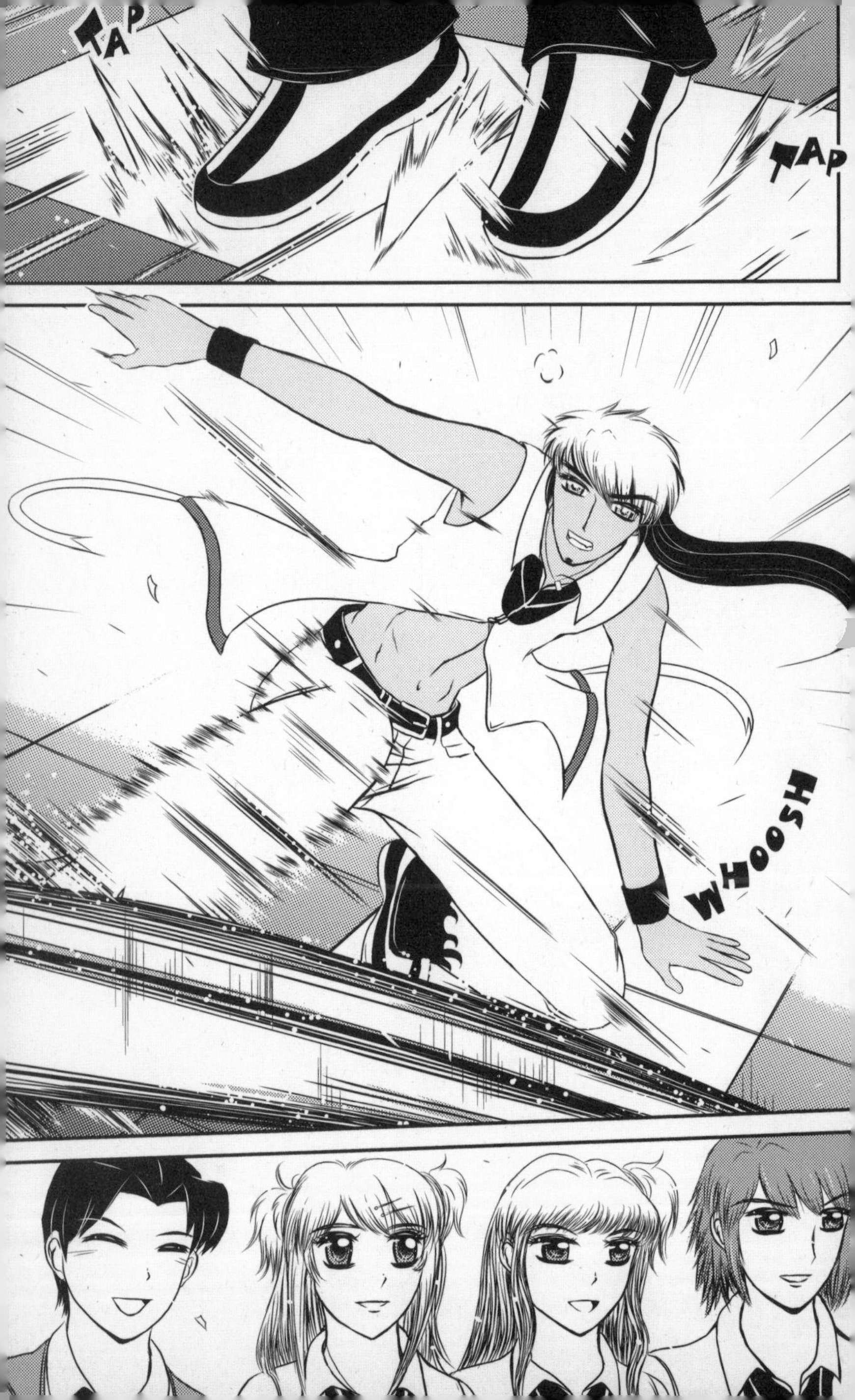
TAP
TAP
WHOOSH

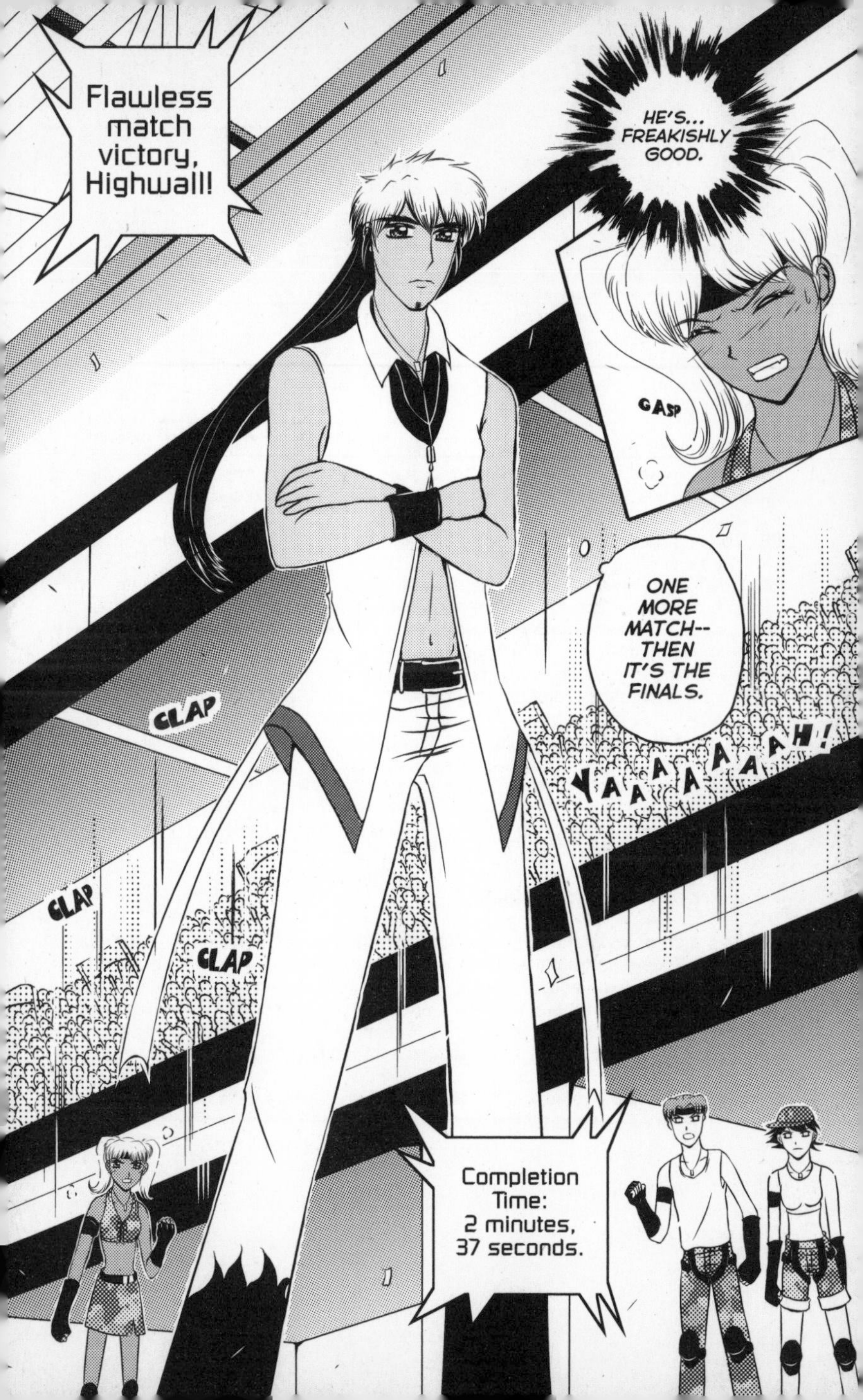

Flawless match victory, Highwall!
HE'S... FREAKISHLY GOOD.
GASP
ONE MORE MATCH-- THEN IT'S THE FINALS.
CLAP
YAAAAAAAH!
CLAP
CLAP
Completion Time: 2 minutes, 37 seconds.

RHYSMYTH

FROM PAGE C 1 --

I caught up with local high school athlete Renaldo Guarin for his thoughts on the growing mania surrounding Rhysmyth.

FELIPE ABBOTT: When Rhysmyth debuted, many dismissed it as a glorified arcade video game, not a real sport. But the professional league has been sizably successful after its first two full seasons. Why do you think Rhysmyth is what it is?

Renaldo Guarin, last year's MVP from Mountain Ridge

RENALDO GUARIN: Passion and creativity. People are naturally drawn to both. Rhysmyth is one hundred percent sport. Rhysmyth is also one hundred percent art.

FA: Do you feel Rhysmyth is a sport on par with football or baseball or basketball?

RG: Definitely. Personally, I feel like Rhysmyth was made for me. When I play or watch other sports, there's no question about what I'm experiencing: fierce competition between amazing athletes. But over the entire period of a game, there are only a limited amount of truly transcendent moments. Moments when I catch myself holding my breath. When I watch a high-level Rhysmyth battle, I can barely breathe the whole way through. And when I play...there's nothing better.

FA: I'm sure many people would have said the same thing about your oft-viewed, Videotube-replayed semifinal match last year. Is it fair to say that you and Highwall High School's Wahzee Zameel are enjoying a bit of a rivalry right now?

RG: Well... I don't really know about that. People toss around the word rivalry pretty easily nowadays.

FA: Would you elaborate, please?

RG: He's a great competitor, for sure. Toughest I've gone up against so far. What separates Rhysmyth from the other sports is the prolonged one-on-one aspect, the sense that the person across the court from you is pushing you to do better than you could alone. Even though tennis is one-on-one, you're still exchanging shots, still reacting to the other person. On the Rhysmyth court, you have to keep pushing the intensity from the start. I'd definitely love to battle him again if it comes to that.

But we've only had one go and that's that, so I don't know if it's fair, in respect to the great rivalries in sports, for someone to say that "Zameel and Guarin" is a rivalry.

FA: And if you meet again in this year's competition?

RG: I'd say bring it on. (laughter)

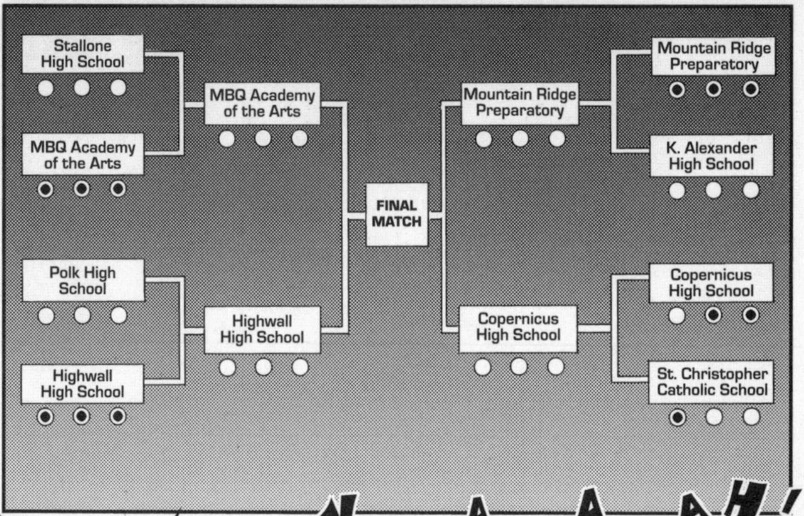
Stallone High School
MBQ Academy of the Arts
MBQ Academy of the Arts
Polk High School
Highwall High School
Highwall High School
FINAL MATCH
Mountain Ridge Preparatory
Mountain Ridge Preparatory
K. Alexander High School
Copernicus High School
Copernicus High School
St. Christopher Catholic School
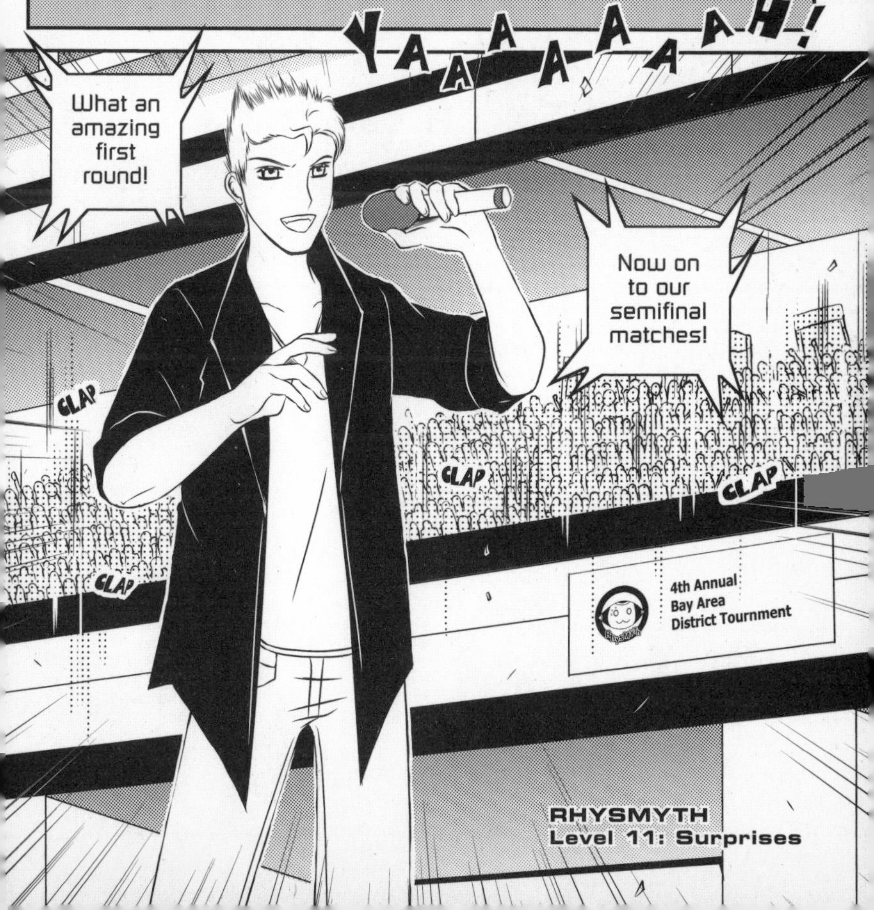
YAAAAAAAH!
What an amazing first round!
Now on to our semifinal matches!
CLAP
CLAP
CLAP
CLAP
4th Annual Bay Area District Tournment
RhysMYTh
RHYSMYTH
Level 11: Surprises

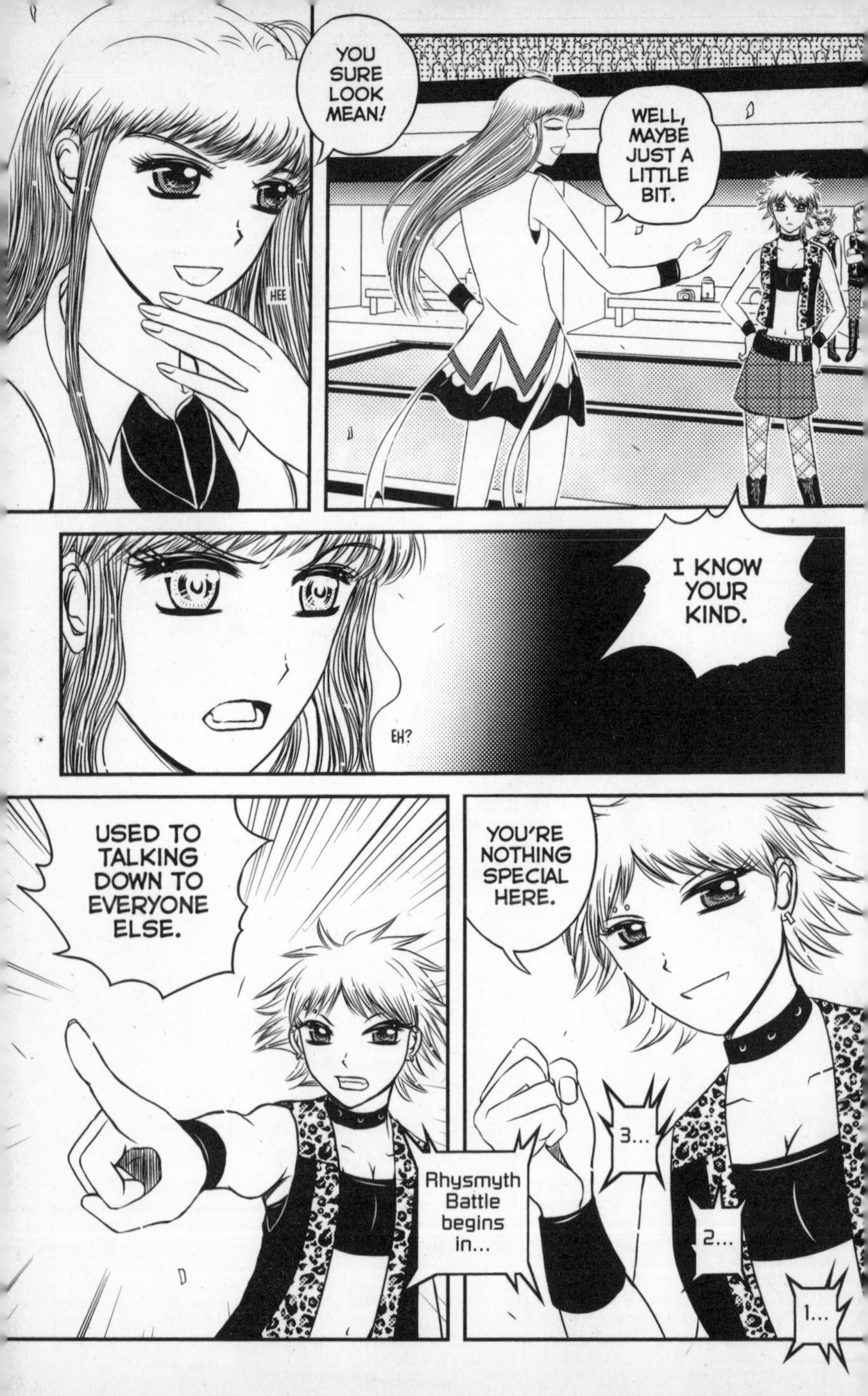
YOU SURE LOOK MEAN!
HEE
WELL, MAYBE JUST A LITTLE BIT.
I KNOW YOUR KIND.
EH?
USED TO TALKING DOWN TO EVERYONE ELSE.
YOU'RE NOTHING SPECIAL HERE.
Rhysmyth Battle begins in...
3...
2...
1...

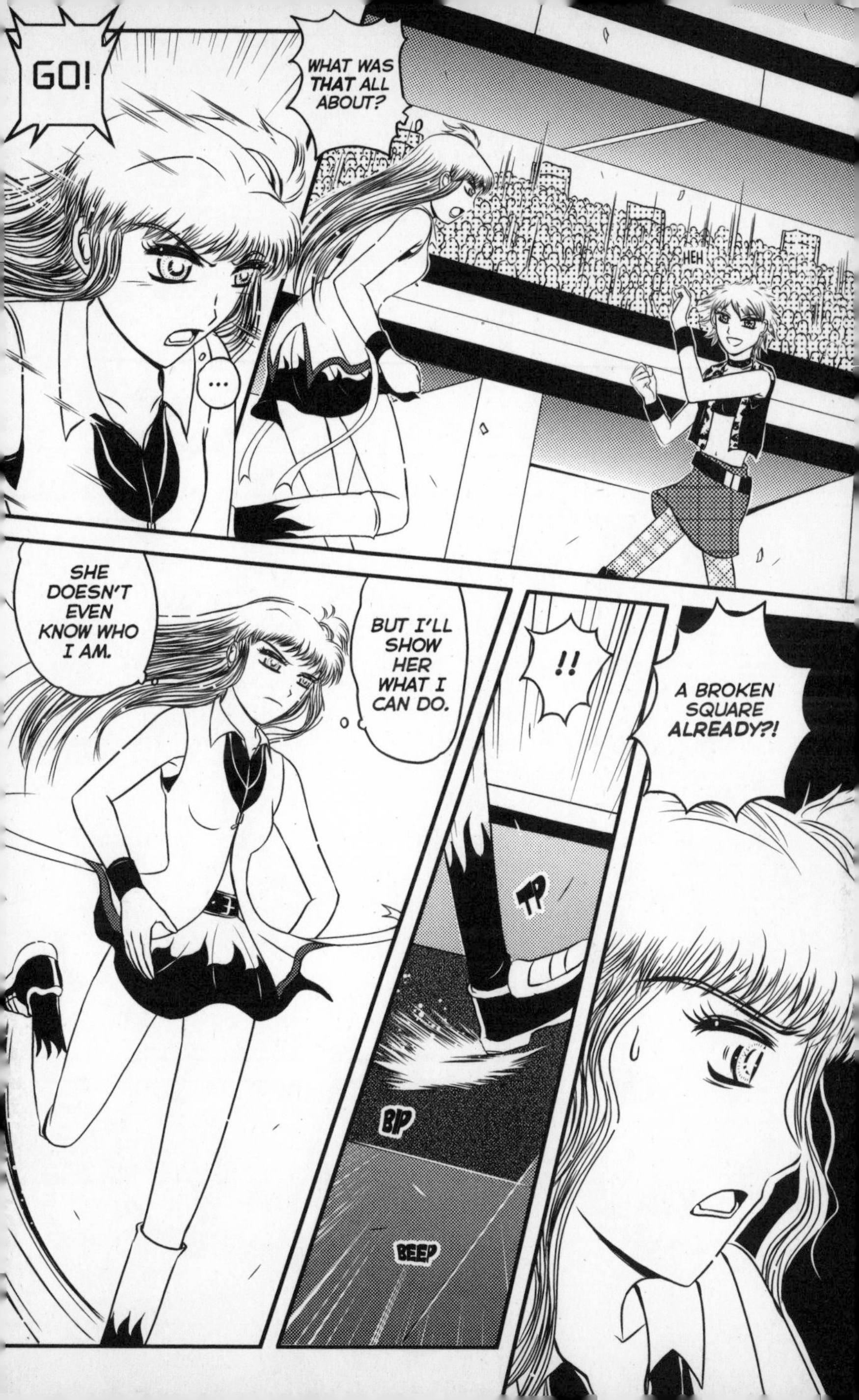
GO!
WHAT WAS THAT ALL ABOUT?
HEH
...
SHE DOESN'T EVEN KNOW WHO I AM.
BUT I'LL SHOW HER WHAT I CAN DO.
!!
TP
BIP
BEEP
A BROKEN SQUARE ALREADY?!

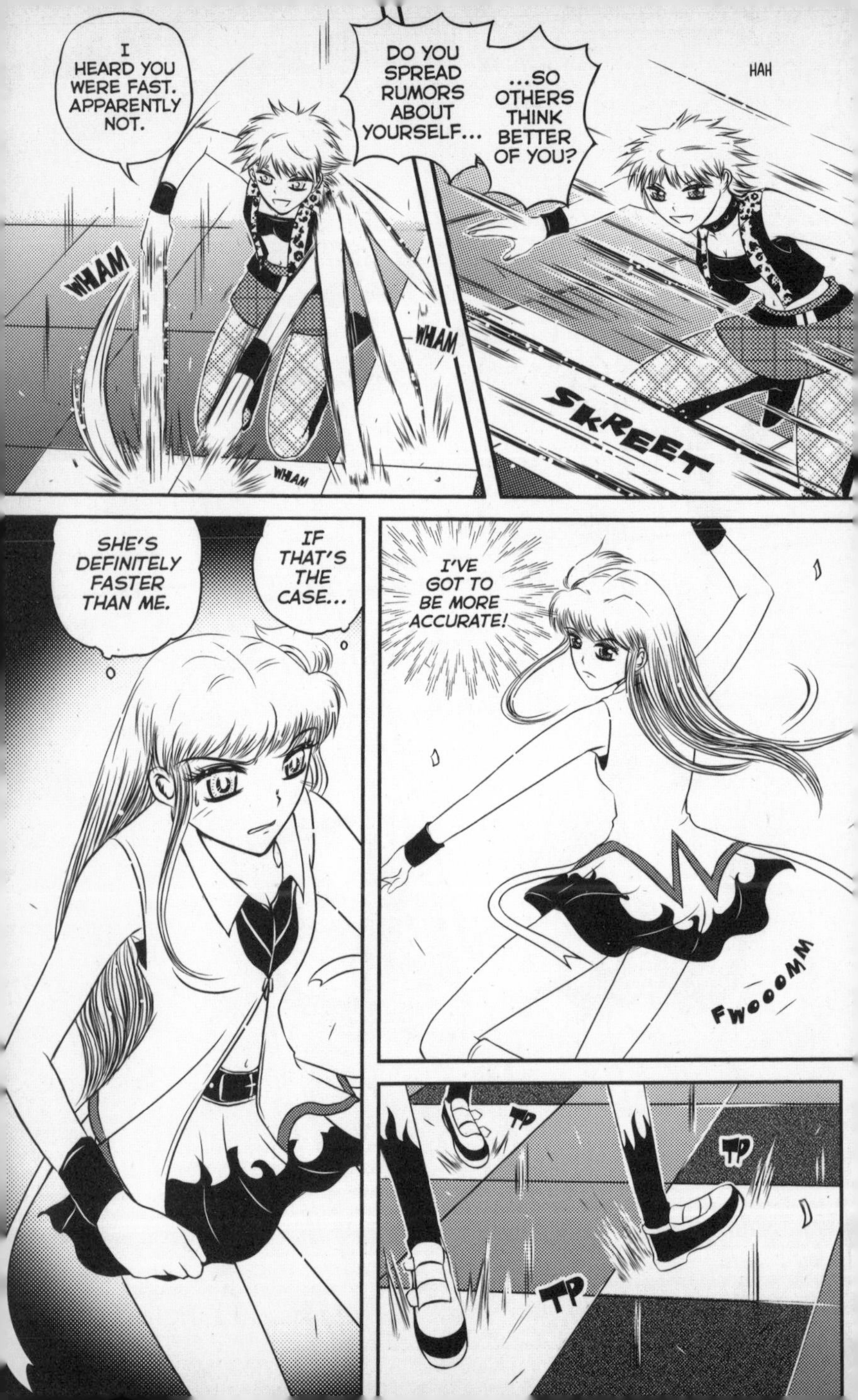
I HEARD YOU WERE FAST. APPARENTLY NOT.
DO YOU SPREAD RUMORS ABOUT YOURSELF...
WHAM
WHAM
WHAM
...SO OTHERS THINK BETTER OF YOU?
HAH
SKREEET
SHE'S DEFINITELY FASTER THAN ME.
IF THAT'S THE CASE...
I'VE GOT TO BE MORE ACCURATE!
FWOOOMM
TP
TP
TP

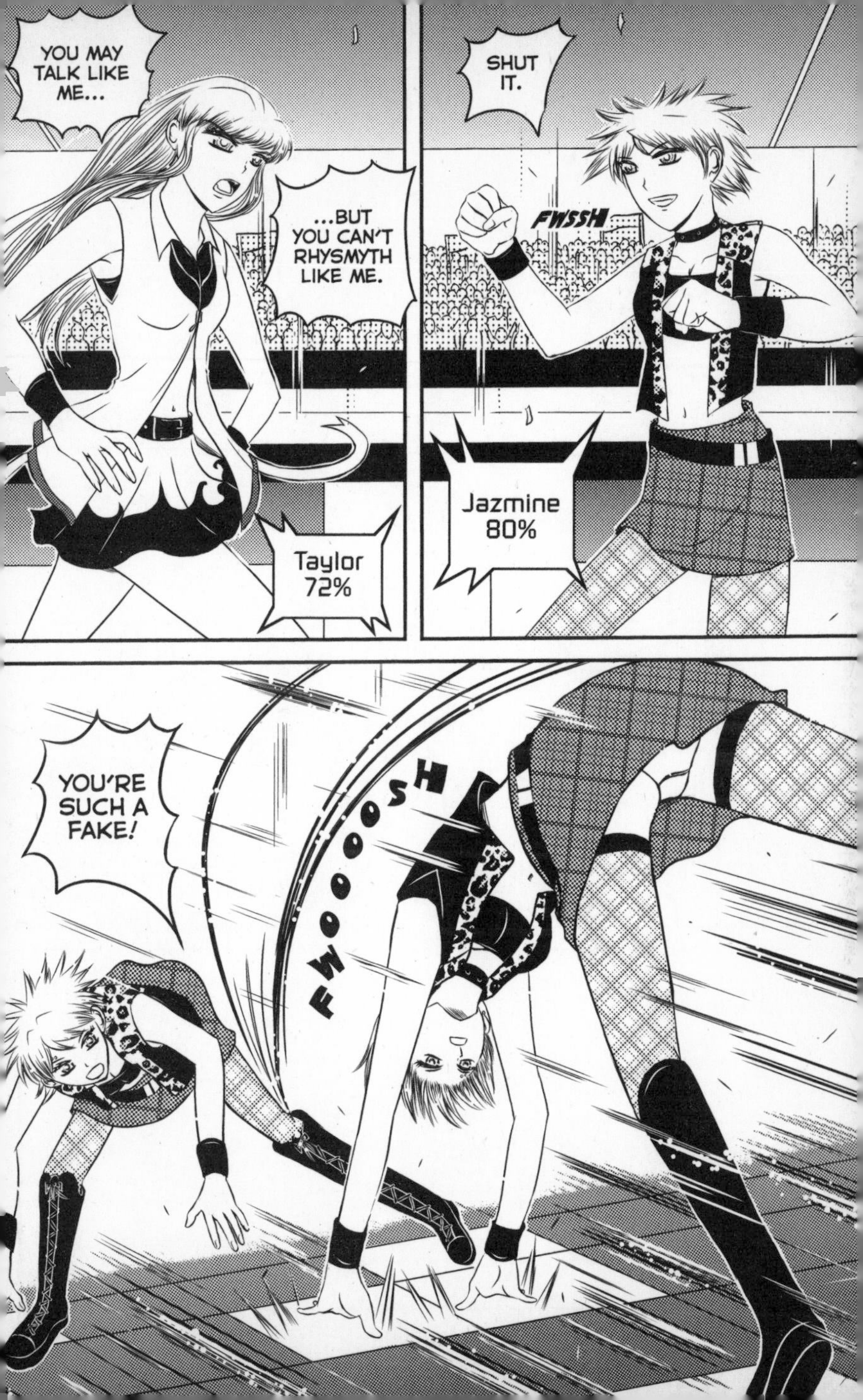
YOU MAY TALK LIKE ME...
...BUT YOU CAN'T RHYSMYTH LIKE ME.
Taylor 72%
SHUT IT.
FWSSH
Jazmine 80%
YOU'RE SUCH A FAKE!
FWOOOOSH

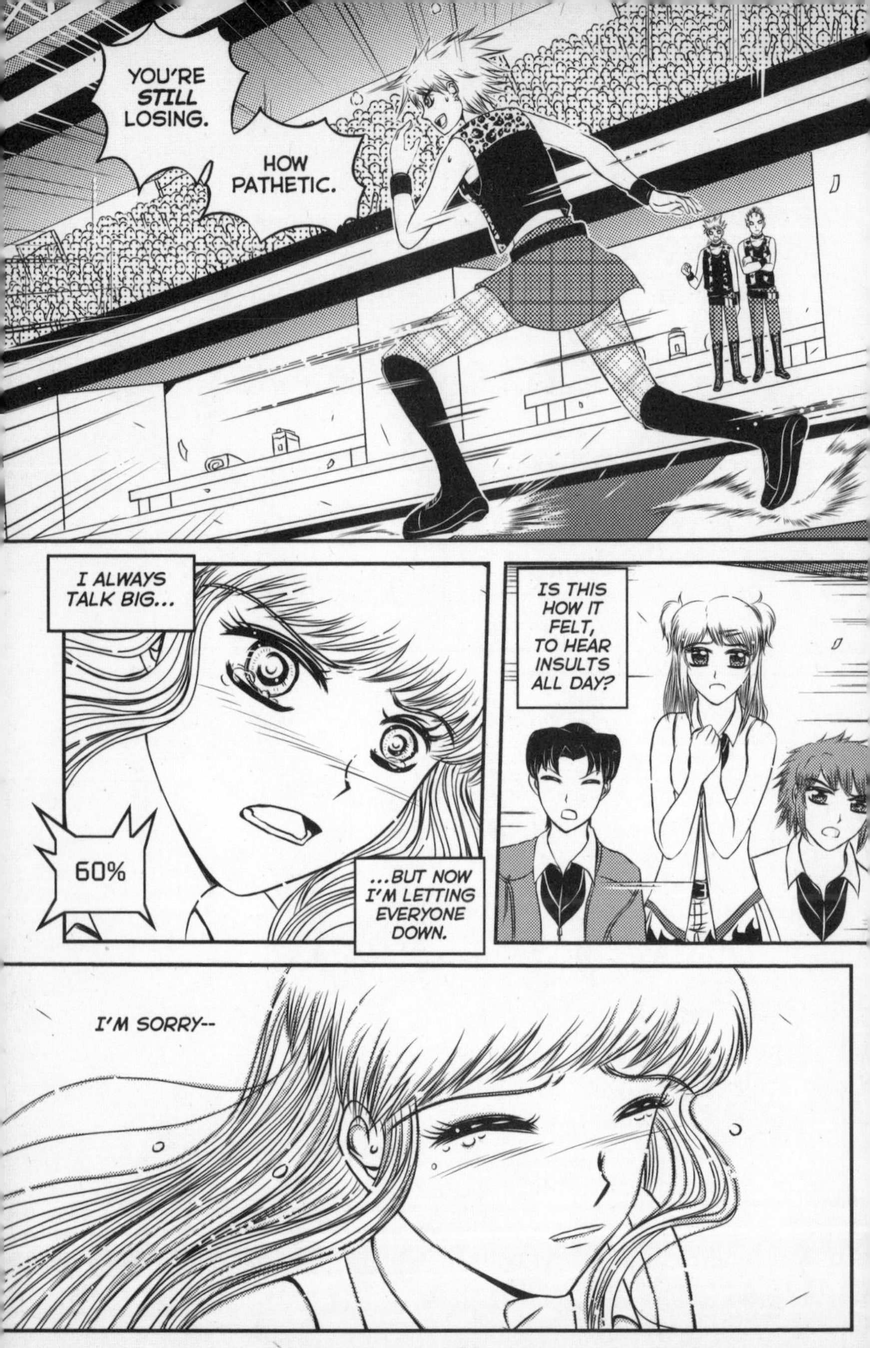
YOU'RE STILL LOSING.
HOW PATHETIC.
I ALWAYS TALK BIG...
60%
...BUT NOW I'M LETTING EVERYONE DOWN.
IS THIS HOW IT FELT, TO HEAR INSULTS ALL DAY?
I'M SORRY--

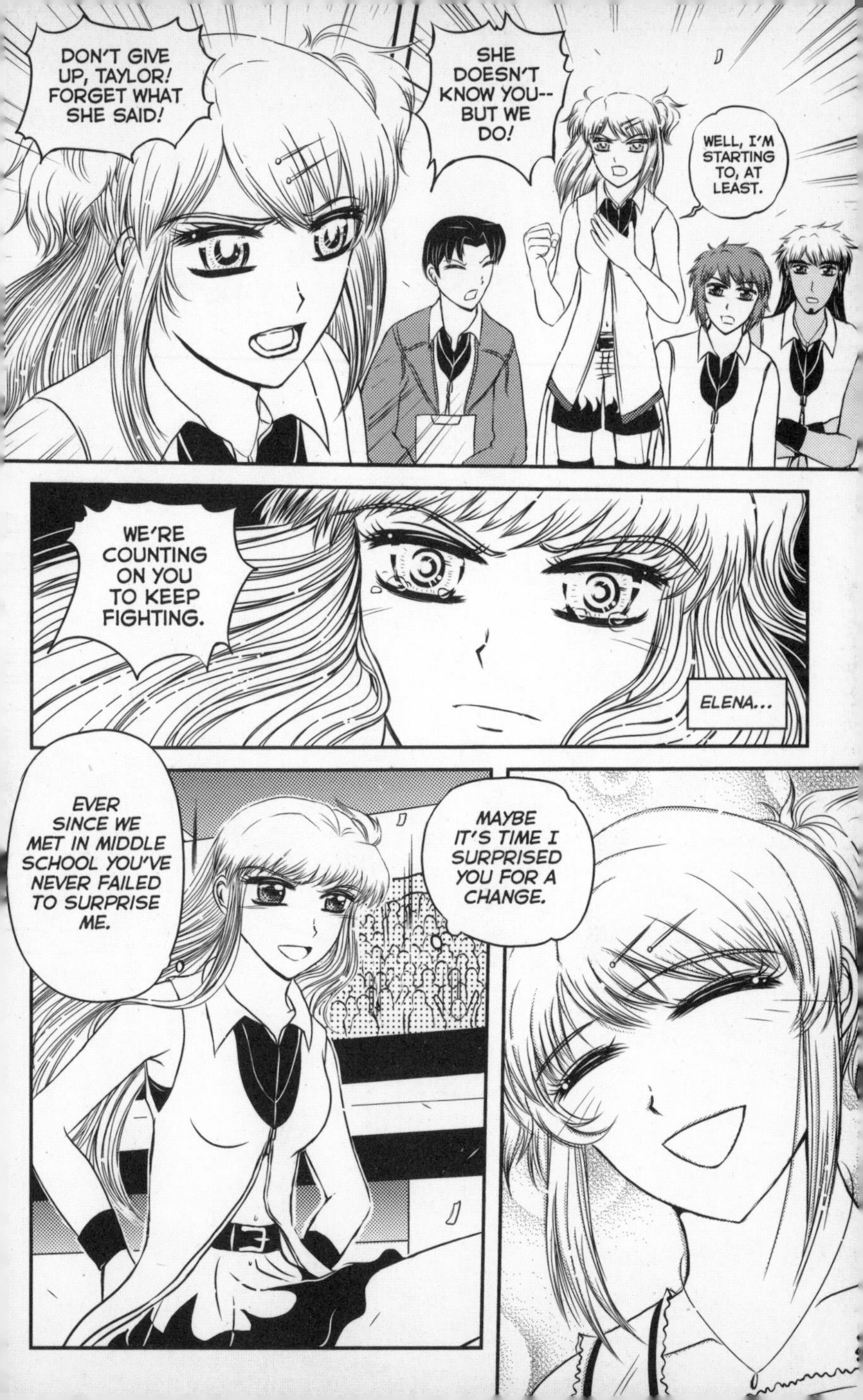
DON'T GIVE UP, TAYLOR! FORGET WHAT SHE SAID!
SHE DOESN'T KNOW YOU-- BUT WE DO!
WELL, I'M STARTING TO, AT LEAST.
WE'RE COUNTING ON YOU TO KEEP FIGHTING.
ELENA...
EVER SINCE WE MET IN MIDDLE SCHOOL YOU'VE NEVER FAILED TO SURPRISE ME.
MAYBE IT'S TIME I SURPRISED YOU FOR A CHANGE.

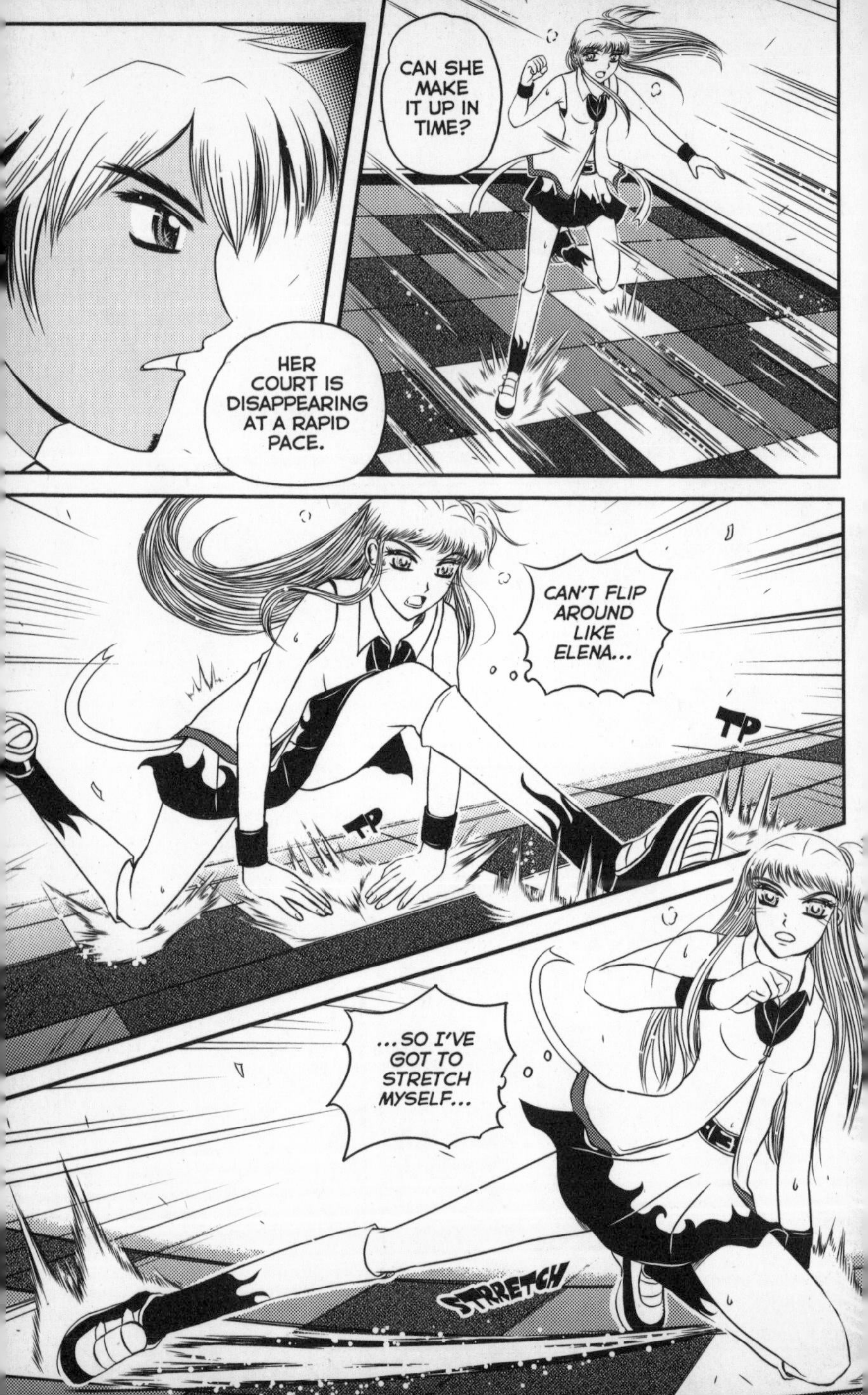
HER COURT IS DISAPPEARING AT A RAPID PACE.
CAN SHE MAKE IT UP IN TIME?
CAN'T FLIP AROUND LIKE ELENA...
TP
TP
...SO I'VE GOT TO STRETCH MYSELF...
STRRETCH

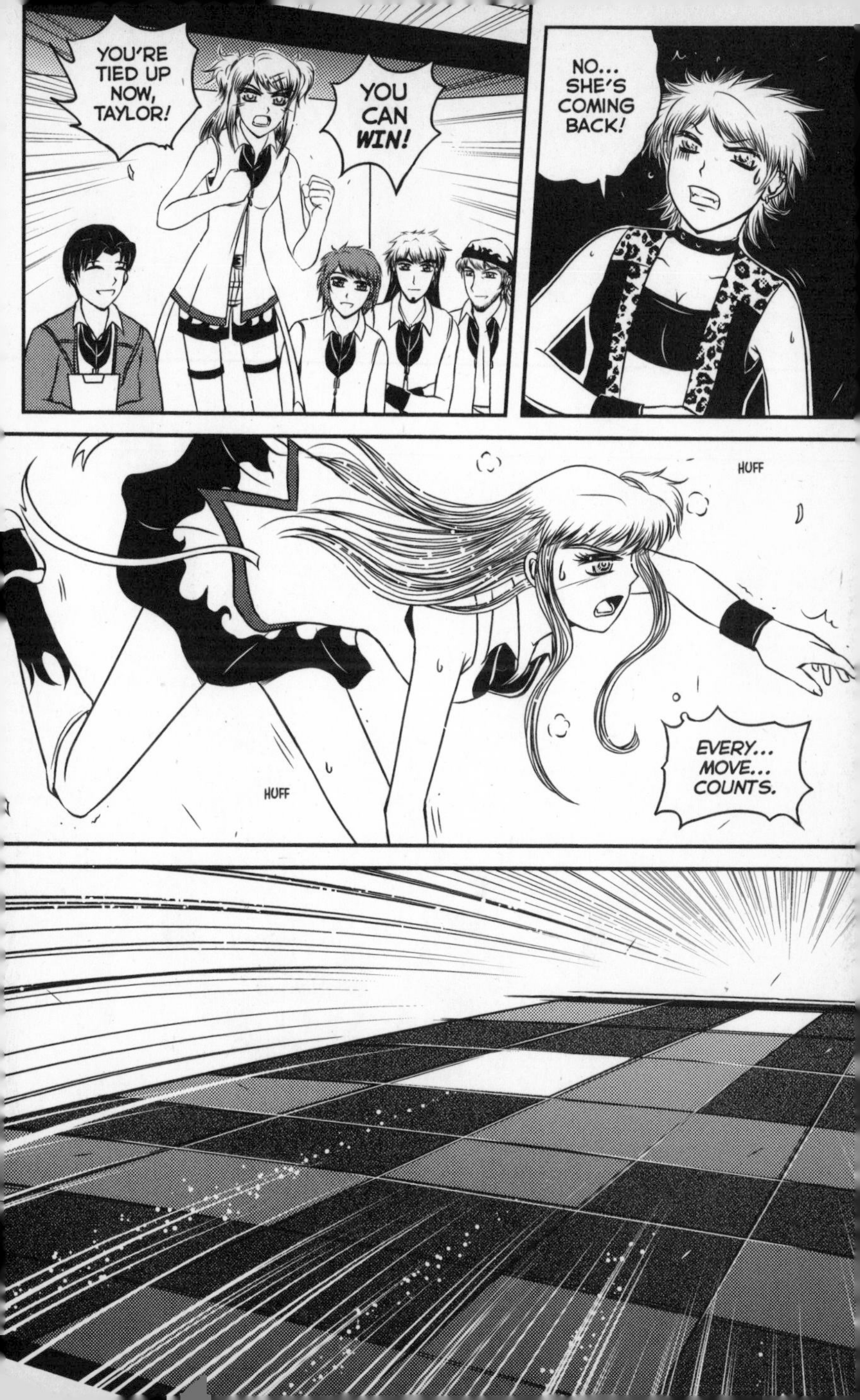

YOU'RE TIED UP NOW, TAYLOR!
YOU CAN WIN!
NO... SHE'S COMING BACK!
HUFF
HUFF
EVERY... MOVE... COUNTS.

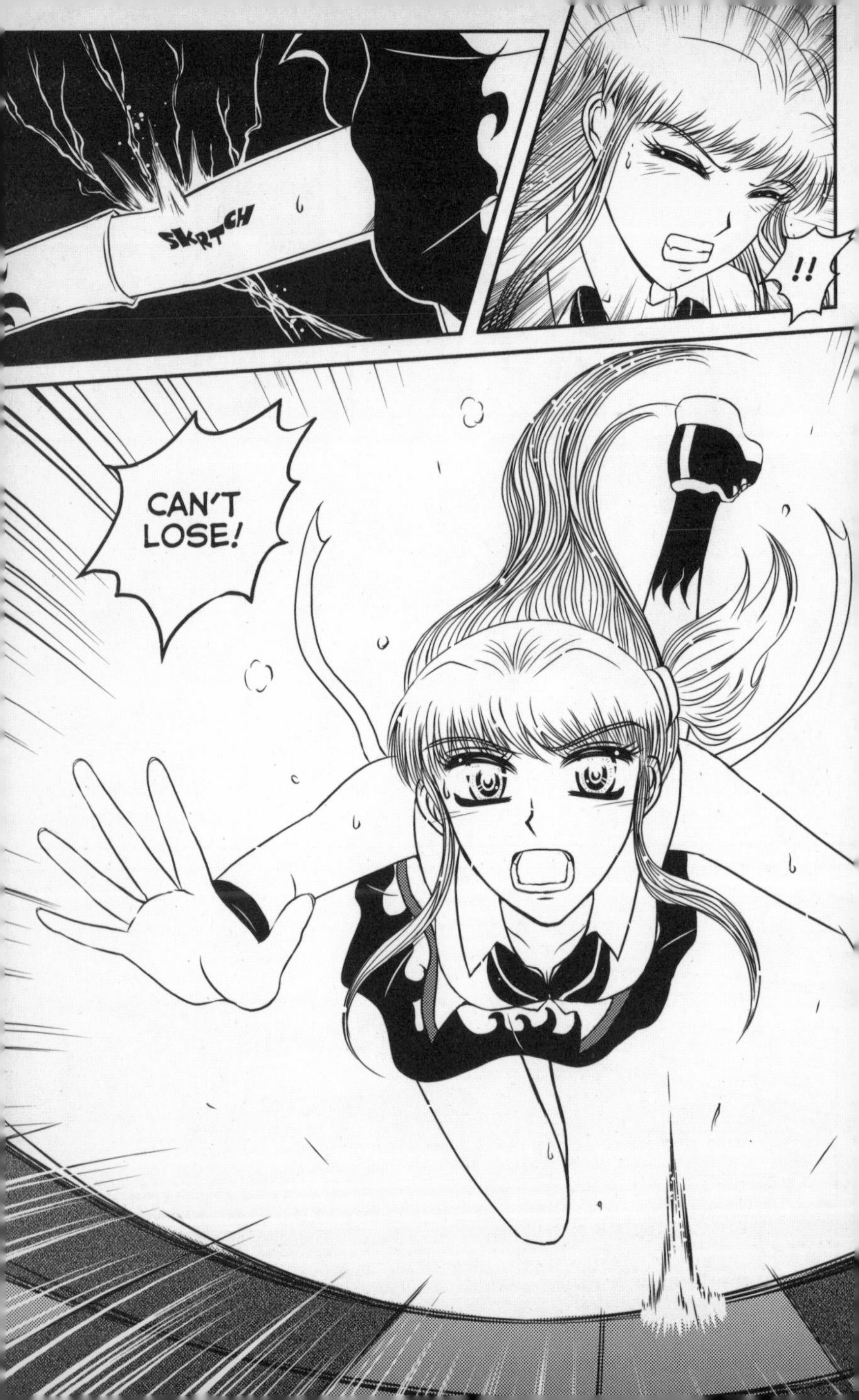
SKRTCH
!!
CAN'T LOSE!

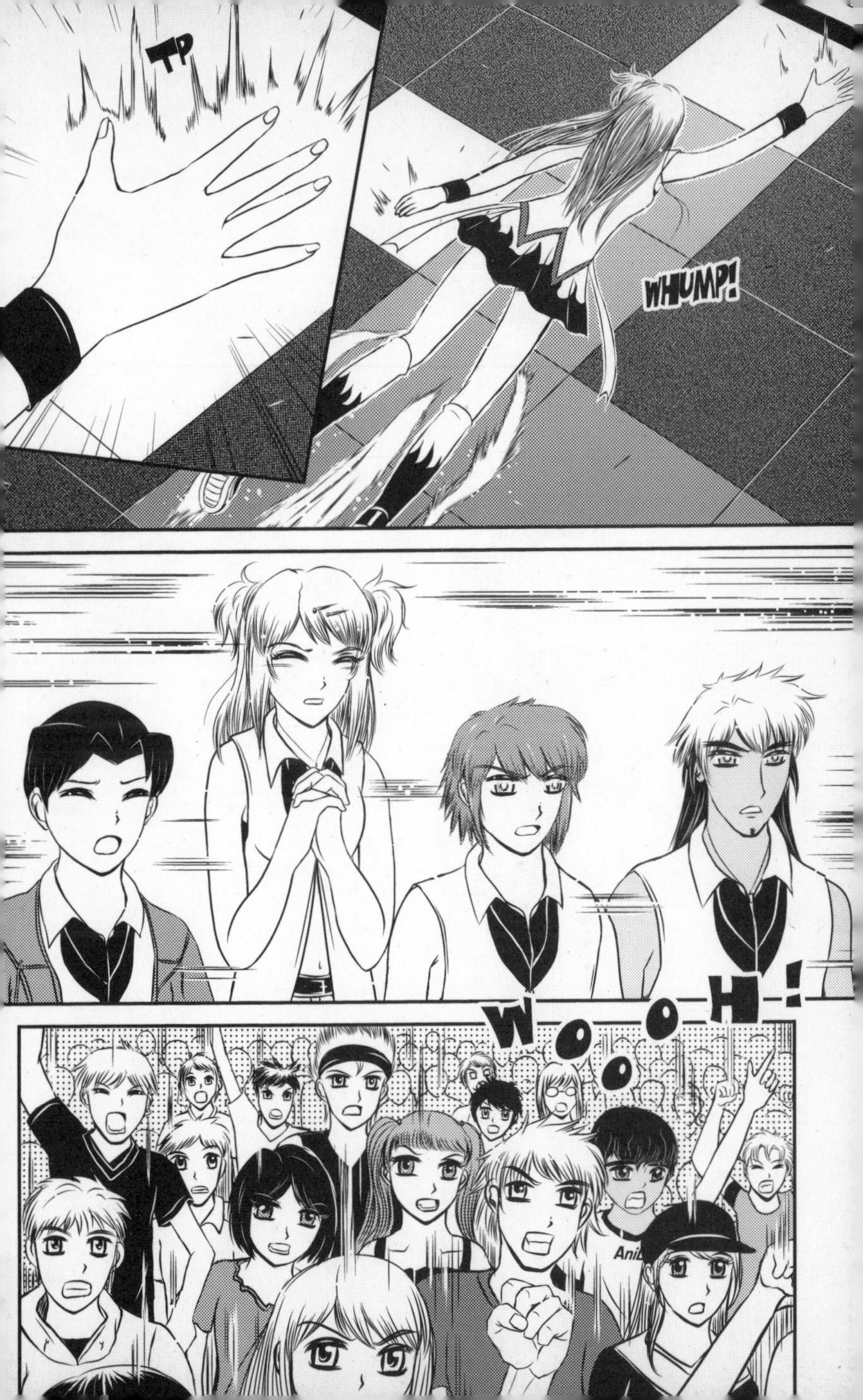
TP
WHUMP!
WOOOH!

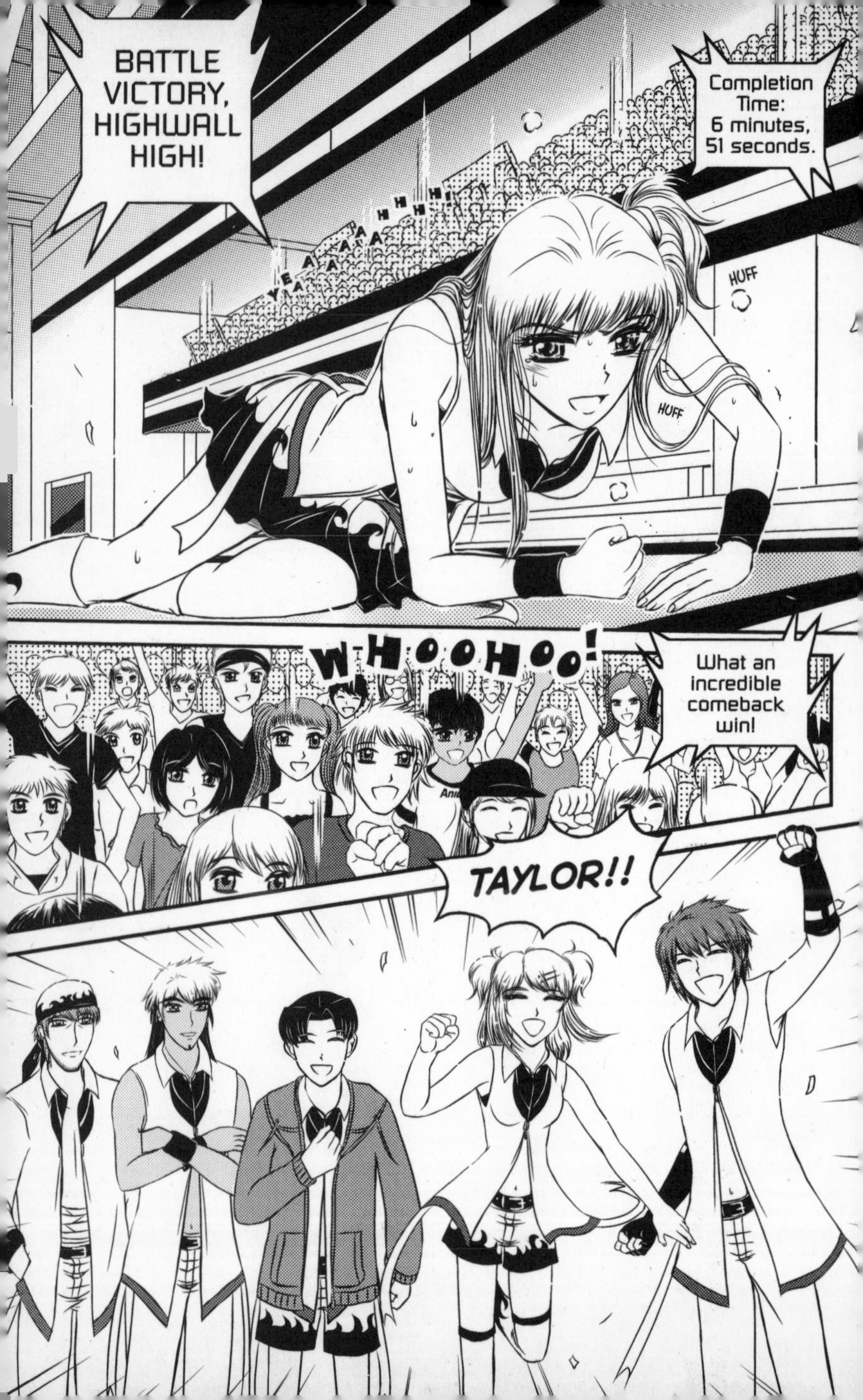
BATTLE VICTORY, HIGHWALL HIGH!
Completion Time: 6 minutes, 51 seconds.
YEAAAAAAAHHHH!
HUFF
HUFF
WHOOOHOO!
What an incredible comeback win!
TAYLOR!!

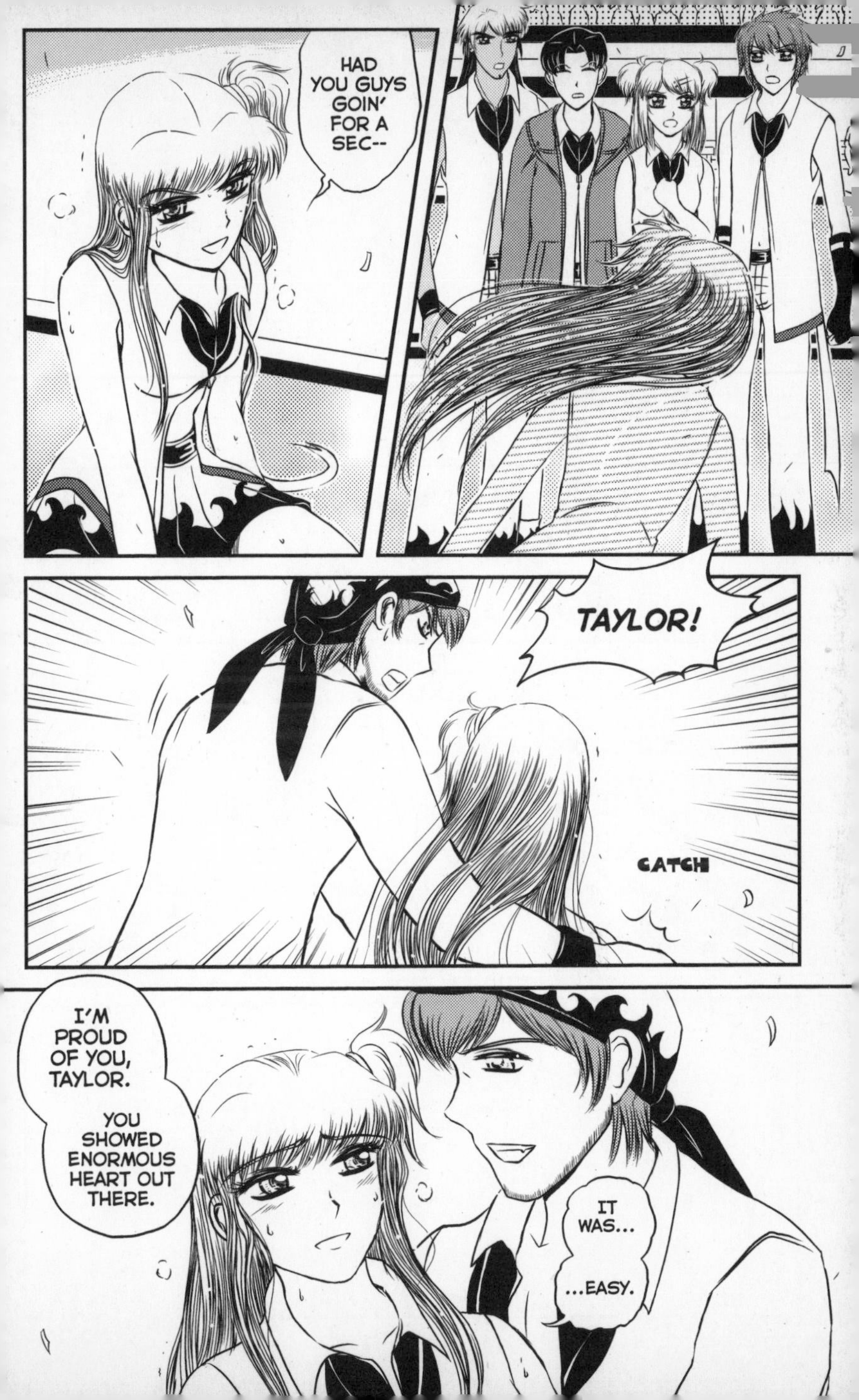
HAD YOU GUYS GOIN' FOR A SEC--
TAYLOR!
CATCH
I'M PROUD OF YOU, TAYLOR.
YOU SHOWED ENORMOUS HEART OUT THERE.
IT WAS...
...EASY.

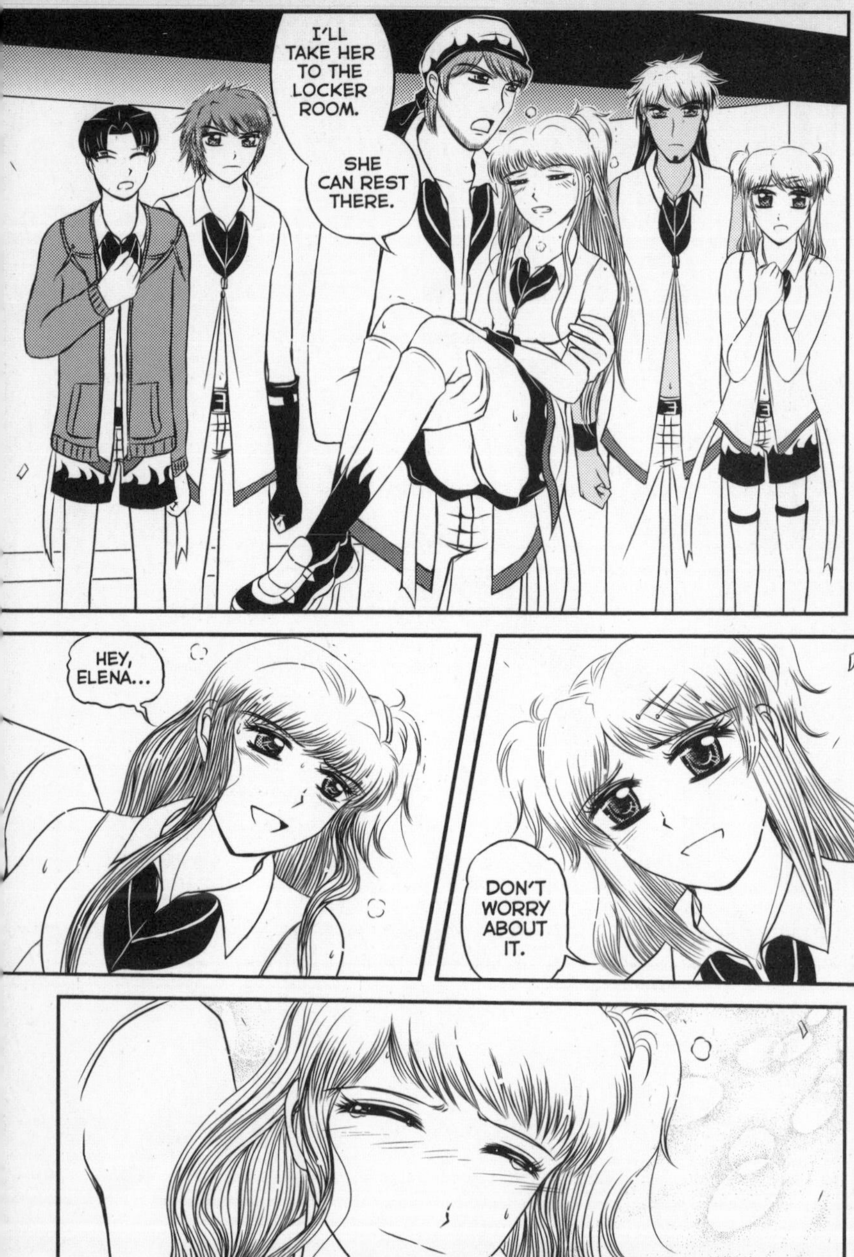
I'LL TAKE HER TO THE LOCKER ROOM.
SHE CAN REST THERE.
HEY, ELENA...
DON'T WORRY ABOUT IT.

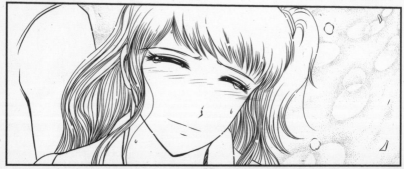

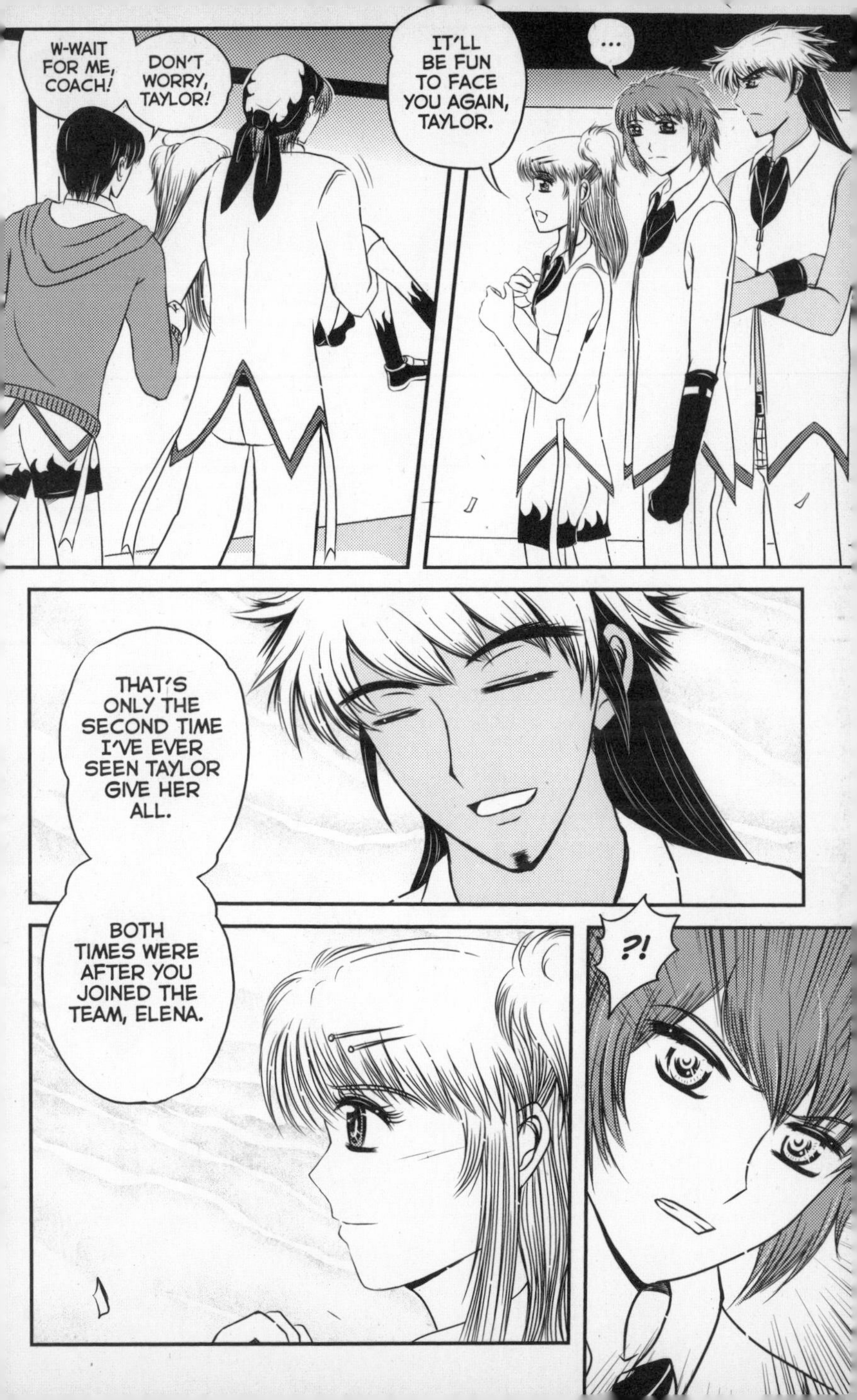
W-WAIT FOR ME, COACH!
DON'T WORRY, TAYLOR!
IT'LL BE FUN TO FACE YOU AGAIN, TAYLOR.
...
THAT'S ONLY THE SECOND TIME I'VE EVER SEEN TAYLOR GIVE HER ALL.
BOTH TIMES WERE AFTER YOU JOINED THE TEAM, ELENA.
?!

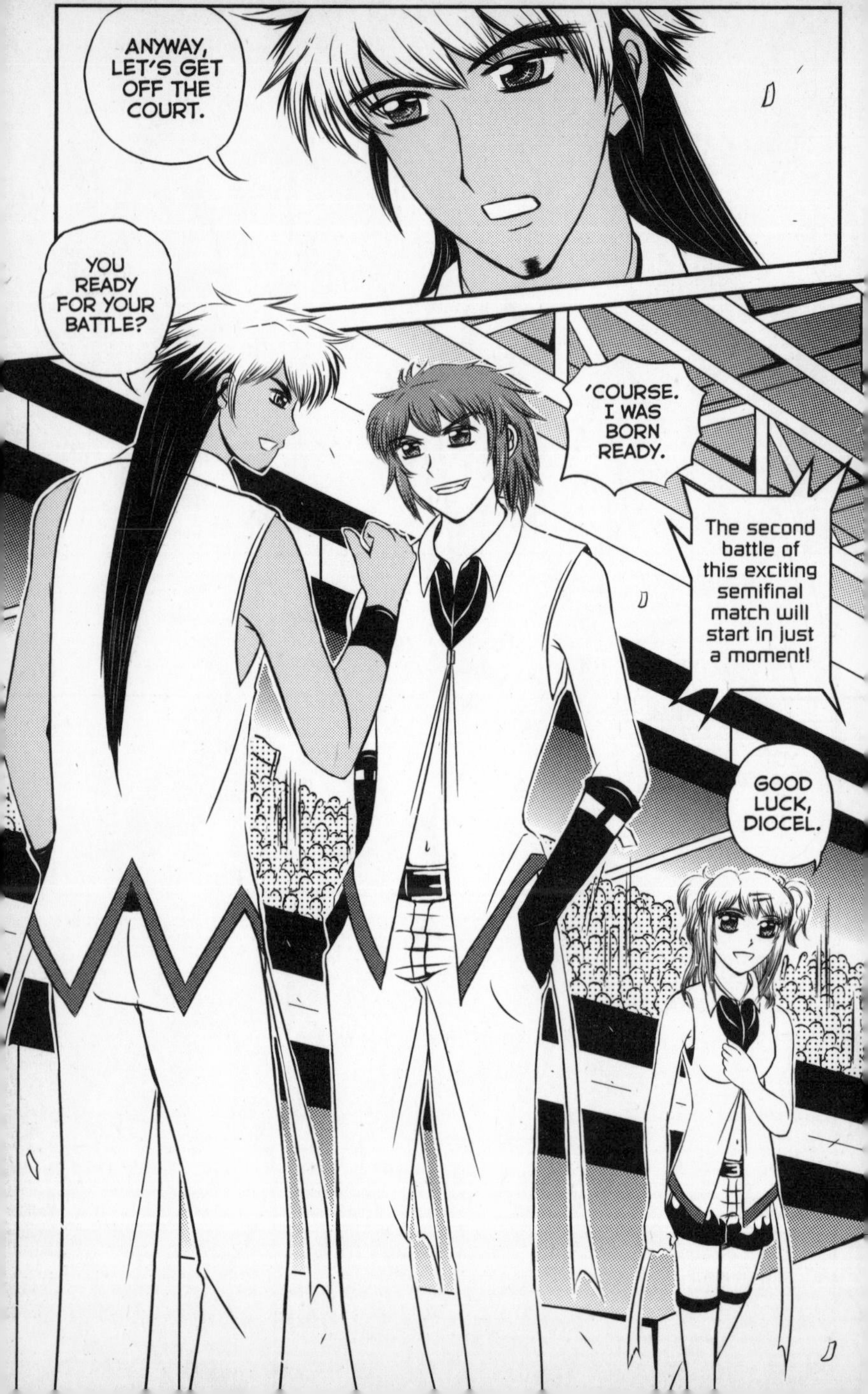
ANYWAY, LET'S GET OFF THE COURT.
YOU READY FOR YOUR BATTLE?
'COURSE. I WAS BORN READY.
The second battle of this exciting semifinal match will start in just a moment!
GOOD LUCK, DIOCEL.

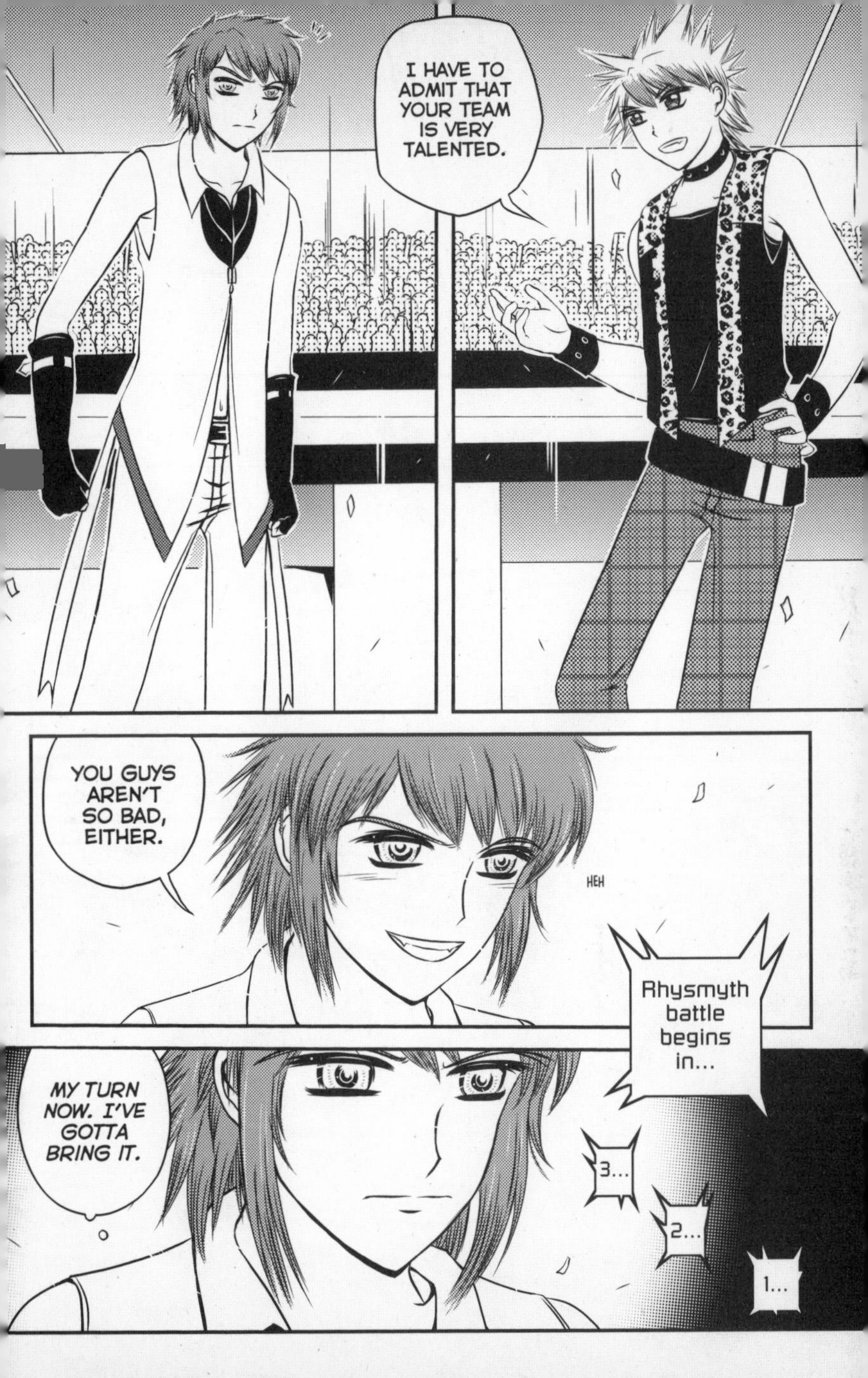
I HAVE TO ADMIT THAT YOUR TEAM IS VERY TALENTED.
YOU GUYS AREN'T SO BAD, EITHER.
HEH
MY TURN NOW. I'VE GOTTA BRING IT.
Rhysmyth battle begins in...
3...
2...
1...

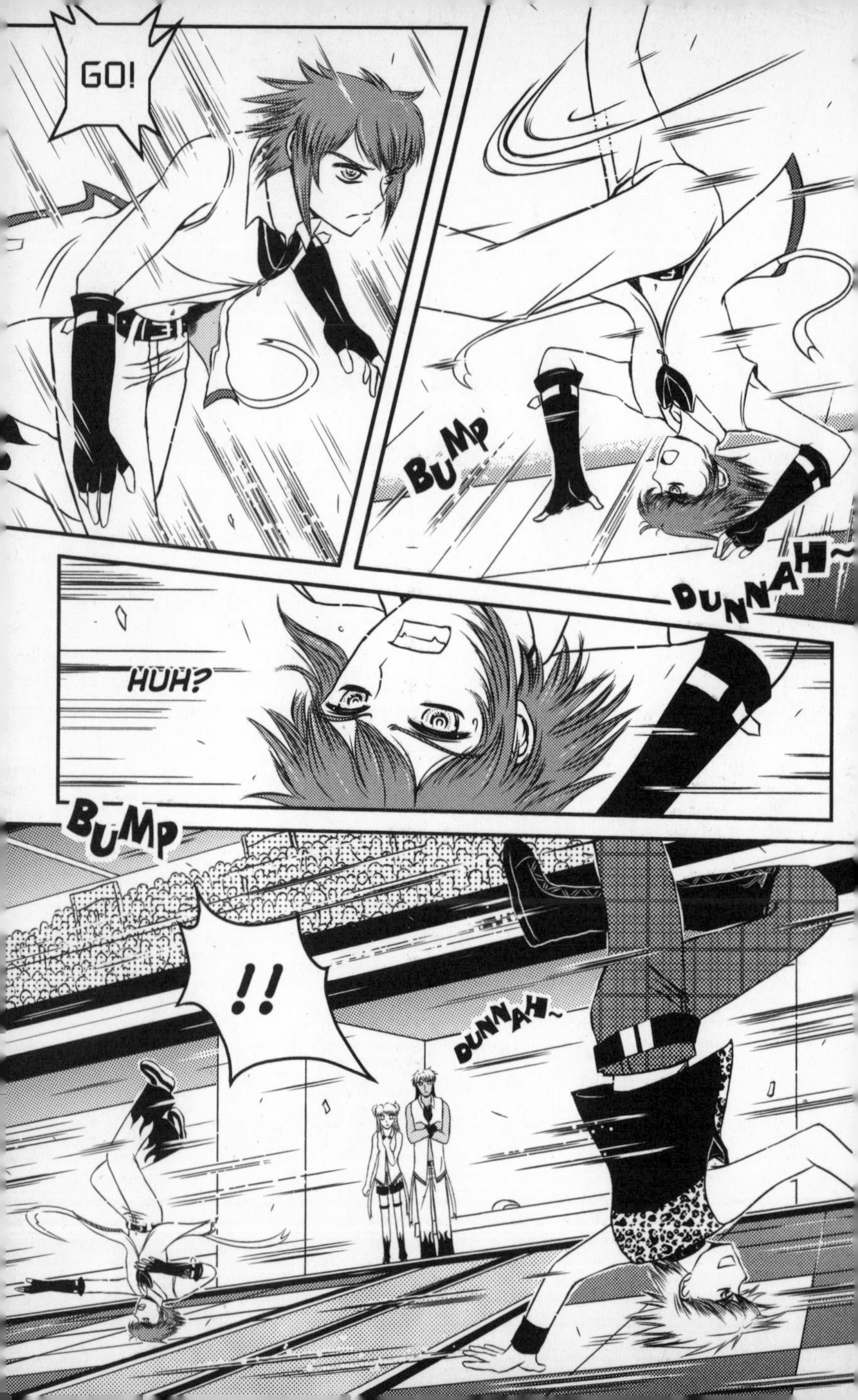
GO!
BUMP
DUNNAH~
HUH?
BUMP
!!
DUNNAH~

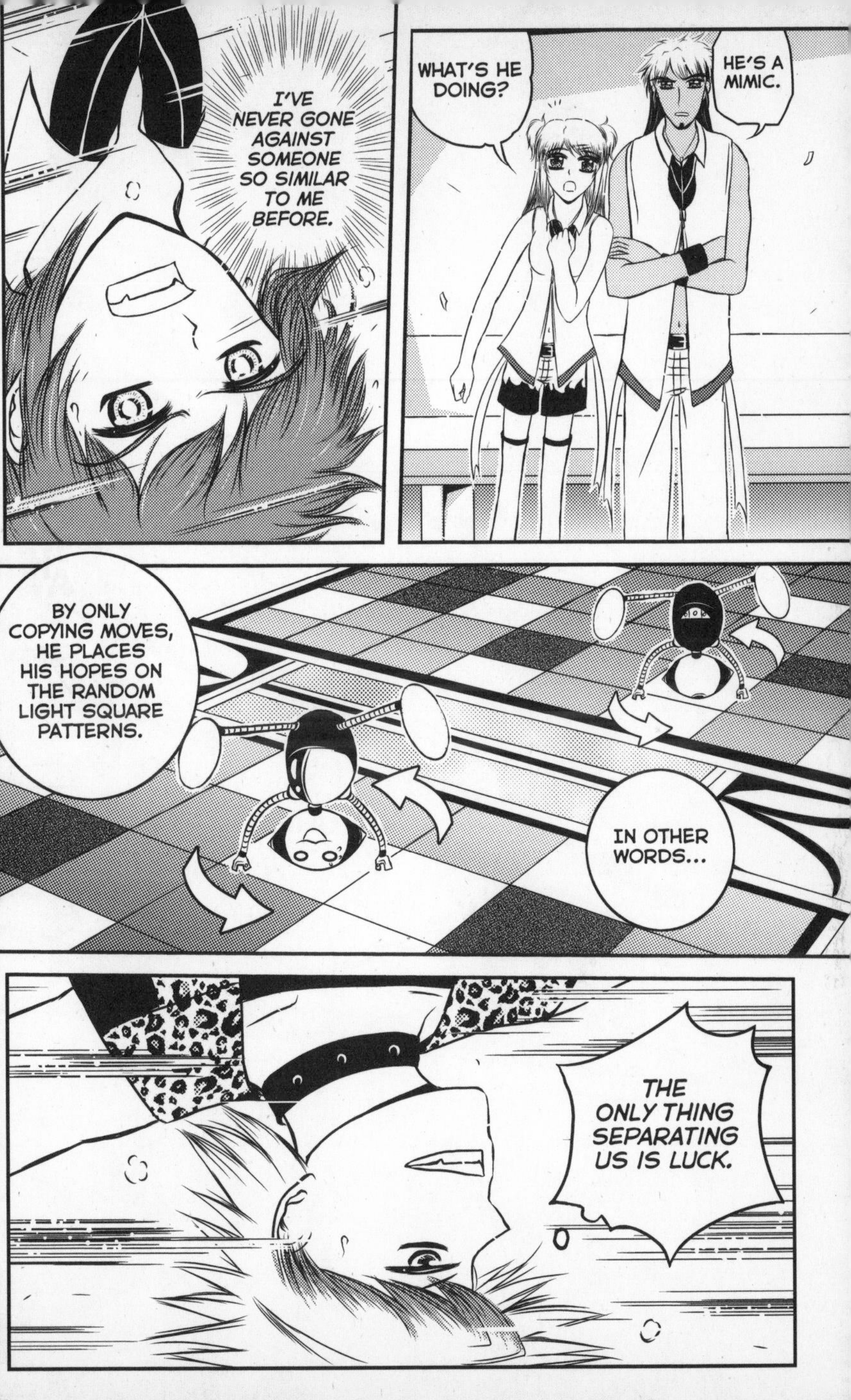
I'VE NEVER GONE AGAINST SOMEONE SO SIMILAR TO ME BEFORE.
WHAT'S HE DOING?
HE'S A MIMIC.
BY ONLY COPYING MOVES, HE PLACES HIS HOPES ON THE RANDOM LIGHT SQUARE PATTERNS.
IN OTHER WORDS...
THE ONLY THING SEPARATING US IS LUCK.

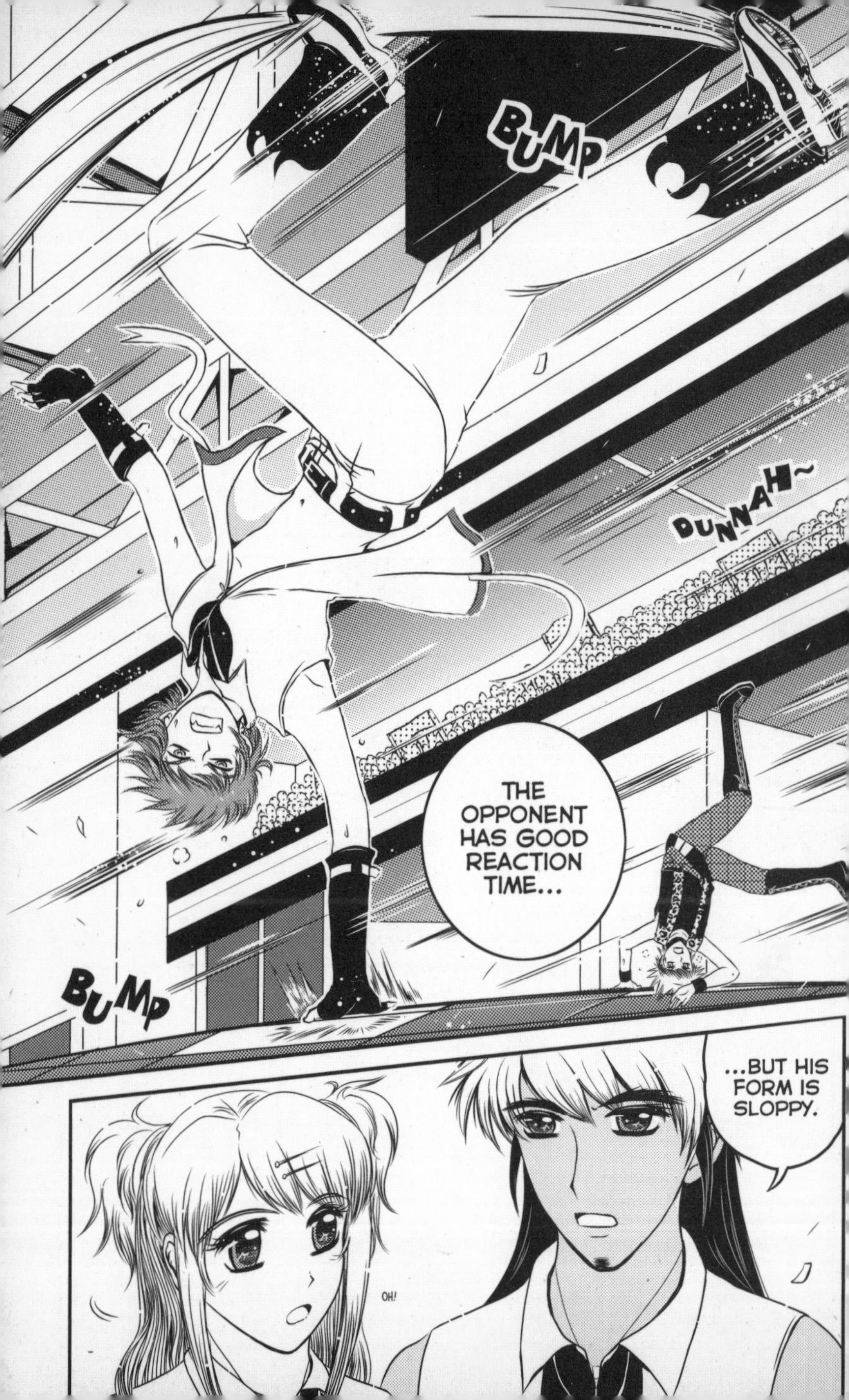
BUMP
DUNNAH~
THE OPPONENT HAS GOOD REACTION TIME...
BUMP
...BUT HIS FORM IS SLOPPY.
OH!

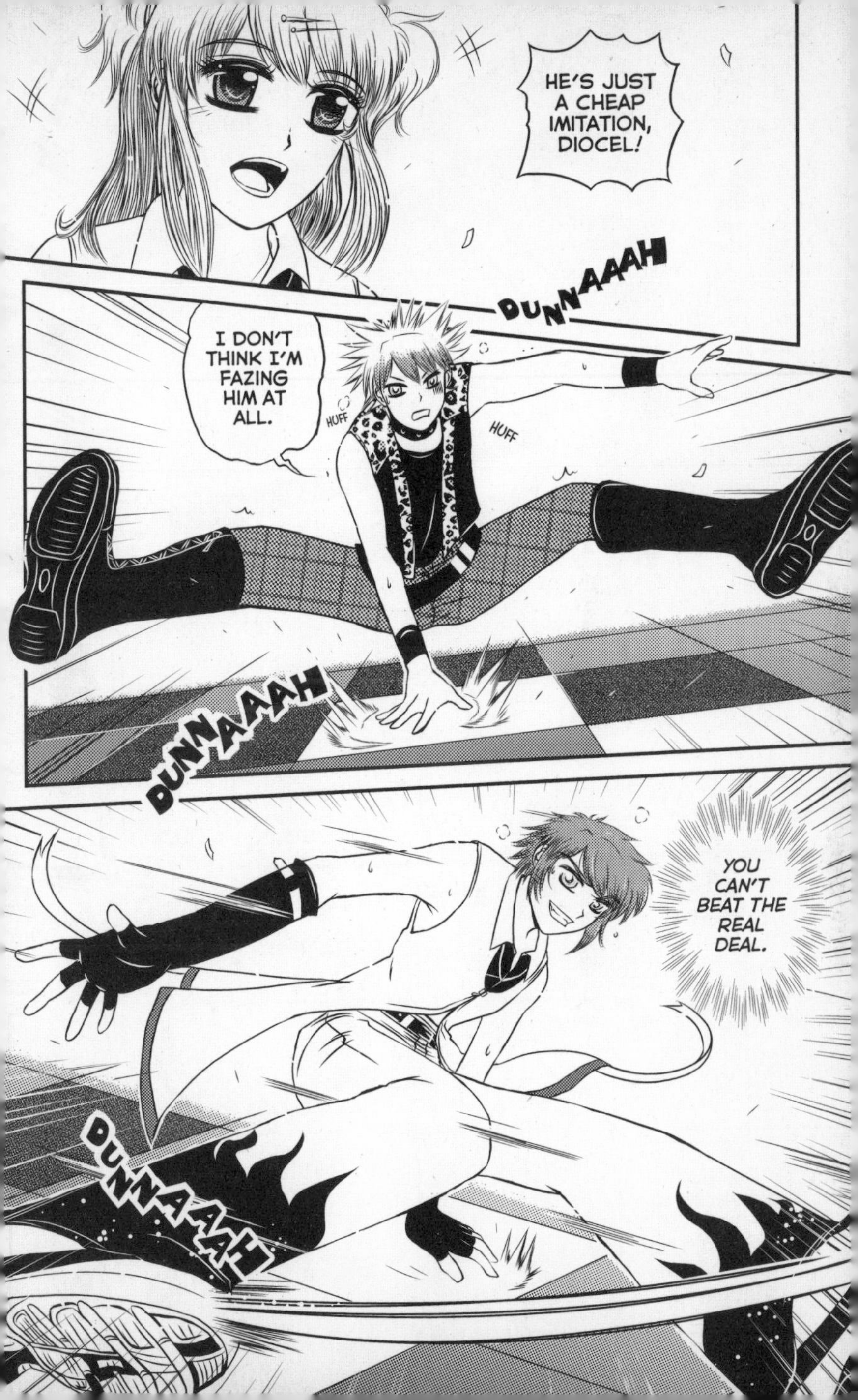
HE'S JUST A CHEAP IMITATION, DIOCEL!
DUNNAAAH
I DON'T THINK I'M FAZING HIM AT ALL.
HUFF
HUFF
DUNNAAAH
YOU CAN'T BEAT THE REAL DEAL.
DUNNAAAH

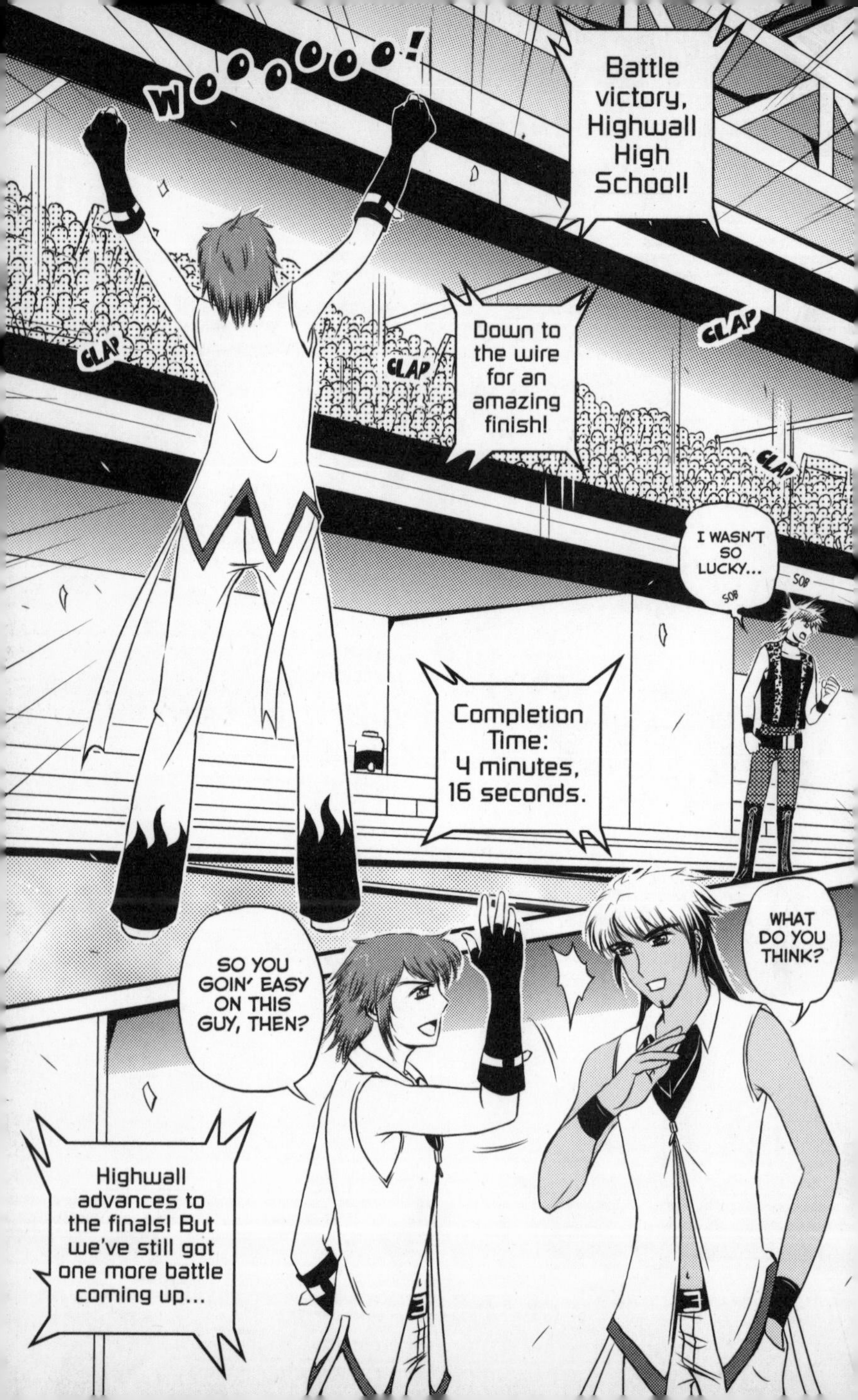
WOOOOOOO!
Battle victory, Highwall High School!
CLAP
CLAP
Down to the wire for an amazing finish!
CLAP
CLAP
I WASN'T SO LUCKY...
SOB
SOB
Completion Time: 4 minutes, 16 seconds.
SO YOU GOIN' EASY ON THIS GUY, THEN?
WHAT DO YOU THINK?
Highwall advances to the finals! But we've still got one more battle coming up...

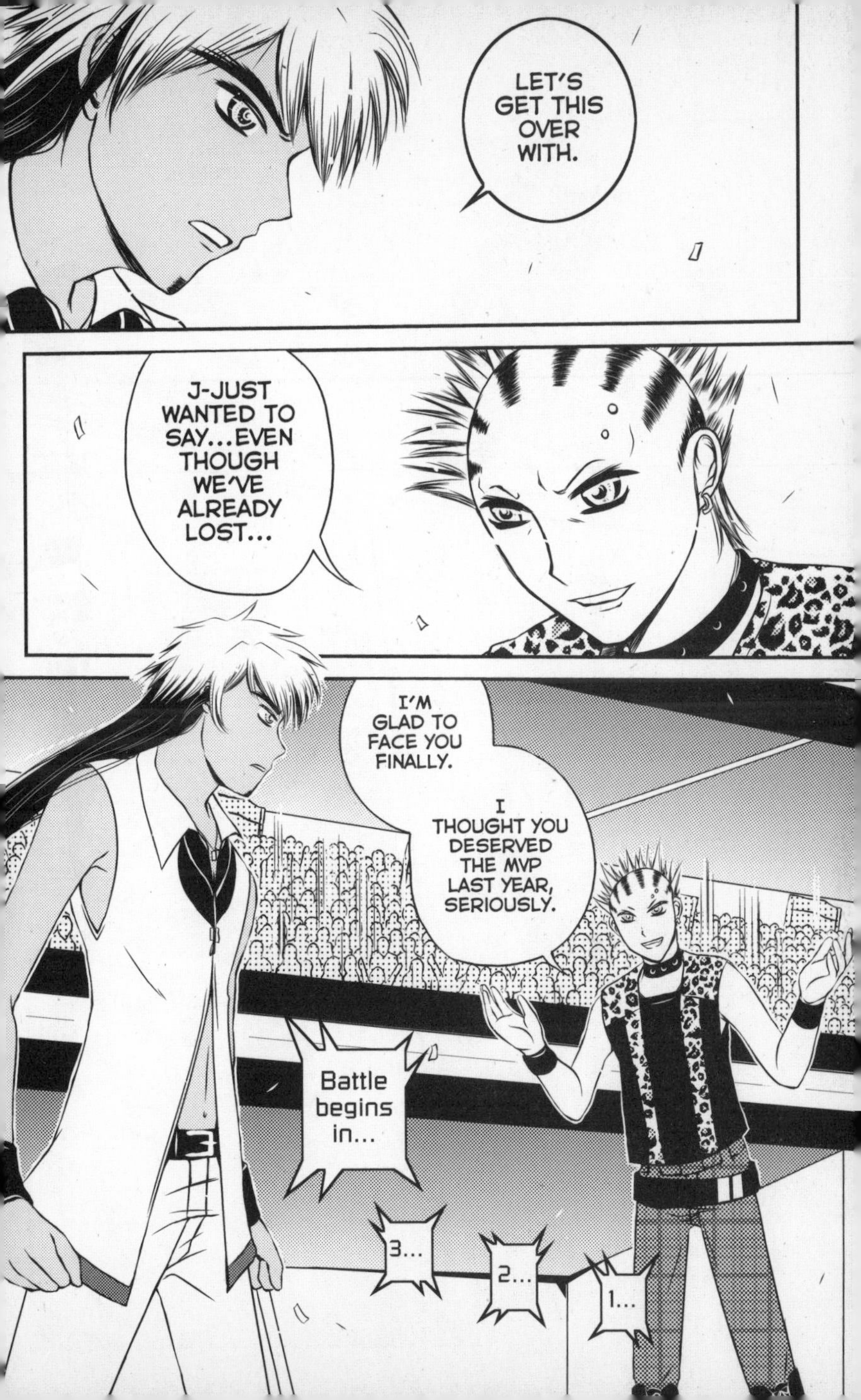
LET'S GET THIS OVER WITH.
J-JUST WANTED TO SAY...EVEN THOUGH WE'VE ALREADY LOST...
I'M GLAD TO FACE YOU FINALLY.
I THOUGHT YOU DESERVED THE MVP LAST YEAR, SERIOUSLY.
Battle begins in...
3...
2...
1...

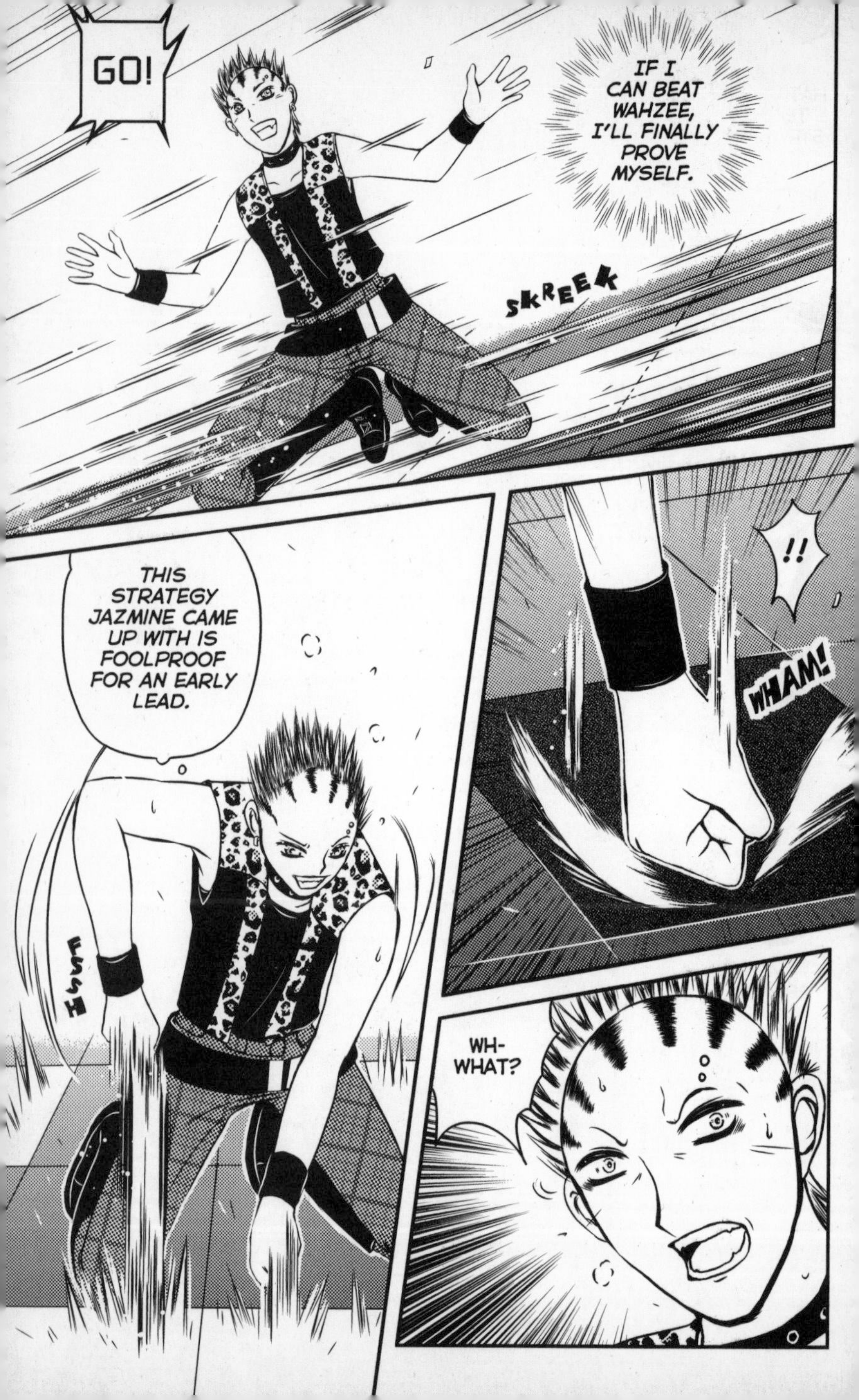
GO!
IF I CAN BEAT WAHZEE, I'LL FINALLY PROVE MYSELF.
SKREEEK
THIS STRATEGY JAZMINE CAME UP WITH IS FOOLPROOF FOR AN EARLY LEAD.
FSSH
!!
WHAM!
WH-WHAT?

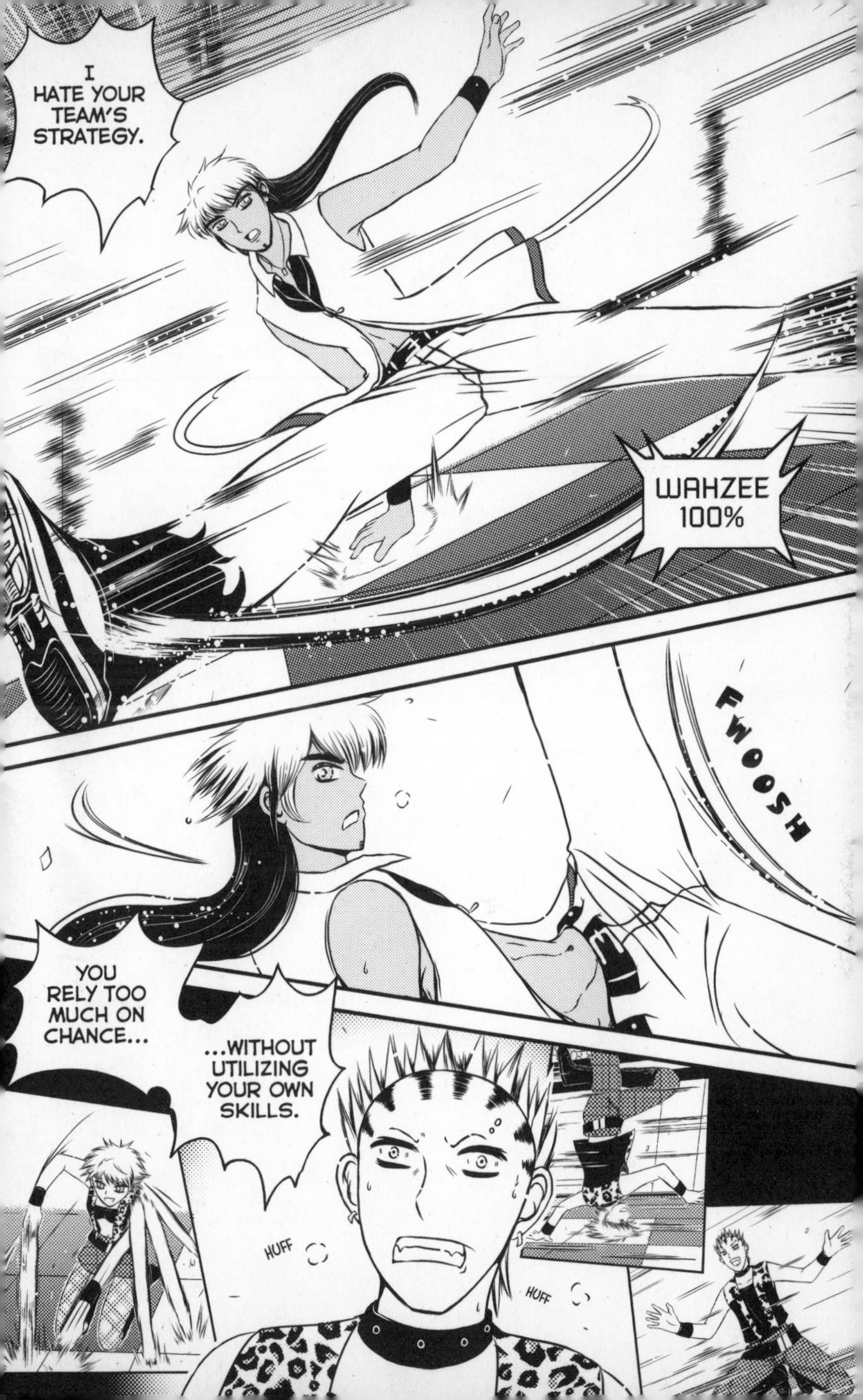
I HATE YOUR TEAM'S STRATEGY.
WAHZEE 100%
FWOOSH
YOU RELY TOO MUCH ON CHANCE...
...WITHOUT UTILIZING YOUR OWN SKILLS.
HUFF
HUFF

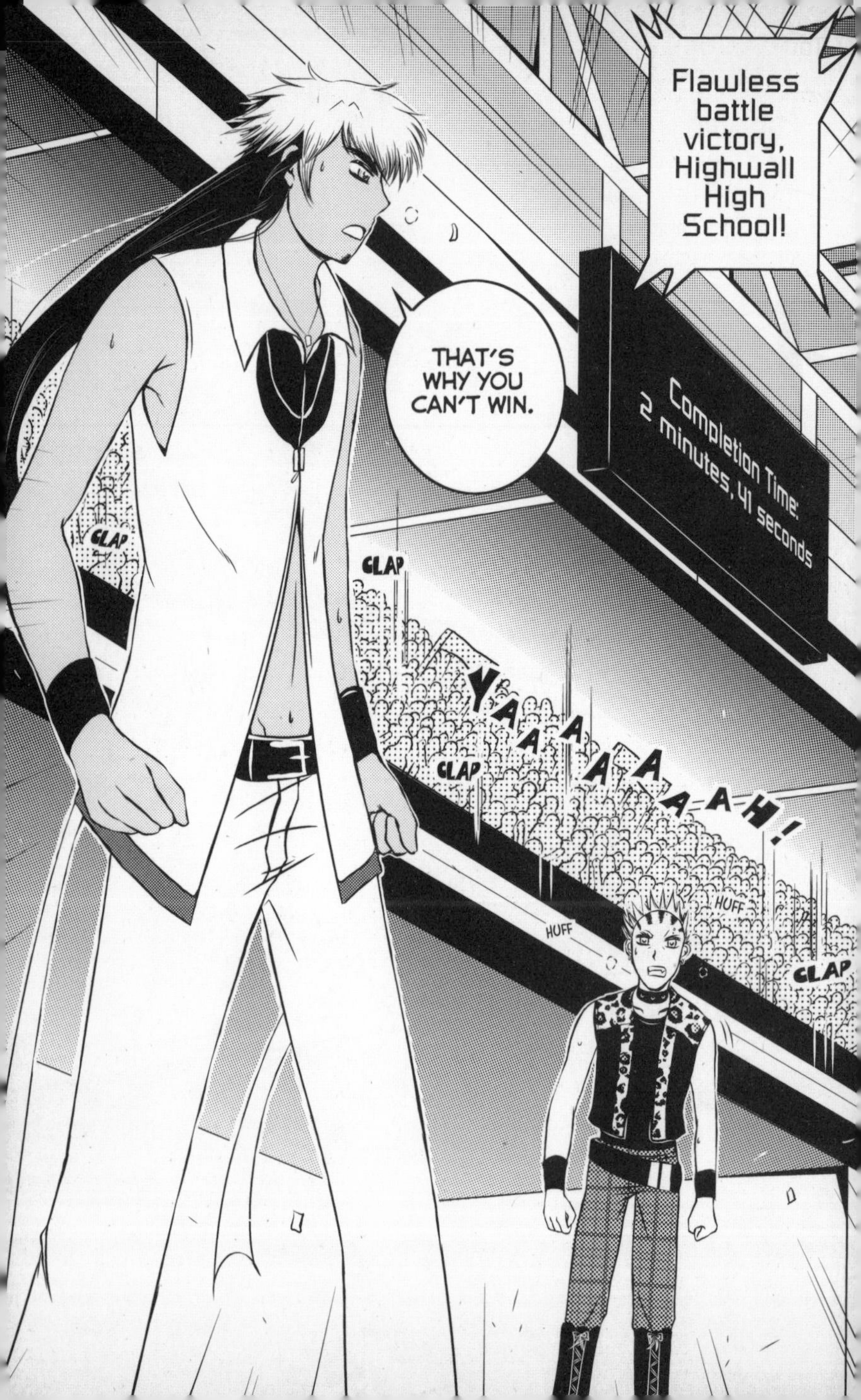
Flawless battle victory, Highwall High School!
THAT'S WHY YOU CAN'T WIN.
Completion Time: 2 minutes, 41 seconds
CLAP
CLAP
YAAAAAAAAAH!
CLAP
HUFF
HUFF
CLAP

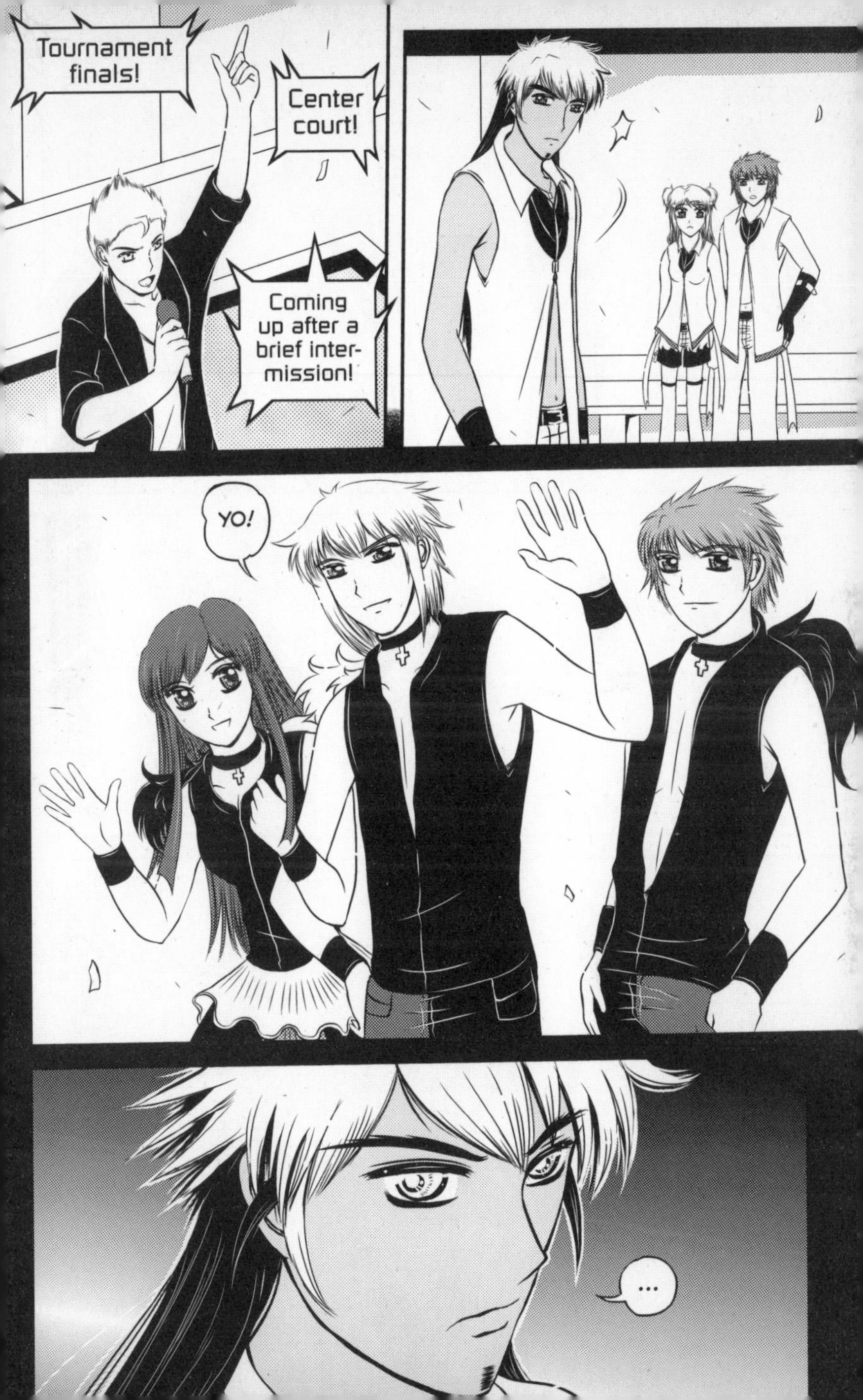

Tournament finals!
Center court!
Coming up after a brief inter-mission!
YO!
...

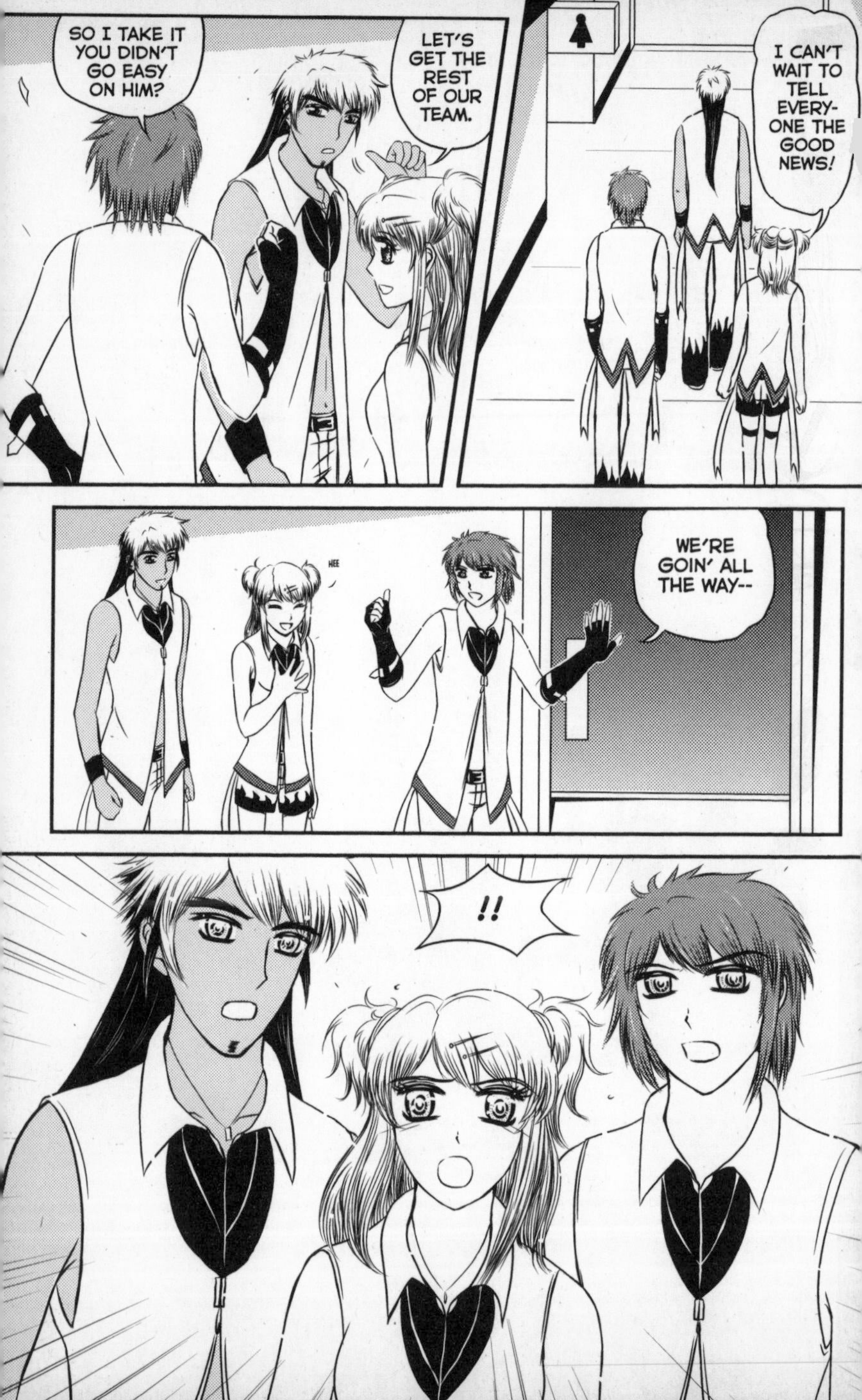
SO I TAKE IT YOU DIDN'T GO EASY ON HIM?
LET'S GET THE REST OF OUR TEAM.
I CAN'T WAIT TO TELL EVERY-ONE THE GOOD NEWS!
HEE
WE'RE GOIN' ALL THE WAY--
!!

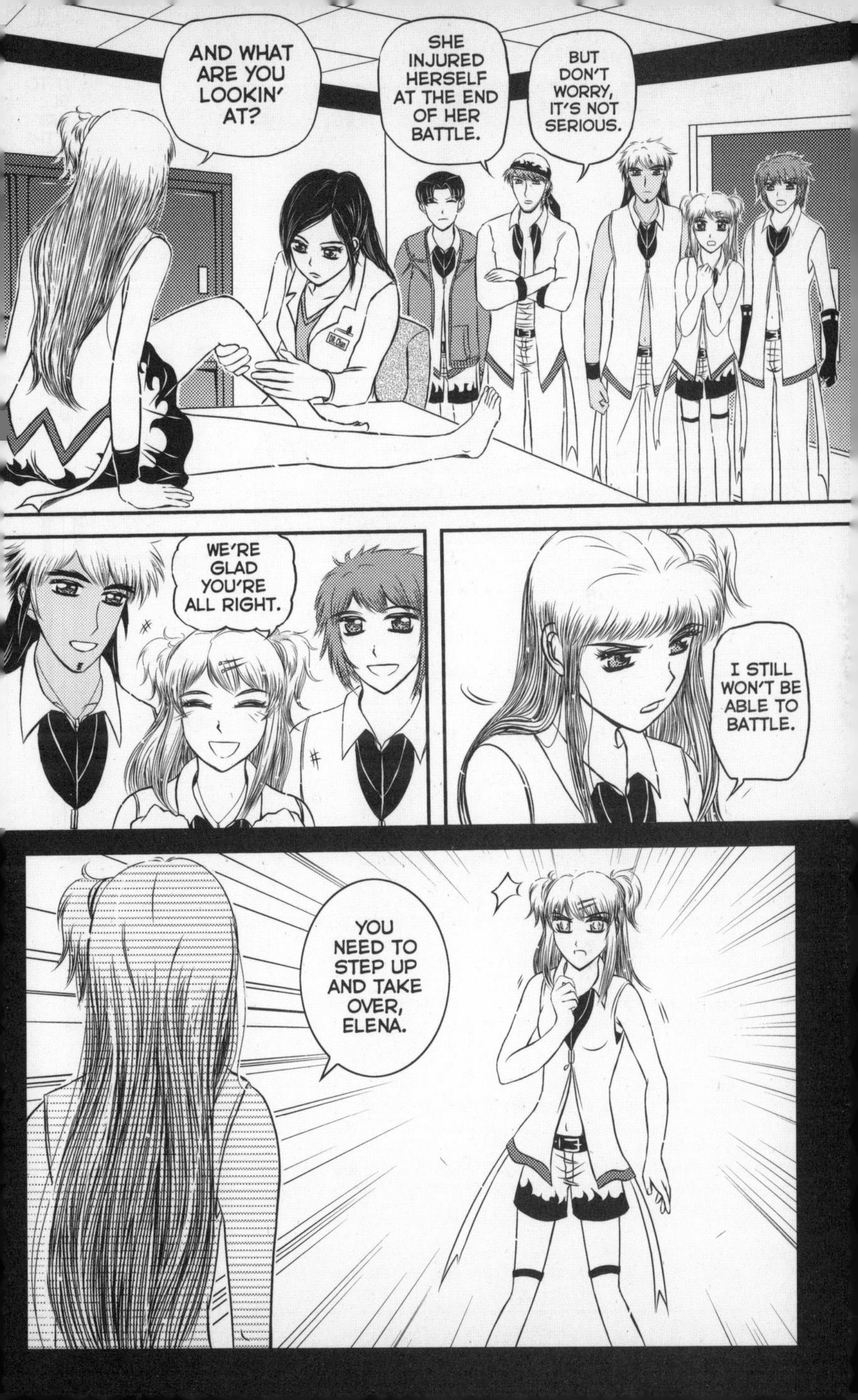
AND WHAT ARE YOU LOOKIN' AT?
SHE INJURED HERSELF AT THE END OF HER BATTLE.
BUT DON'T WORRY, IT'S NOT SERIOUS.
DR. Chan
WE'RE GLAD YOU'RE ALL RIGHT.
I STILL WON'T BE ABLE TO BATTLE.
YOU NEED TO STEP UP AND TAKE OVER, ELENA.

Bigtime Intense RHYSMYTh BattLe!

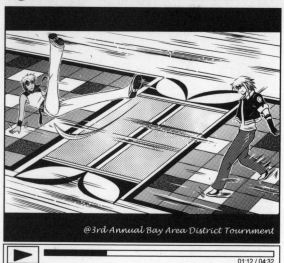

@3rd Annual Bay Area District Tournment

▶ |━━━━━━━━━━━━━━━━━━━━━━━━━━━|
01:12 / 04:32

Added: May 08, 2008
From: hiei9934

Semi-final battle between
two local legends ... (more)

Category: Sports

Tags: Rhysmyth, bishies,
HSD (more)

Rate this video:

 ★ ★ ★ ★ ⯪

123 ratings

Views: 62,303
Comments: 247
Clip: 12,133 times

Email this video

Comments & Responses

hiei9934 (29 minutes ago)   (Mark as Spam)
I hope to get even better battle vids this weekend =D

YamPuff (3 hours ago)   (Mark as Spam)
!!!!! this is t3h AWESOME battle vids! Their in high school ??/

Kaoru (12 hours ago)   (Mark as Spam)
O RLY?

Animedudde (12 hours ago)   (Mark as Spam)
This vid is GHEY. Where's all the hawt rhysmythers? aka GIRLZ!

Mintley (14 hours ago)   (Mark as Spam)
Hmmm...so the one with more impressive "SKILLZ" loses. Ugh, I'm goin with the winner. Ren goes
pro fo SHO. wahz maybe.
highwall's capt is way better then both.

Arcademan (1 day ago)   (Mark as Spam)
wahzee was more impressive in this one. did you even WATCH the whole video? he absolutely
has more skills.

MizRobyn (1 day ago)   (Mark as Spam)
Uhh wahzee LOST this one. What about renaldo pro?

ahianiki (1 day ago)   (Mark as Spam)
Anyone here SERIOUS about Rhysmyth? Sure the guys are hot but this is REAL, intense sport.
I'm seriously thinking about tryin out for my school's team next year. I love watching these videos.
Seriously Wahzee will be pro one day.

KaYoKitten (2 days ago)   (Mark as Spam)
@ booboos -- yer SOOOOO lucky! if i evar saw wahzee in real life...zOMG i'd kidnap him and...
well, you know...

Page: 1 2 3 ..... Oldest   Next

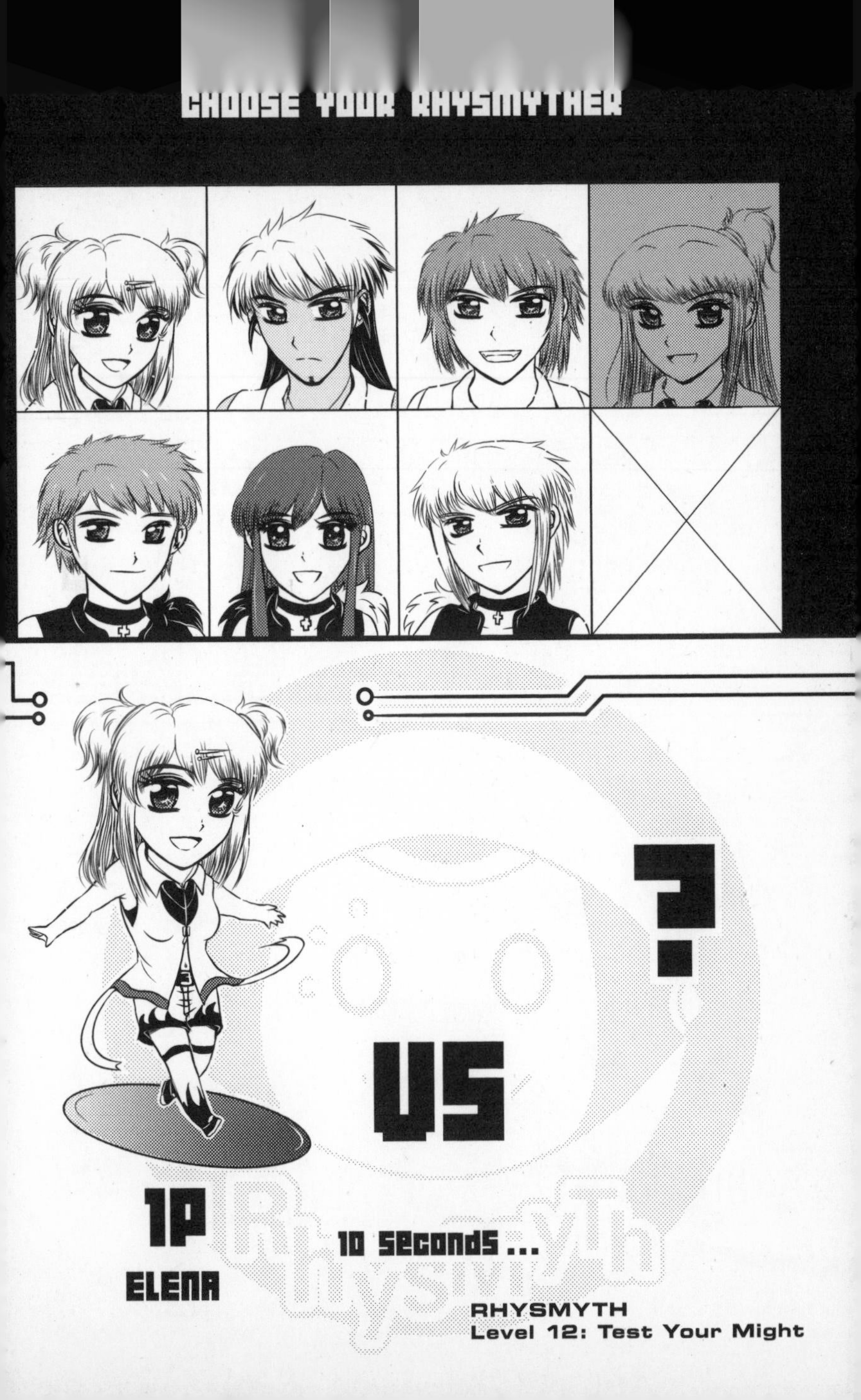
CHOOSE YOUR RHYSMYTHER
?
VS
1P
ELENA
10 seconds...
Rhysmyth
RHYSMYTH
Level 12: Test Your Might

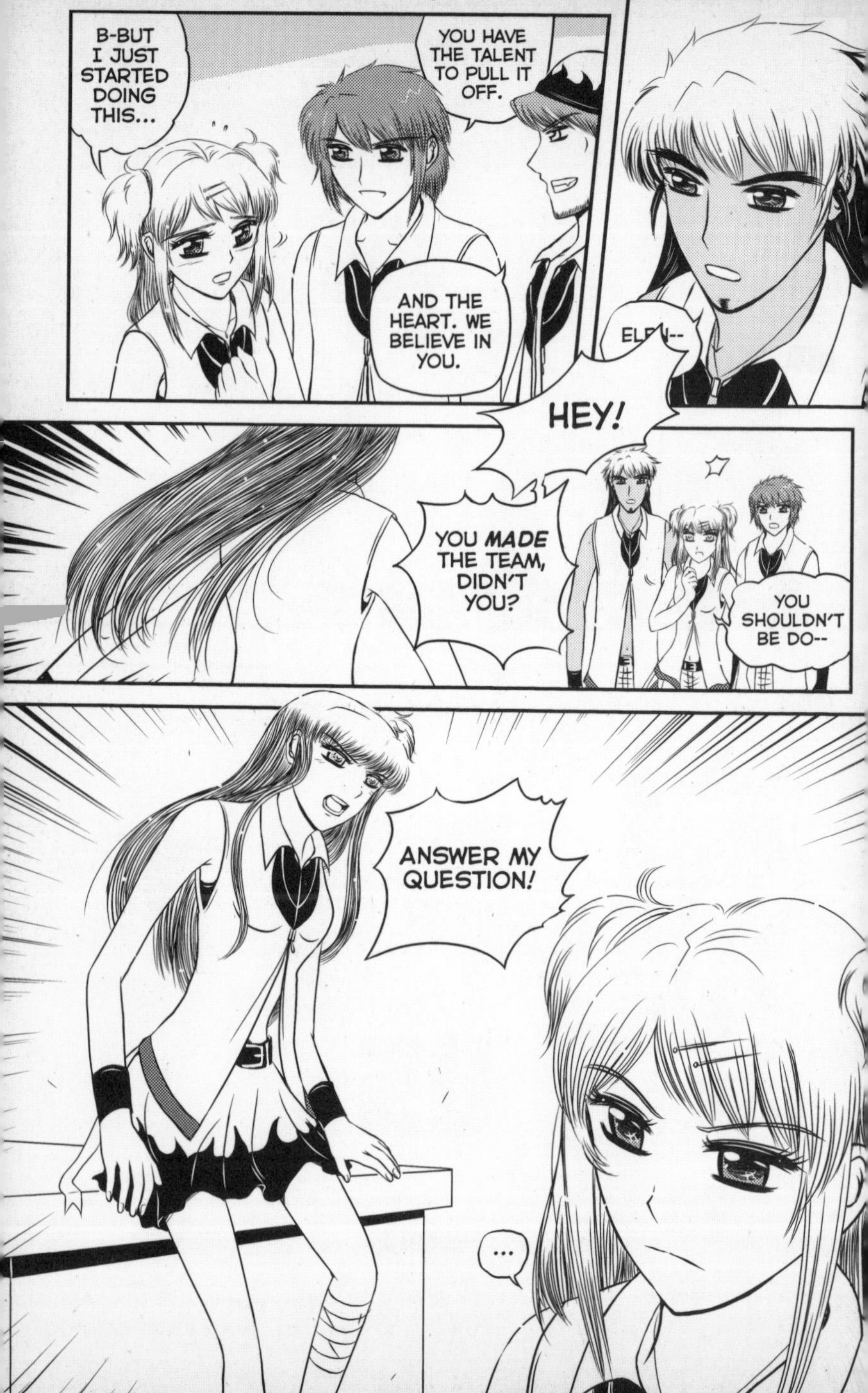

B-BUT I JUST STARTED DOING THIS...
YOU HAVE THE TALENT TO PULL IT OFF.
AND THE HEART. WE BELIEVE IN YOU.
ELEN--
HEY!
YOU *MADE* THE TEAM, DIDN'T YOU?
YOU SHOULDN'T BE DO--
ANSWER MY QUESTION!
...

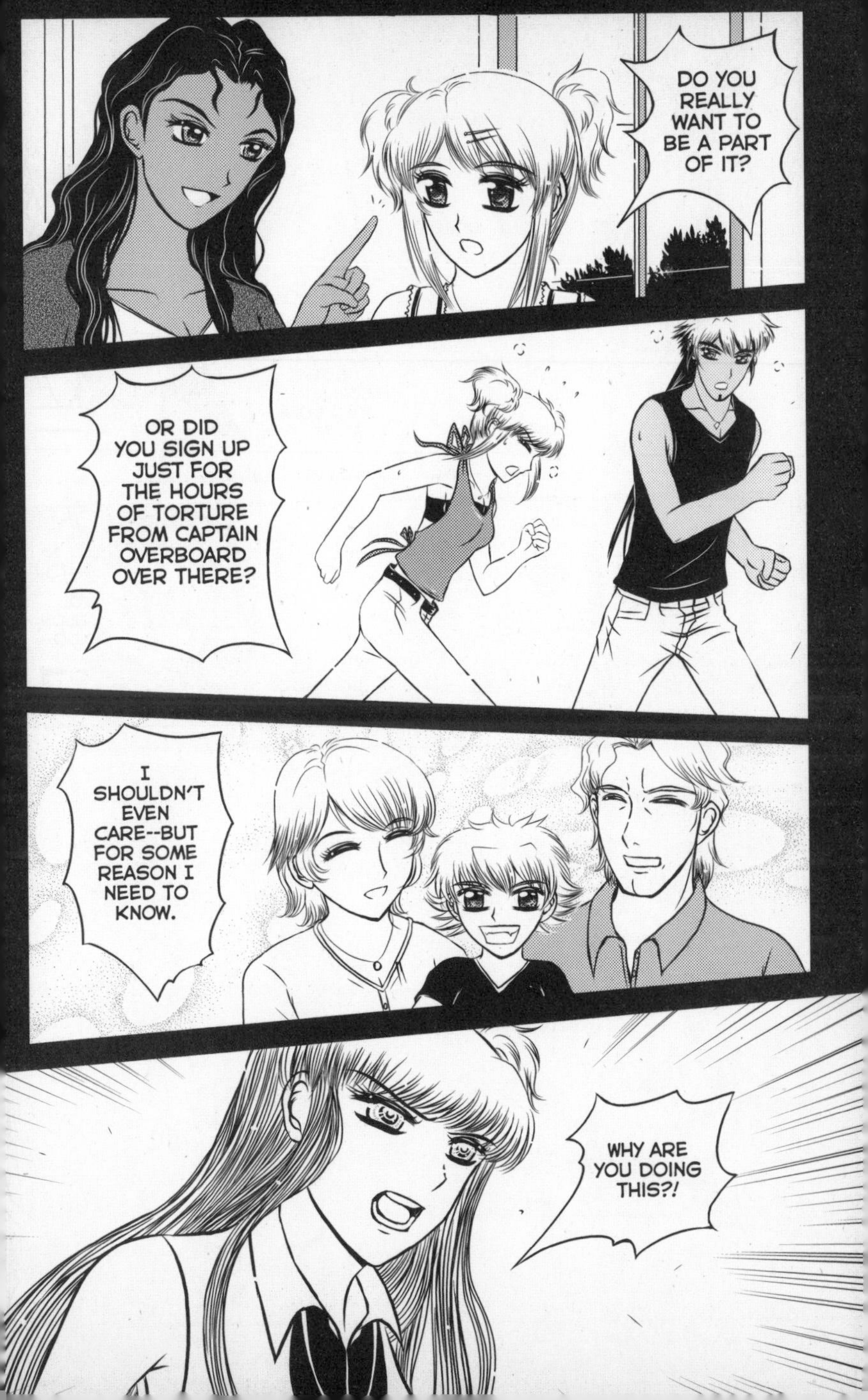
DO YOU REALLY WANT TO BE A PART OF IT?
OR DID YOU SIGN UP JUST FOR THE HOURS OF TORTURE FROM CAPTAIN OVERBOARD OVER THERE?
I SHOULDN'T EVEN CARE--BUT FOR SOME REASON I NEED TO KNOW.
WHY ARE YOU DOING THIS?!

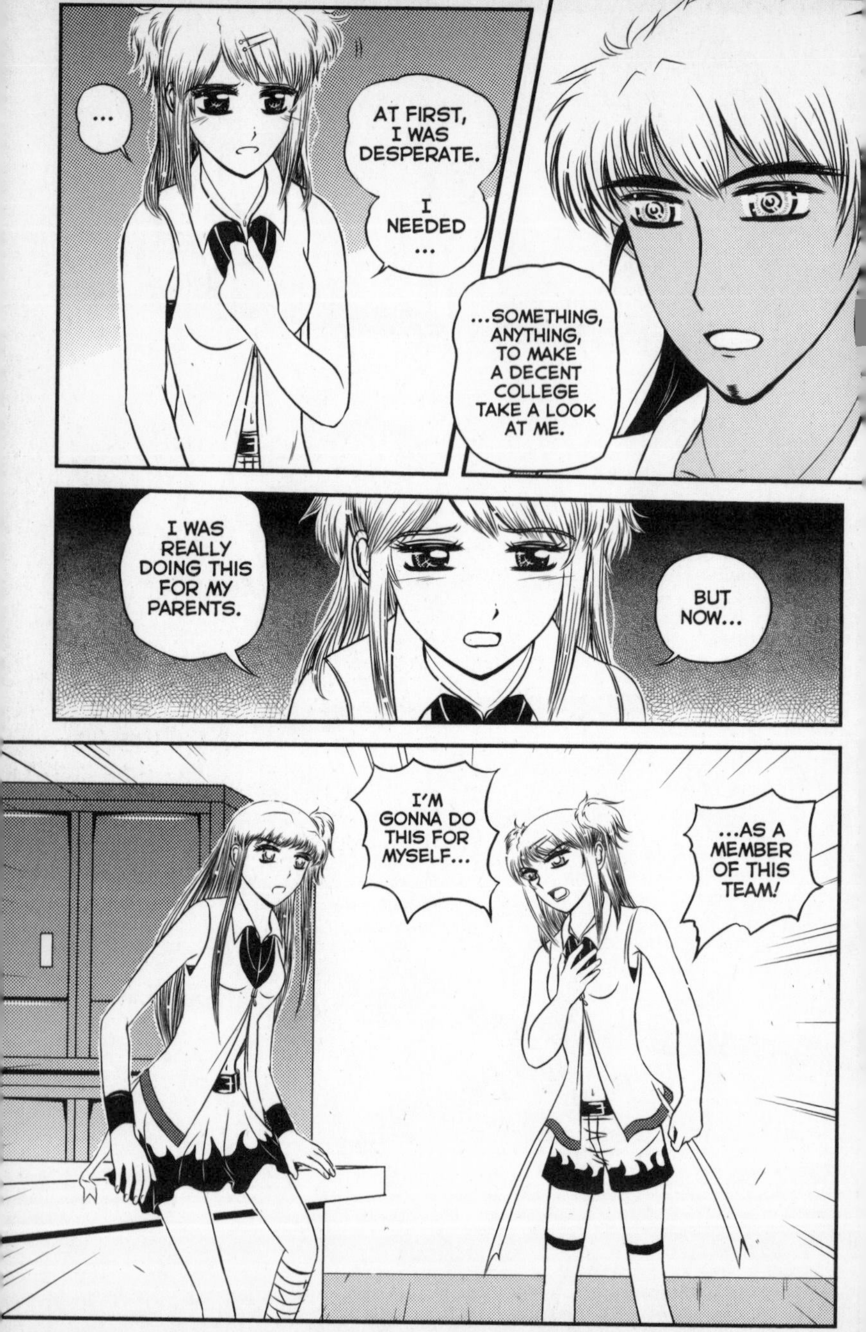
...
AT FIRST, I WAS DESPERATE.
I NEEDED ...
...SOMETHING, ANYTHING, TO MAKE A DECENT COLLEGE TAKE A LOOK AT ME.
I WAS REALLY DOING THIS FOR MY PARENTS.
BUT NOW...
I'M GONNA DO THIS FOR MYSELF...
...AS A MEMBER OF THIS TEAM!

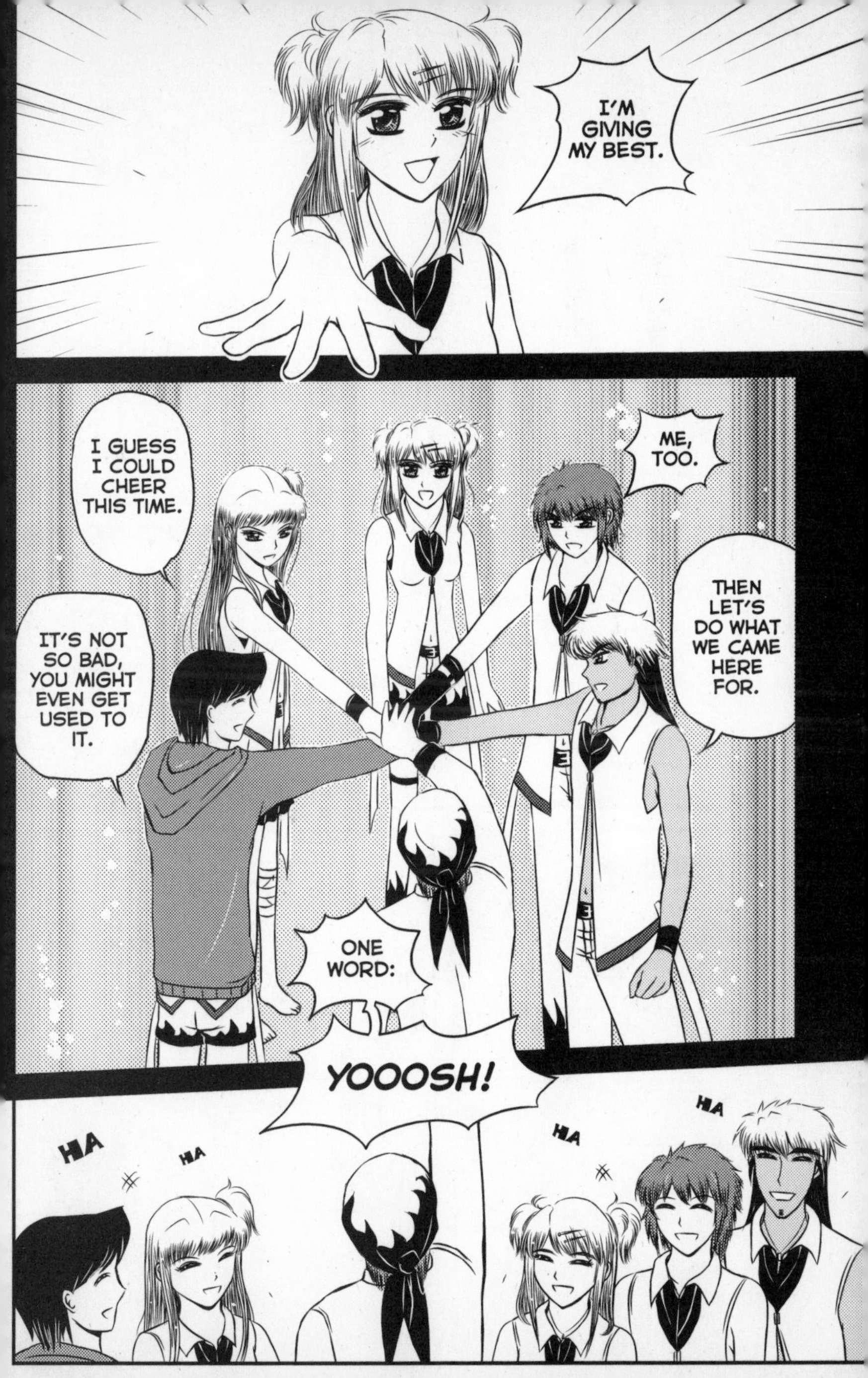
I'M GIVING MY BEST.
I GUESS I COULD CHEER THIS TIME.
ME, TOO.
IT'S NOT SO BAD, YOU MIGHT EVEN GET USED TO IT.
THEN LET'S DO WHAT WE CAME HERE FOR.
ONE WORD:
YOOOSH!
HA
HA
HA
HA

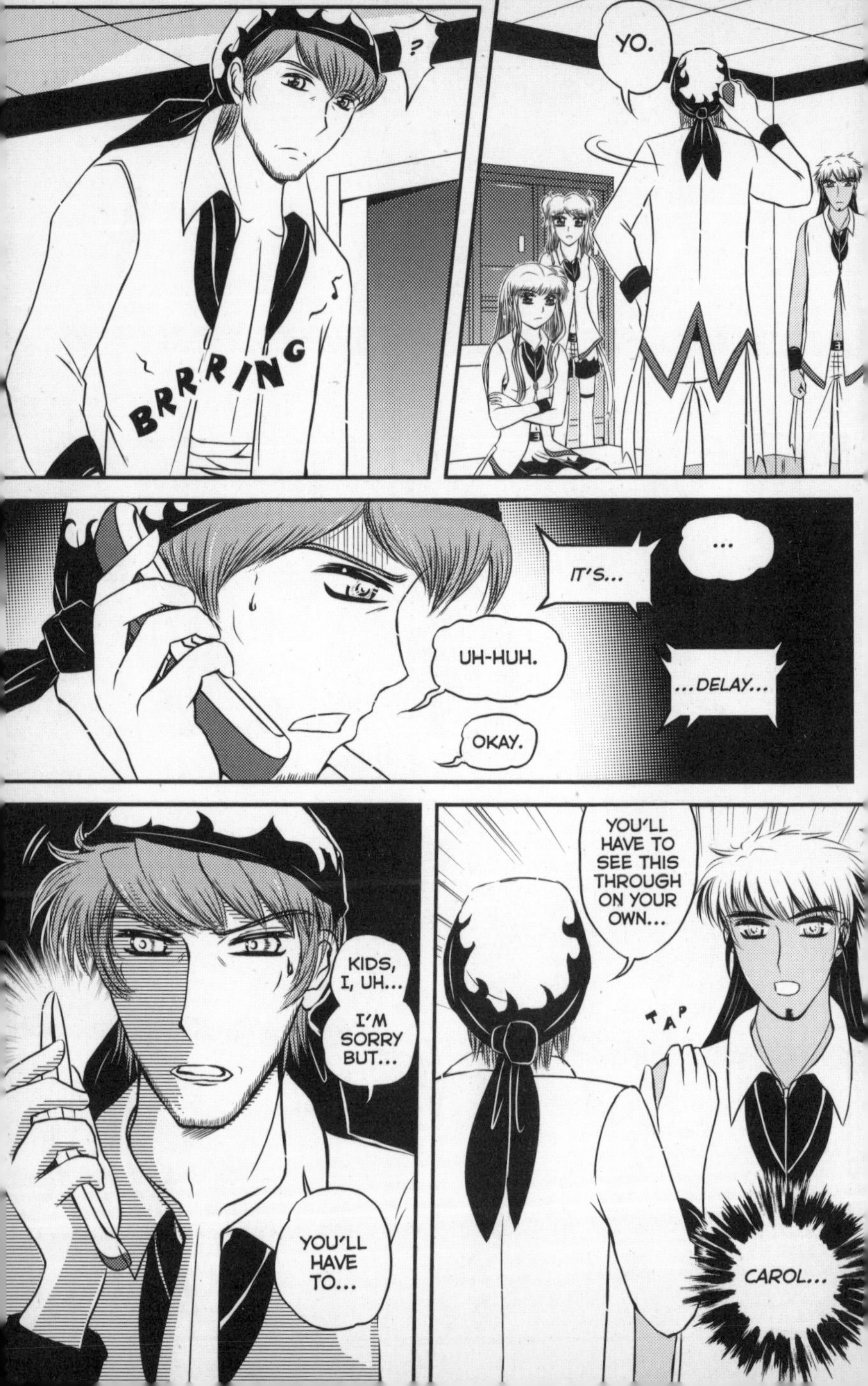
?
BRRRING
YO.
UH-HUH.
OKAY.
IT'S...
...
...DELAY...
KIDS, I, UH...
I'M SORRY BUT...
YOU'LL HAVE TO...
YOU'LL HAVE TO SEE THIS THROUGH ON YOUR OWN...
TAP
CAROL...

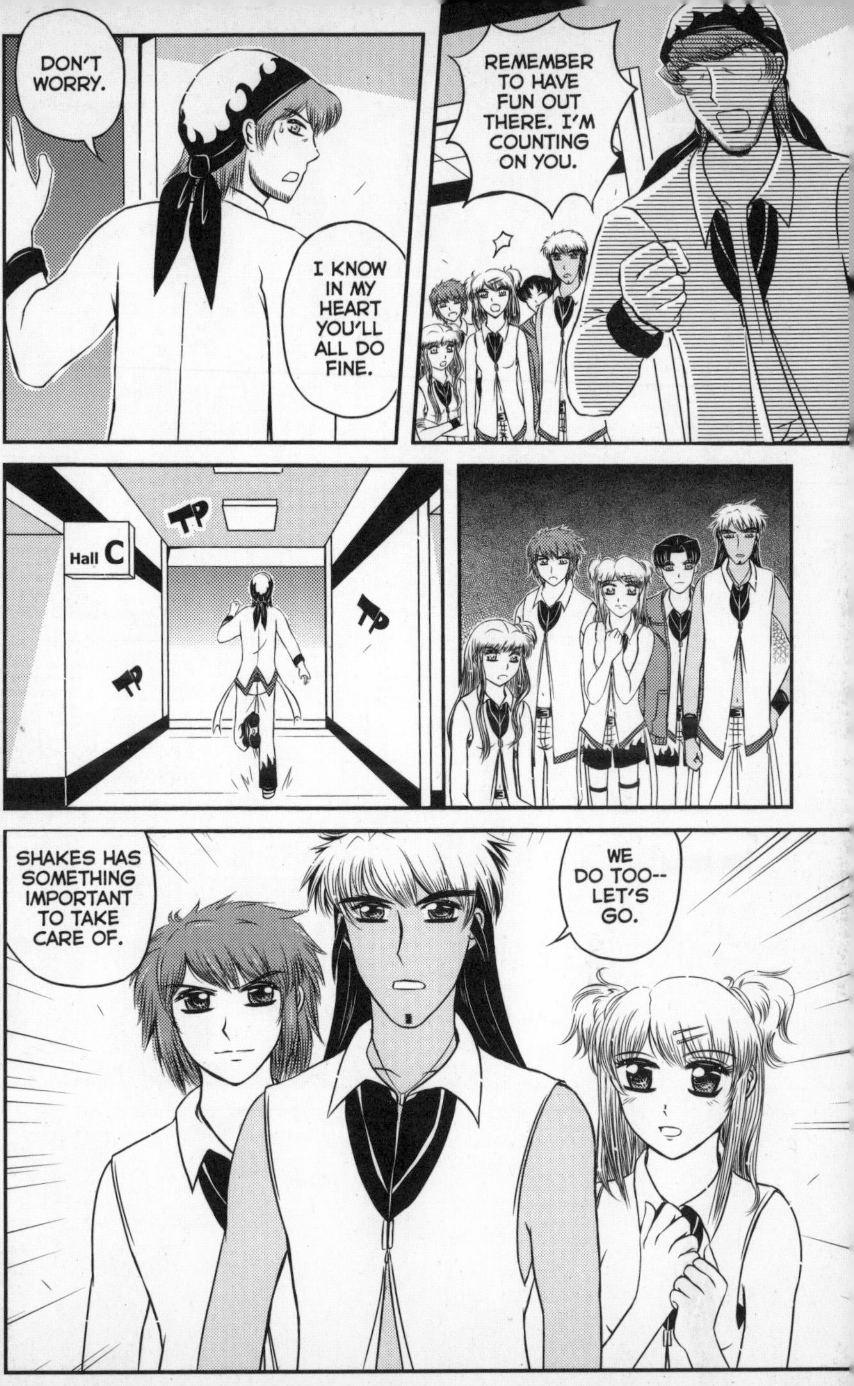
DON'T WORRY.
I KNOW IN MY HEART YOU'LL ALL DO FINE.
REMEMBER TO HAVE FUN OUT THERE. I'M COUNTING ON YOU.
Hall C
TP
TP
TP
SHAKES HAS SOMETHING IMPORTANT TO TAKE CARE OF.
WE DO TOO-- LET'S GO.

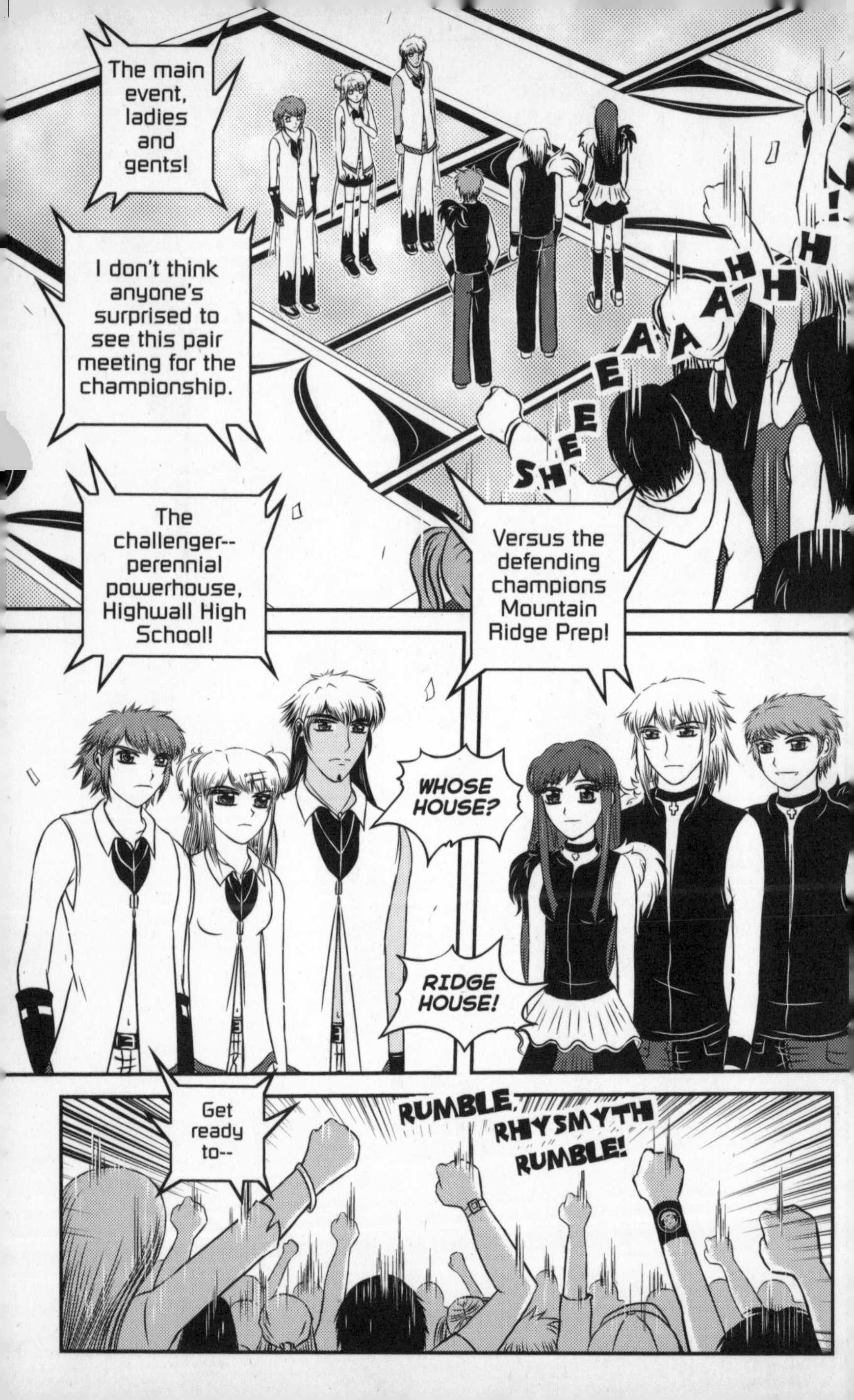
The main event, ladies and gents!
I don't think anyone's surprised to see this pair meeting for the championship.
SHEEEAAAAHHHH!
The challenger-- perennial powerhouse, Highwall High School!
Versus the defending champions Mountain Ridge Prep!
WHOSE HOUSE?
RIDGE HOUSE!
Get ready to--
RUMBLE, RHYSMYTH RUMBLE!

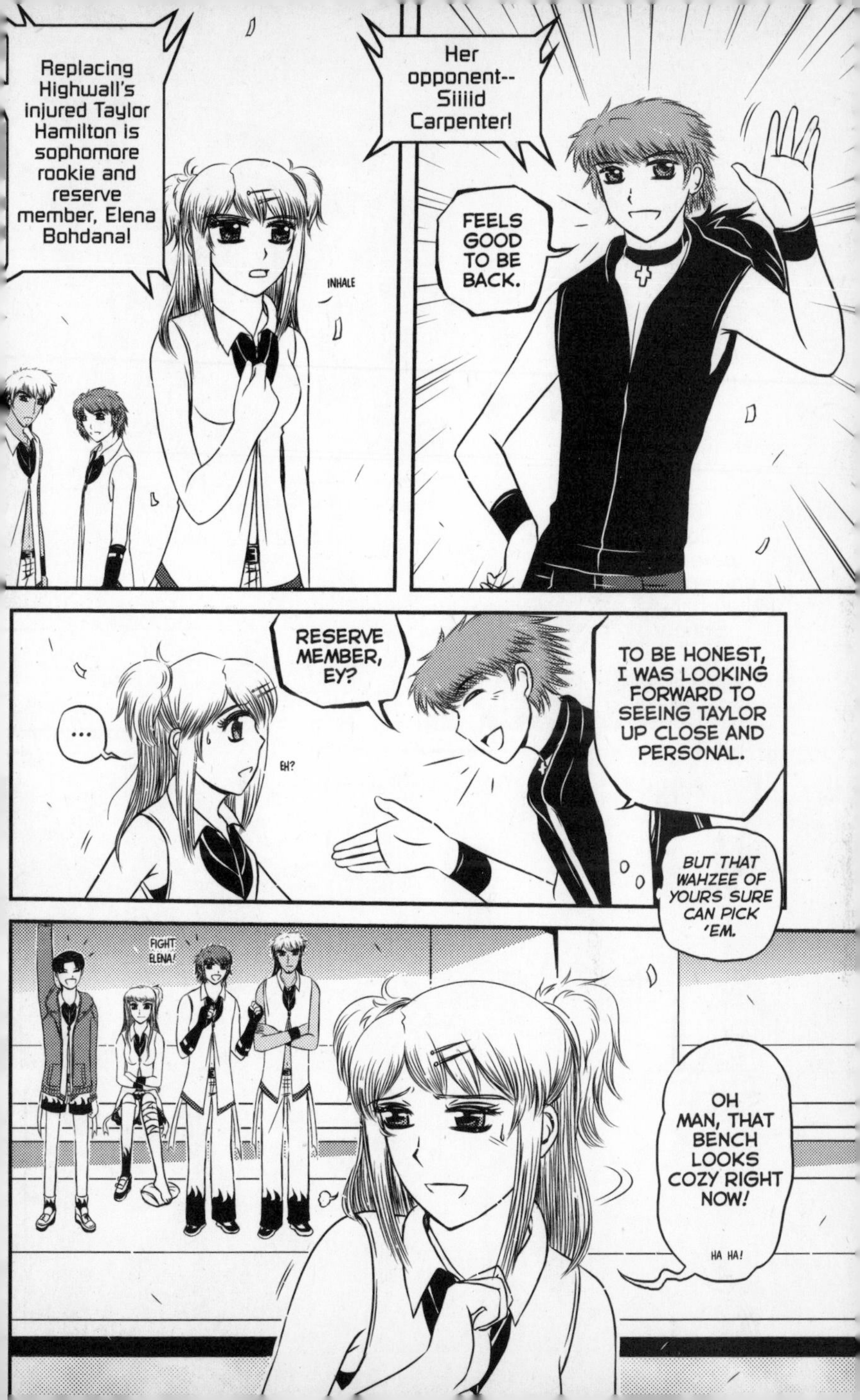
Replacing Highwall's injured Taylor Hamilton is sophomore rookie and reserve member, Elena Bohdana!
INHALE
Her opponent-- Siiiid Carpenter!
FEELS GOOD TO BE BACK.
...
EH?
RESERVE MEMBER, EY?
TO BE HONEST, I WAS LOOKING FORWARD TO SEEING TAYLOR UP CLOSE AND PERSONAL.
BUT THAT WAHZEE OF YOURS SURE CAN PICK 'EM.
FIGHT ELENA!
OH MAN, THAT BENCH LOOKS COZY RIGHT NOW!
HA HA!

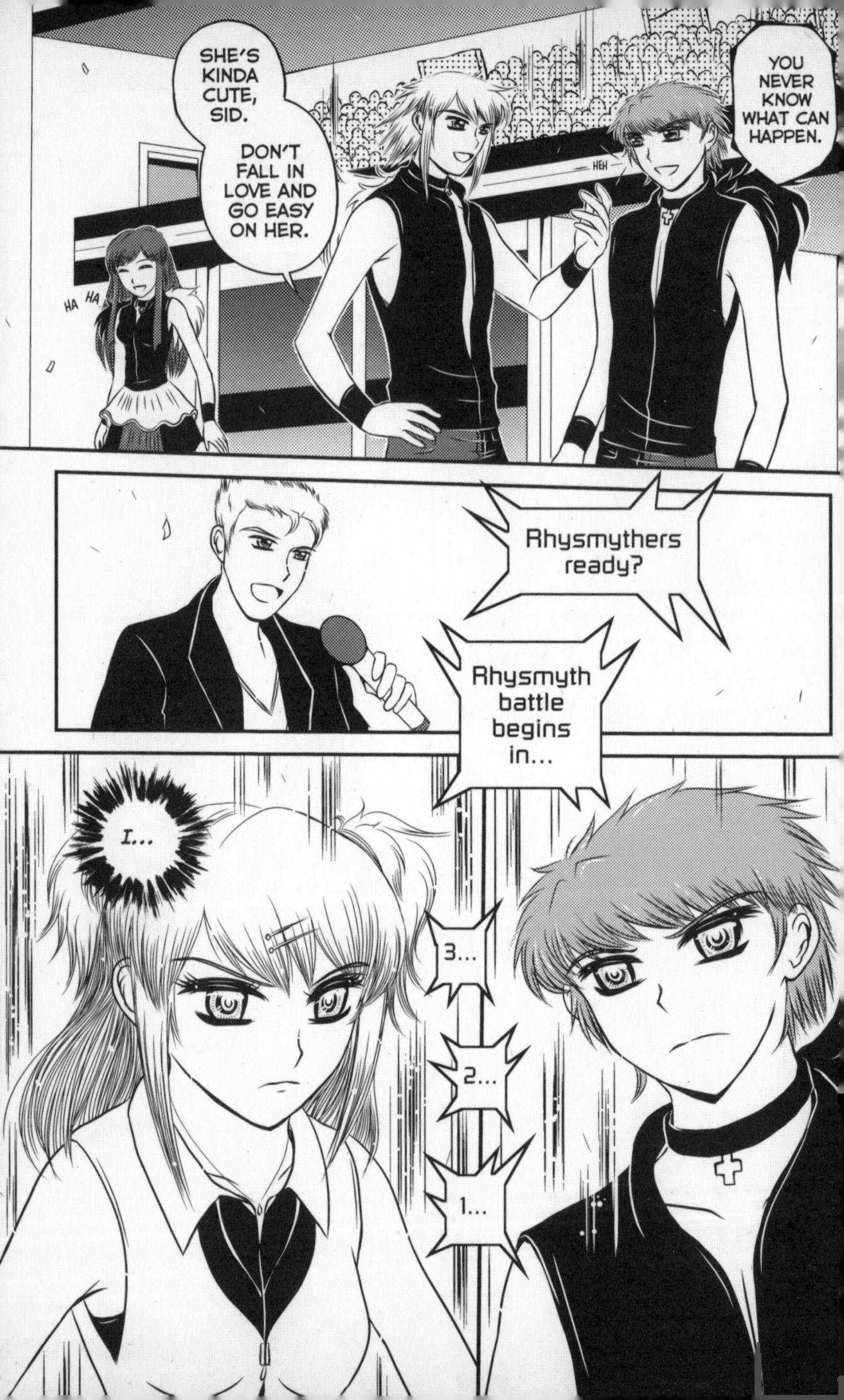
HA HA
SHE'S KINDA CUTE, SID.
DON'T FALL IN LOVE AND GO EASY ON HER.
HEH
YOU NEVER KNOW WHAT CAN HAPPEN.
Rhysmythers ready?
Rhysmyth battle begins in...
I...
3...
2...
1...

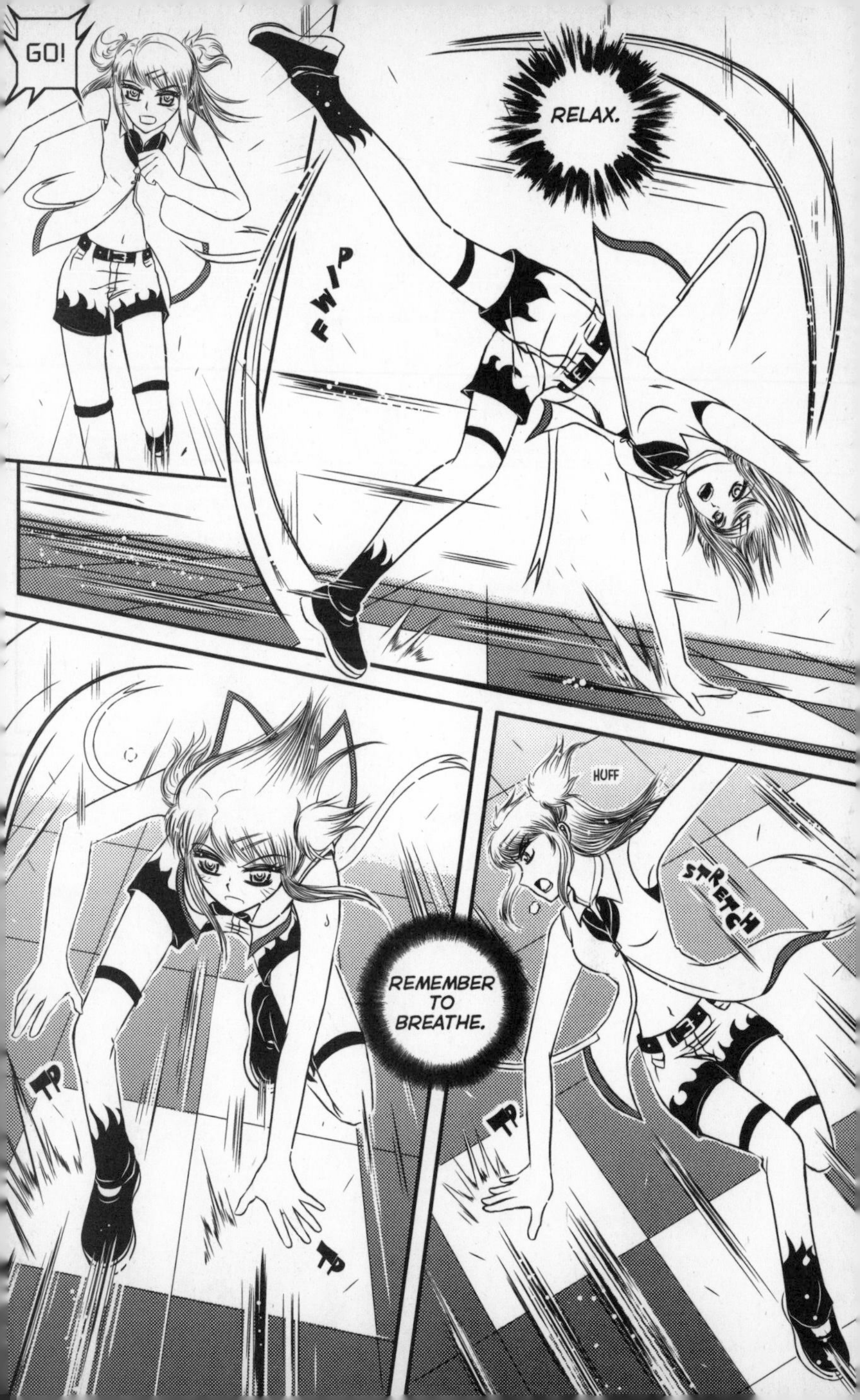
GO!
RELAX.
FWIP
HUFF
STRETCH
REMEMBER TO BREATHE.
TP
TP
TP

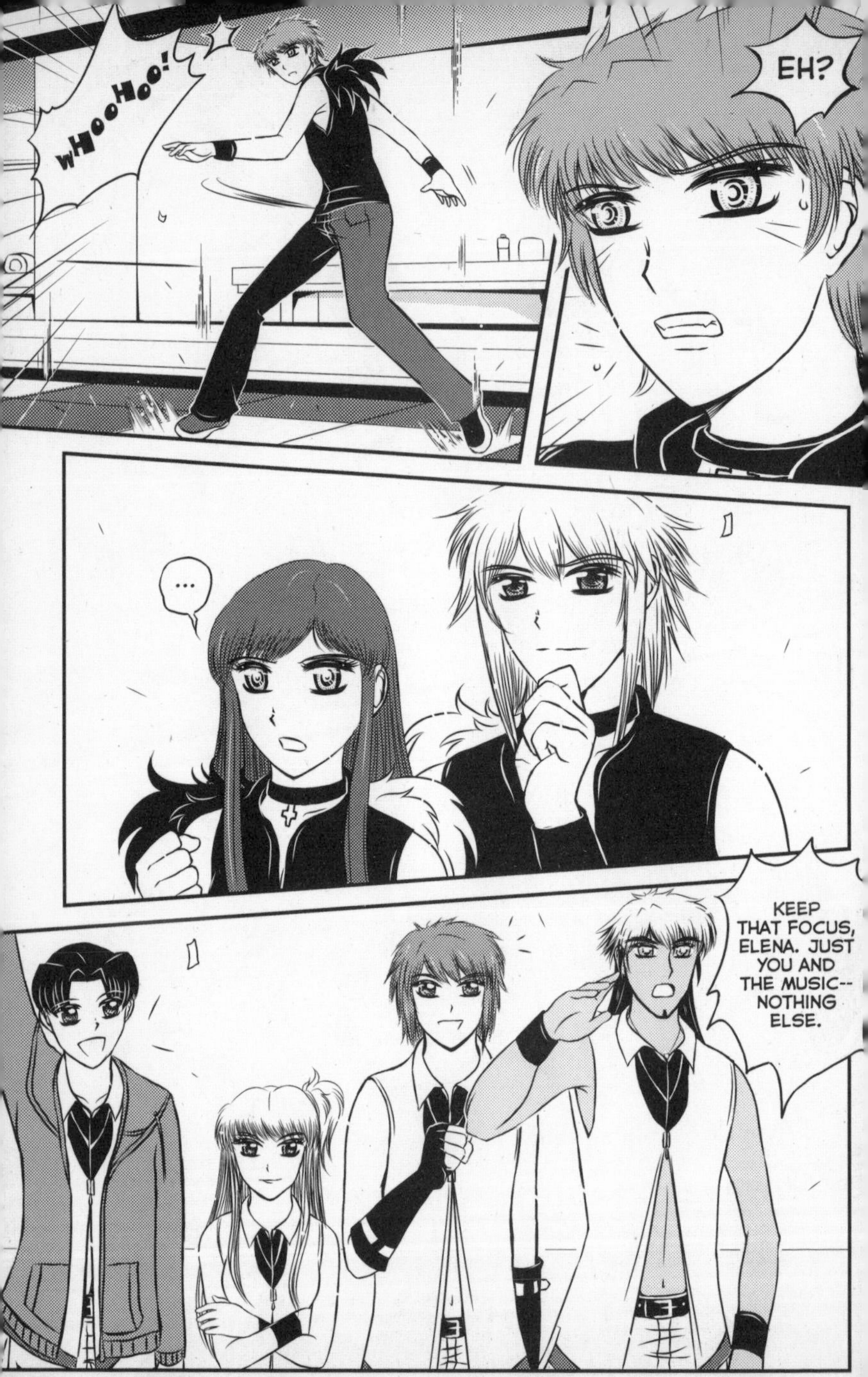
WHOOHOO!
EH?
...
KEEP THAT FOCUS, ELENA. JUST YOU AND THE MUSIC-- NOTHING ELSE.

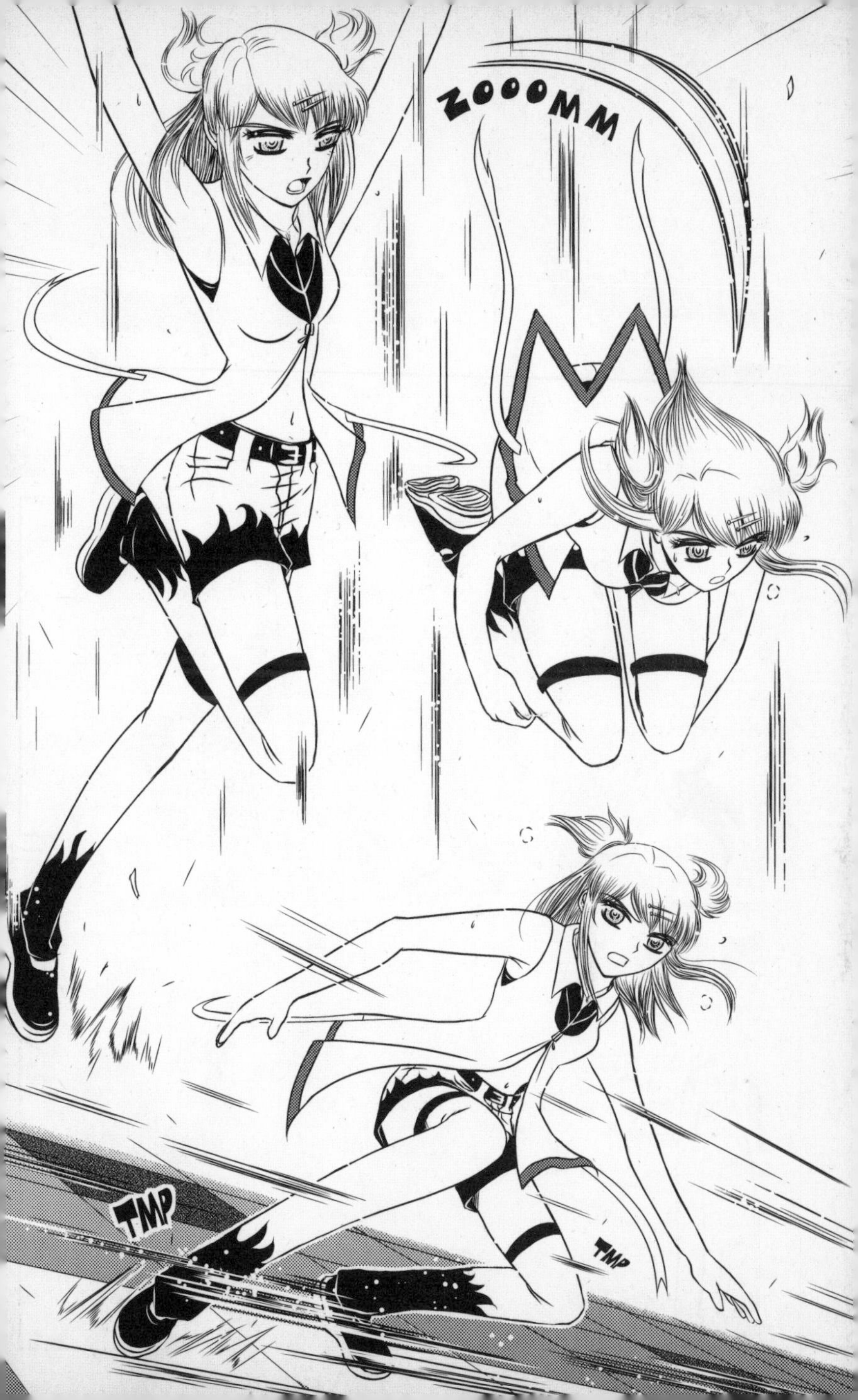
ZOOOMM
TMP
TMP

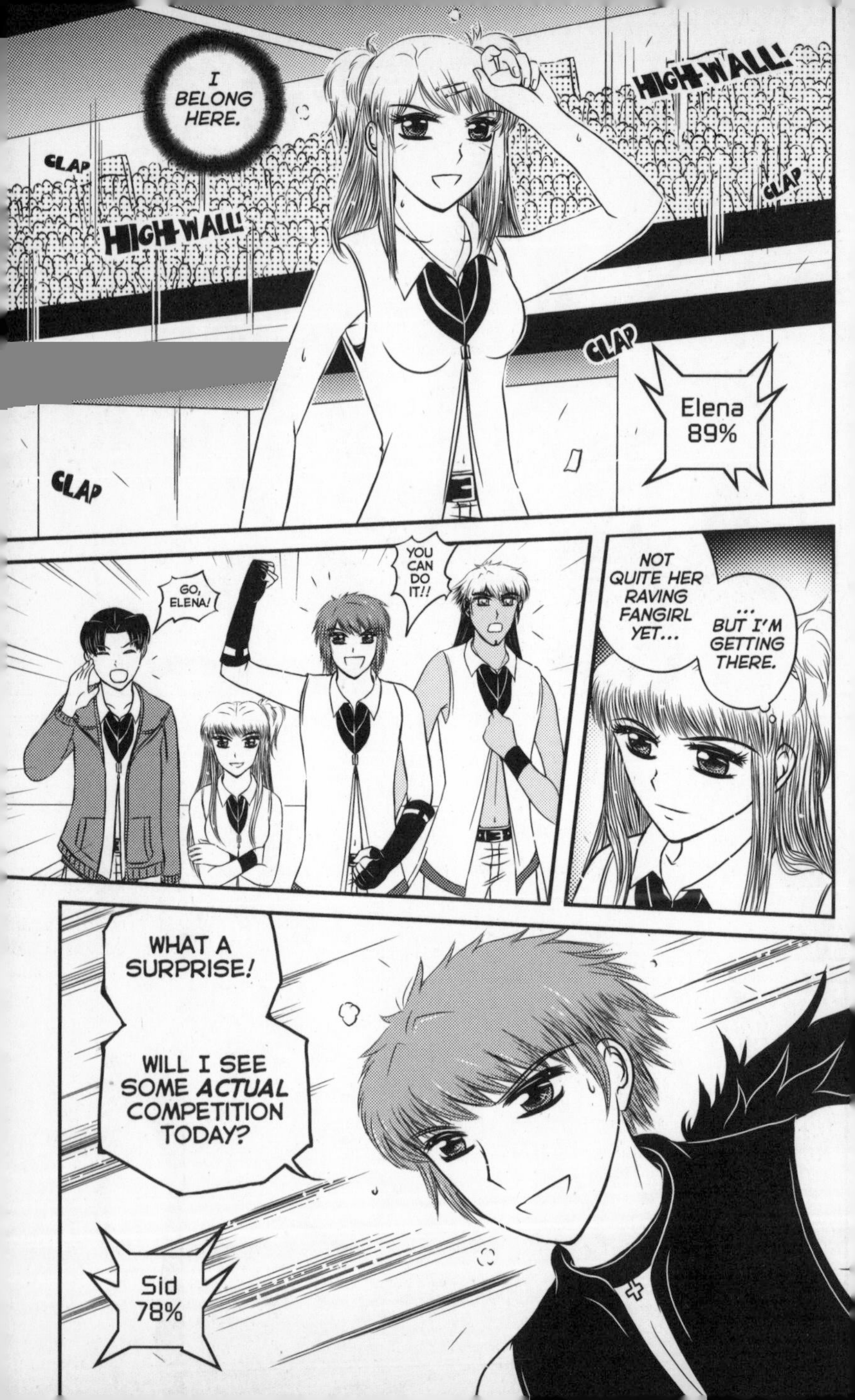

I BELONG HERE.
HIGH-WALL!
CLAP
CLAP
HIGH-WALL!
CLAP
CLAP
Elena 89%
GO, ELENA!
YOU CAN DO IT!!
NOT QUITE HER RAVING FANGIRL YET...
... BUT I'M GETTING THERE.
WHAT A SURPRISE!
WILL I SEE SOME *ACTUAL* COMPETITION TODAY?
Sid 78%

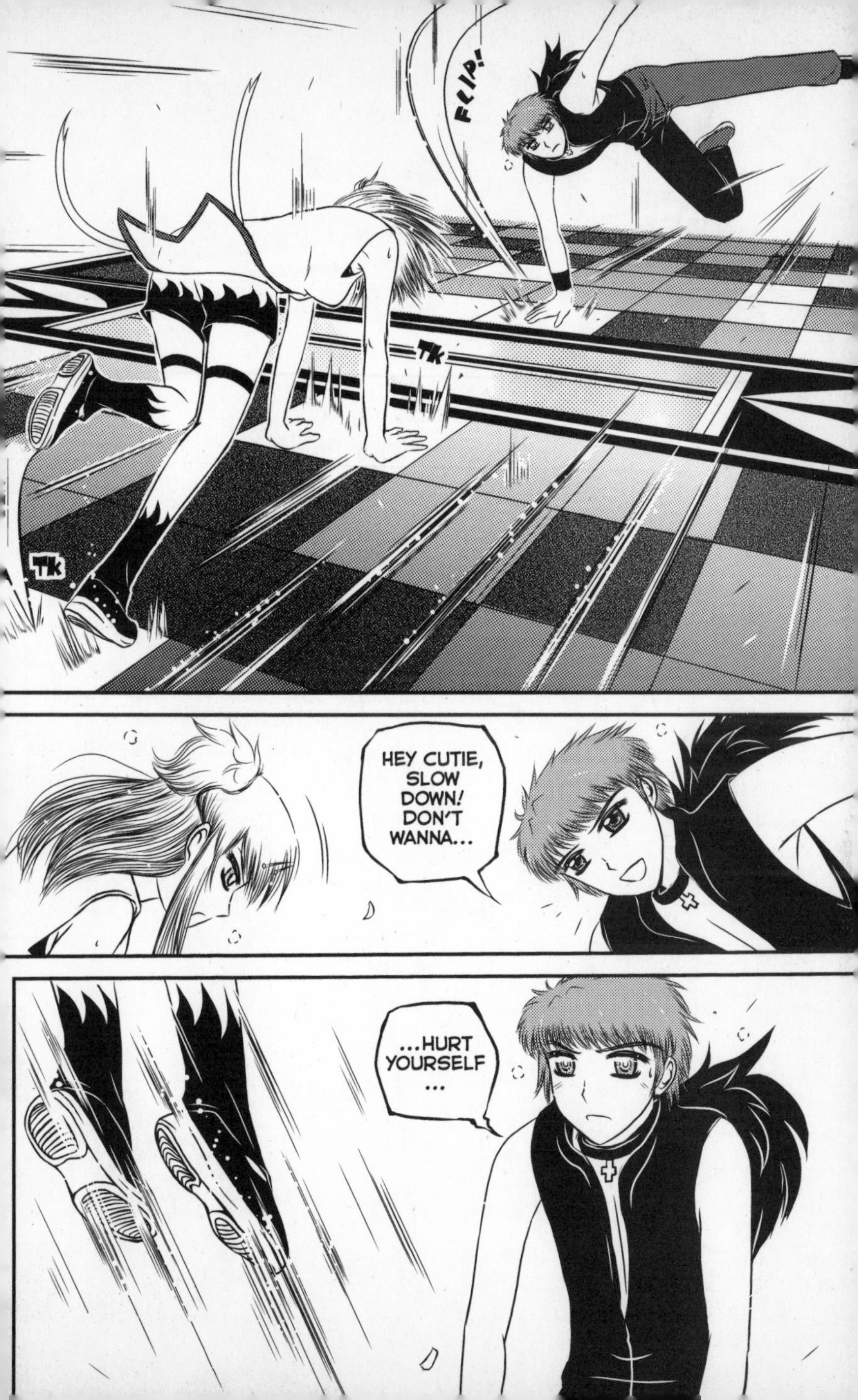
FLIP!
TK
TK
HEY CUTIE, SLOW DOWN! DON'T WANNA...
...HURT YOURSELF ...

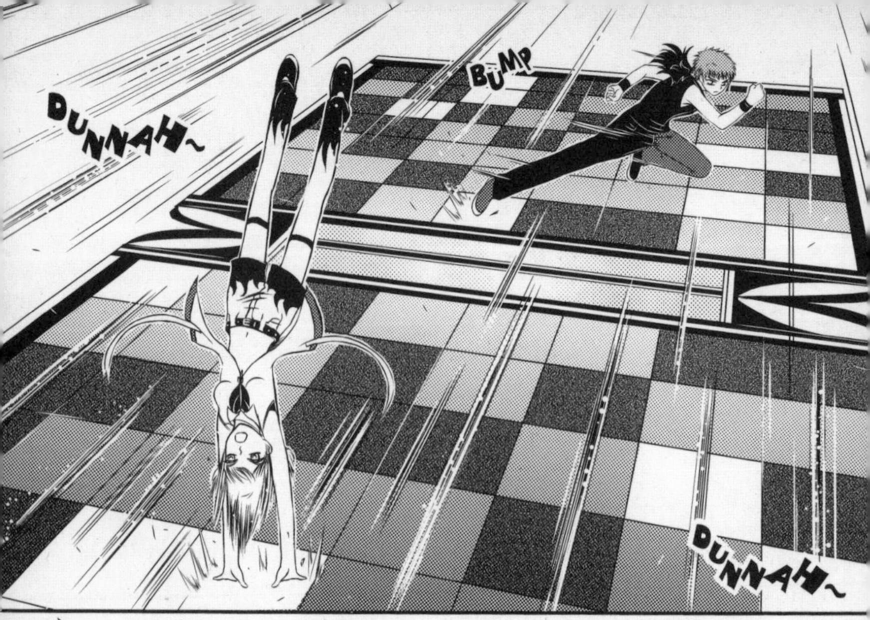
DUNNAH~
BUMP
DUNNAH~

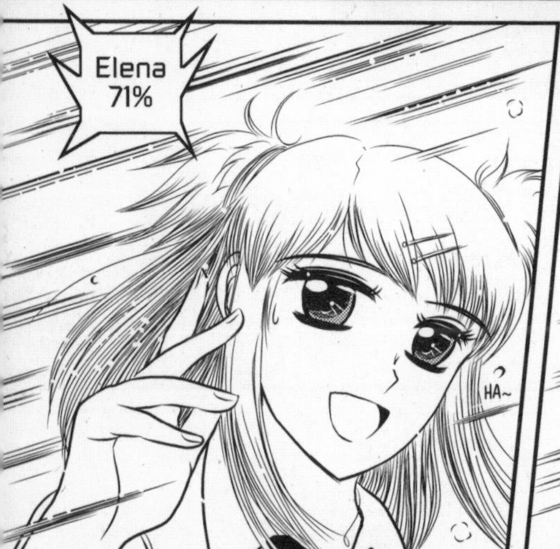
Elena 71%
HA~

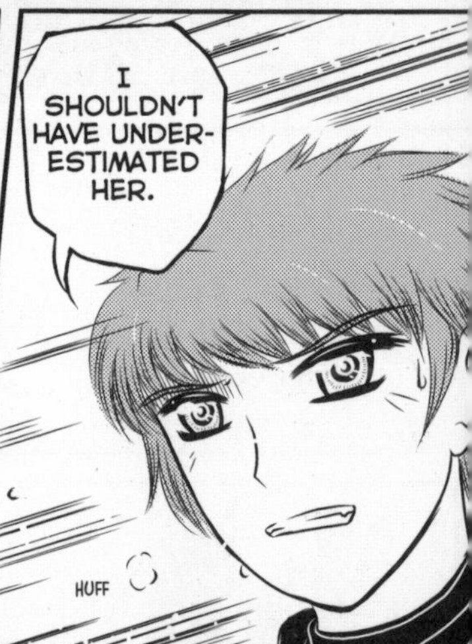
I SHOULDN'T HAVE UNDER-ESTIMATED HER.
HUFF
Sid 57%

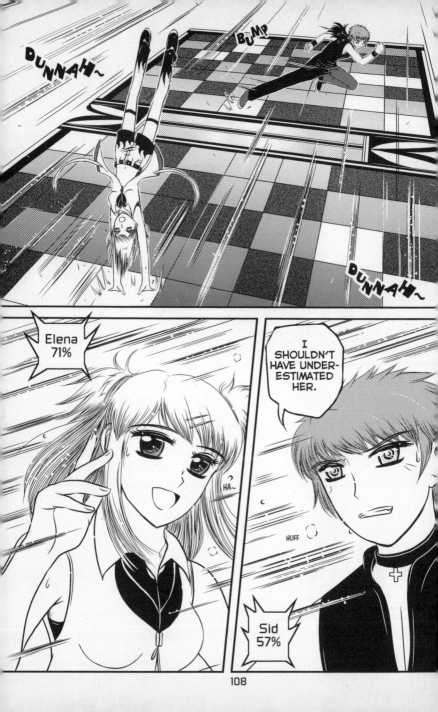

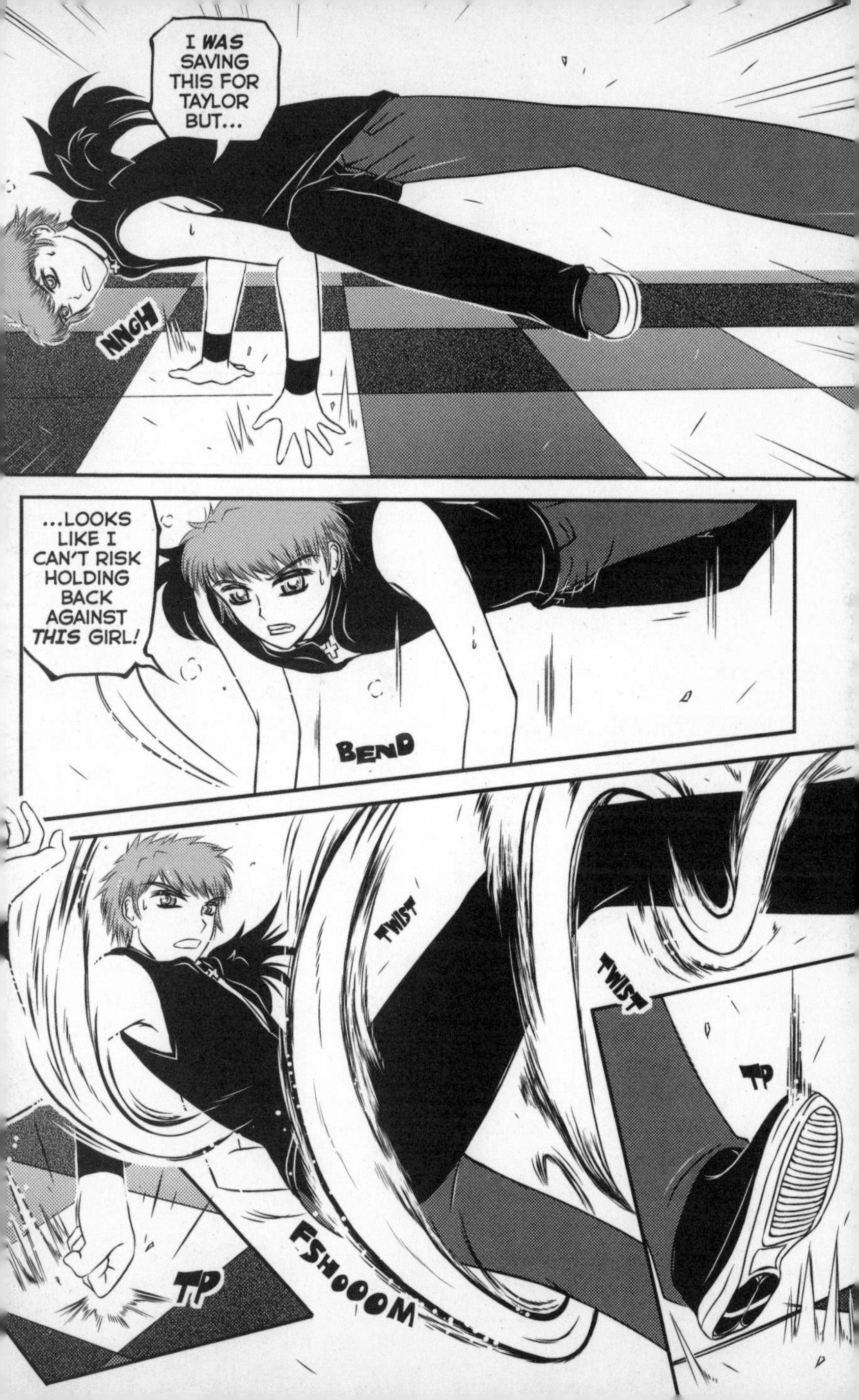
I WAS SAVING THIS FOR TAYLOR BUT...
NNGH
...LOOKS LIKE I CAN'T RISK HOLDING BACK AGAINST THIS GIRL!
BEND
TWIST
TWIST
TP
FSHOOOM
TP

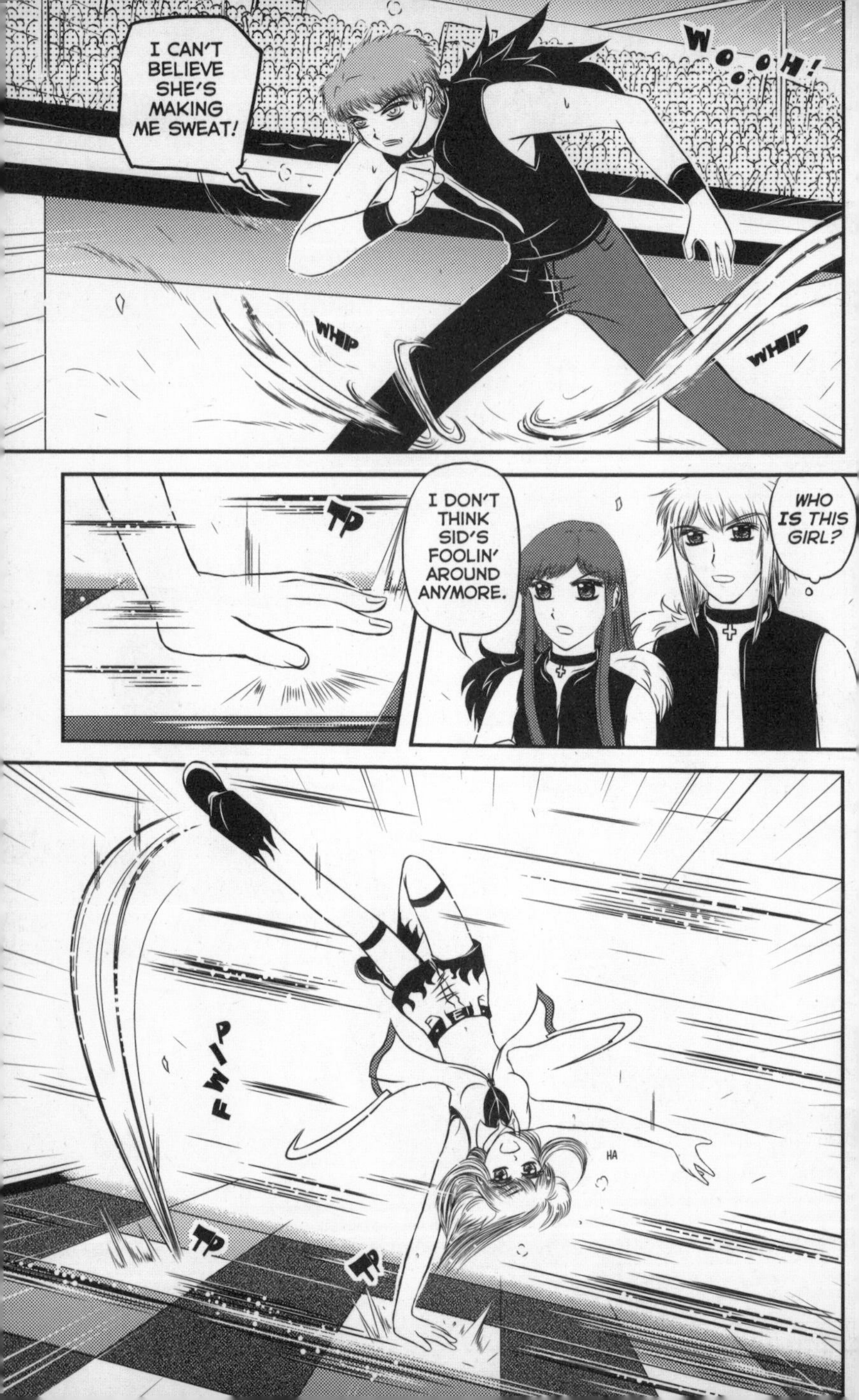
I CAN'T BELIEVE SHE'S MAKING ME SWEAT!
WOOOH!
WHIP
WHIP
TP
I DON'T THINK SID'S FOOLIN' AROUND ANYMORE.
WHO IS THIS GIRL?
FWIP
HA
TP
TP

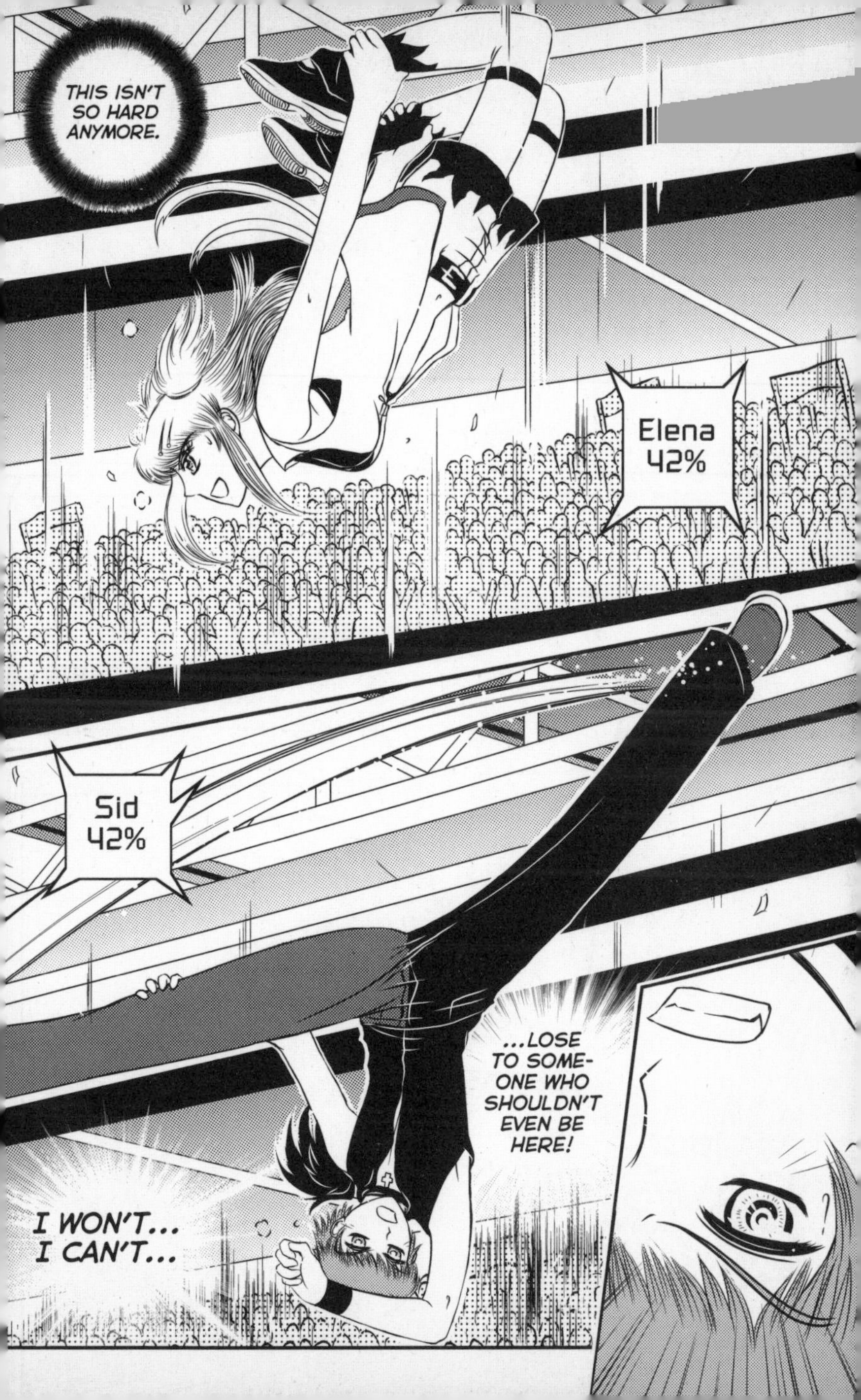
THIS ISN'T SO HARD ANYMORE.
Elena 42%
Sid 42%
I WON'T... I CAN'T...
...LOSE TO SOME-ONE WHO SHOULDN'T EVEN BE HERE!

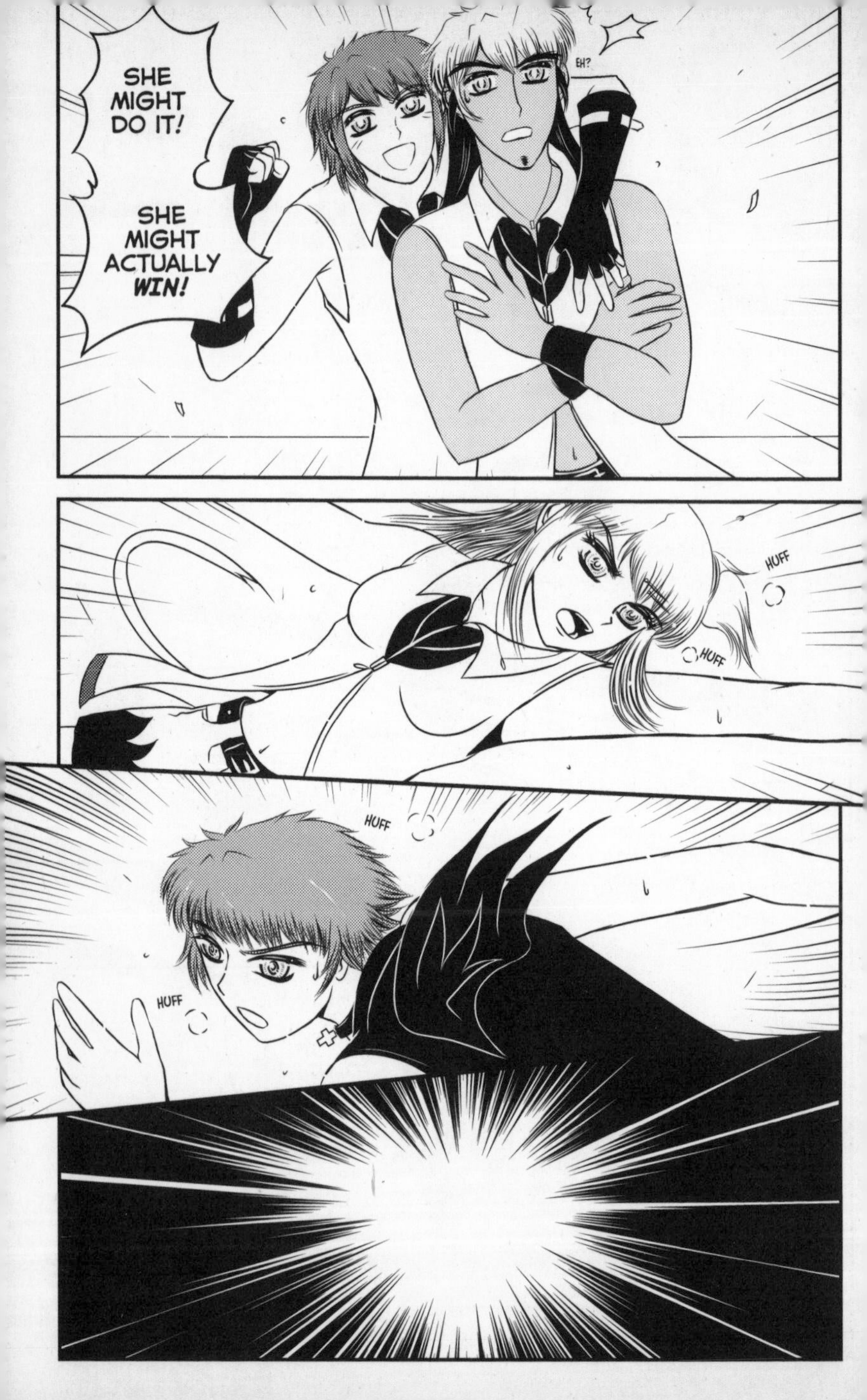
SHE MIGHT DO IT!
SHE MIGHT ACTUALLY WIN!
EH?
HUFF
HUFF
HUFF
HUFF

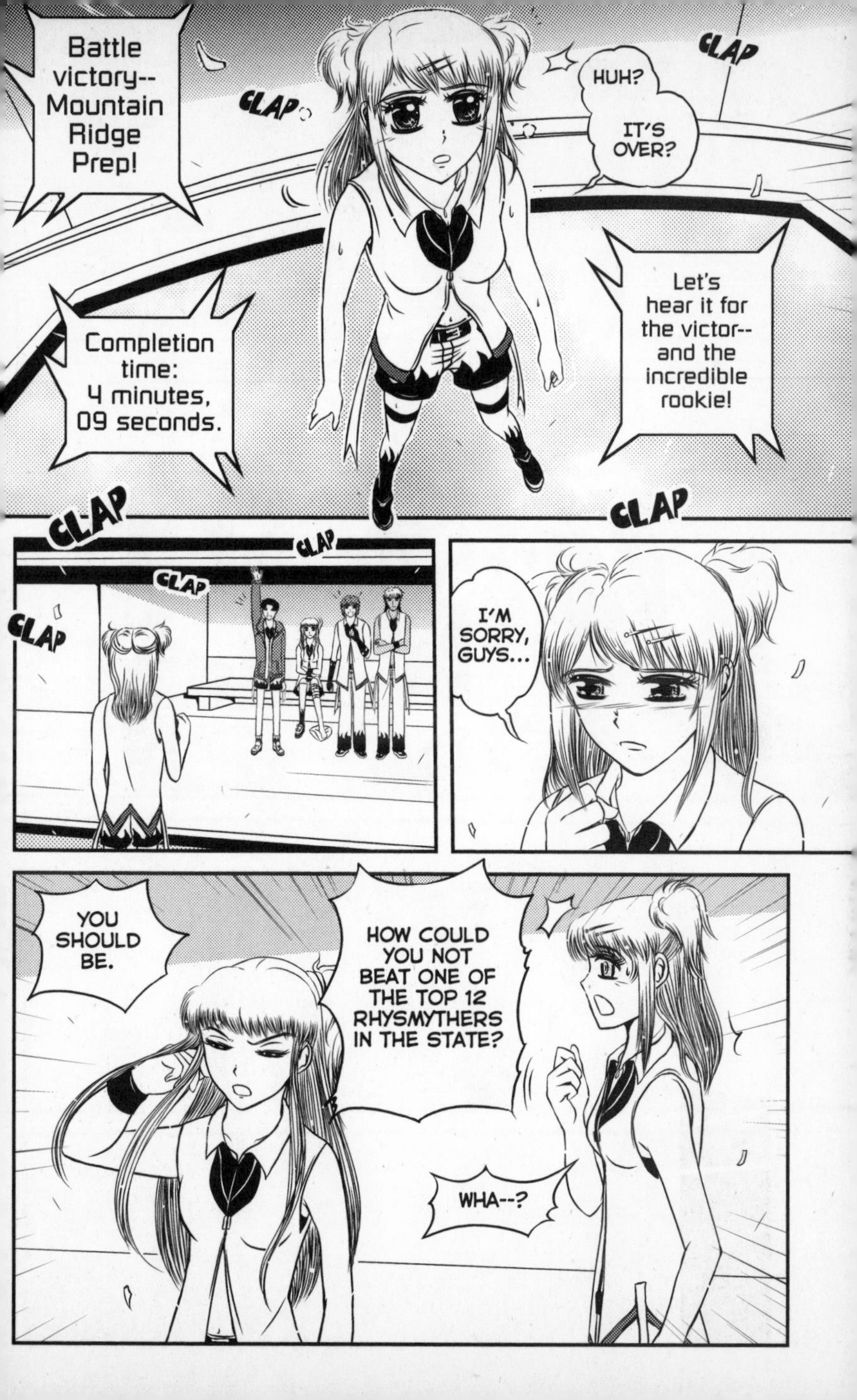
Battle victory--Mountain Ridge Prep!
CLAP
HUH?
IT'S OVER?
CLAP
Completion time: 4 minutes, 09 seconds.
Let's hear it for the victor--and the incredible rookie!
CLAP
CLAP
CLAP
CLAP
CLAP
CLAP
I'M SORRY, GUYS...
YOU SHOULD BE.
HOW COULD YOU NOT BEAT ONE OF THE TOP 12 RHYSMYTHERS IN THE STATE?
WHA--?

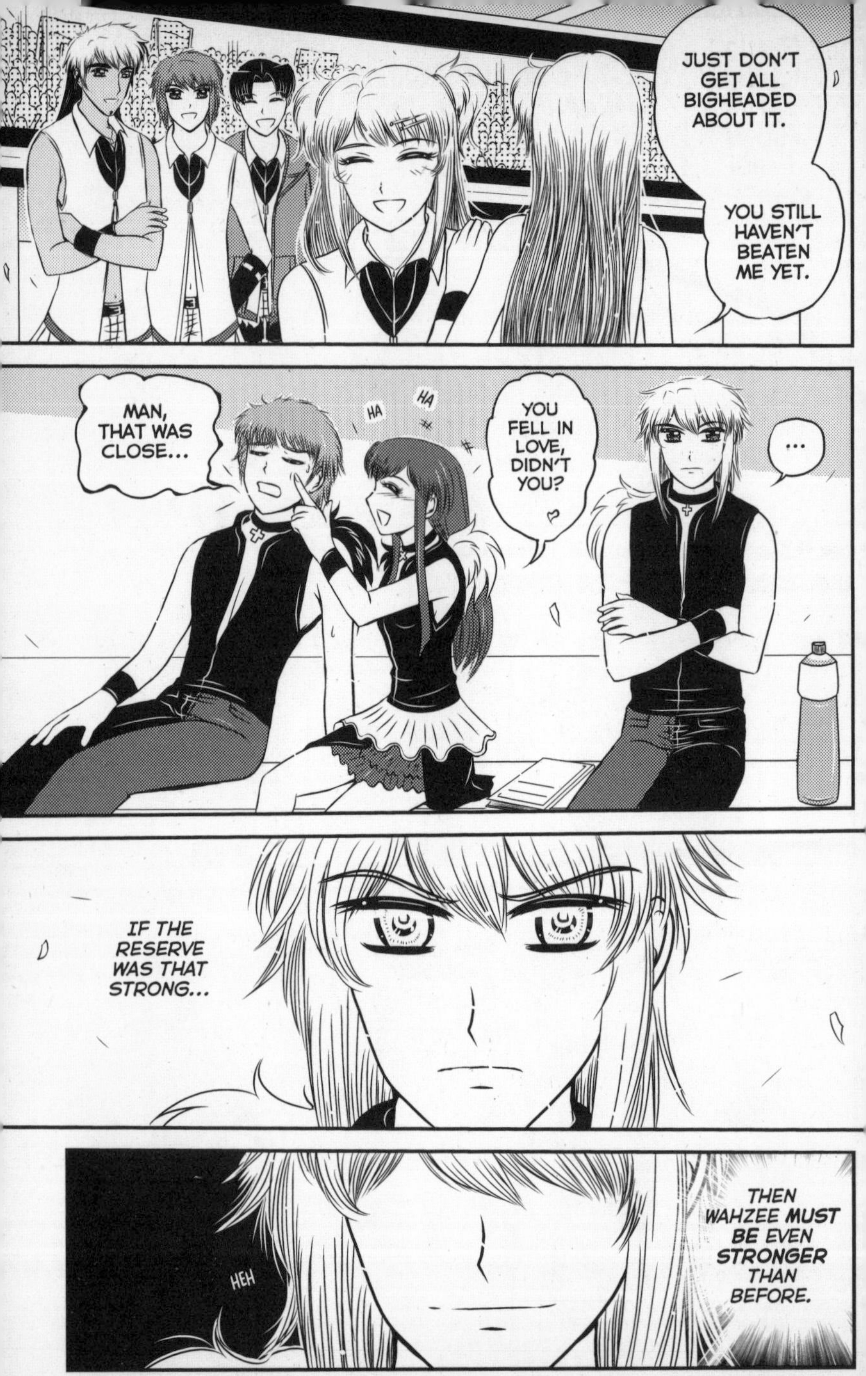
JUST DON'T GET ALL BIGHEADED ABOUT IT.
YOU STILL HAVEN'T BEATEN ME YET.
MAN, THAT WAS CLOSE...
HA
HA
YOU FELL IN LOVE, DIDN'T YOU?
...
IF THE RESERVE WAS THAT STRONG...
HEH
THEN WAHZEE MUST BE EVEN STRONGER THAN BEFORE.

hiei9934
Head Spinner

Joined: May 07 2007
Posts: 303

Best local Rhysmyther?
October 6, 2008 9:12 pm

Hey guys!! I was wondering what everyone thinks about the local Rhysmyth scene here in the Bay area. Specifically--who do you think is best?

[Quote] [Edit]

Naruru
Moon Walker

Joined: Aug 15 2007
Posts: 140

Re: Best local Rhysmyther?
October 6, 2008 9:15 pm

My school doesn't have a Rhysmyth team... but I have been to one comp since my cousin dances for MBQ. I like it so far. How many schools are there? That do it, I mean.

[Quote] [Edit]

---

omittchi
Cabbage Patcher

Joined: Nov 26 2007
Posts: 47

Re: Best local Rhysmyther?
October 7, 2008 1:03 am

Uh, 2 words, a billion syllables, 1 hottie: Diocel manibusan! FTW !!!! ⟨+_+⟩

[Quote] [Edit]

---

hiei9934
Head Spinner

Joined: May 07 2007
Posts: 303

Re: Best local Rhysmyther?
October 7, 2008 9:12 am

@ Naruru: We've got really strong schools, 8 in our district but there are more that come in for interleague matches. The top two of course are Mountain Ridge and Highwall. Click on my profile button and you'll find a link to my vidtube account. WATCH WATCH WATCH!

@ omi: Diocel IS good. But Wahzee is SO much better. That is why he's captain of course :: wink ::

[Quote] [Edit]

---

midorihebi
Rhysmyth Captain

Joined: Oct 21 2006
Posts: 1528

Re: Best local Rhysmyther?
October 7, 2008 9:36 pm

wow--lotsa 'Myth newbs here, but don't mean in a bad way, i'm just saying no one has mentioned Carol yet, the old HWH captain going back to 2 years ago when the team just started. as good as wahzee is--she was ten times better. and that just means wahzee is that good nowadays.

[Quote] [Edit]

---

hiei9934
Head Spinner

Joined: May 07 2007
Posts: 303

Re: Best local Rhysmyther?
October 7, 2008 11:09 pm

@ midori : Who is that?
Renaldo is VERY good. When he and Wahzee go at it zOMG!!!! I can't even express it! But I heard Ren has been trained in dance since DAY ONE. I heard from a friend that he even toured across the world aspart of a dance troupe. If that's the case, I think my dear Wahwah has more talent--everyone knows he's never done ANYTHING before Rhysmyth but he's a NATURAL!

[Quote] [Edit]

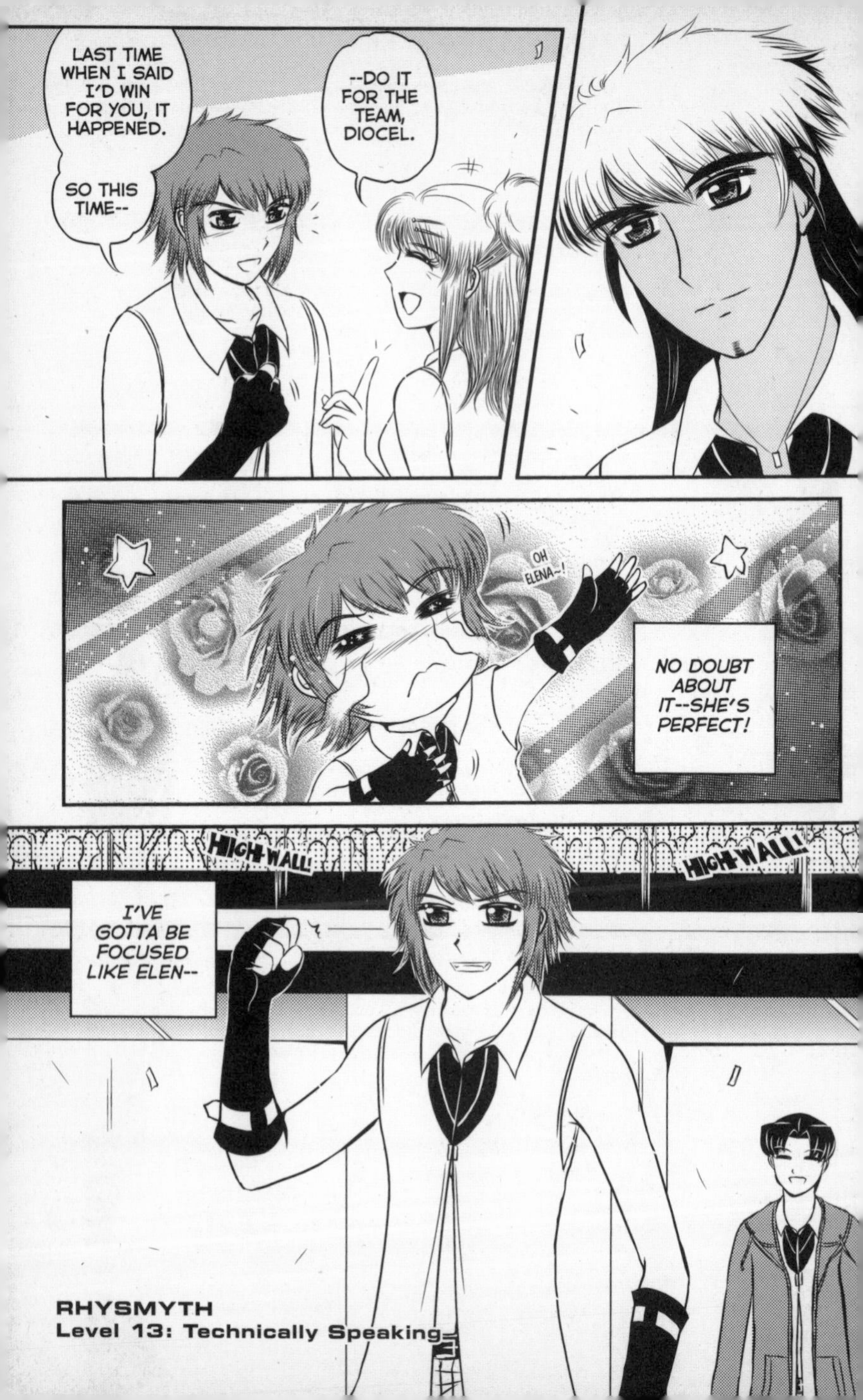

LAST TIME WHEN I SAID I'D WIN FOR YOU, IT HAPPENED.
SO THIS TIME--
--DO IT FOR THE TEAM, DIOCEL.
OH ELENA~!
NO DOUBT ABOUT IT--SHE'S PERFECT!
HIGH-WALL!
HIGH-WALL!
I'VE GOTTA BE FOCUSED LIKE ELEN--
RHYSMYTH
Level 13: Technically Speaking

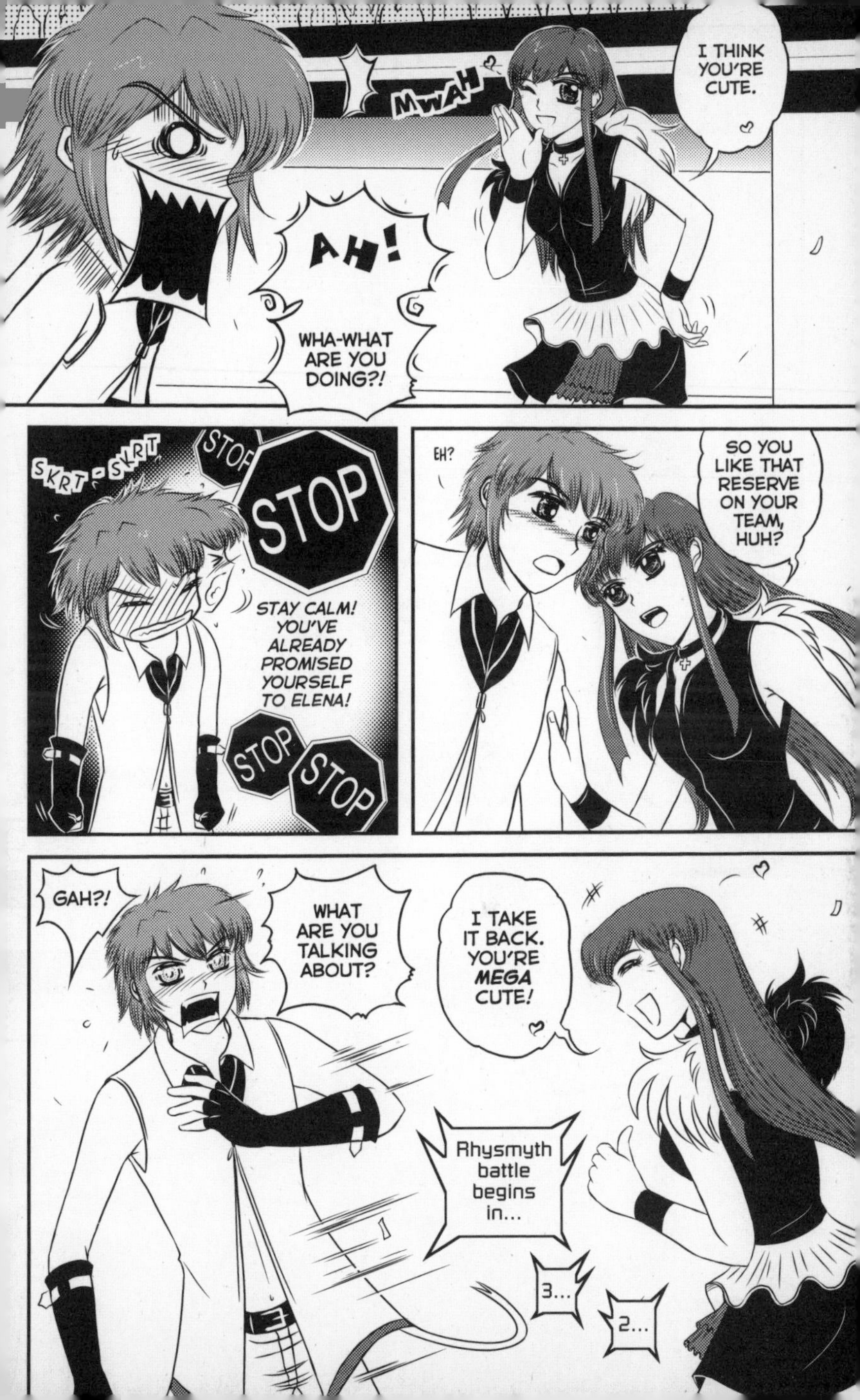
MWAH
I THINK YOU'RE CUTE.
AH!
WHA-WHAT ARE YOU DOING?!
SKRT-SKRT
STOP
STOP
STAY CALM! YOU'VE ALREADY PROMISED YOURSELF TO ELENA!
STOP
STOP
EH?
SO YOU LIKE THAT RESERVE ON YOUR TEAM, HUH?
GAH?!
WHAT ARE YOU TALKING ABOUT?
I TAKE IT BACK. YOU'RE *MEGA* CUTE!
Rhysmyth battle begins in...
3...
2...

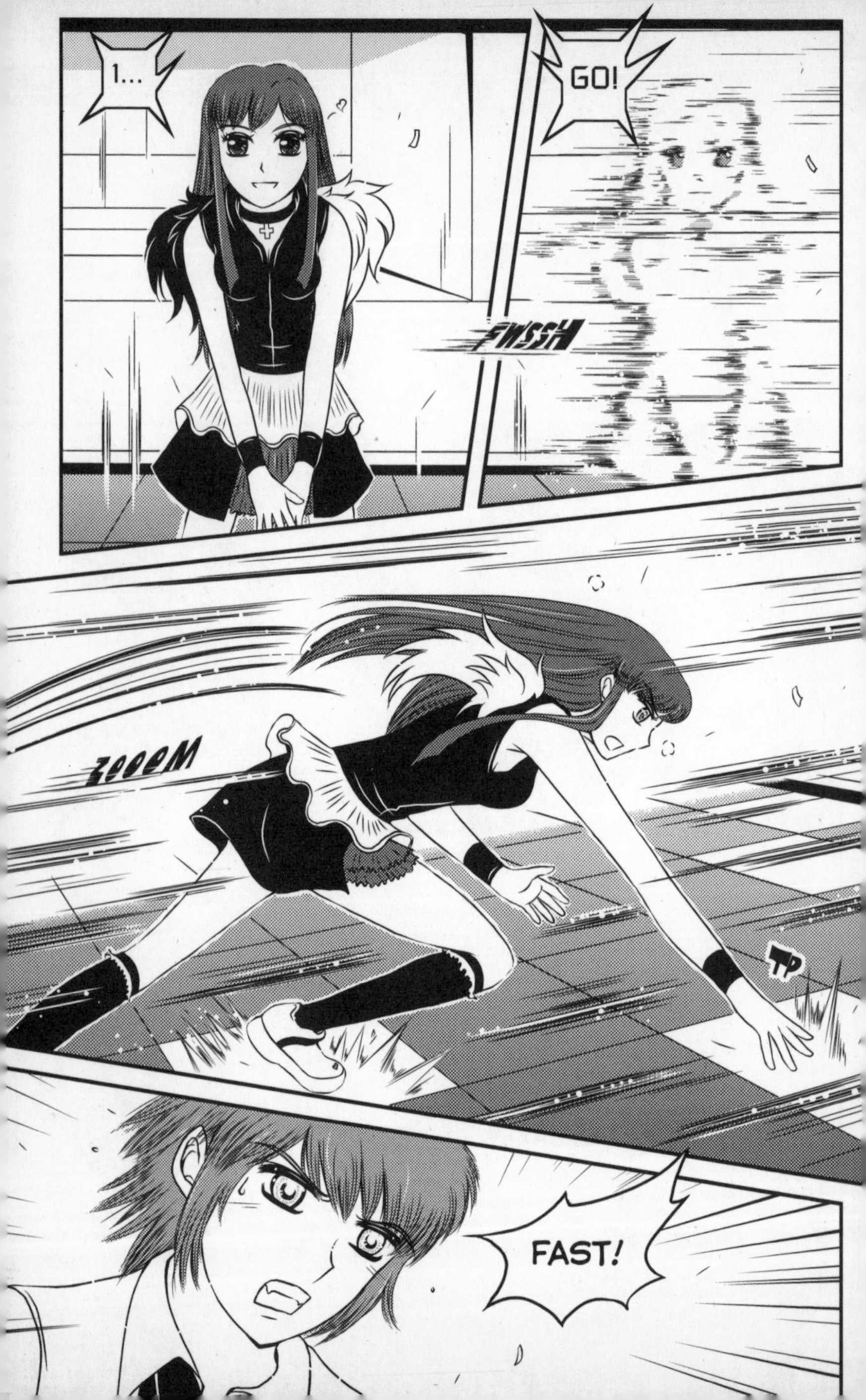
1...
GO!
FWSSH
ZOOOM
TP
FAST!

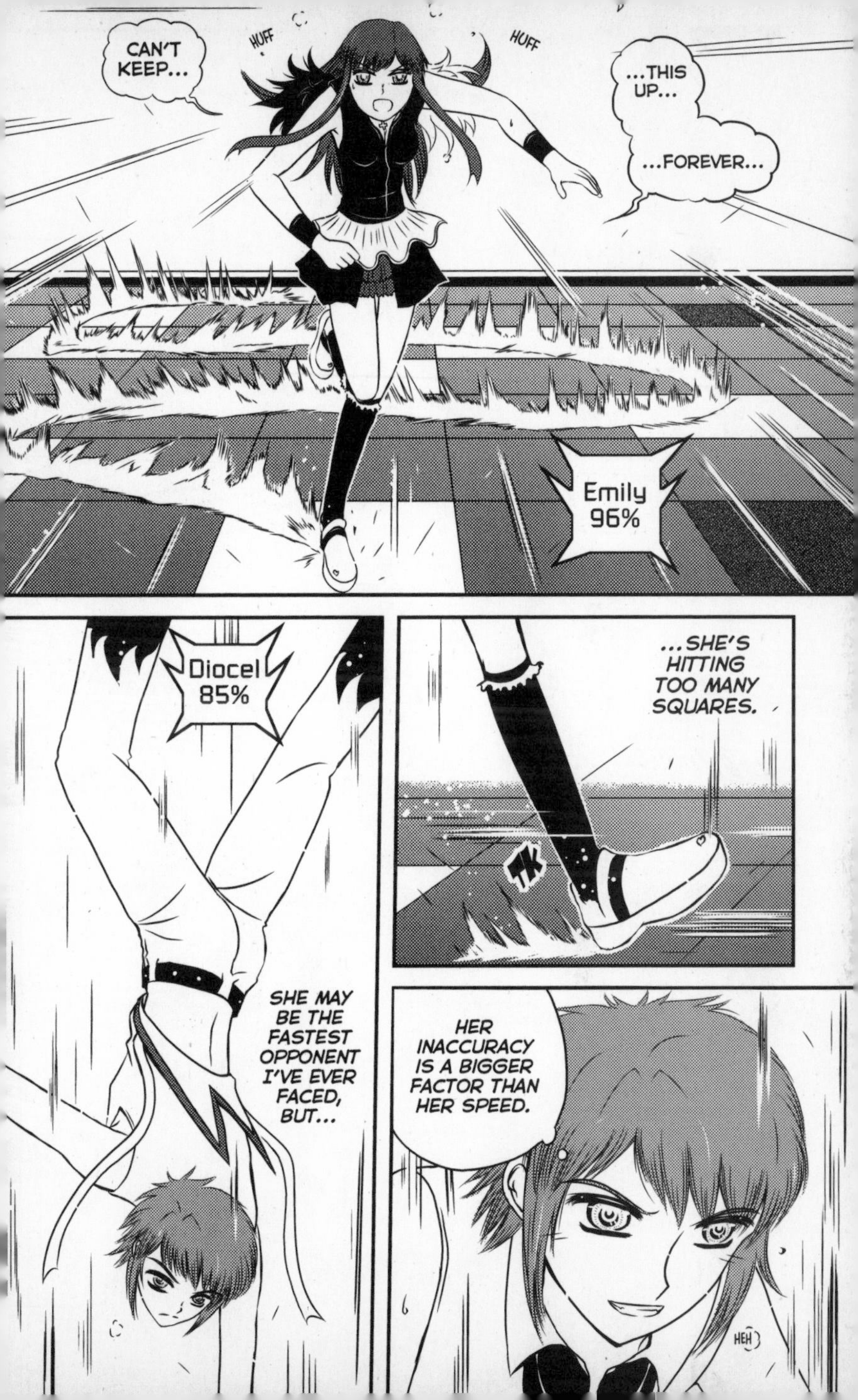
CAN'T KEEP...
HUFF
HUFF
...THIS UP...
...FOREVER...
Emily 96%
Diocel 85%
...SHE'S HITTING TOO MANY SQUARES.
TK
SHE MAY BE THE FASTEST OPPONENT I'VE EVER FACED, BUT...
HER INACCURACY IS A BIGGER FACTOR THAN HER SPEED.
HEH

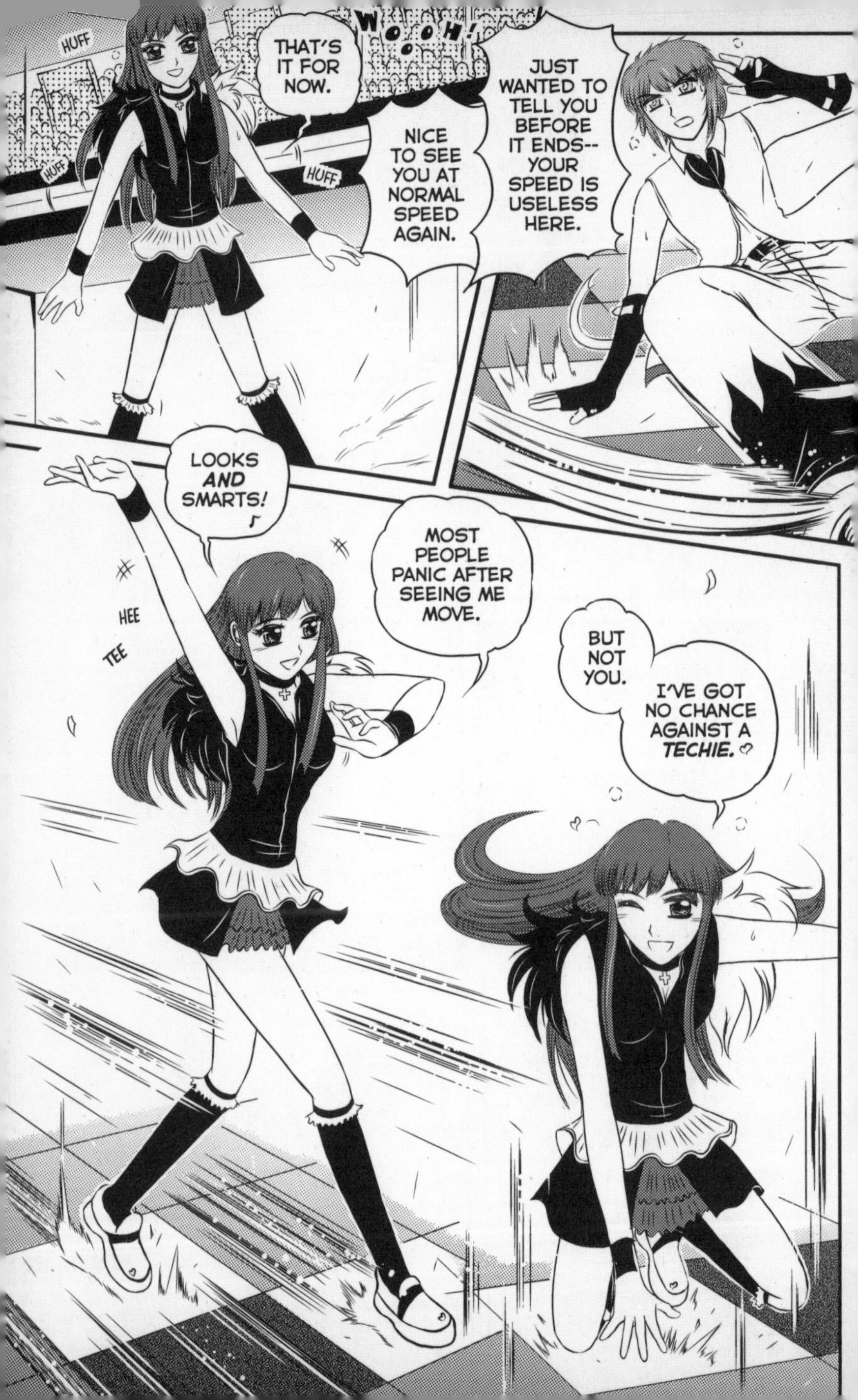
HUFF
THAT'S IT FOR NOW.
WOOOH!
HUFF
HUFF
NICE TO SEE YOU AT NORMAL SPEED AGAIN.
JUST WANTED TO TELL YOU BEFORE IT ENDS-- YOUR SPEED IS USELESS HERE.
LOOKS AND SMARTS!
MOST PEOPLE PANIC AFTER SEEING ME MOVE.
HEE
TEE
BUT NOT YOU.
I'VE GOT NO CHANCE AGAINST A TECHIE.

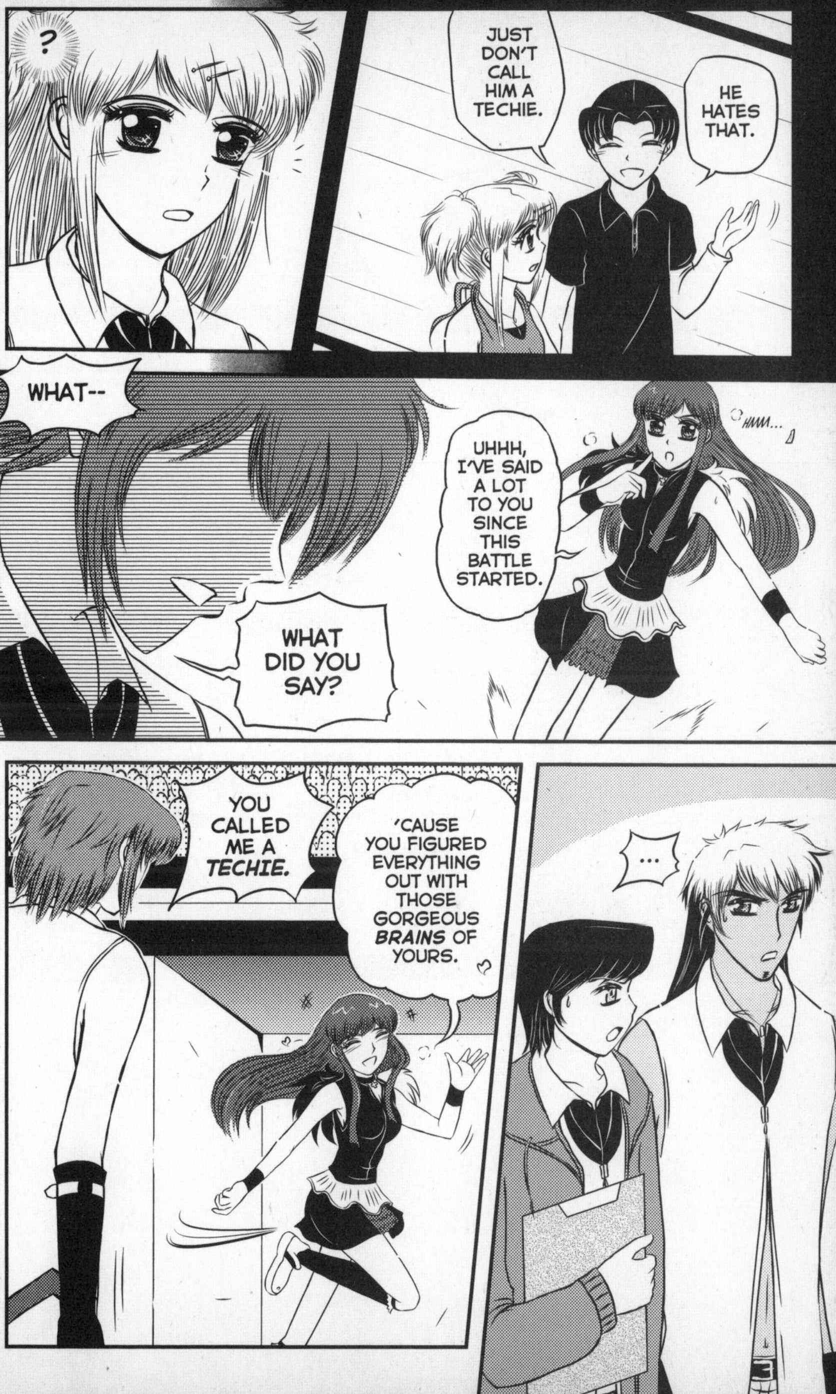
?
JUST DON'T CALL HIM A TECHIE.
HE HATES THAT.
WHAT--
HMM...
UHHH, I'VE SAID A LOT TO YOU SINCE THIS BATTLE STARTED.
WHAT DID YOU SAY?
YOU CALLED ME A *TECHIE.*
'CAUSE YOU FIGURED EVERYTHING OUT WITH THOSE GORGEOUS *BRAINS* OF YOURS.
...

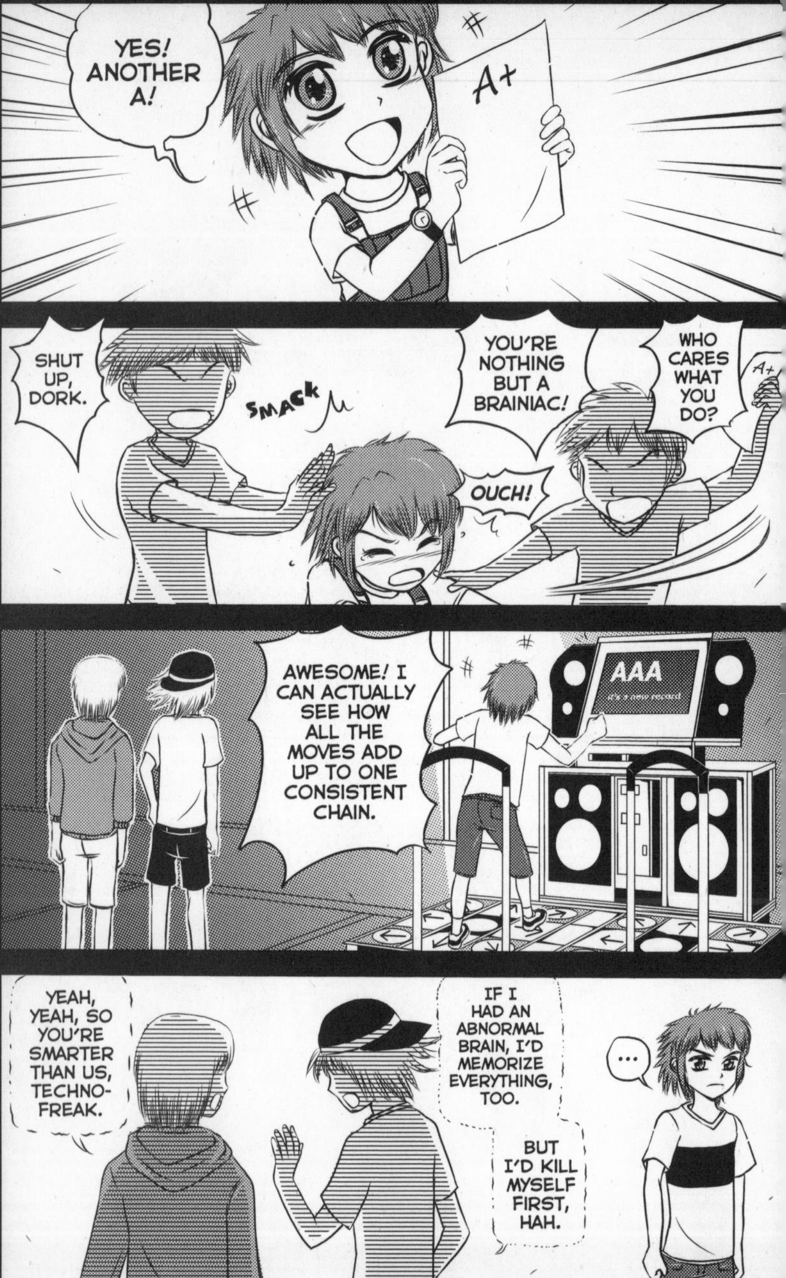
YES! ANOTHER A!
A+
SHUT UP, DORK.
SMACK
YOU'RE NOTHING BUT A BRAINIAC!
WHO CARES WHAT YOU DO?
A+
OUCH!
AWESOME! I CAN ACTUALLY SEE HOW ALL THE MOVES ADD UP TO ONE CONSISTENT CHAIN.
AAA
it's a new record
YEAH, YEAH, SO YOU'RE SMARTER THAN US, TECHNO-FREAK.
IF I HAD AN ABNORMAL BRAIN, I'D MEMORIZE EVERYTHING, TOO.
BUT I'D KILL MYSELF FIRST, HAH.
...

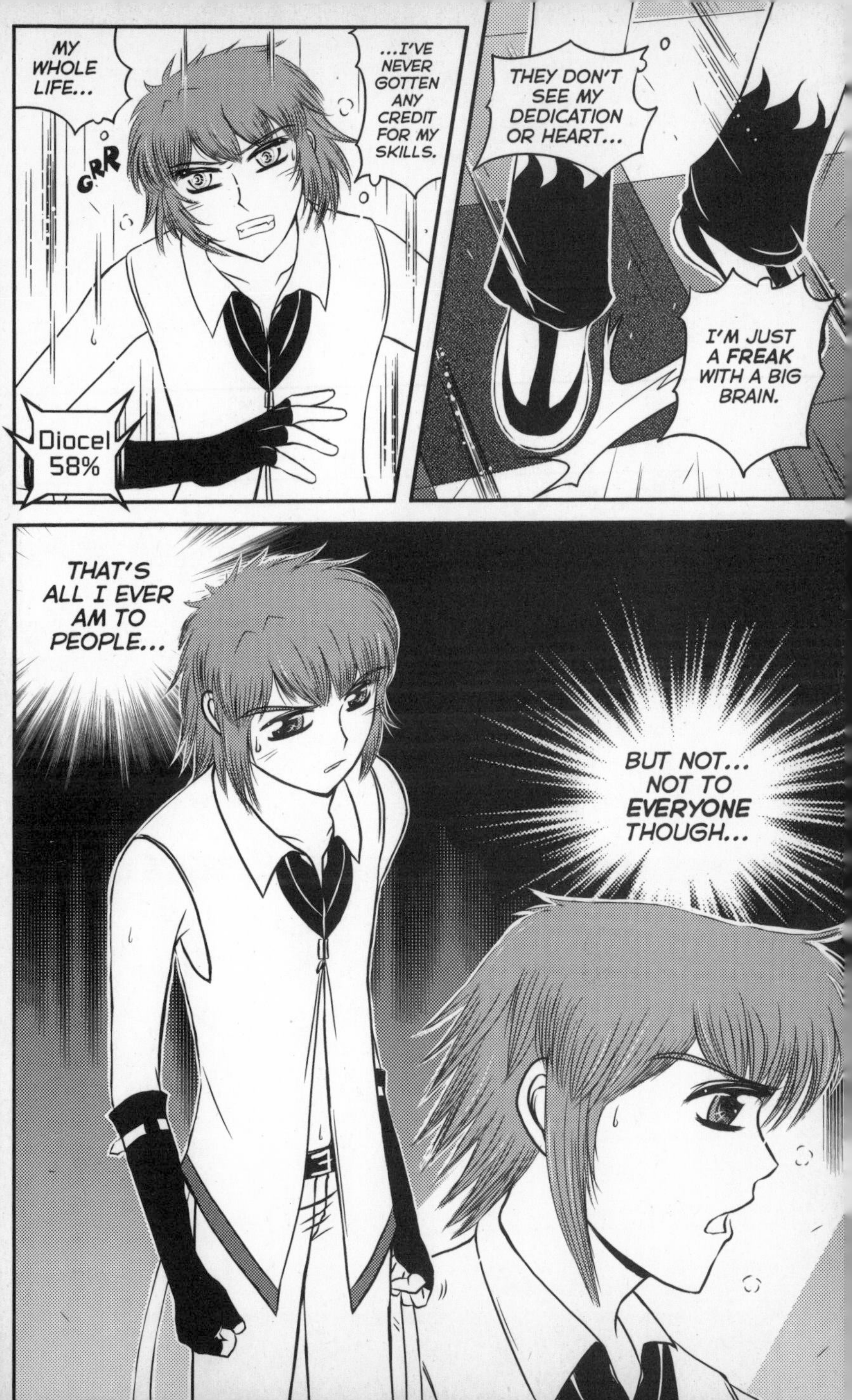
MY WHOLE LIFE...
GRR
...I'VE NEVER GOTTEN ANY CREDIT FOR MY SKILLS.
Diocel 58%
THEY DON'T SEE MY DEDICATION OR HEART...
I'M JUST A FREAK WITH A BIG BRAIN.
THAT'S ALL I EVER AM TO PEOPLE...
BUT NOT... NOT TO EVERYONE THOUGH...

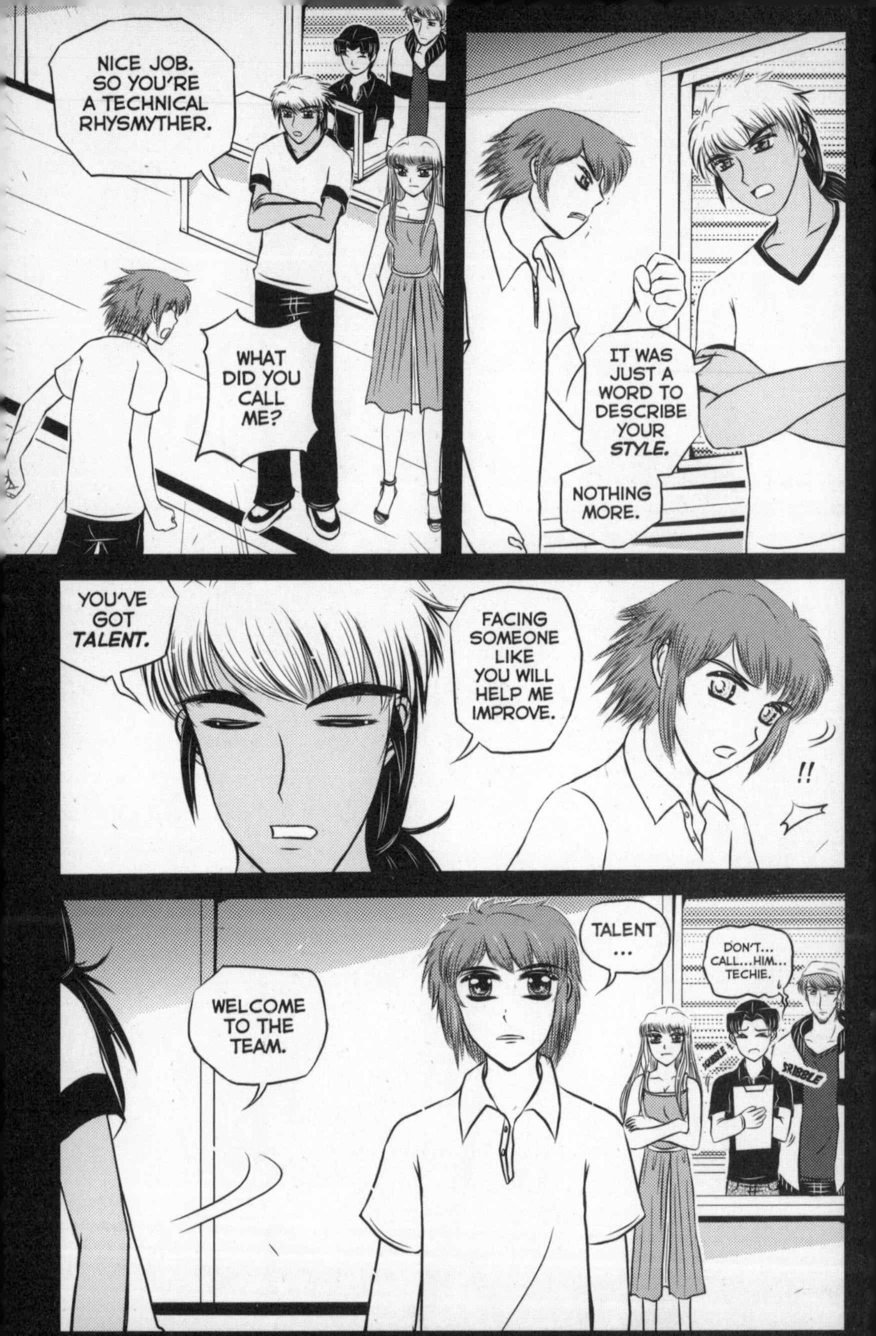
NICE JOB. SO YOU'RE A TECHNICAL RHYSMYTHER.
WHAT DID YOU CALL ME?
IT WAS JUST A WORD TO DESCRIBE YOUR STYLE.
NOTHING MORE.
YOU'VE GOT TALENT.
FACING SOMEONE LIKE YOU WILL HELP ME IMPROVE.
!!
WELCOME TO THE TEAM.
TALENT ...
DON'T... CALL...HIM... TECHIE.
SRIBBLE
SRIBBLE

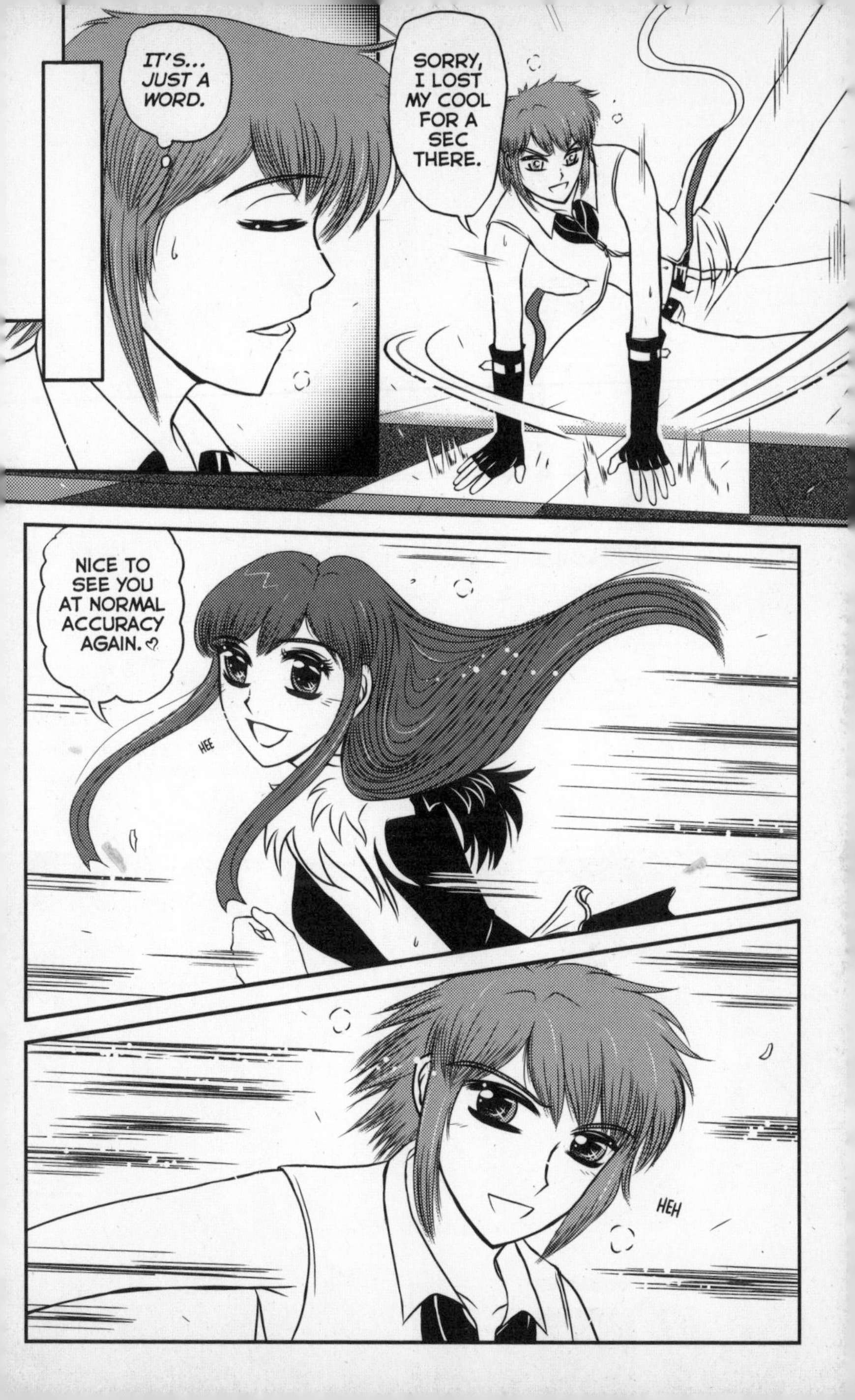

IT'S... JUST A WORD.
SORRY, I LOST MY COOL FOR A SEC THERE.
NICE TO SEE YOU AT NORMAL ACCURACY AGAIN. ♡
HEE
HEH

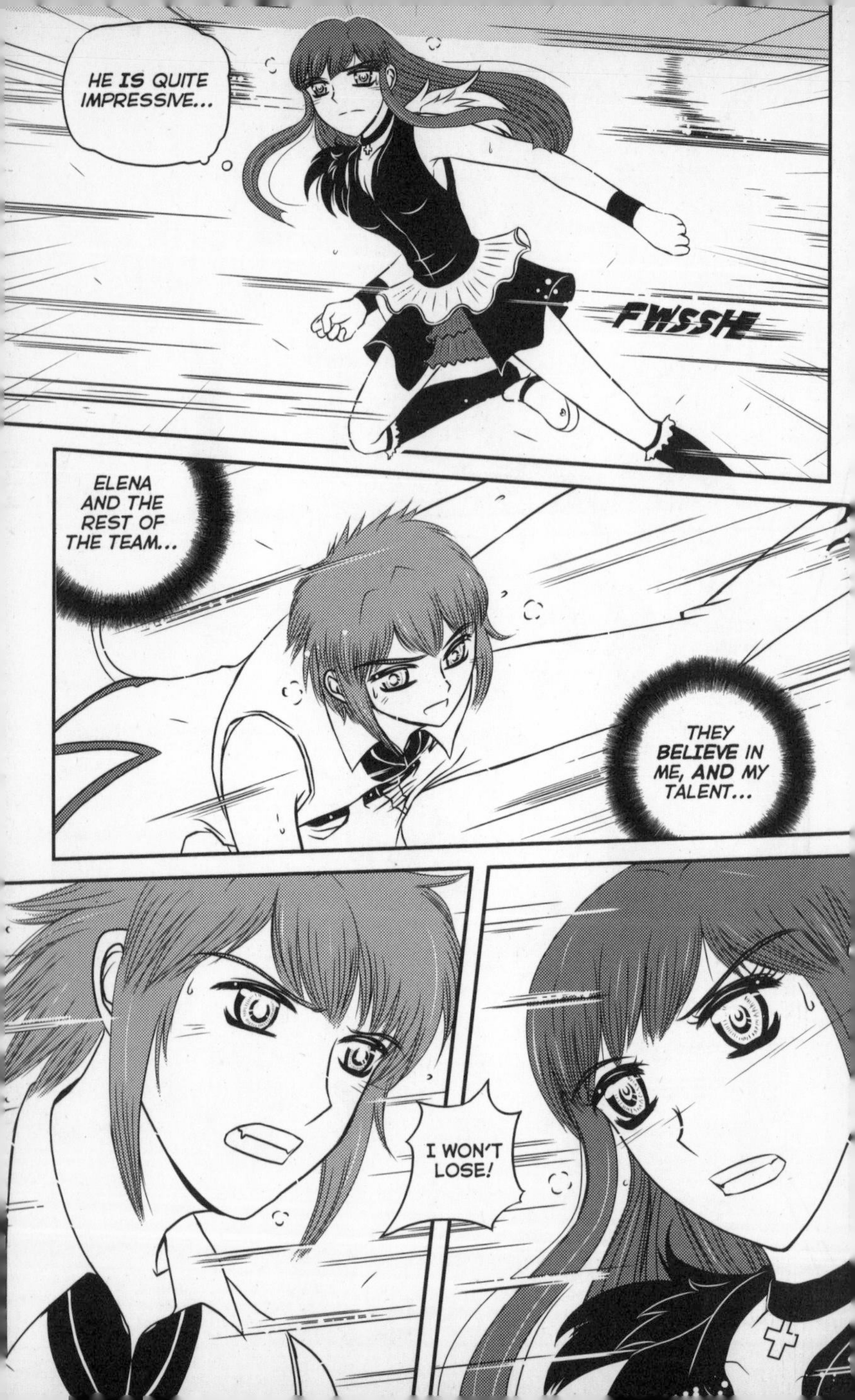
HE IS QUITE IMPRESSIVE...
FWSSH
ELENA AND THE REST OF THE TEAM...
THEY BELIEVE IN ME, AND MY TALENT...
I WON'T LOSE!

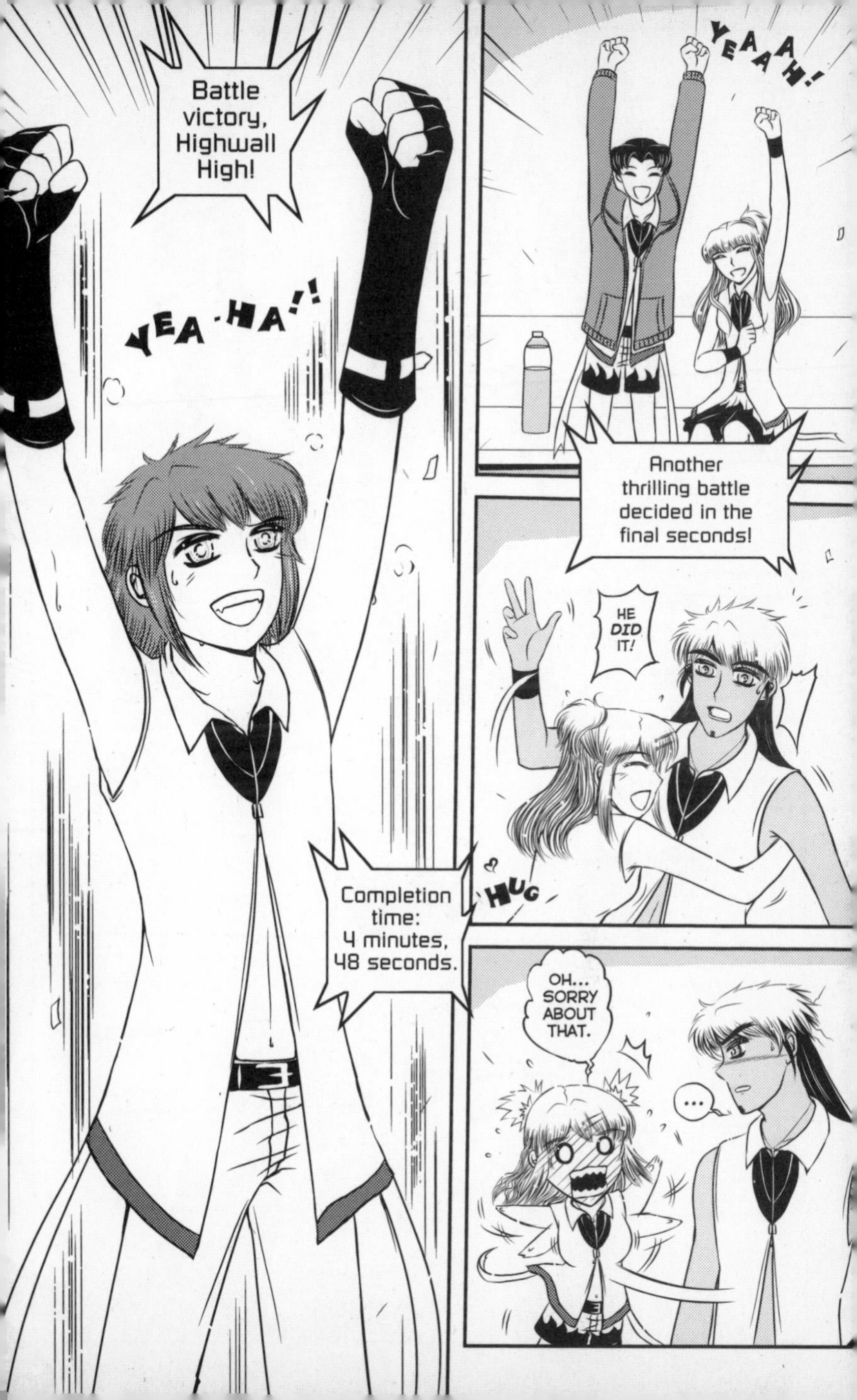
Battle victory, Highwall High!
YEA-HA!!
Completion time: 4 minutes, 48 seconds.
YEAAAH!
Another thrilling battle decided in the final seconds!
HE *DID* IT!
HUG
OH... SORRY ABOUT THAT.
...

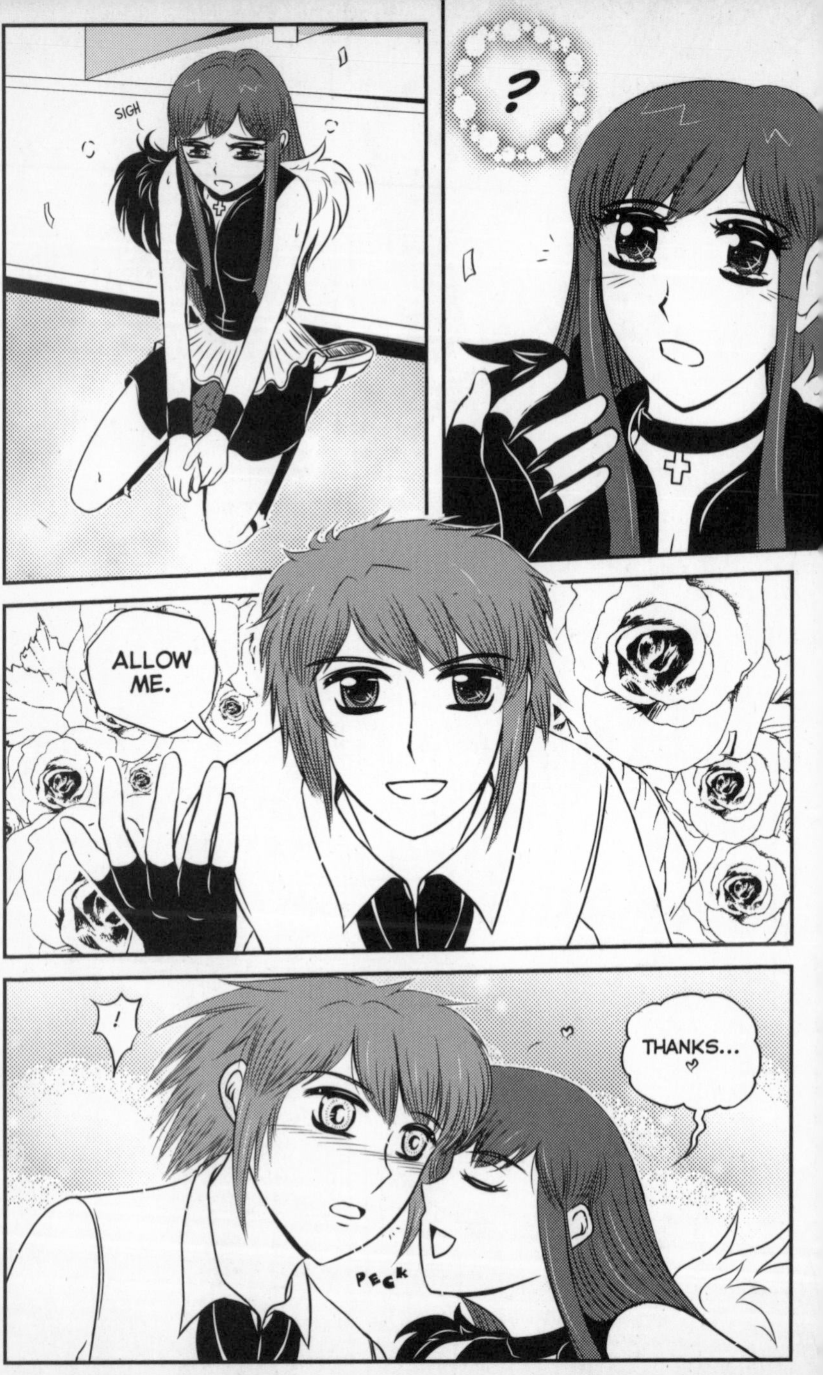
SIGH
?
ALLOW ME.
!
THANKS...
PECK

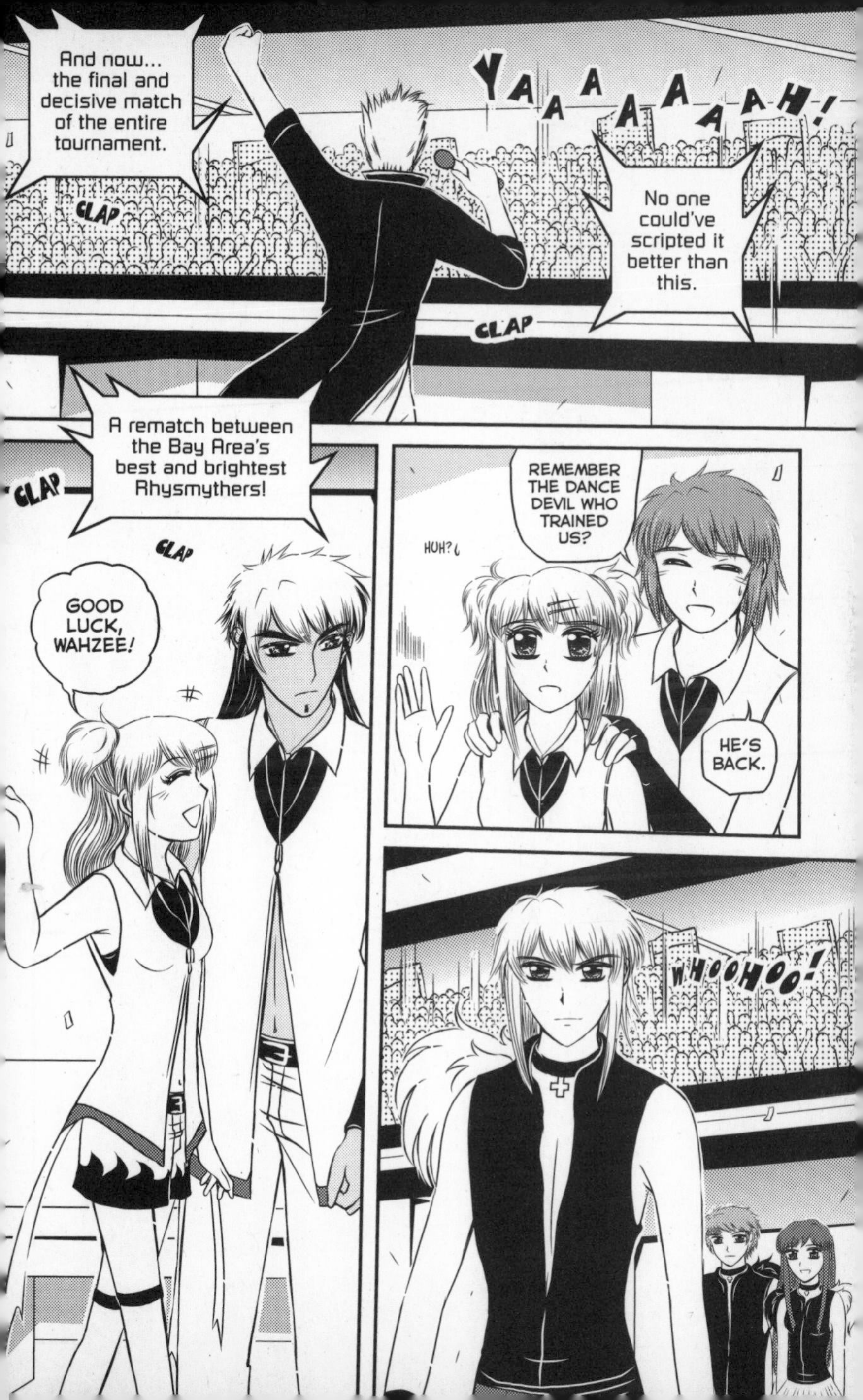
And now... the final and decisive match of the entire tournament.
YAAAAAAAH!
CLAP
No one could've scripted it better than this.
CLAP
A rematch between the Bay Area's best and brightest Rhysmythers!
CLAP
CLAP
GOOD LUCK, WAHZEE!
HUH?
REMEMBER THE DANCE DEVIL WHO TRAINED US?
HE'S BACK.
WHOOHOO!

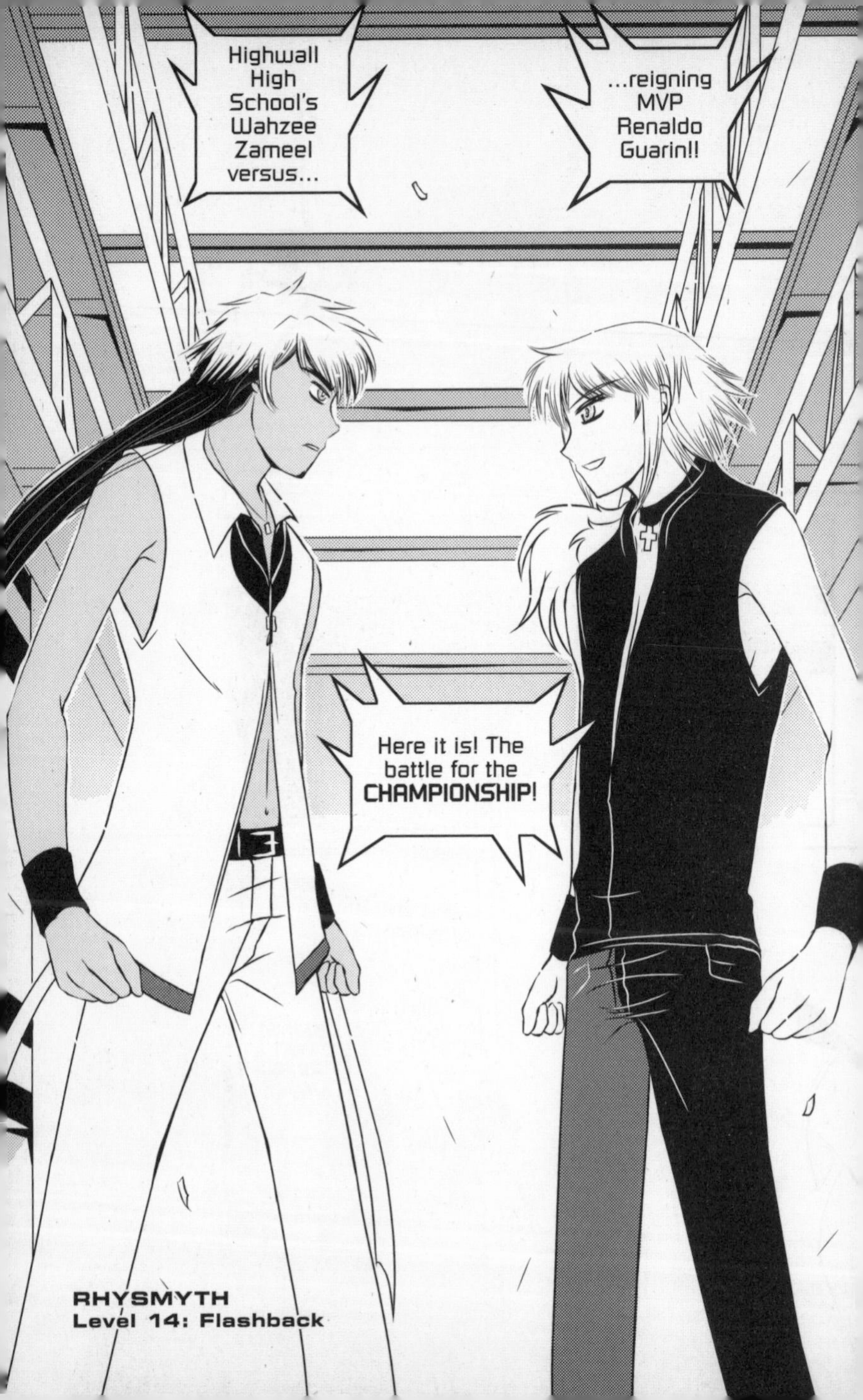
Highwall High School's Wahzee Zameel versus...
...reigning MVP Renaldo Guarin!!
Here it is! The battle for the CHAMPIONSHIP!

RHYSMYTH
Level 14: Flashback

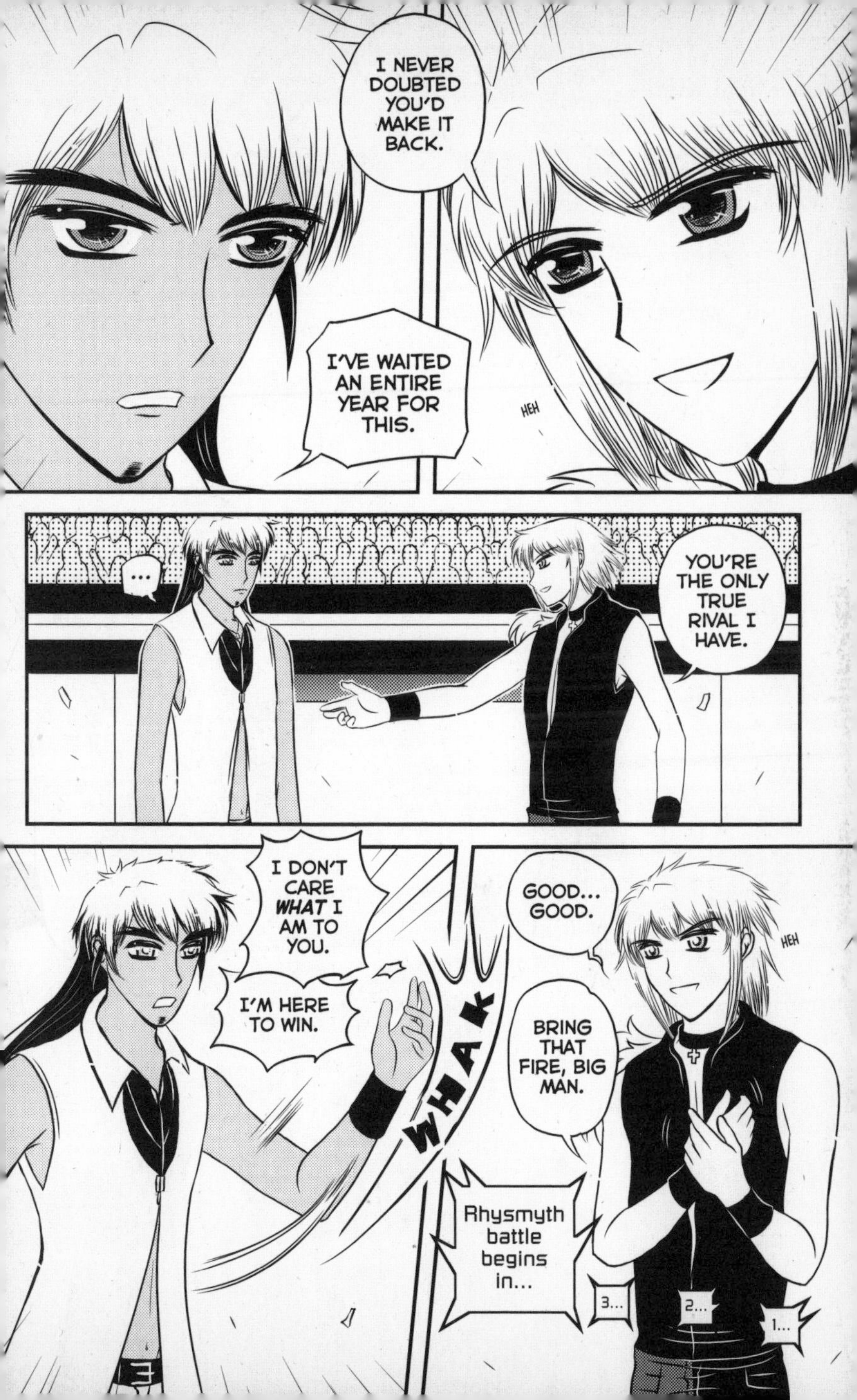
I NEVER DOUBTED YOU'D MAKE IT BACK.
I'VE WAITED AN ENTIRE YEAR FOR THIS.
HEH
...
YOU'RE THE ONLY TRUE RIVAL I HAVE.
I DON'T CARE *WHAT* I AM TO YOU.
I'M HERE TO WIN.
WHAK
GOOD... GOOD.
HEH
BRING THAT FIRE, BIG MAN.
Rhysmyth battle begins in...
3...
2...
1...

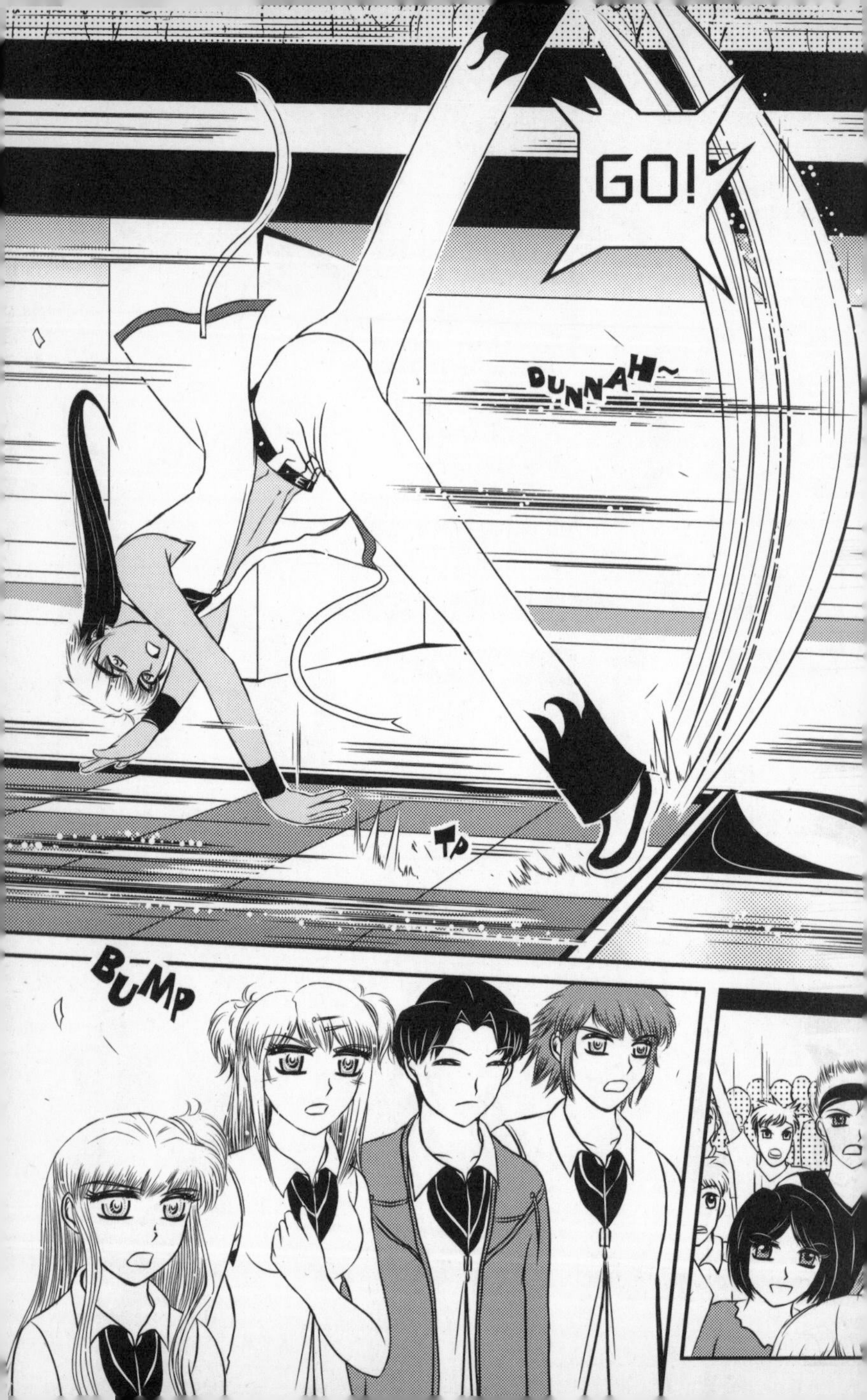
GO!
DUNNAH~
TP
BUMP

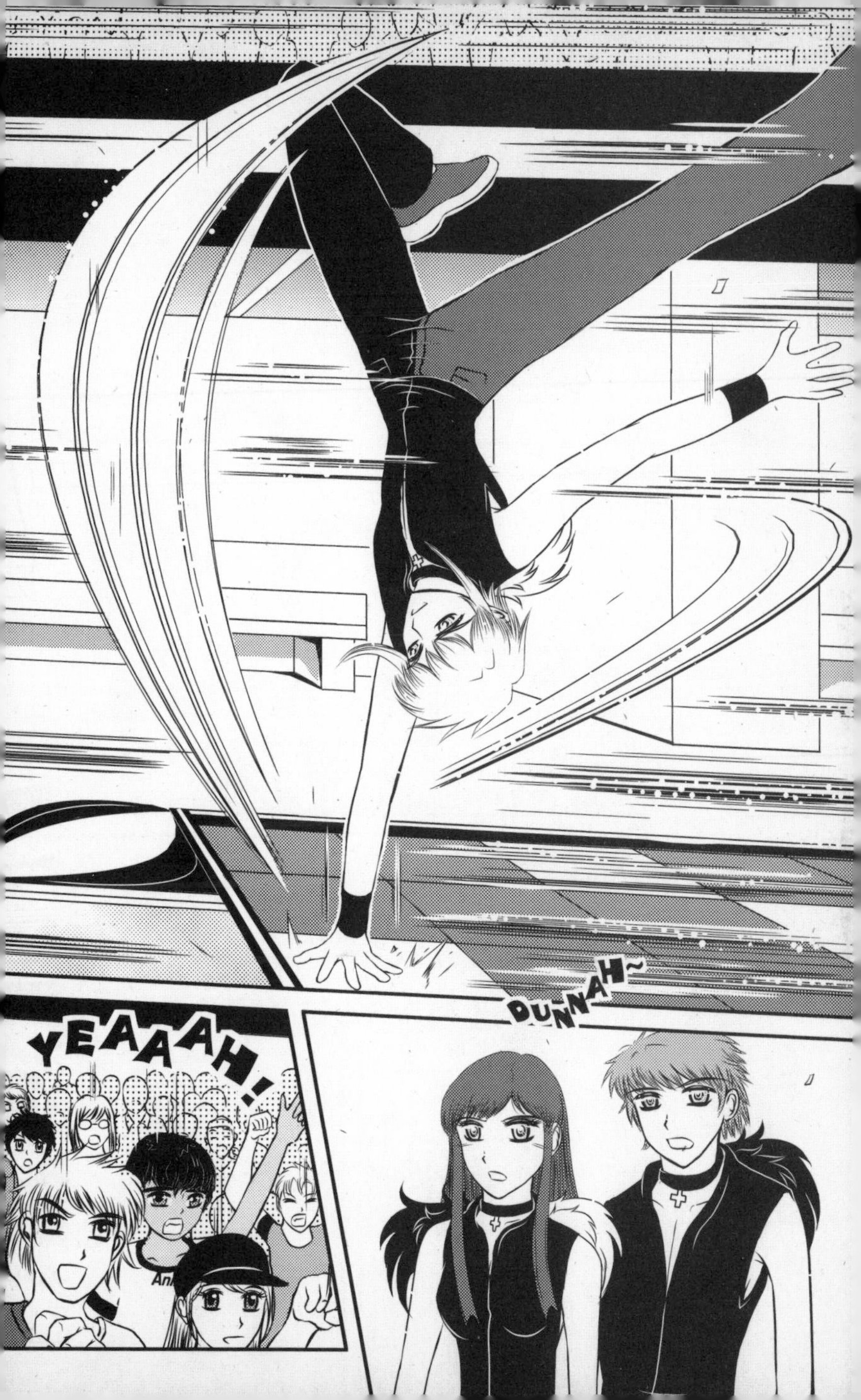
DUNNAH~
YEAAAH!

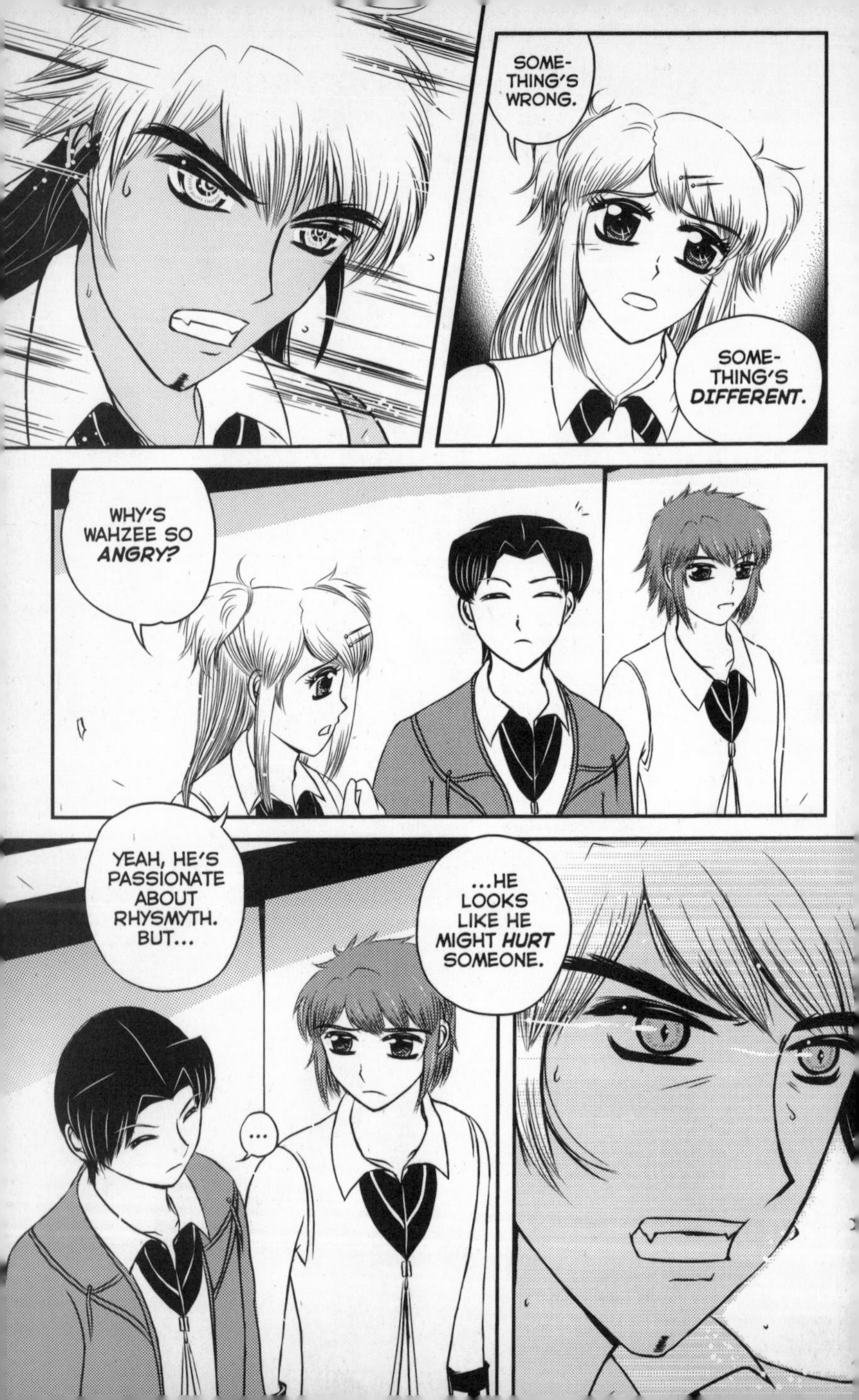
SOME-THING'S WRONG.
SOME-THING'S DIFFERENT.
WHY'S WAHZEE SO ANGRY?
YEAH, HE'S PASSIONATE ABOUT RHYSMYTH. BUT...
...HE LOOKS LIKE HE MIGHT HURT SOMEONE.
...

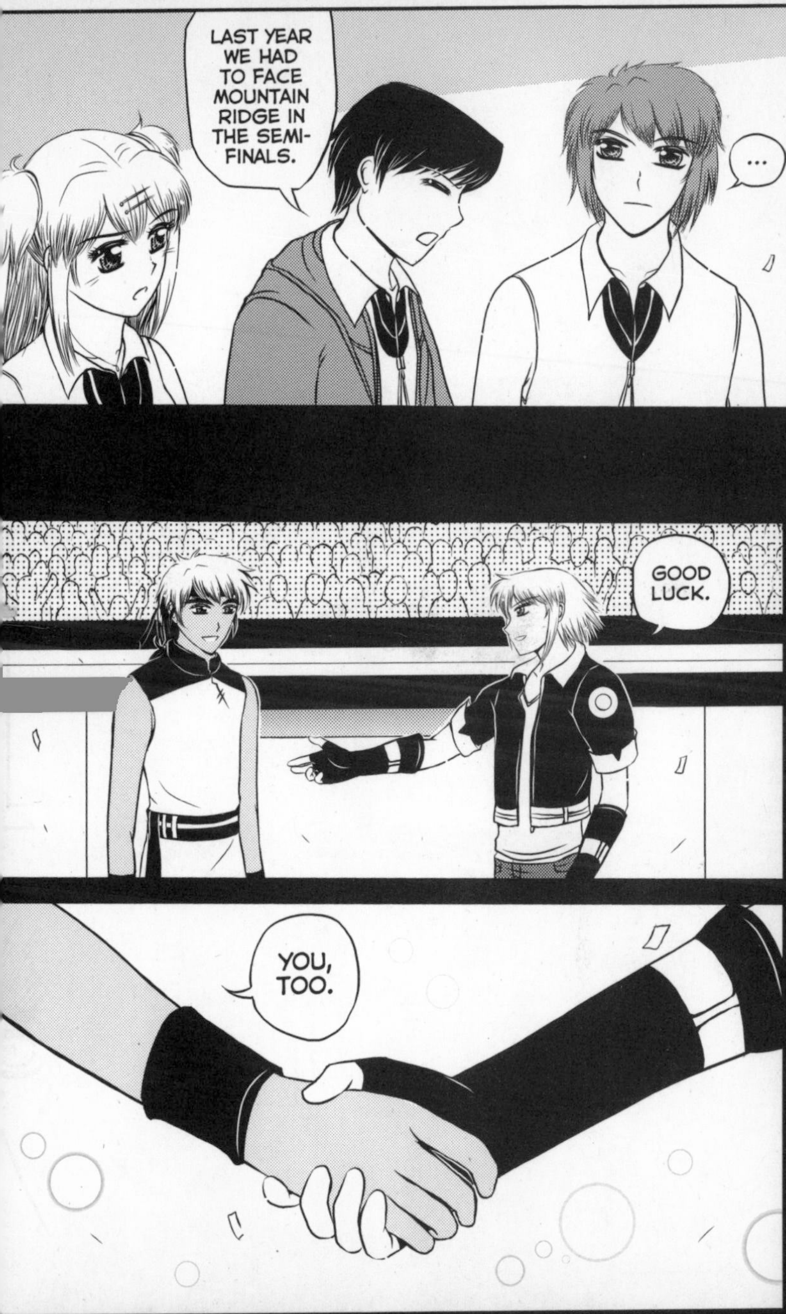
LAST YEAR WE HAD TO FACE MOUNTAIN RIDGE IN THE SEMI-FINALS.
...
GOOD LUCK.
YOU, TOO.

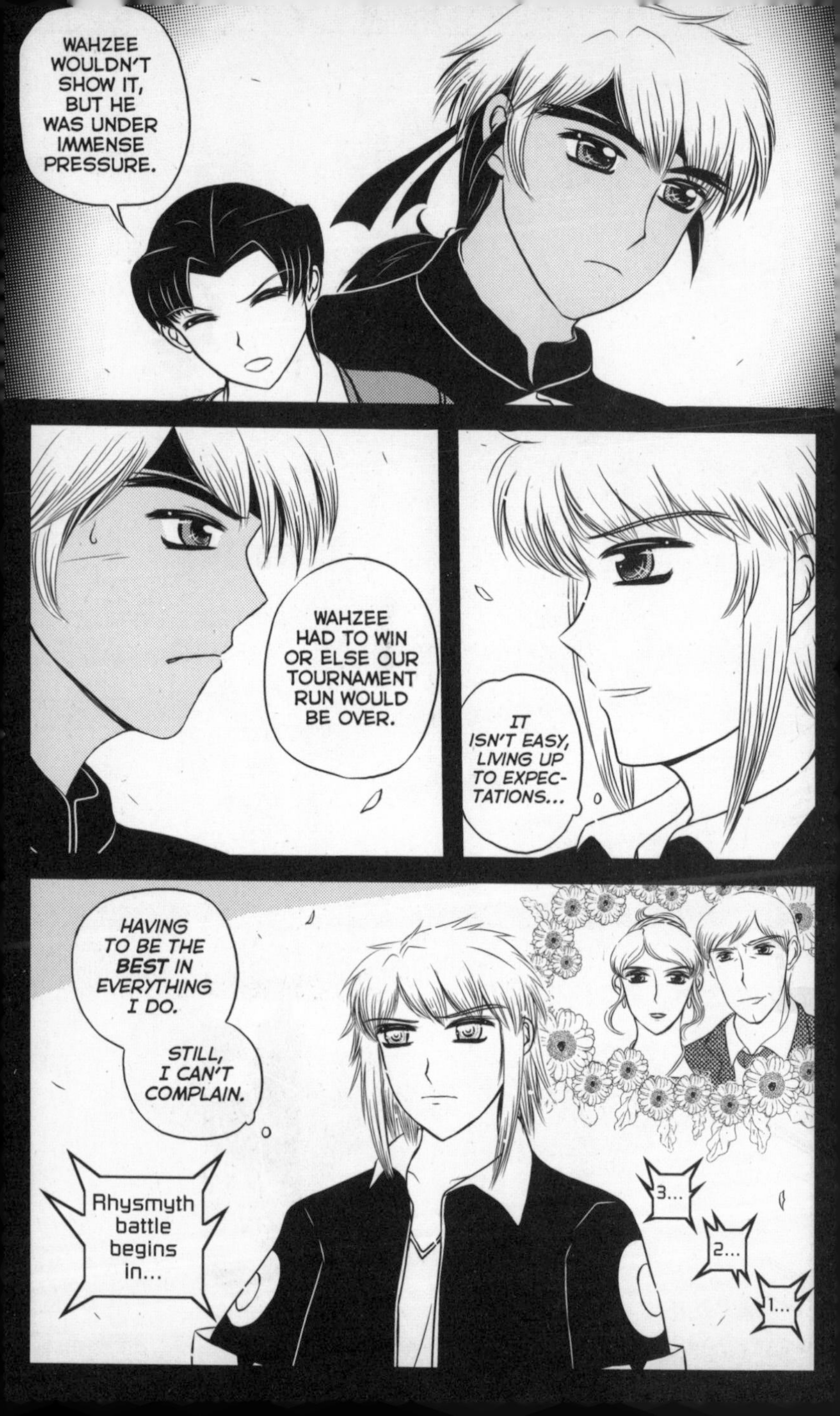
WAHZEE WOULDN'T SHOW IT, BUT HE WAS UNDER IMMENSE PRESSURE.
WAHZEE HAD TO WIN OR ELSE OUR TOURNAMENT RUN WOULD BE OVER.
IT ISN'T EASY, LIVING UP TO EXPEC-TATIONS...
HAVING TO BE THE BEST IN EVERYTHING I DO.
STILL, I CAN'T COMPLAIN.
Rhysmyth battle begins in...
3...
2...
1...

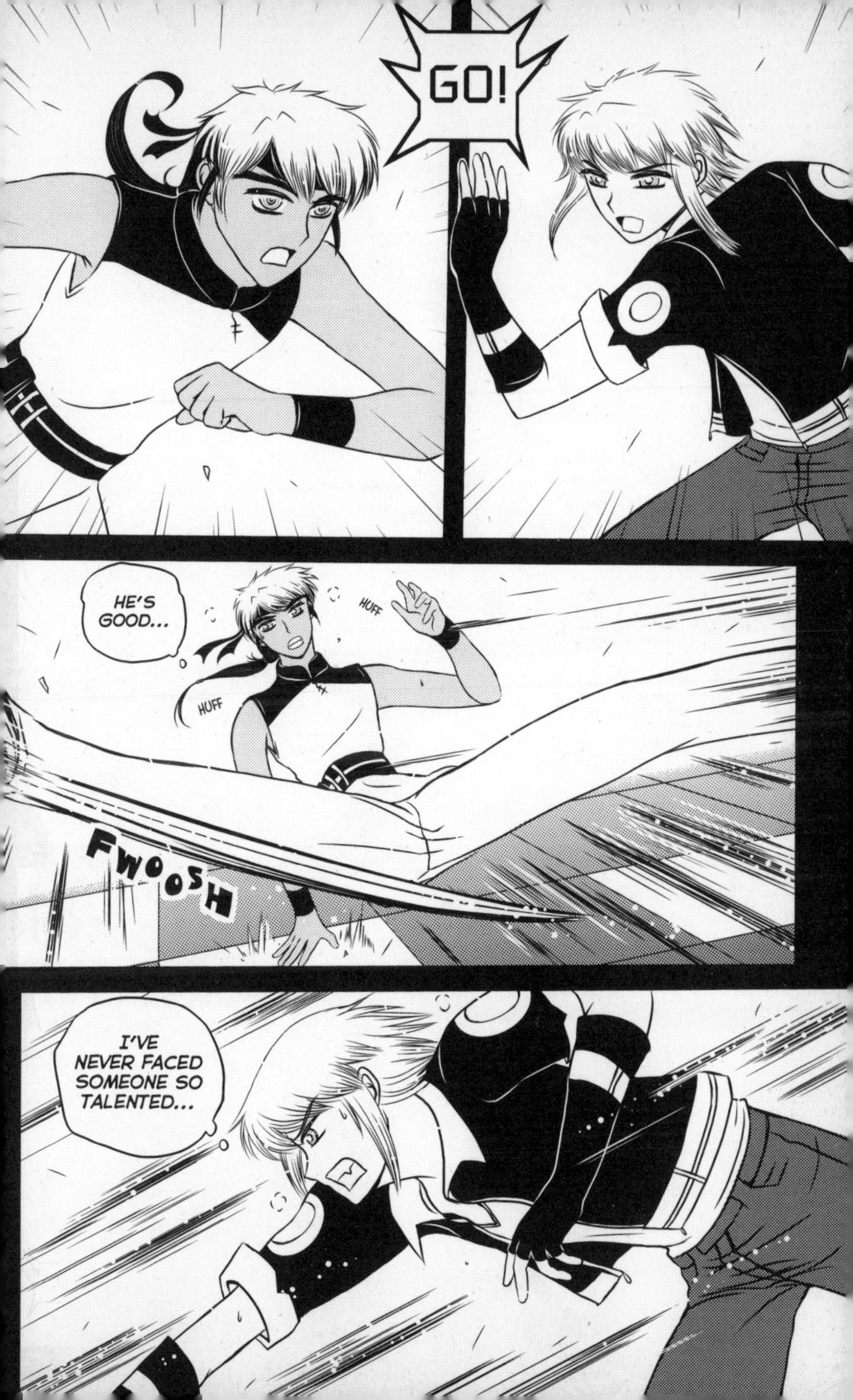
GO!
HE'S GOOD...
HUFF
HUFF
FWOOSH
I'VE NEVER FACED SOMEONE SO TALENTED...

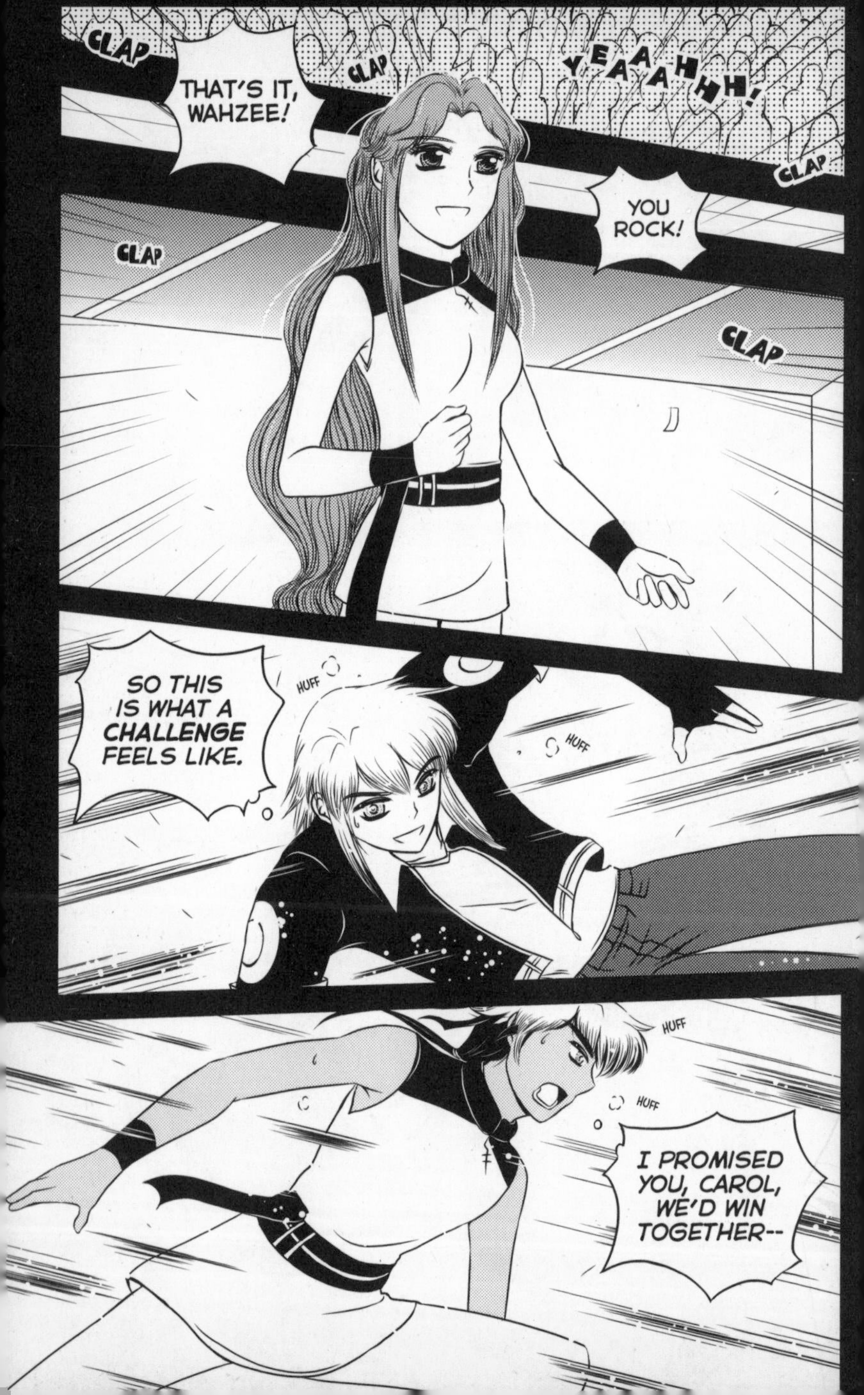
CLAP
THAT'S IT, WAHZEE!
CLAP
YEAAAHHH!
CLAP
YOU ROCK!
CLAP
CLAP
SO THIS IS WHAT A CHALLENGE FEELS LIKE.
HUFF
HUFF
HUFF
HUFF
I PROMISED YOU, CAROL, WE'D WIN TOGETHER--

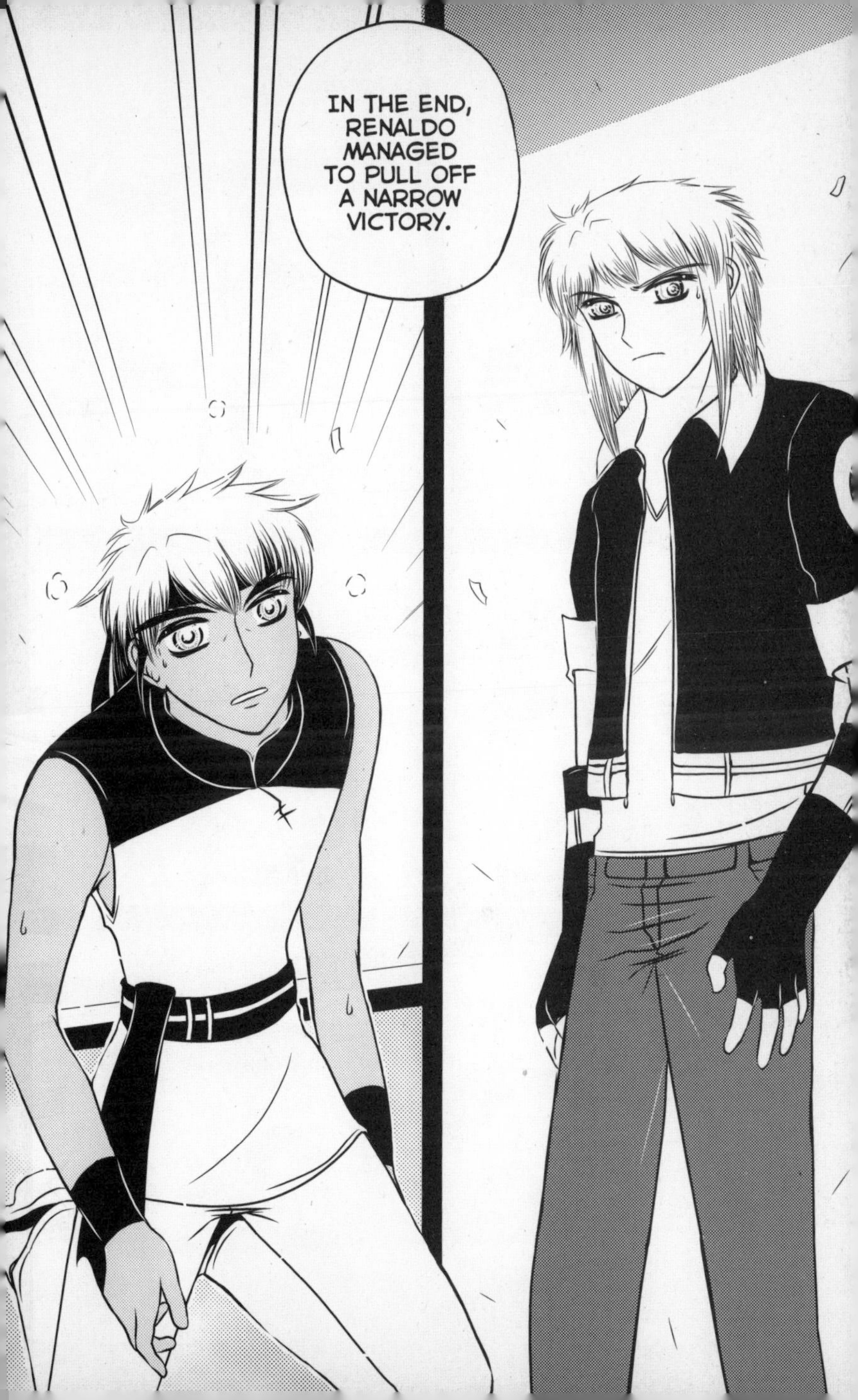
IN THE END, RENALDO MANAGED TO PULL OFF A NARROW VICTORY.

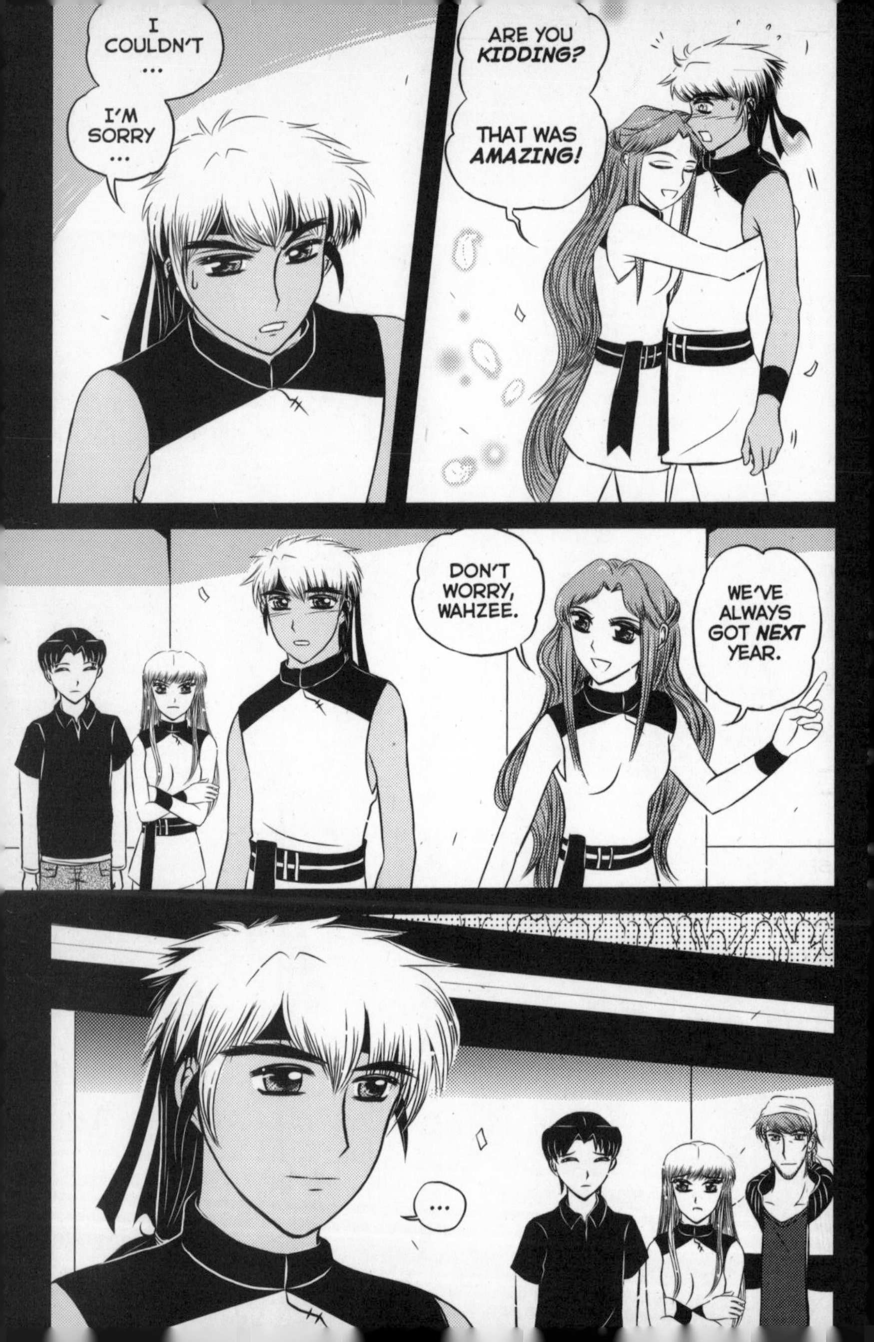
I COULDN'T ...
I'M SORRY ...
ARE YOU *KIDDING?*
THAT WAS *AMAZING!*
DON'T WORRY, WAHZEE.
WE'VE ALWAYS GOT *NEXT* YEAR.
...

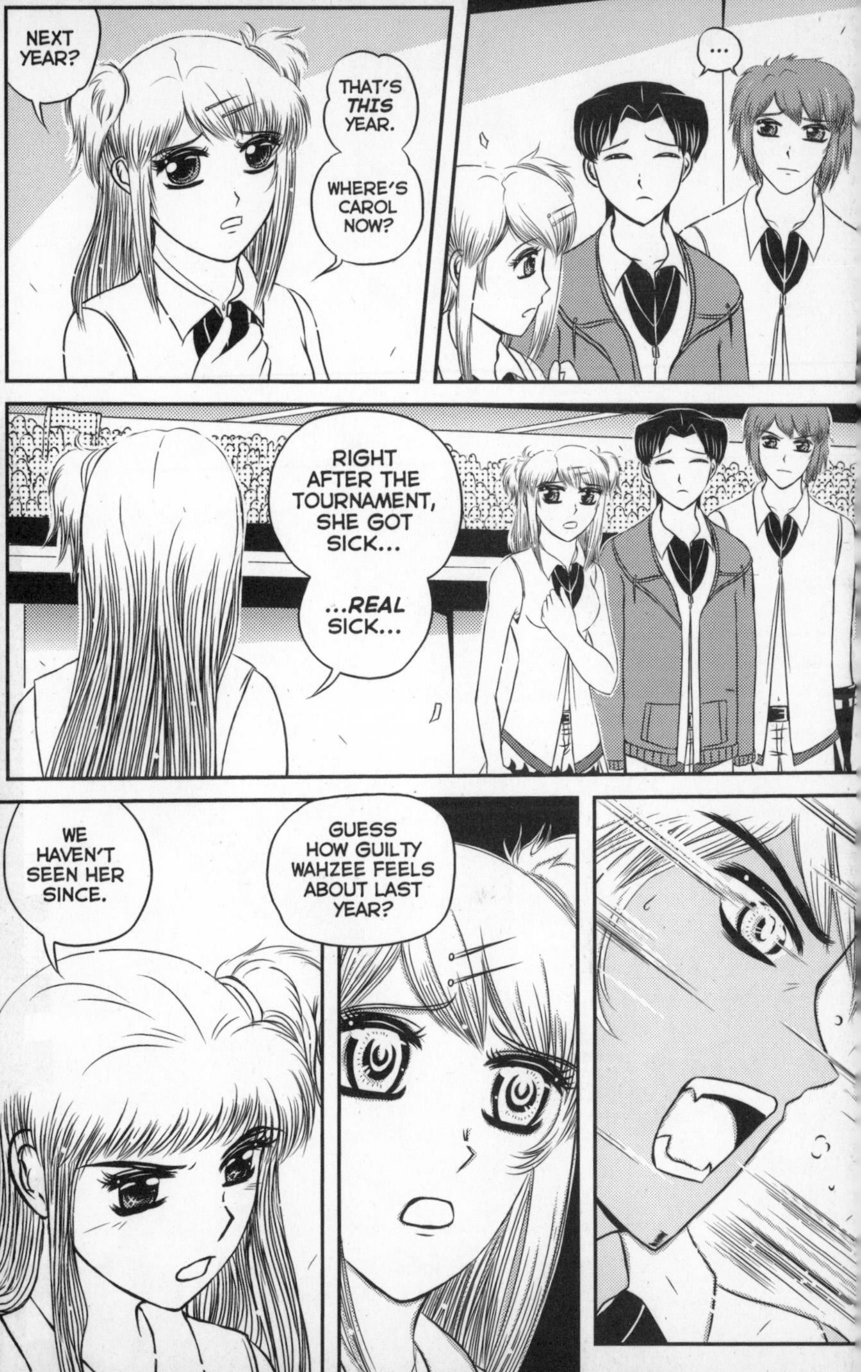
NEXT YEAR?
THAT'S *THIS* YEAR.
WHERE'S CAROL NOW?
...
RIGHT AFTER THE TOURNAMENT, SHE GOT SICK...
...*REAL* SICK...
WE HAVEN'T SEEN HER SINCE.
GUESS HOW GUILTY WAHZEE FEELS ABOUT LAST YEAR?

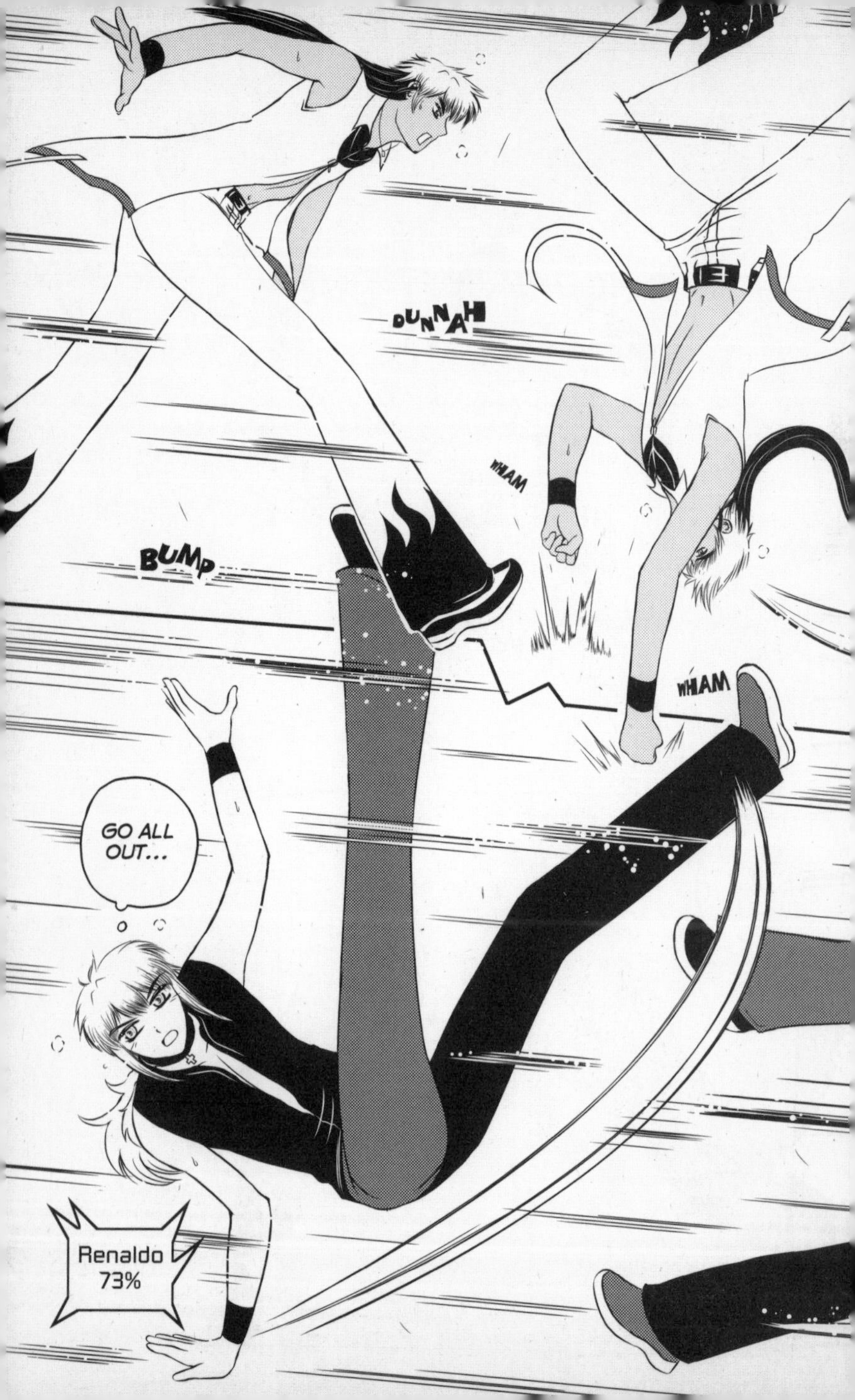
DUNNAH
WHAM
BUMP
WHAM
GO ALL OUT...
Renaldo 73%

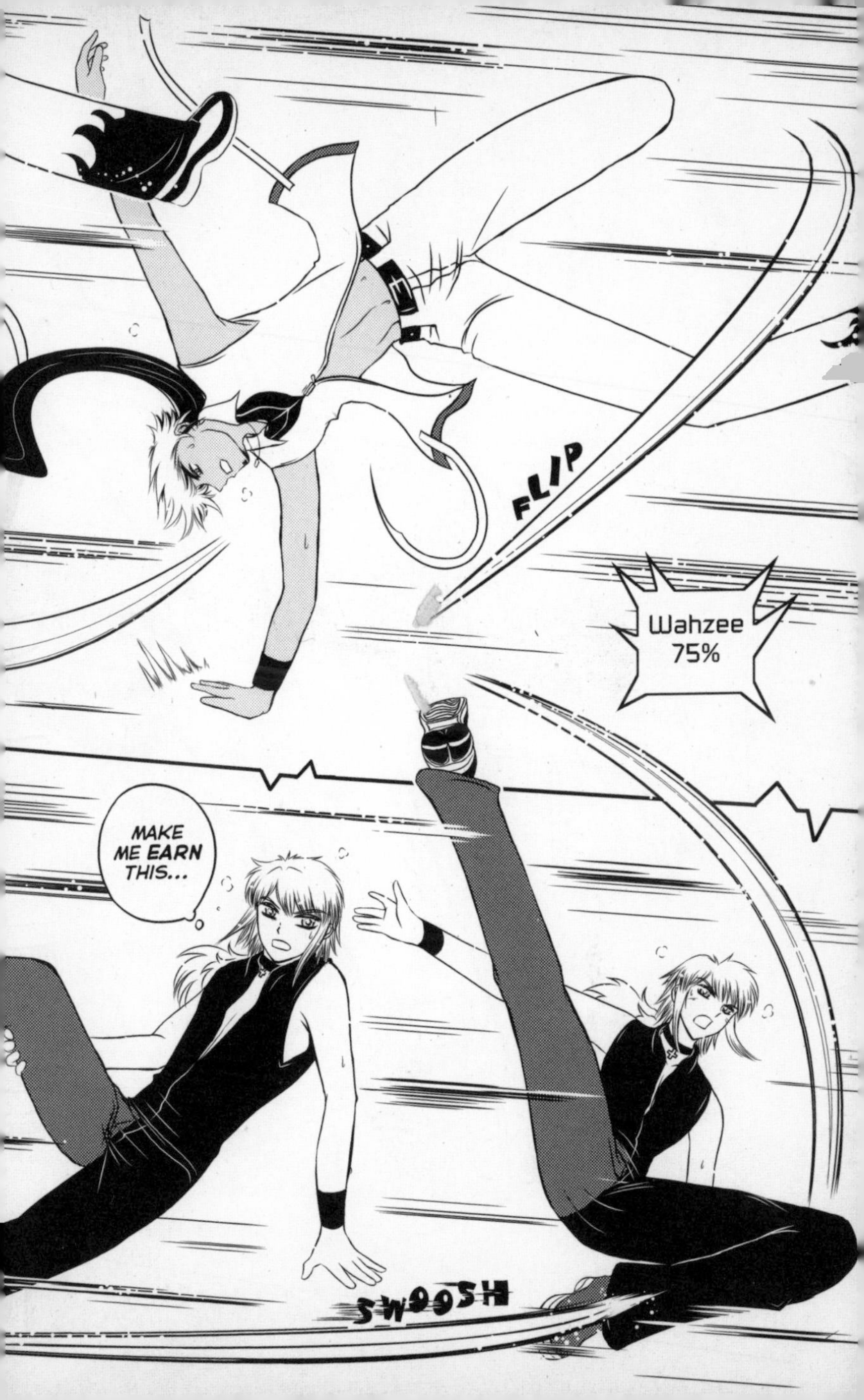
FLIP
Wahzee
75%
MAKE ME EARN THIS...
SWOOSH

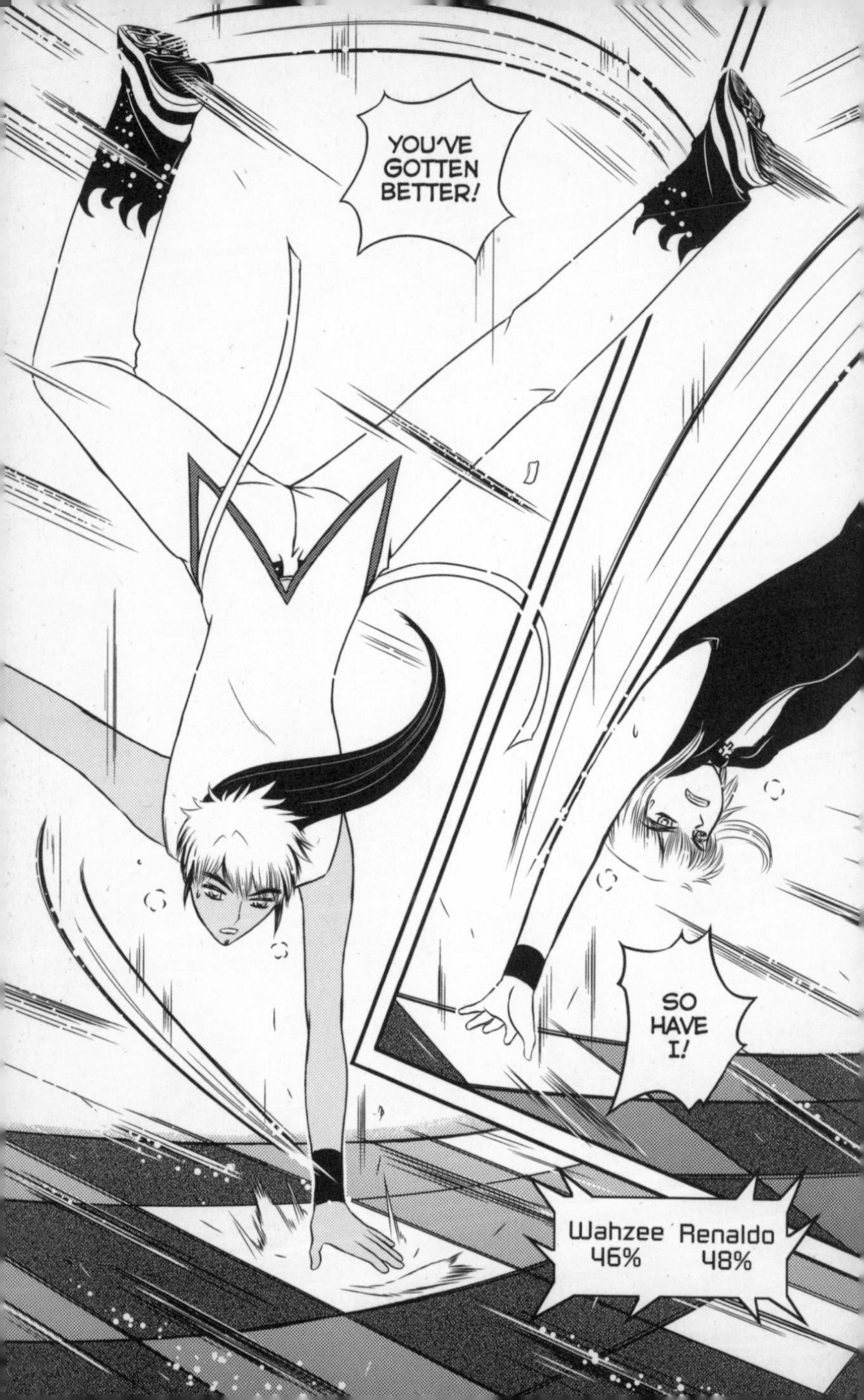
YOU'VE GOTTEN BETTER!
SO HAVE I!
Wahzee 46%
Renaldo 48%

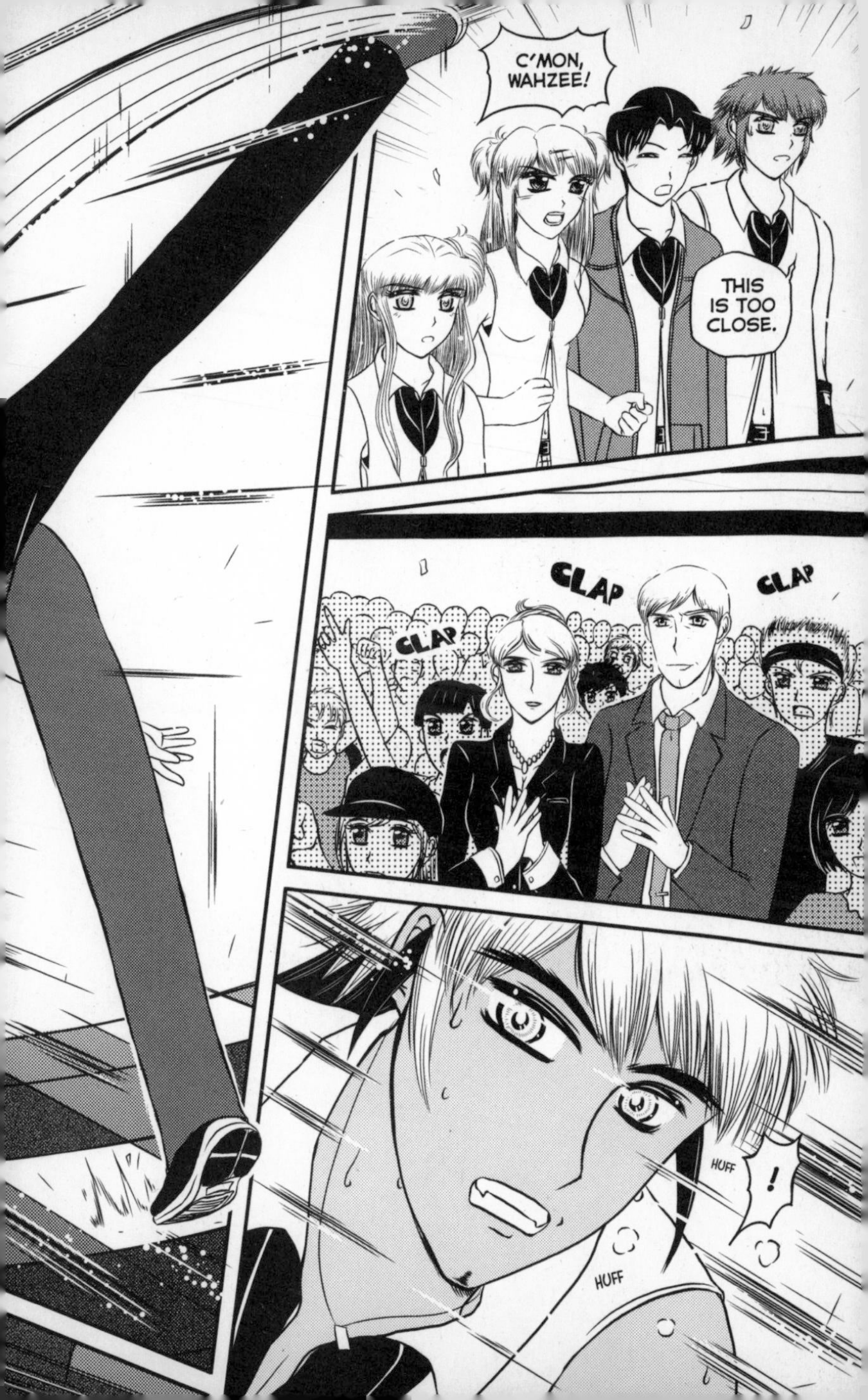
C'MON, WAHZEE!
THIS IS TOO CLOSE.
CLAP
CLAP
CLAP
HUFF
!
HUFF

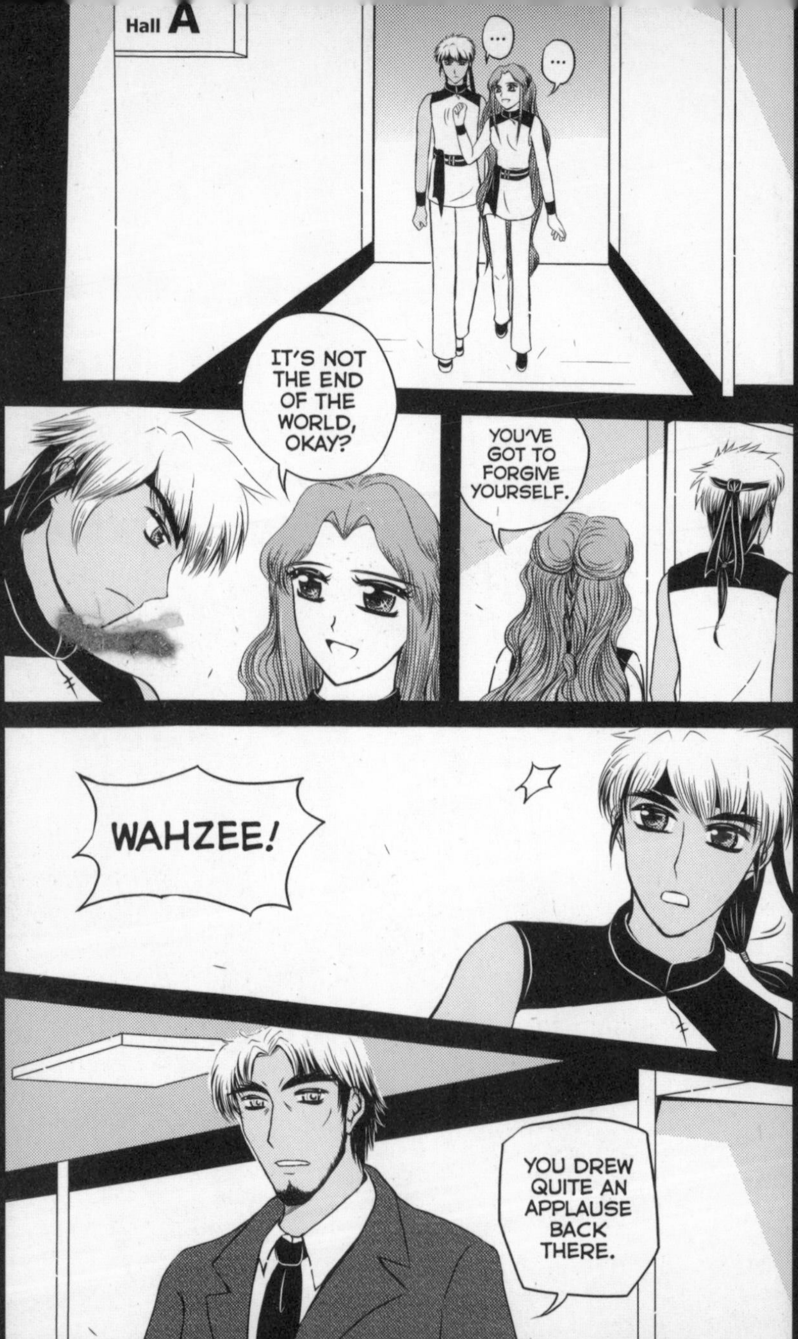
Hall A
...
...
IT'S NOT THE END OF THE WORLD, OKAY?
YOU'VE GOT TO FORGIVE YOURSELF.
WAHZEE!
YOU DREW QUITE AN APPLAUSE BACK THERE.

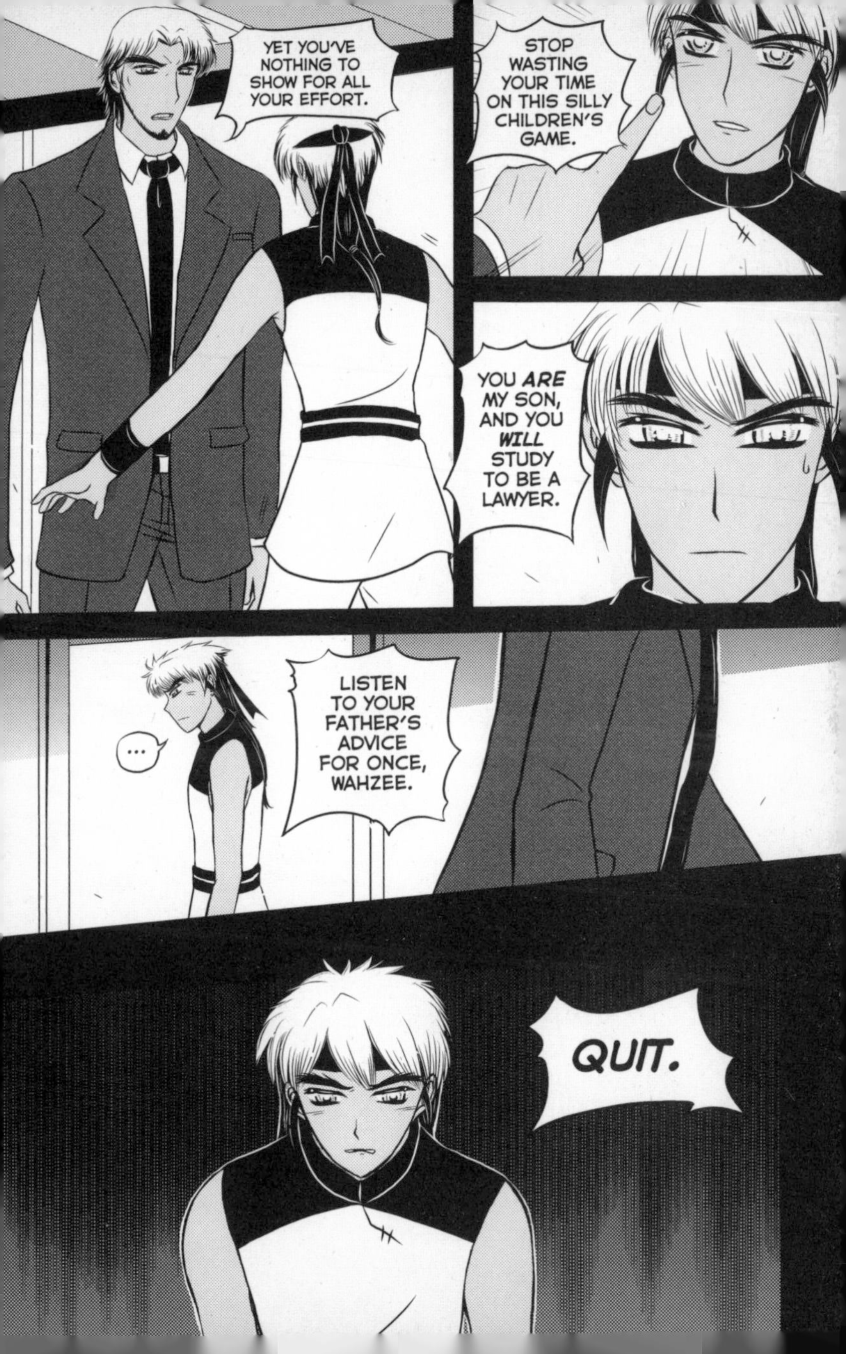
YET YOU'VE NOTHING TO SHOW FOR ALL YOUR EFFORT.
STOP WASTING YOUR TIME ON THIS SILLY CHILDREN'S GAME.
YOU *ARE* MY SON, AND YOU *WILL* STUDY TO BE A LAWYER.
...
LISTEN TO YOUR FATHER'S ADVICE FOR ONCE, WAHZEE.
QUIT.

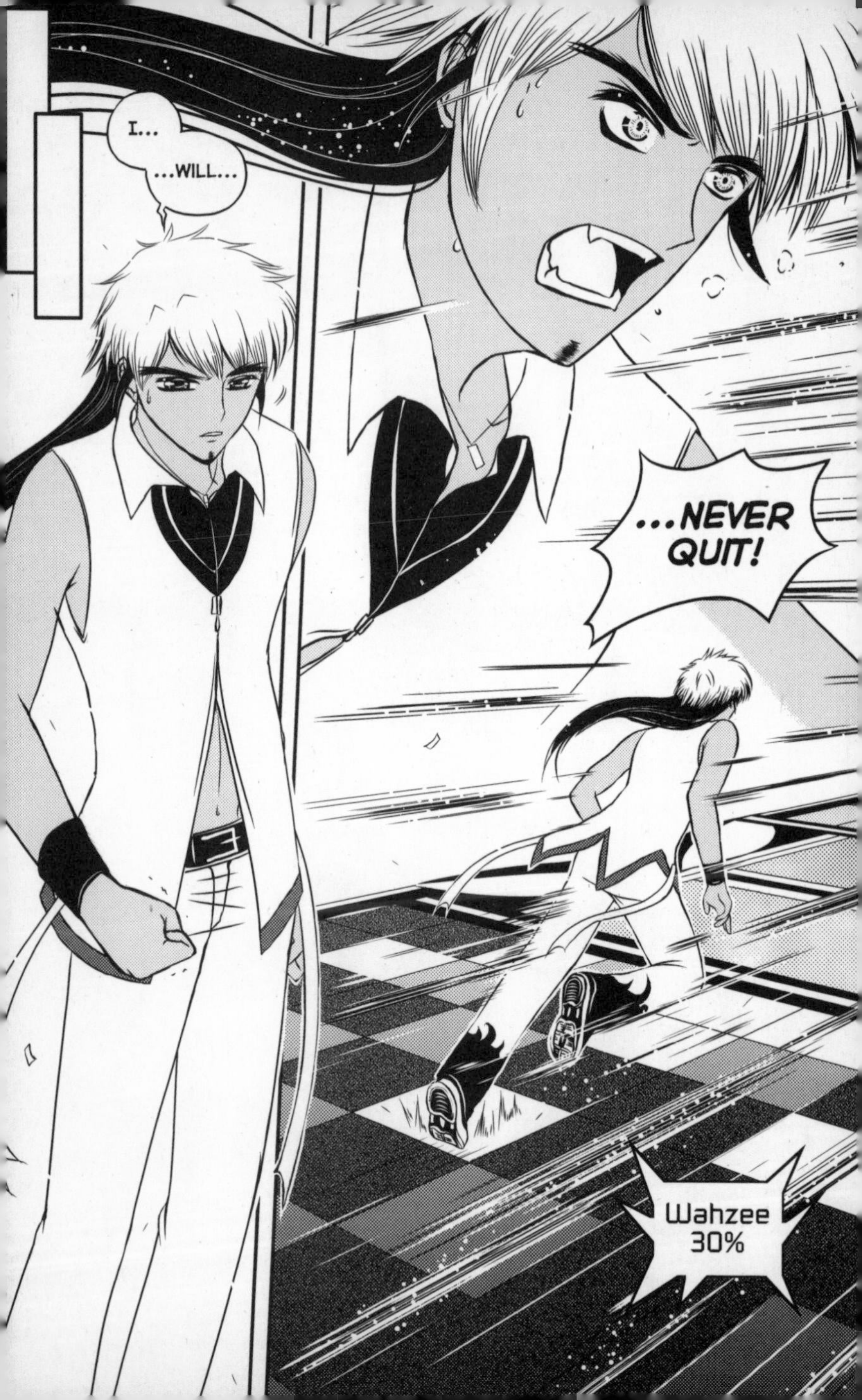
I...
...WILL...
...NEVER QUIT!
Wahzee 30%

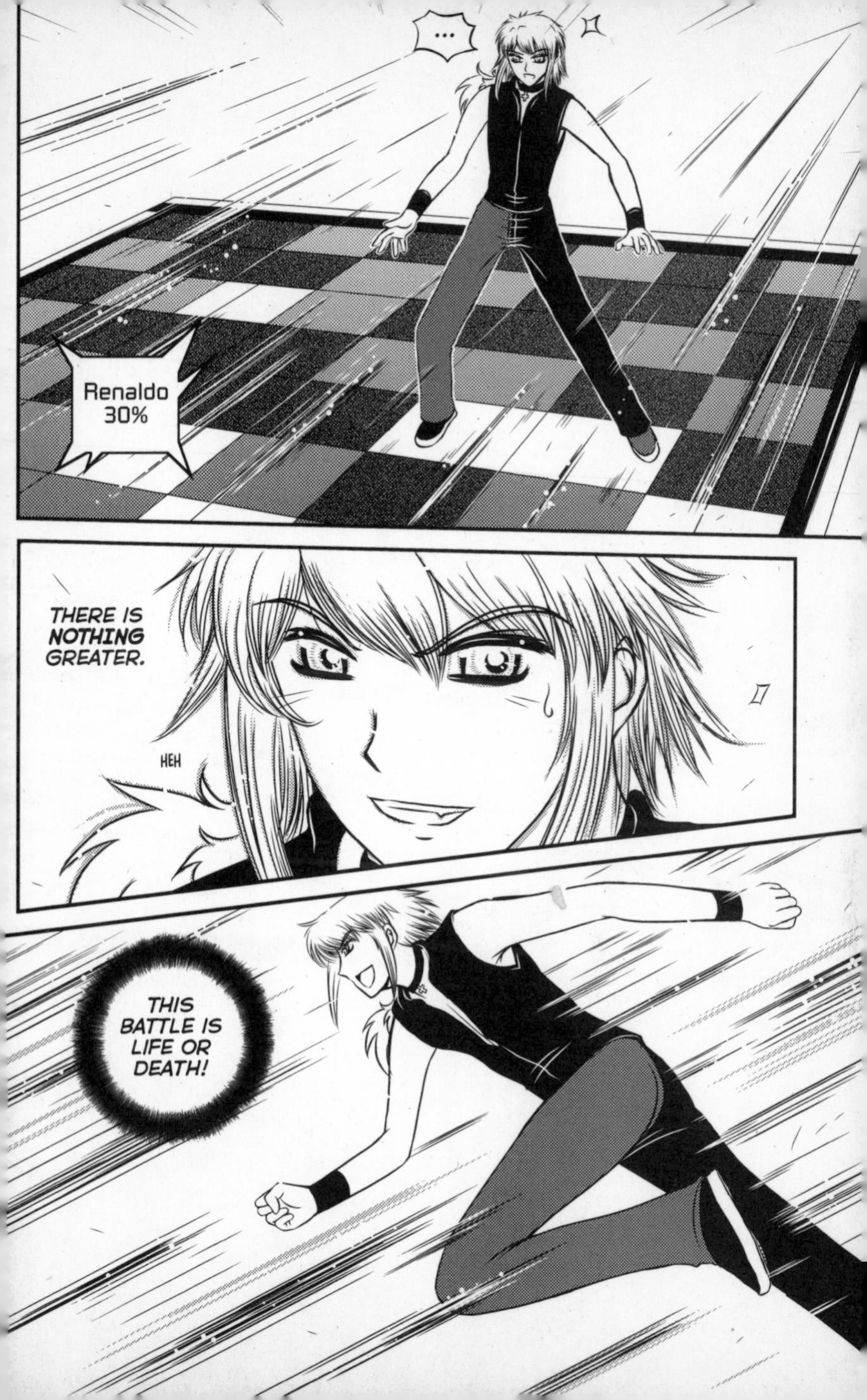
...
Renaldo 30%
THERE IS NOTHING GREATER.
HEH
THIS BATTLE IS LIFE OR DEATH!

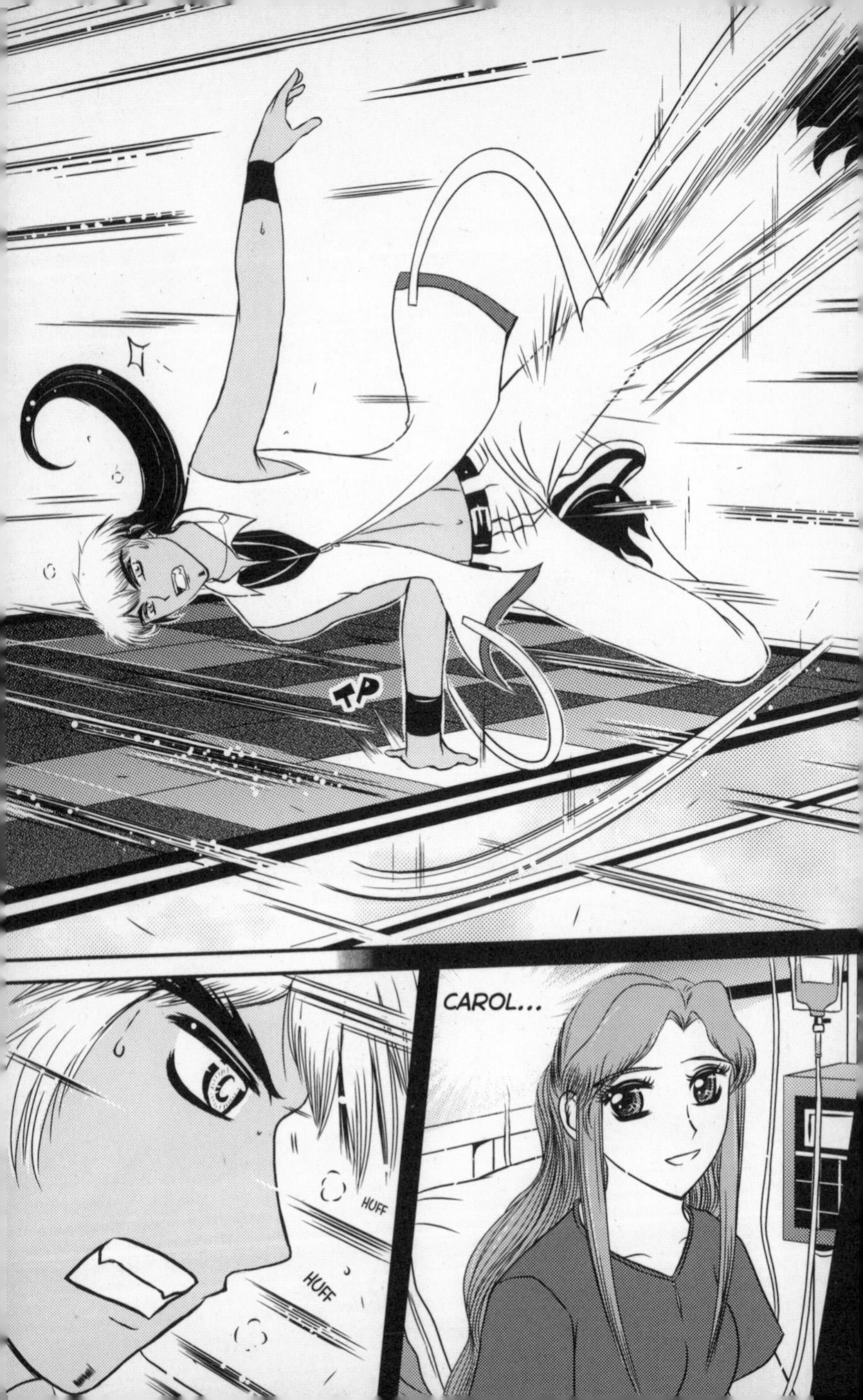
TP
HUFF
HUFF
CAROL...

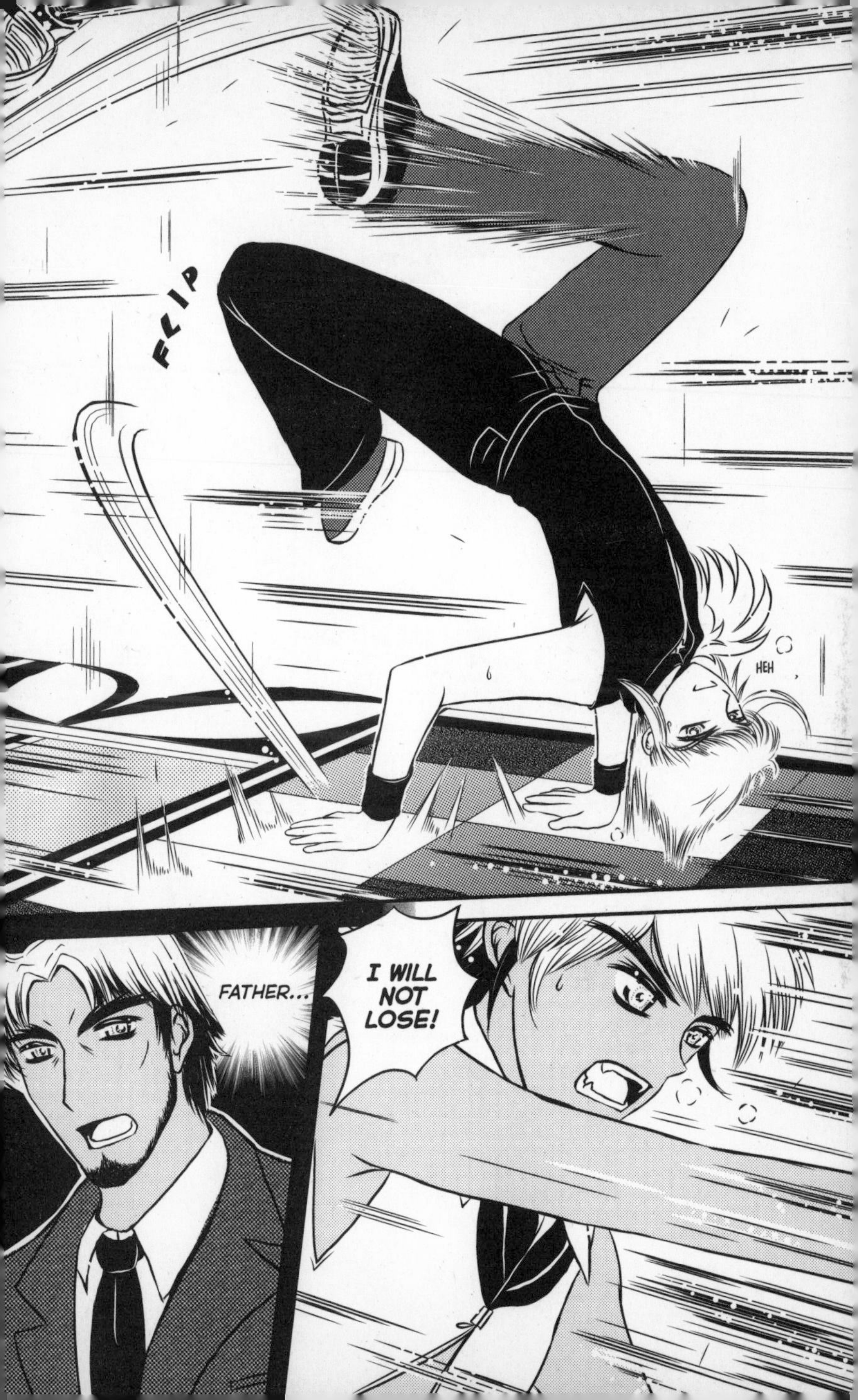
FLIP
HEH
FATHER...
I WILL NOT LOSE!

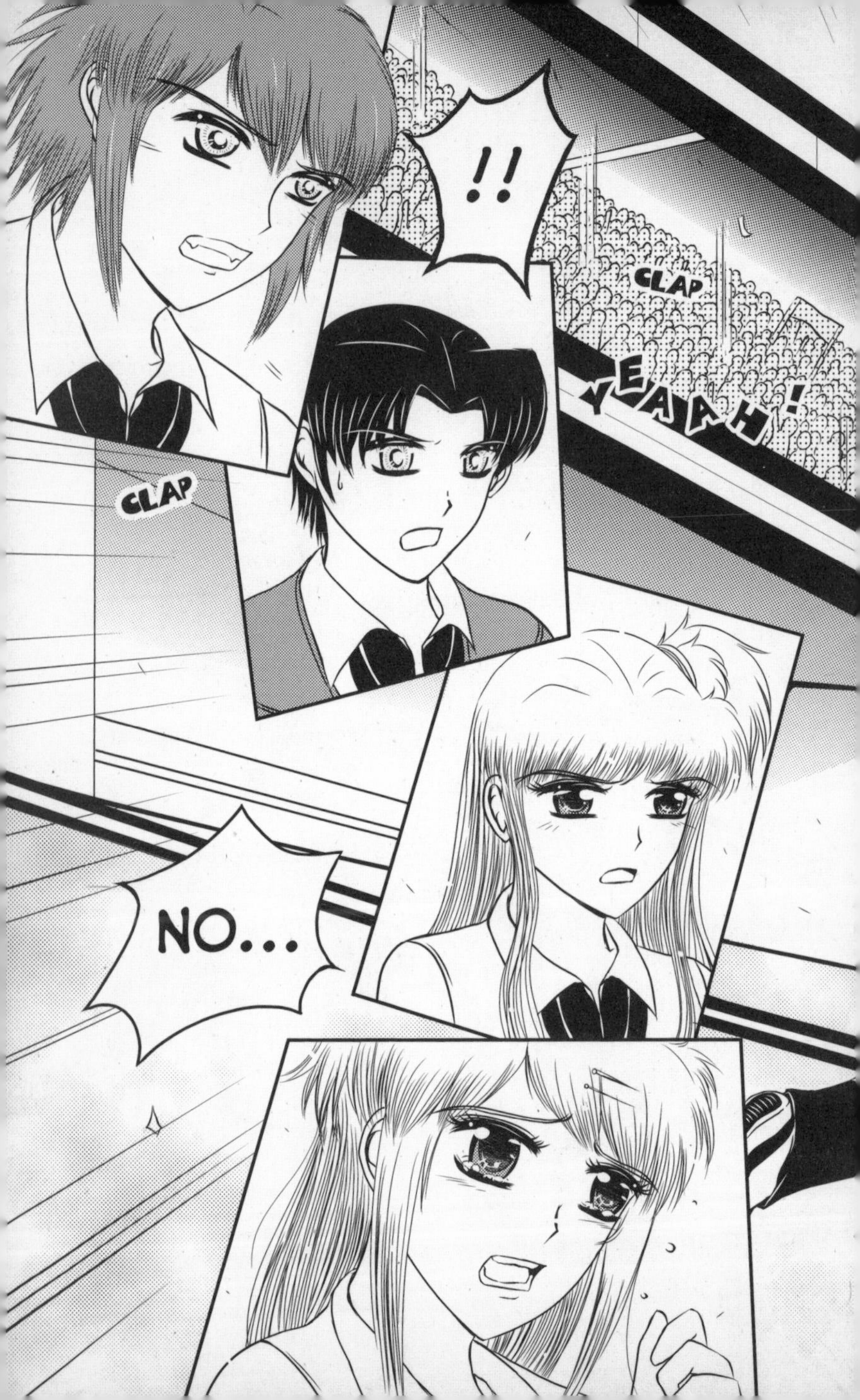
!!
CLAP
YEAAH!
CLAP
NO...

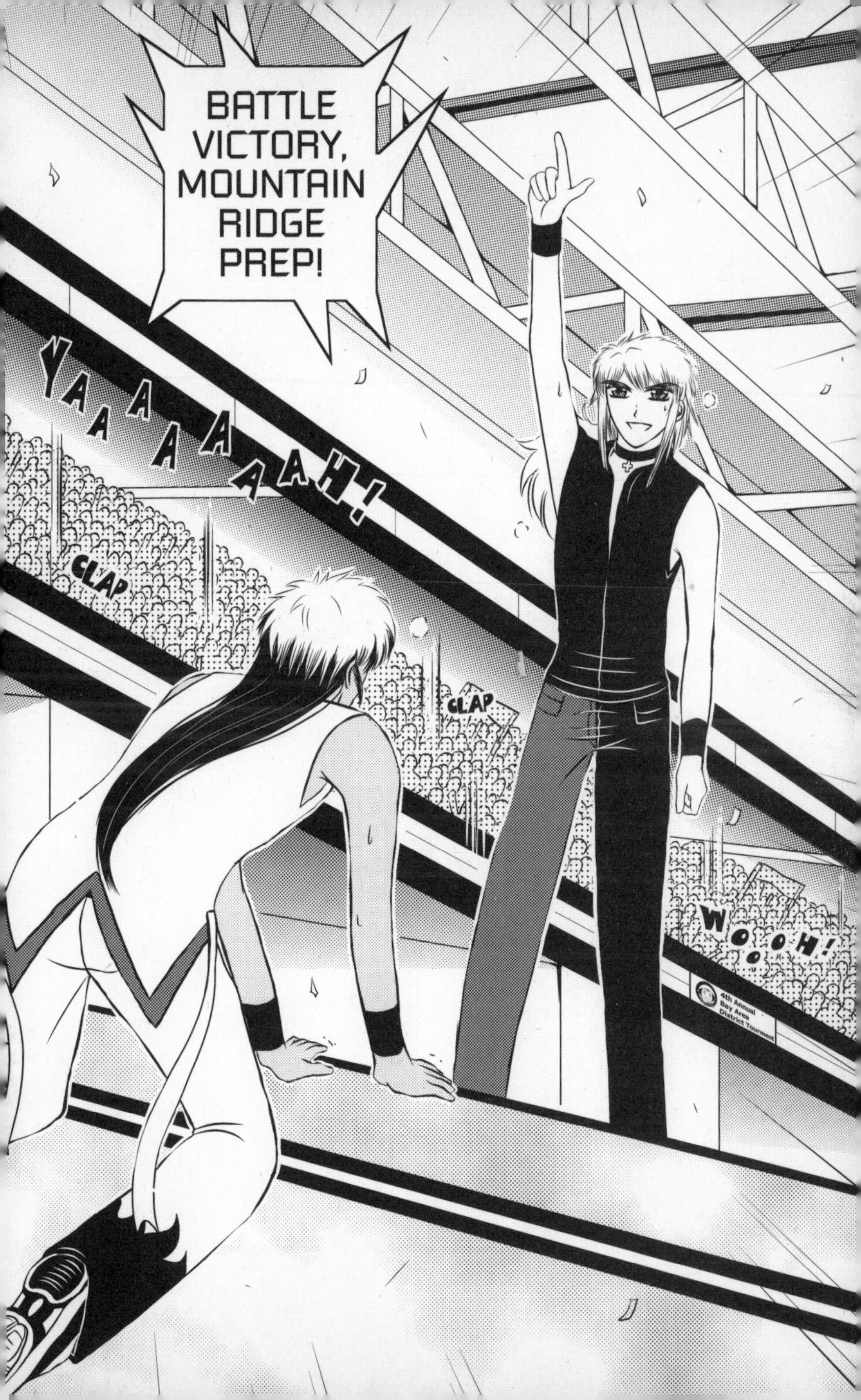
BATTLE VICTORY, MOUNTAIN RIDGE PREP!
YAAAAAAAH!
CLAP
CLAP
WOOOH!
4th Annual Bay Area District Tourment

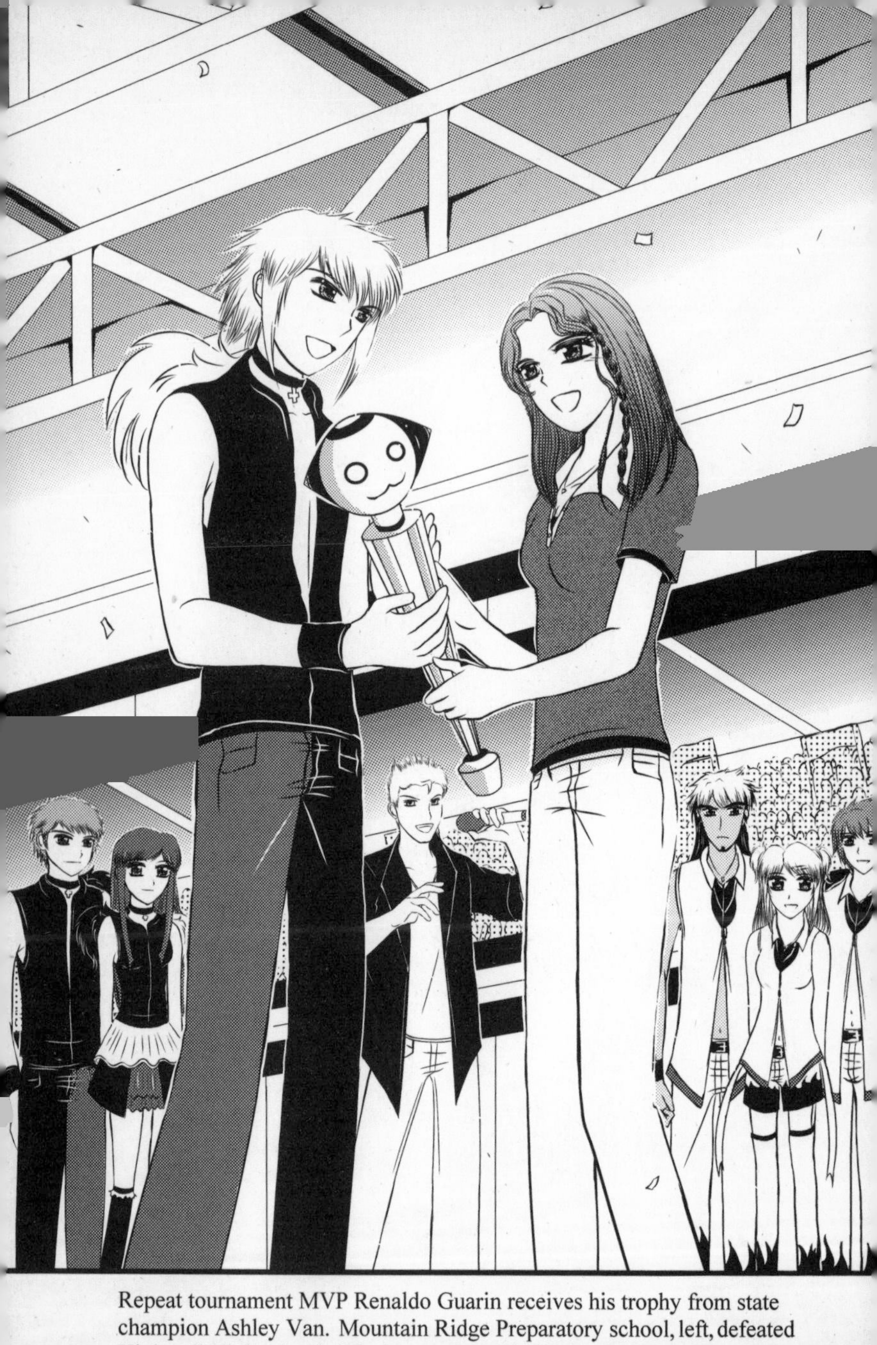

Repeat tournament MVP Renaldo Guarin receives his trophy from state champion Ashley Van. Mountain Ridge Preparatory school, left, defeated Highwall High school, right, in a memorable final round Saturday.

RHYSMYTH
Level 15: Consolation

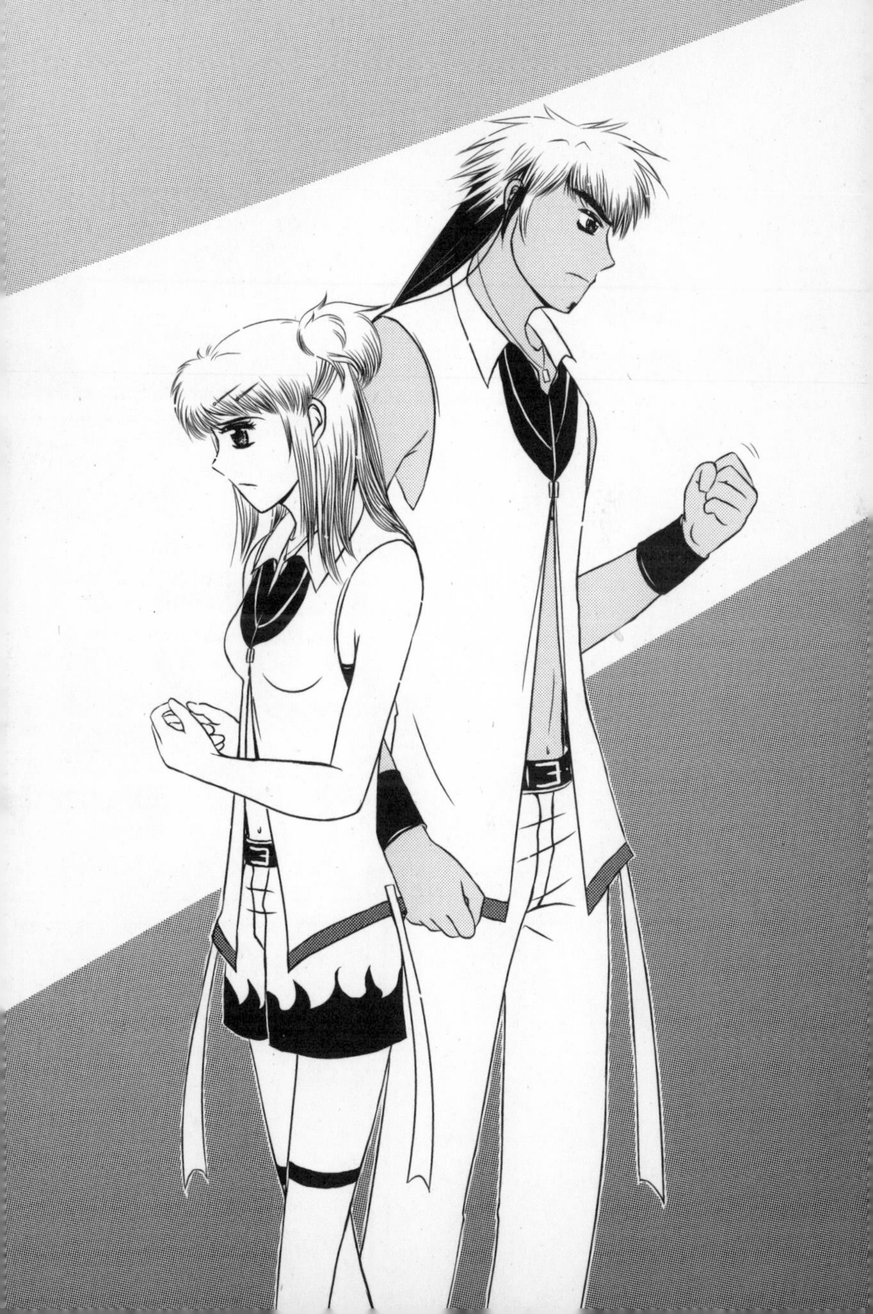

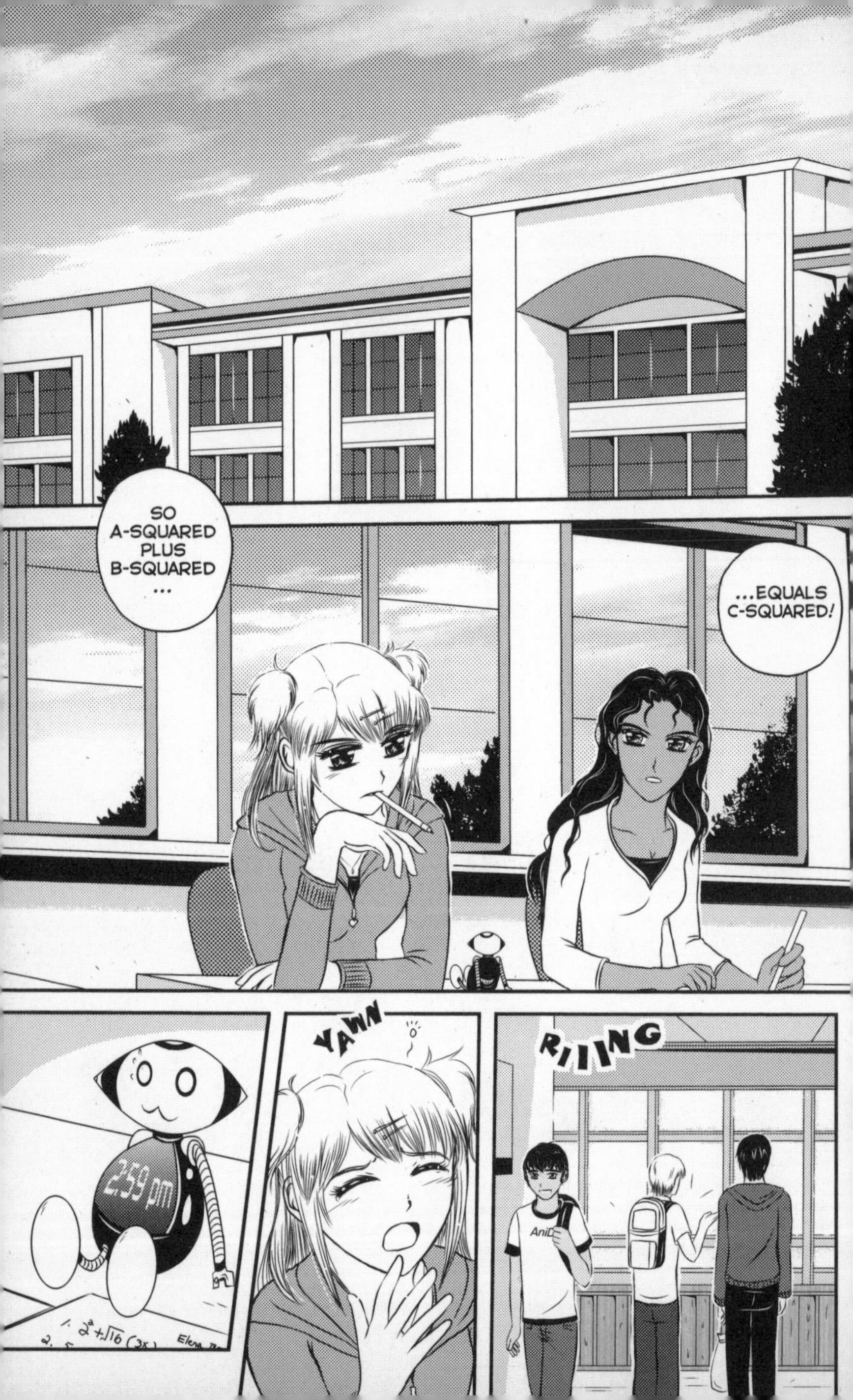
SO A-SQUARED PLUS B-SQUARED ...
...EQUALS C-SQUARED!
2:59 pm
YAWN
RIIING

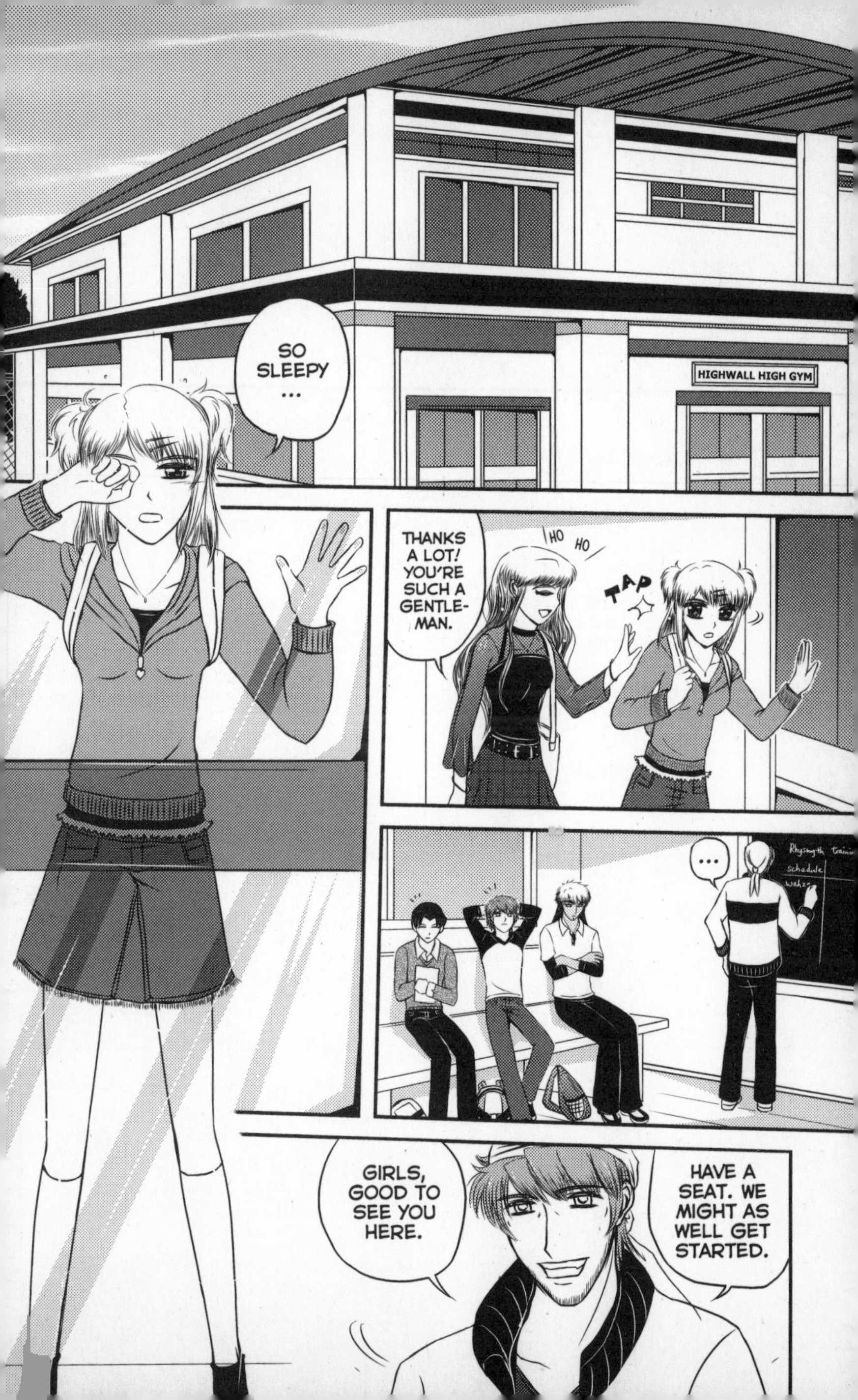
SO SLEEPY ...
HIGHWALL HIGH GYM
THANKS A LOT! YOU'RE SUCH A GENTLE-MAN.
HO HO
TAP
...
GIRLS, GOOD TO SEE YOU HERE.
HAVE A SEAT. WE MIGHT AS WELL GET STARTED.

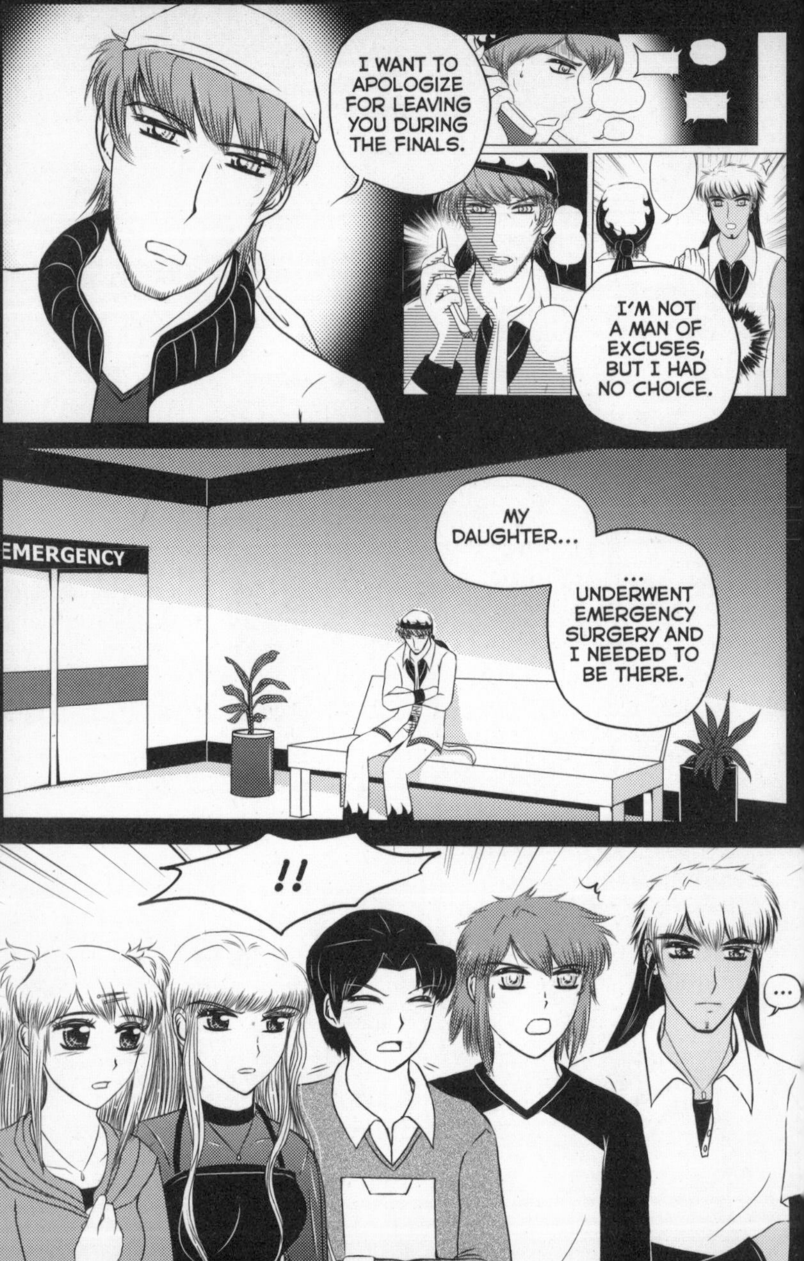
I WANT TO APOLOGIZE FOR LEAVING YOU DURING THE FINALS.
I'M NOT A MAN OF EXCUSES, BUT I HAD NO CHOICE.
EMERGENCY
MY DAUGHTER...
... UNDERWENT EMERGENCY SURGERY AND I NEEDED TO BE THERE.
!!
...

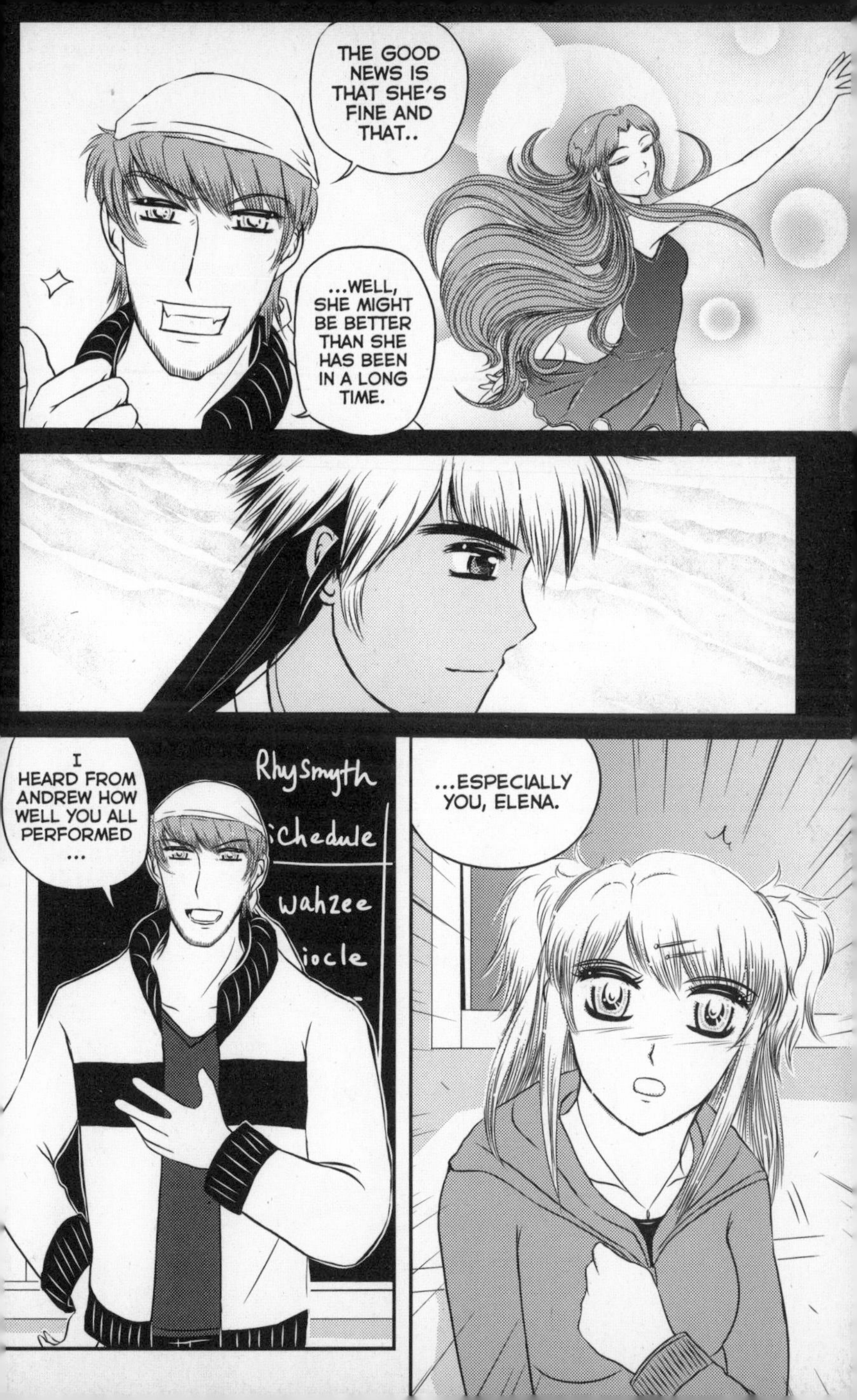
THE GOOD NEWS IS THAT SHE'S FINE AND THAT..
...WELL, SHE MIGHT BE BETTER THAN SHE HAS BEEN IN A LONG TIME.
I HEARD FROM ANDREW HOW WELL YOU ALL PERFORMED ...
Rhysmyth
Schedule
wahzee
iocle
...ESPECIALLY YOU, ELENA.

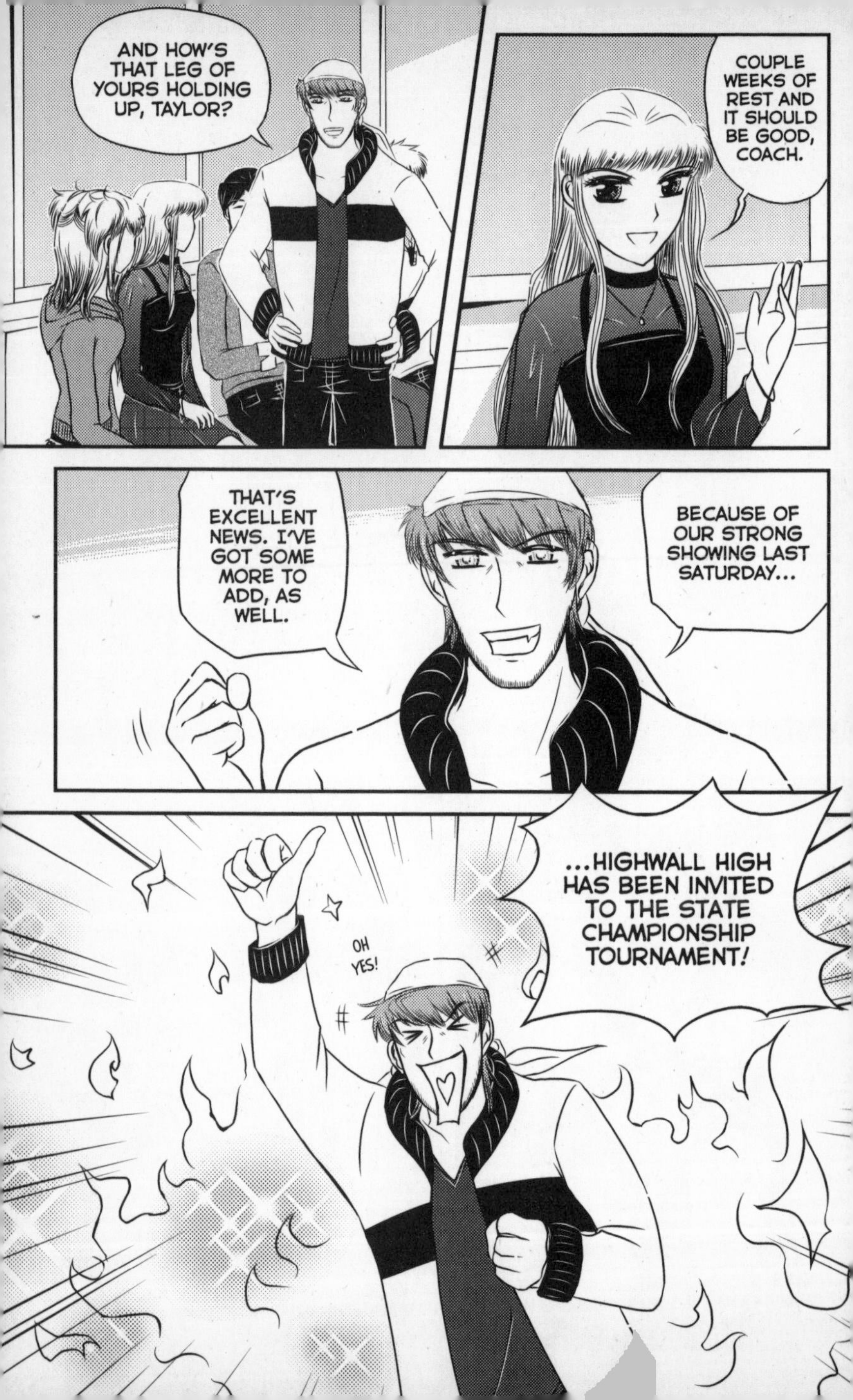
AND HOW'S THAT LEG OF YOURS HOLDING UP, TAYLOR?
COUPLE WEEKS OF REST AND IT SHOULD BE GOOD, COACH.
THAT'S EXCELLENT NEWS. I'VE GOT SOME MORE TO ADD, AS WELL.
BECAUSE OF OUR STRONG SHOWING LAST SATURDAY...
OH YES!
...HIGHWALL HIGH HAS BEEN INVITED TO THE STATE CHAMPIONSHIP TOURNAMENT!

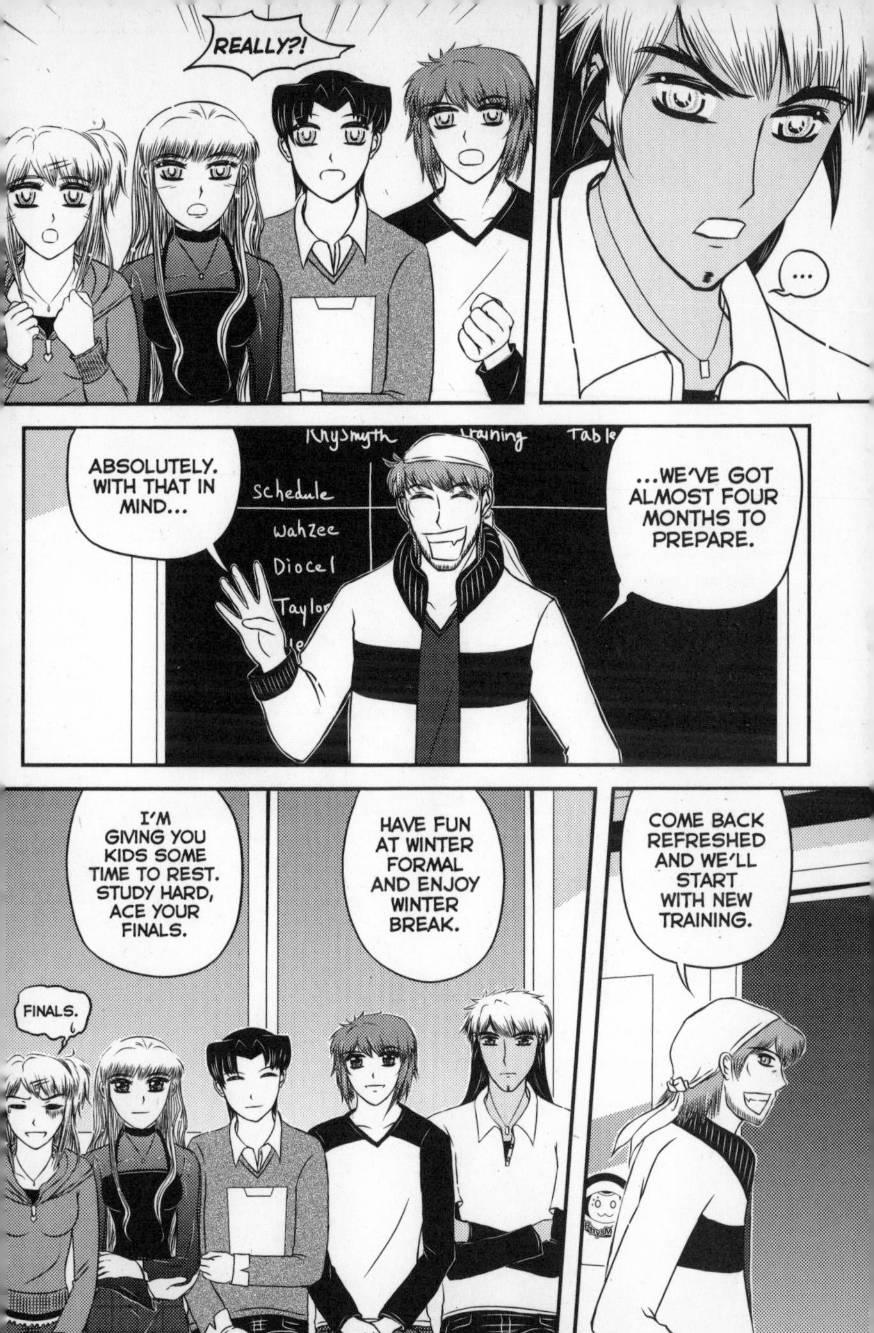
REALLY?!
...
Rhysmyth Training Table
Schedule
Wahzee
Diocel
Taylor
ABSOLUTELY. WITH THAT IN MIND...
...WE'VE GOT ALMOST FOUR MONTHS TO PREPARE.
I'M GIVING YOU KIDS SOME TIME TO REST. STUDY HARD, ACE YOUR FINALS.
HAVE FUN AT WINTER FORMAL AND ENJOY WINTER BREAK.
FINALS.
COME BACK REFRESHED AND WE'LL START WITH NEW TRAINING.

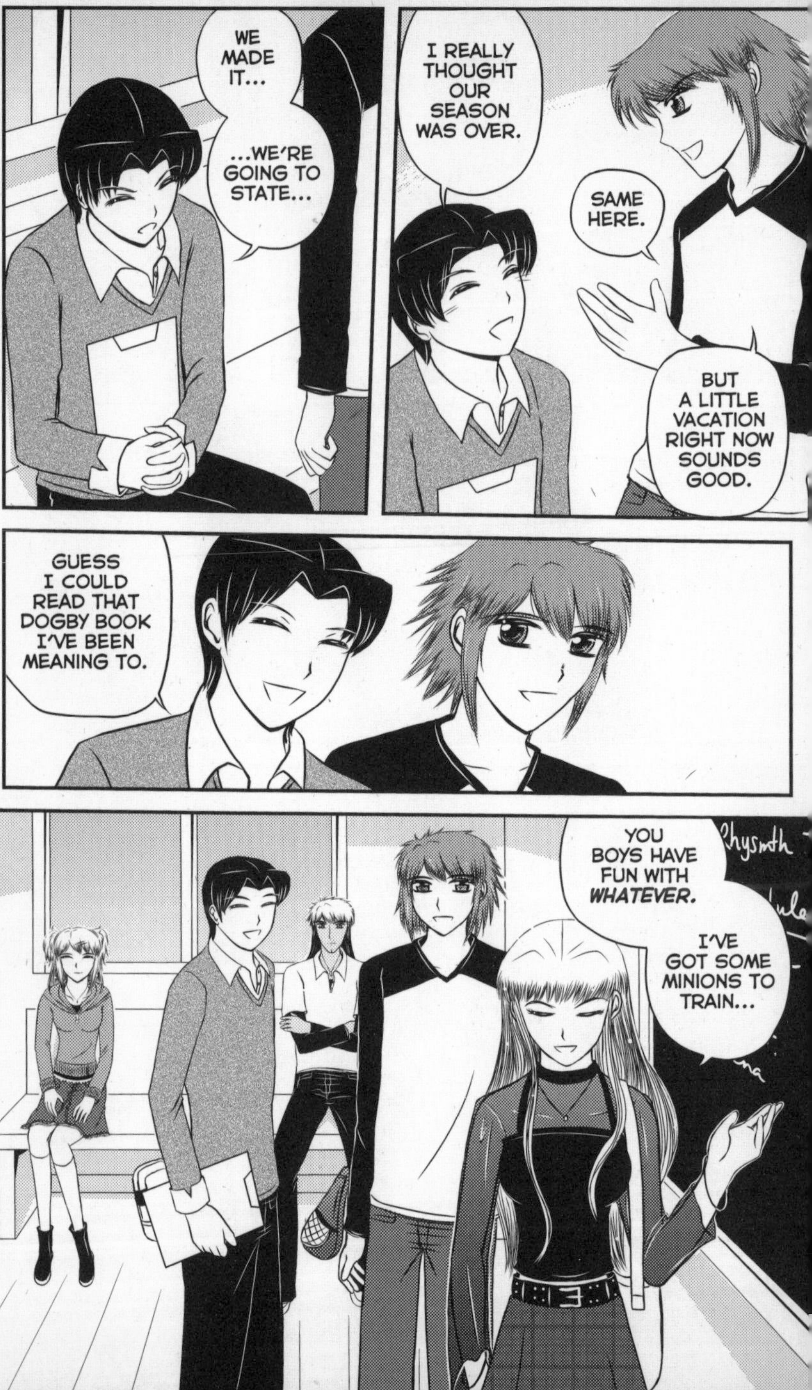
WE MADE IT...
...WE'RE GOING TO STATE...
I REALLY THOUGHT OUR SEASON WAS OVER.
SAME HERE.
BUT A LITTLE VACATION RIGHT NOW SOUNDS GOOD.
GUESS I COULD READ THAT DOGBY BOOK I'VE BEEN MEANING TO.
YOU BOYS HAVE FUN WITH *WHATEVER.*
I'VE GOT SOME MINIONS TO TRAIN...

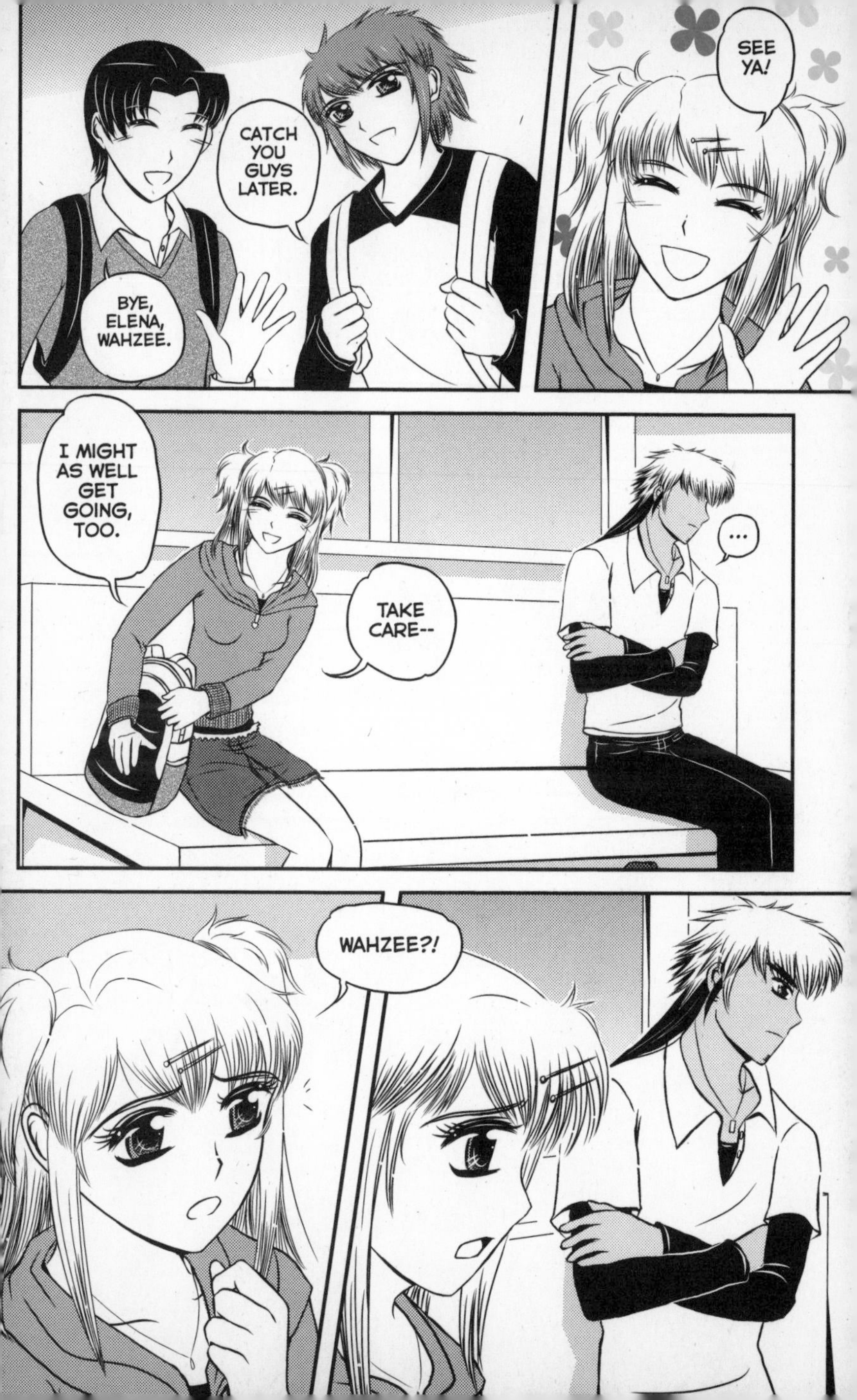
BYE, ELENA, WAHZEE.
CATCH YOU GUYS LATER.
SEE YA!
I MIGHT AS WELL GET GOING, TOO.
TAKE CARE--
...
WAHZEE?!

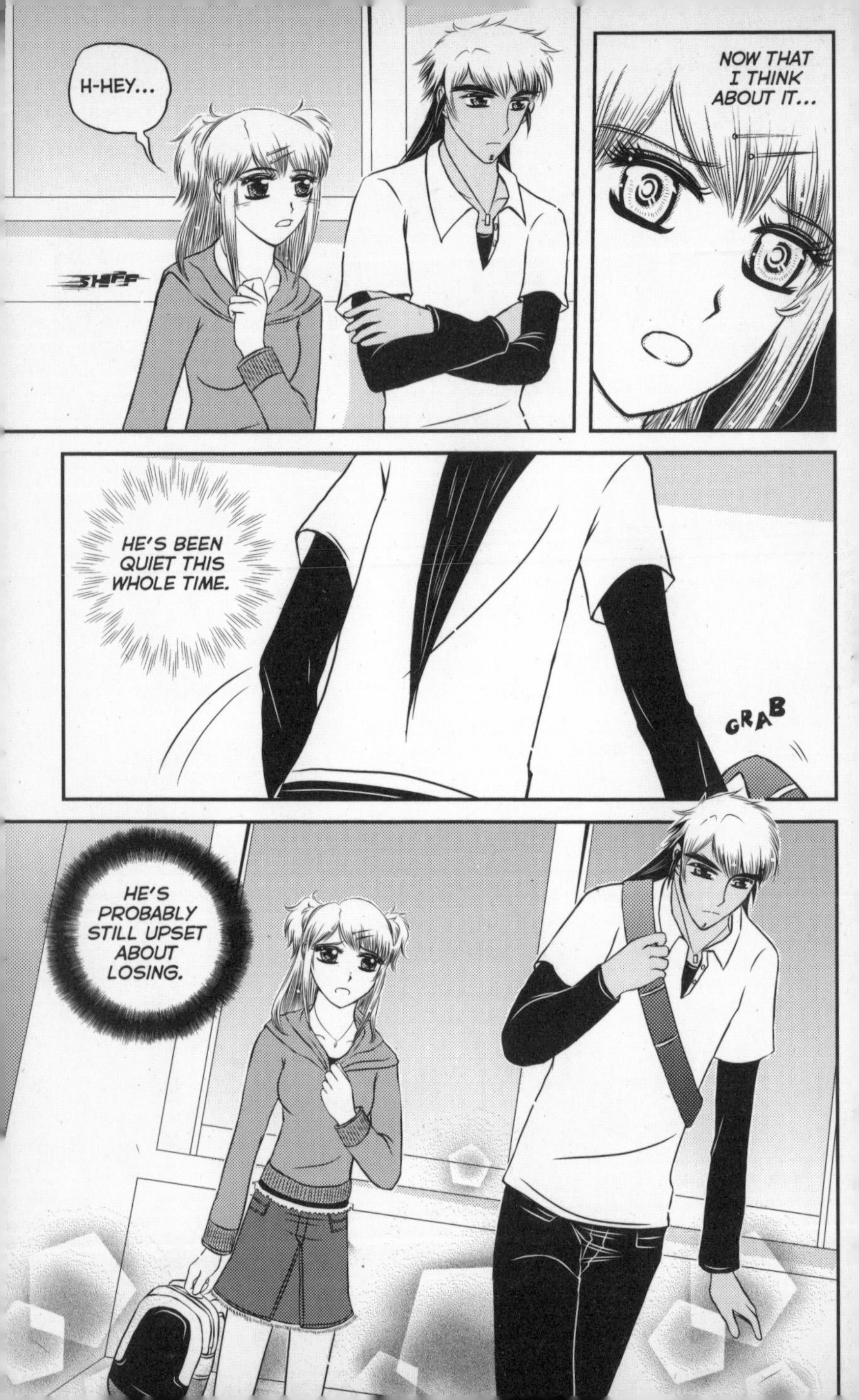
H-HEY...
SHFF
NOW THAT I THINK ABOUT IT...
HE'S BEEN QUIET THIS WHOLE TIME.
GRAB
HE'S PROBABLY STILL UPSET ABOUT LOSING.

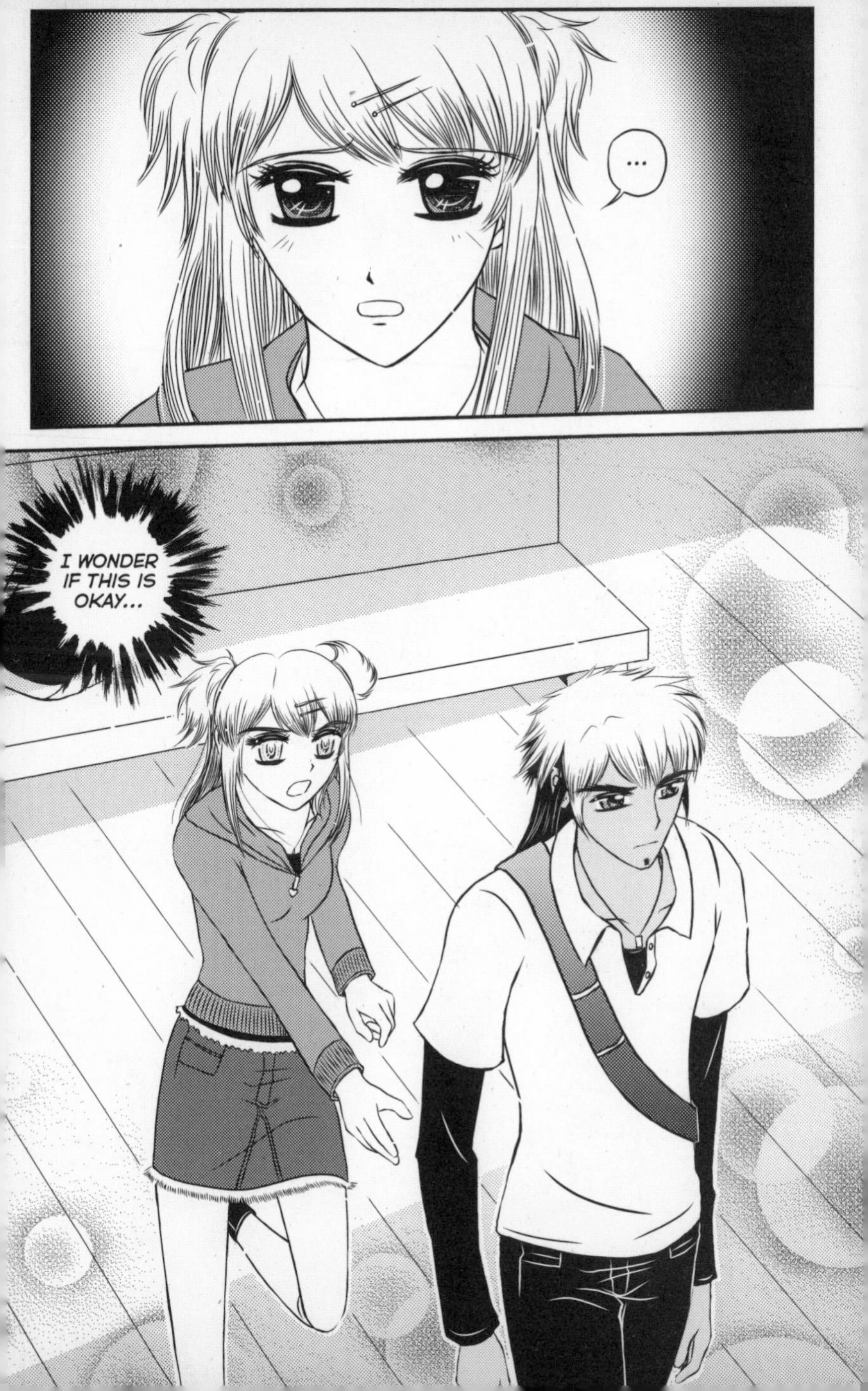
...
I WONDER IF THIS IS OKAY...

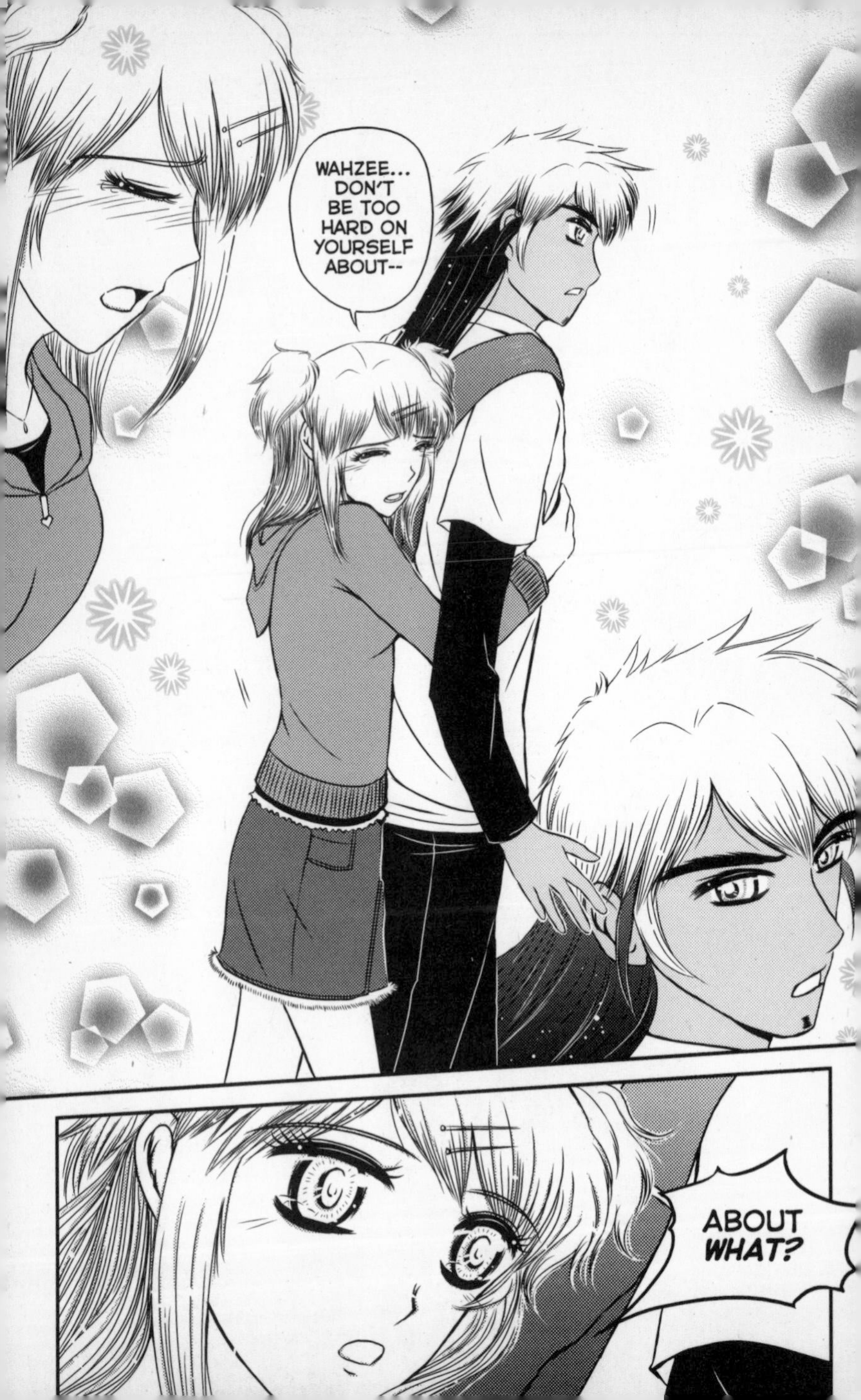
WAHZEE... DON'T BE TOO HARD ON YOURSELF ABOUT--
ABOUT *WHAT?*

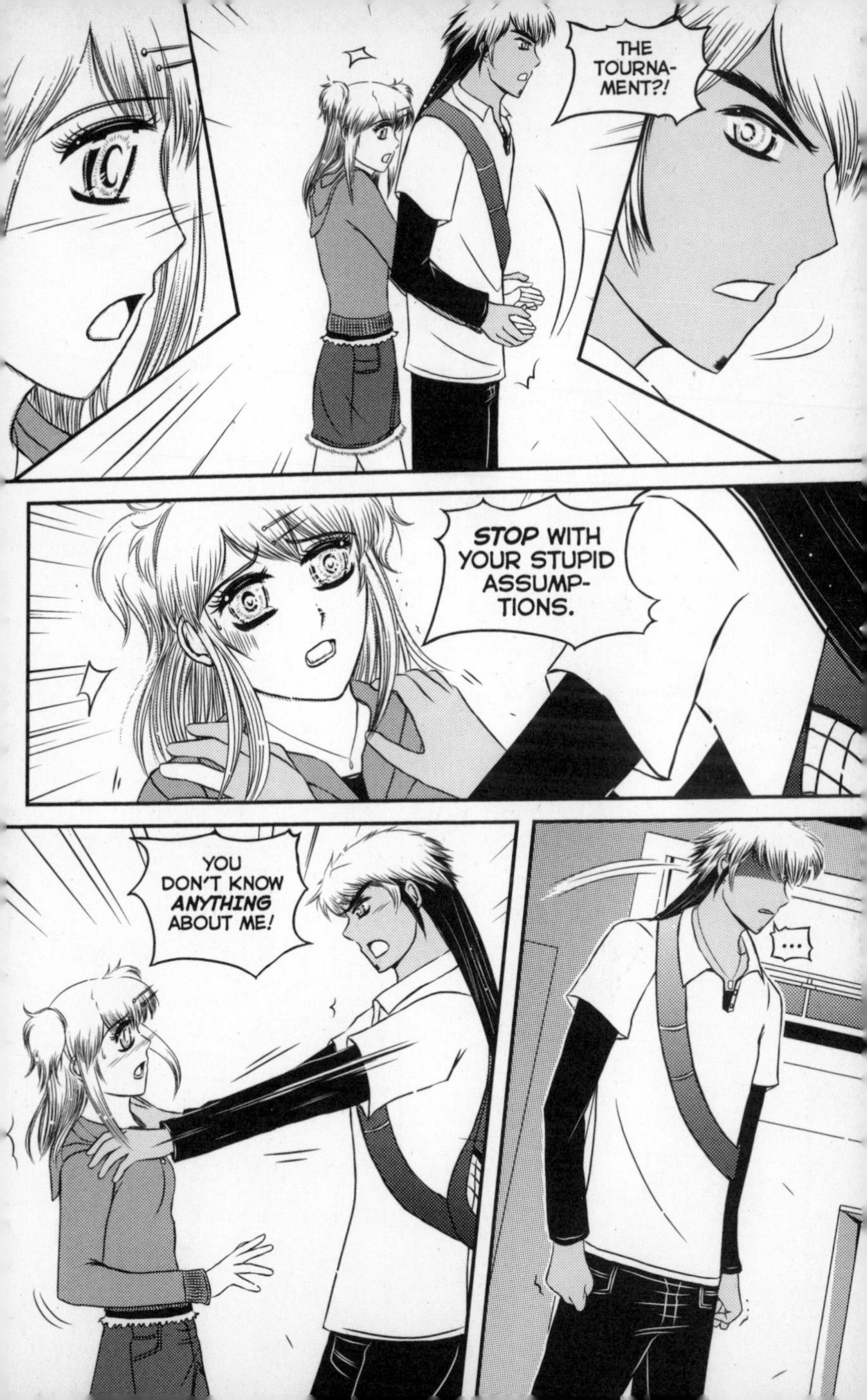
THE TOURNA-MENT?!
STOP WITH YOUR STUPID ASSUMP-TIONS.
YOU DON'T KNOW ANYTHING ABOUT ME!
...

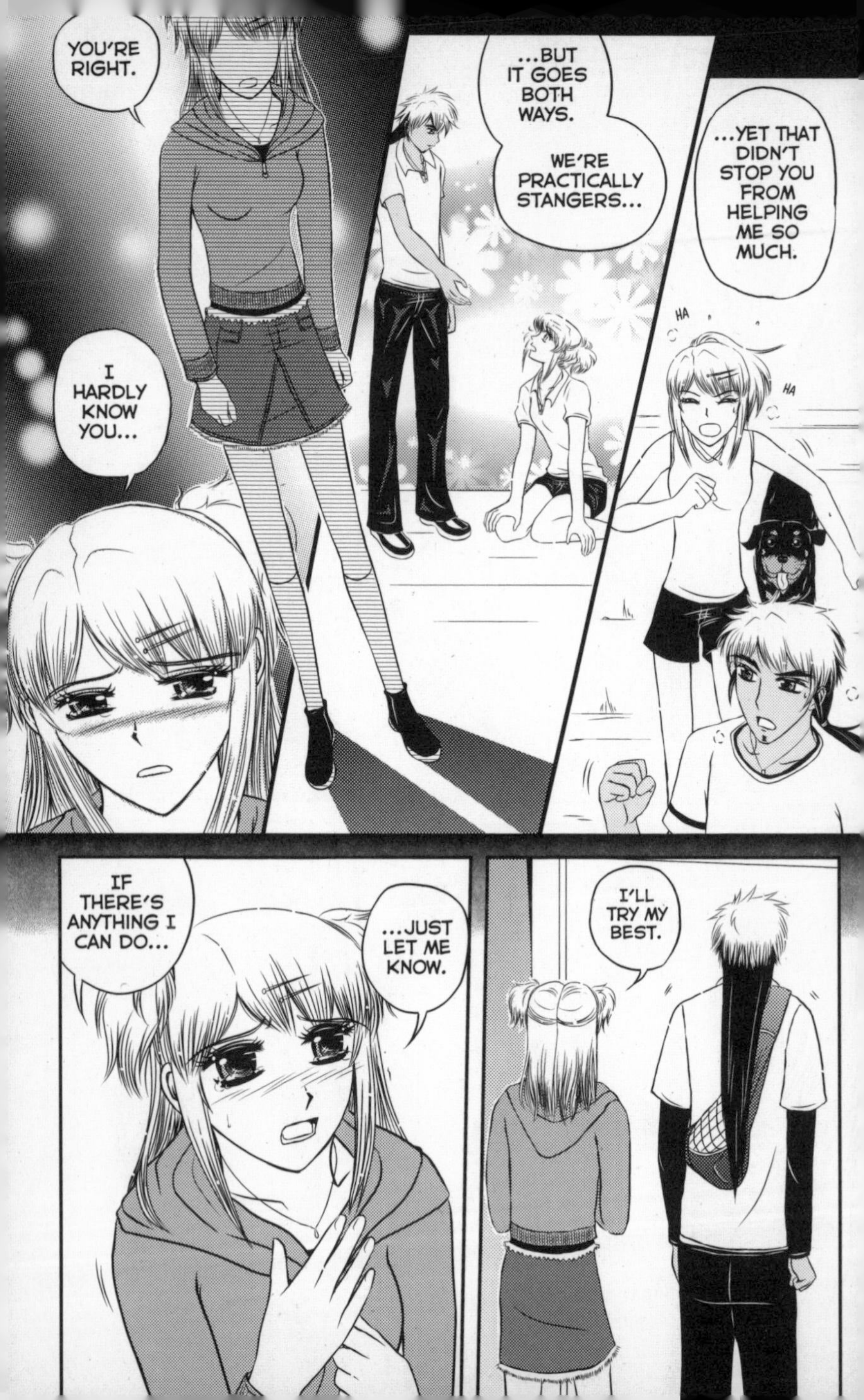
YOU'RE RIGHT.
I HARDLY KNOW YOU...
...BUT IT GOES BOTH WAYS.
WE'RE PRACTICALLY STANGERS...
...YET THAT DIDN'T STOP YOU FROM HELPING ME SO MUCH.
HA
HA
IF THERE'S ANYTHING I CAN DO...
...JUST LET ME KNOW.
I'LL TRY MY BEST.

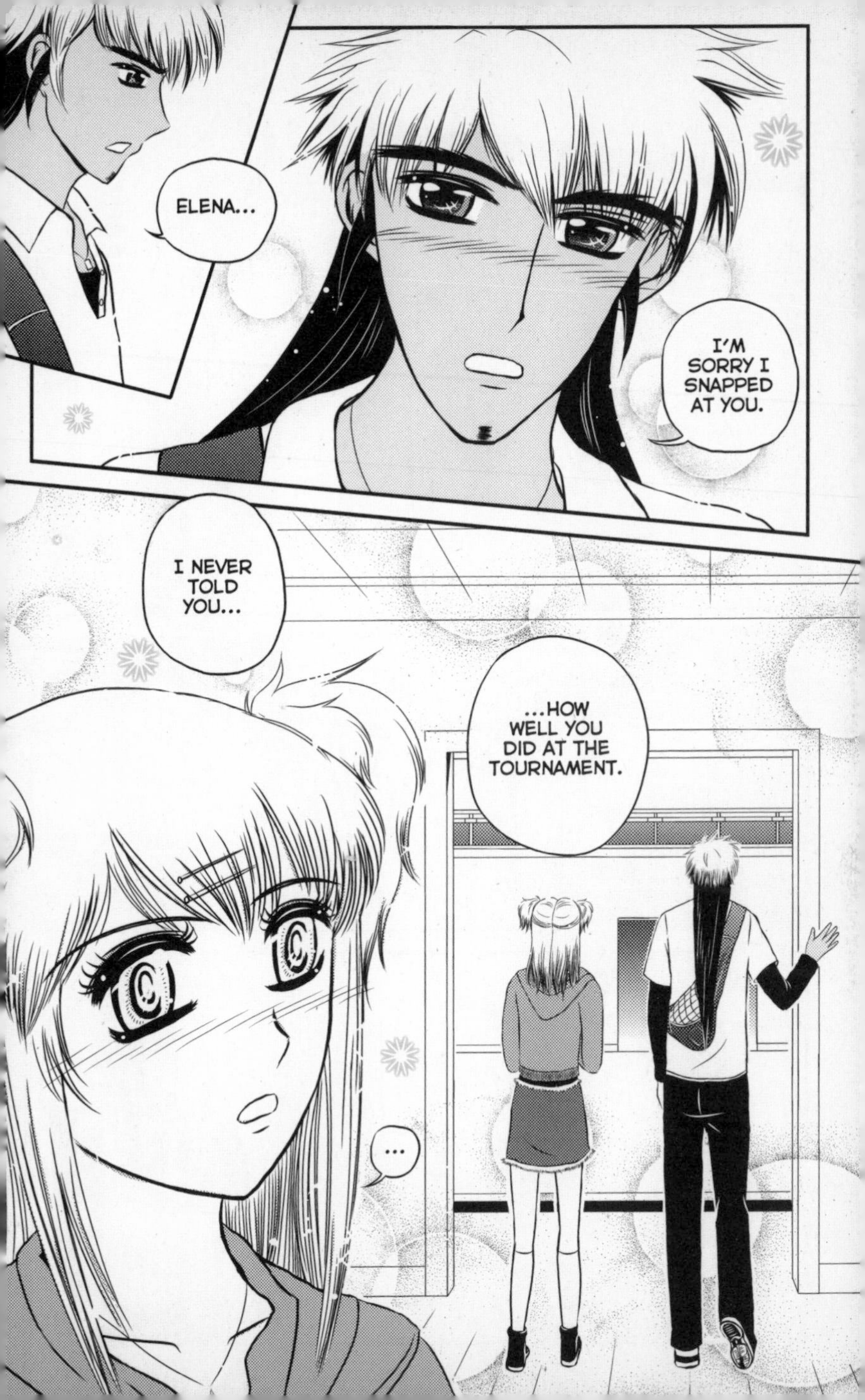
ELENA...
I'M SORRY I SNAPPED AT YOU.
I NEVER TOLD YOU...
...HOW WELL YOU DID AT THE TOURNAMENT.
...

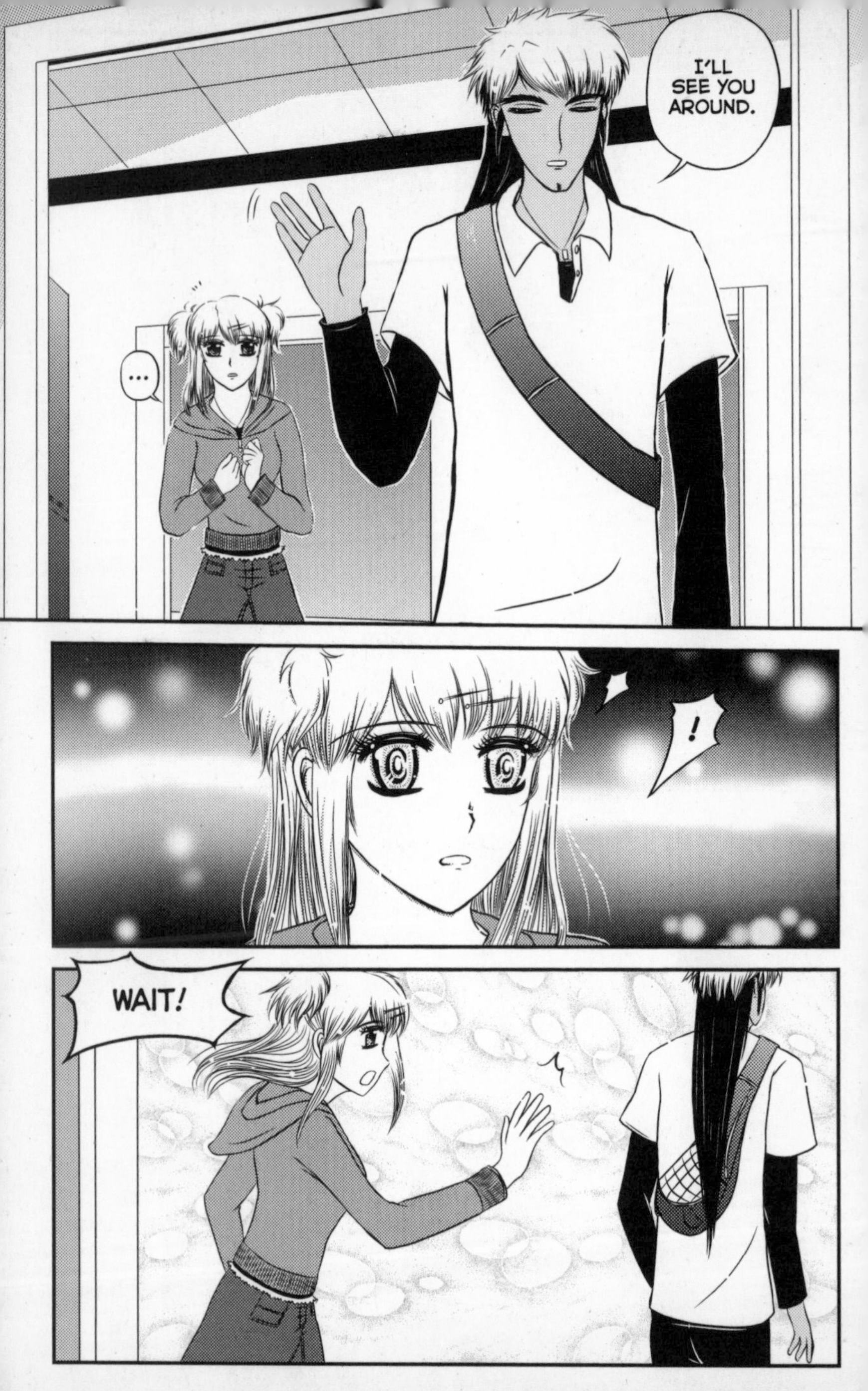
I'LL SEE YOU AROUND.
...
!
WAIT!

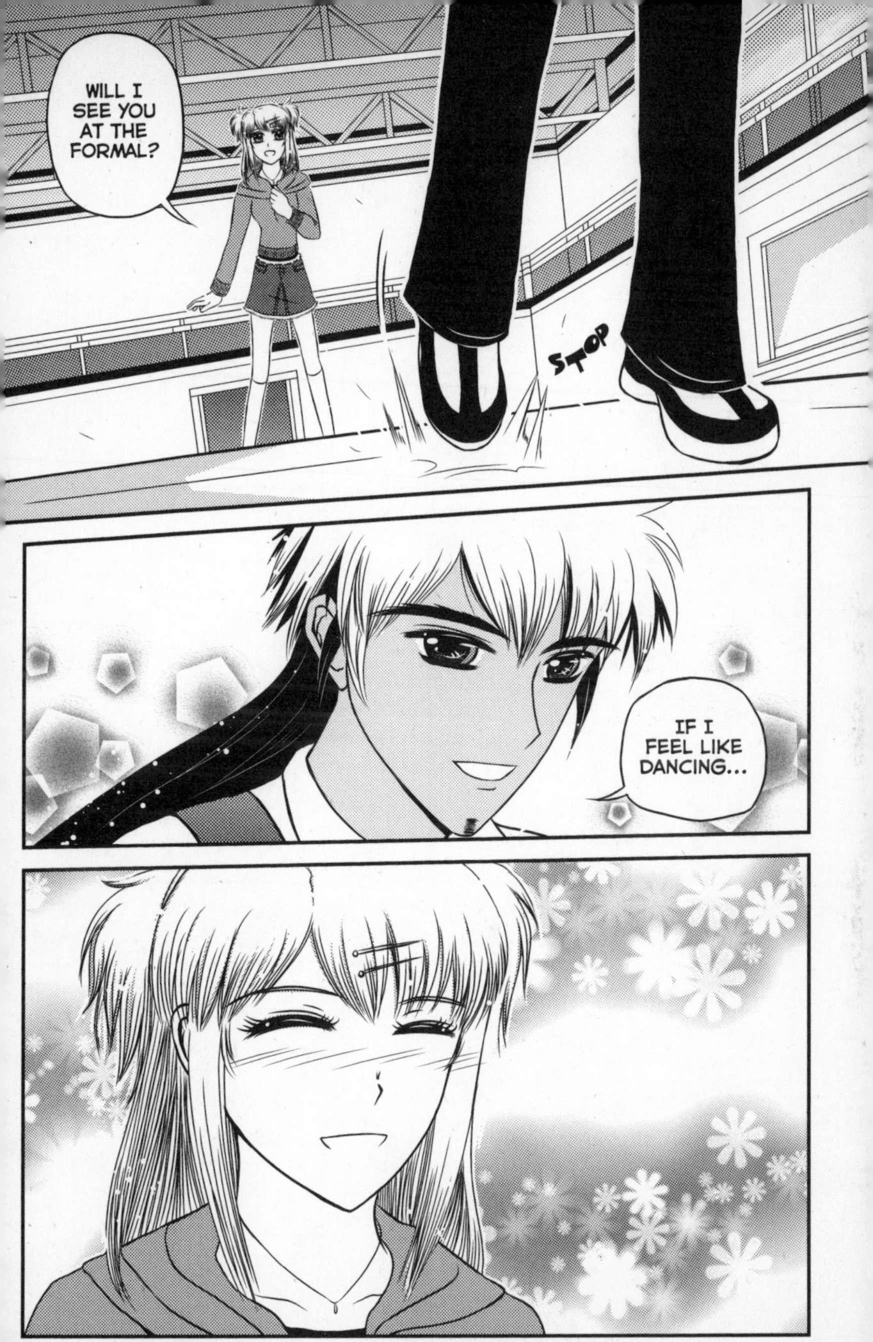
WILL I SEE YOU AT THE FORMAL?
STOP
IF I FEEL LIKE DANCING...

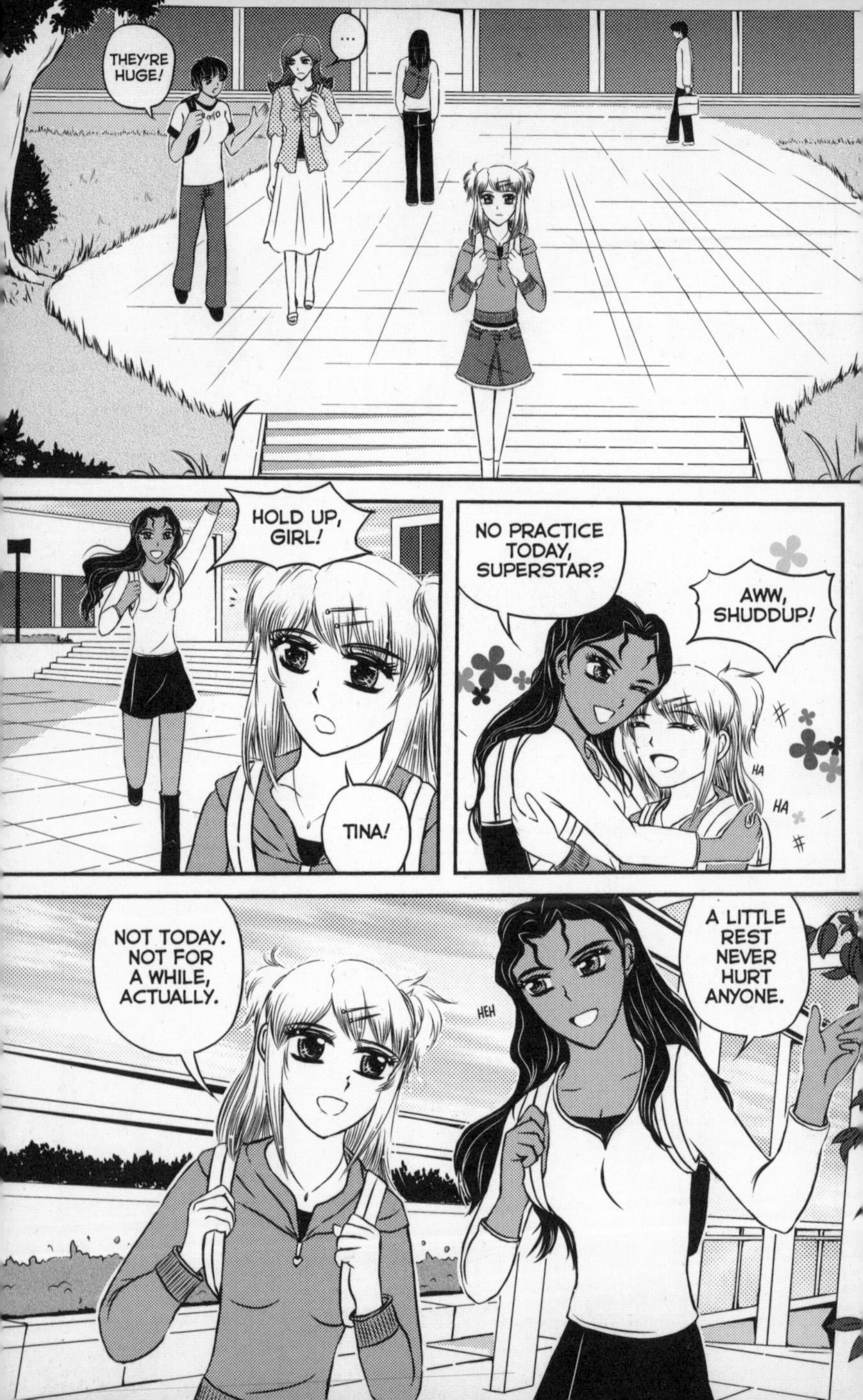
THEY'RE HUGE!
...
HOLD UP, GIRL!
TINA!
NO PRACTICE TODAY, SUPERSTAR?
AWW, SHUDDUP!
HA
HA
NOT TODAY. NOT FOR A WHILE, ACTUALLY.
HEH
A LITTLE REST NEVER HURT ANYONE.

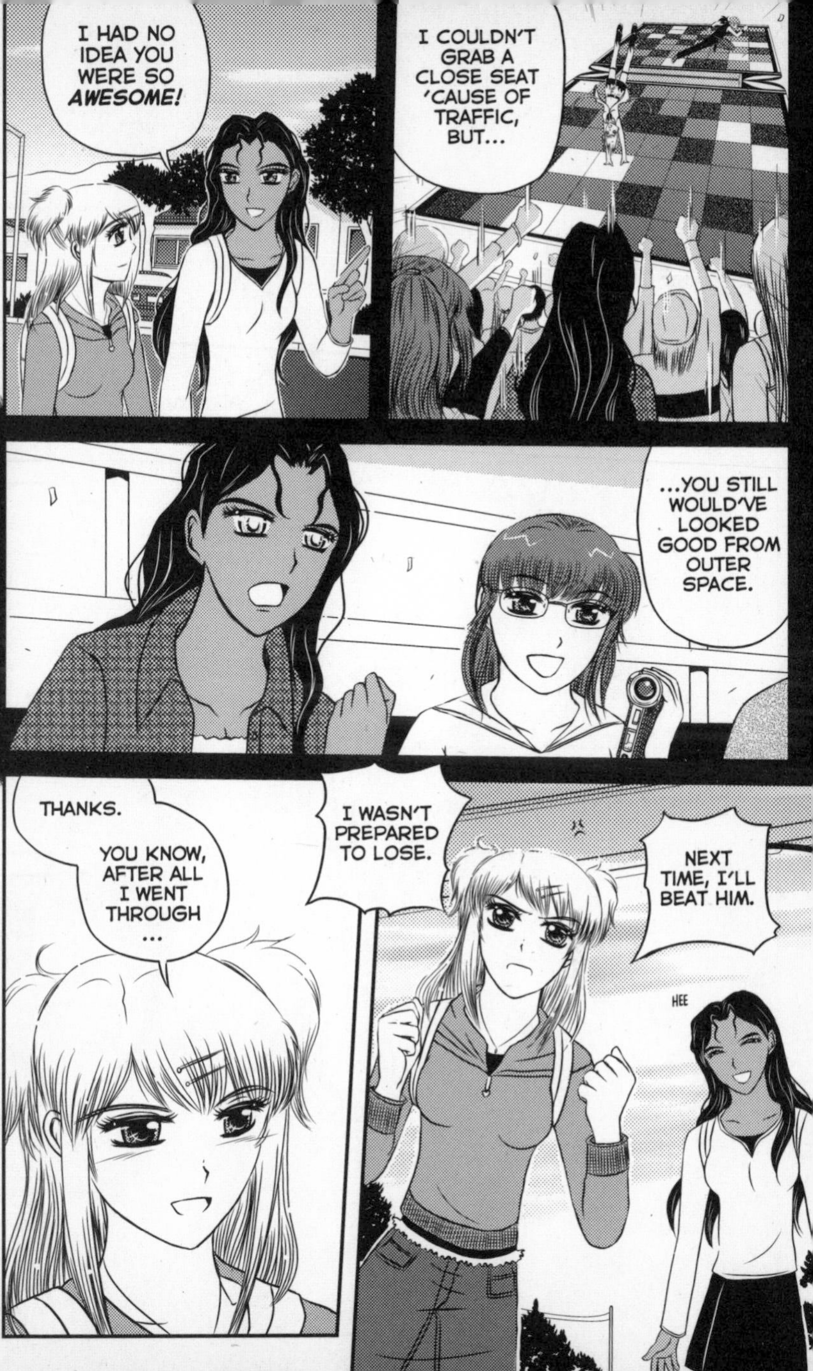
I HAD NO IDEA YOU WERE SO AWESOME!
I COULDN'T GRAB A CLOSE SEAT 'CAUSE OF TRAFFIC, BUT...
...YOU STILL WOULD'VE LOOKED GOOD FROM OUTER SPACE.
THANKS.
YOU KNOW, AFTER ALL I WENT THROUGH ...
I WASN'T PREPARED TO LOSE.
NEXT TIME, I'LL BEAT HIM.
HEE

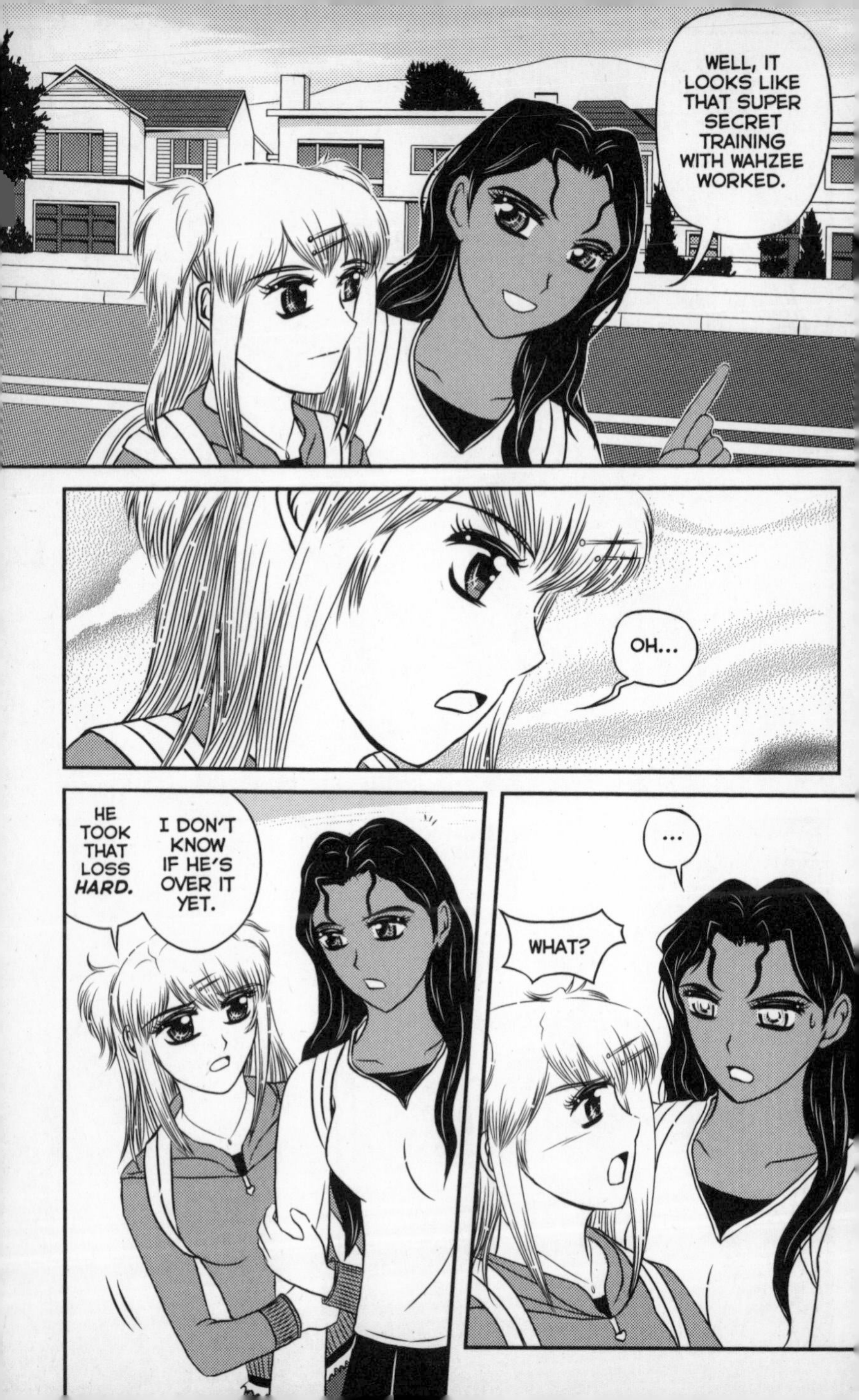

WELL, IT LOOKS LIKE THAT SUPER SECRET TRAINING WITH WAHZEE WORKED.
OH...
HE TOOK THAT LOSS *HARD.*
I DON'T KNOW IF HE'S OVER IT YET.
...
WHAT?

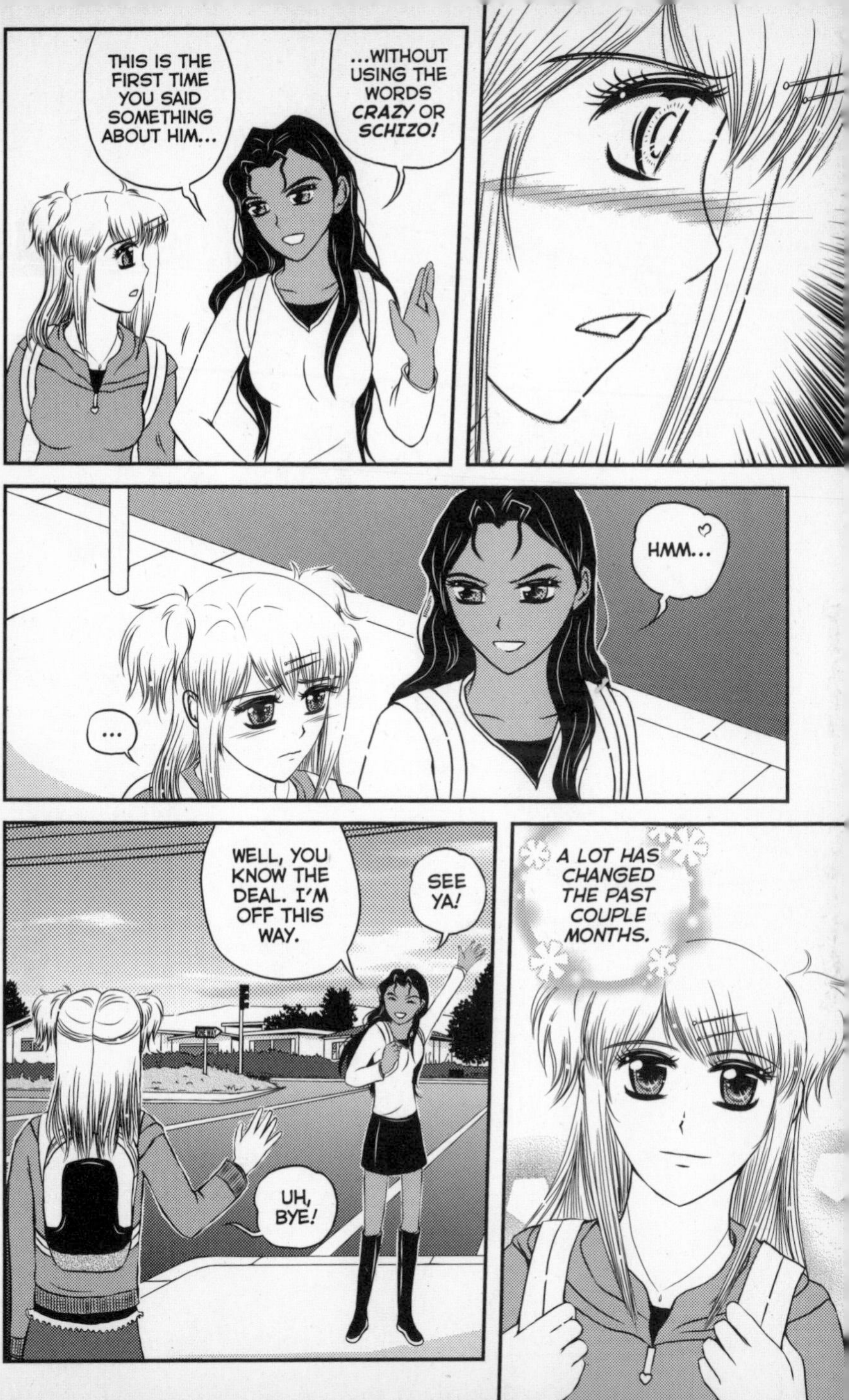
THIS IS THE FIRST TIME YOU SAID SOMETHING ABOUT HIM...
...WITHOUT USING THE WORDS *CRAZY* OR *SCHIZO!*
HMM...
...
WELL, YOU KNOW THE DEAL. I'M OFF THIS WAY.
SEE YA!
UH, BYE!
A LOT HAS CHANGED THE PAST COUPLE MONTHS.

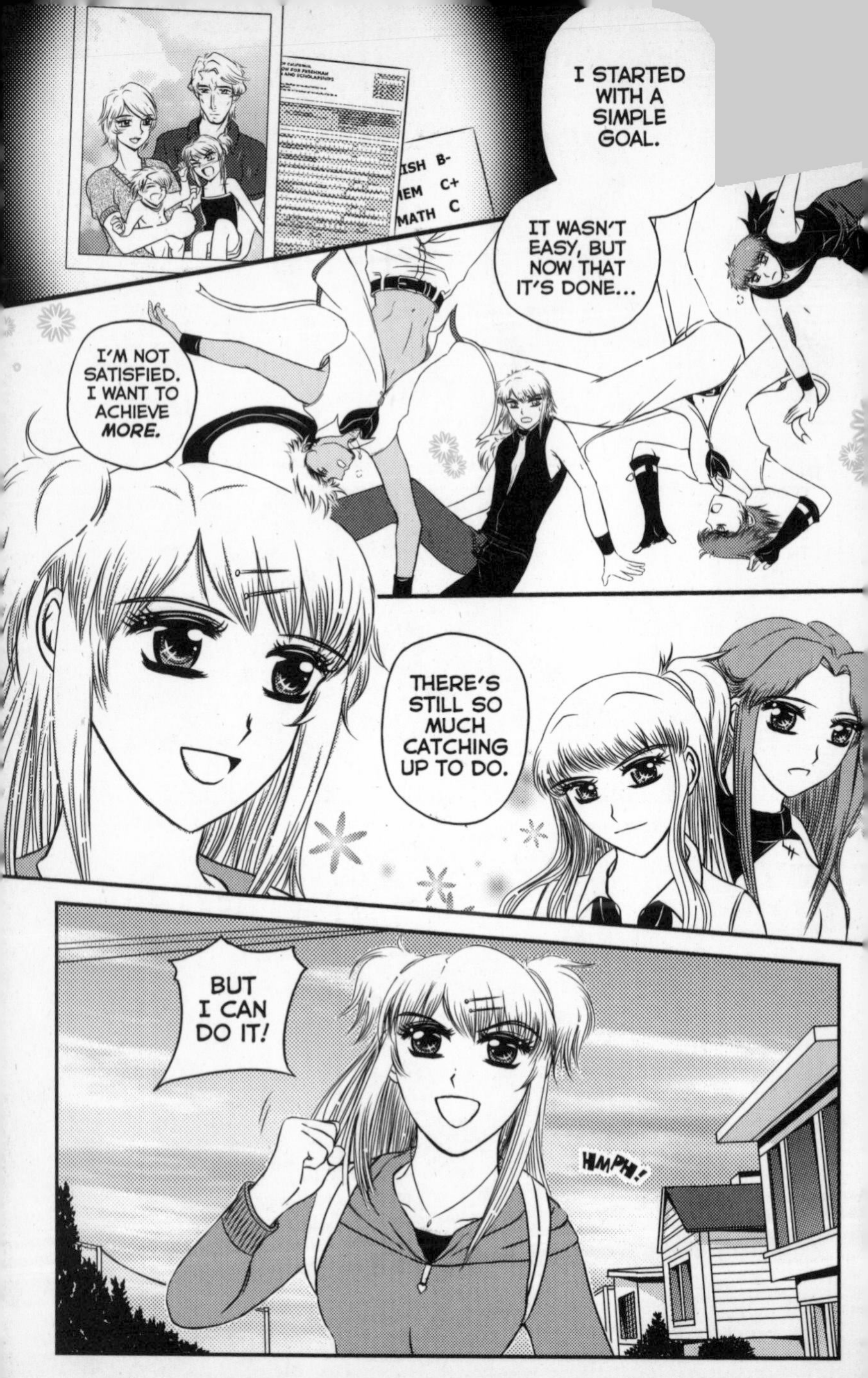
ISH B-
HEM C+
MATH C
I STARTED WITH A SIMPLE GOAL.
IT WASN'T EASY, BUT NOW THAT IT'S DONE...
I'M NOT SATISFIED. I WANT TO ACHIEVE *MORE.*
THERE'S STILL SO MUCH CATCHING UP TO DO.
BUT I CAN DO IT!
HMPH!

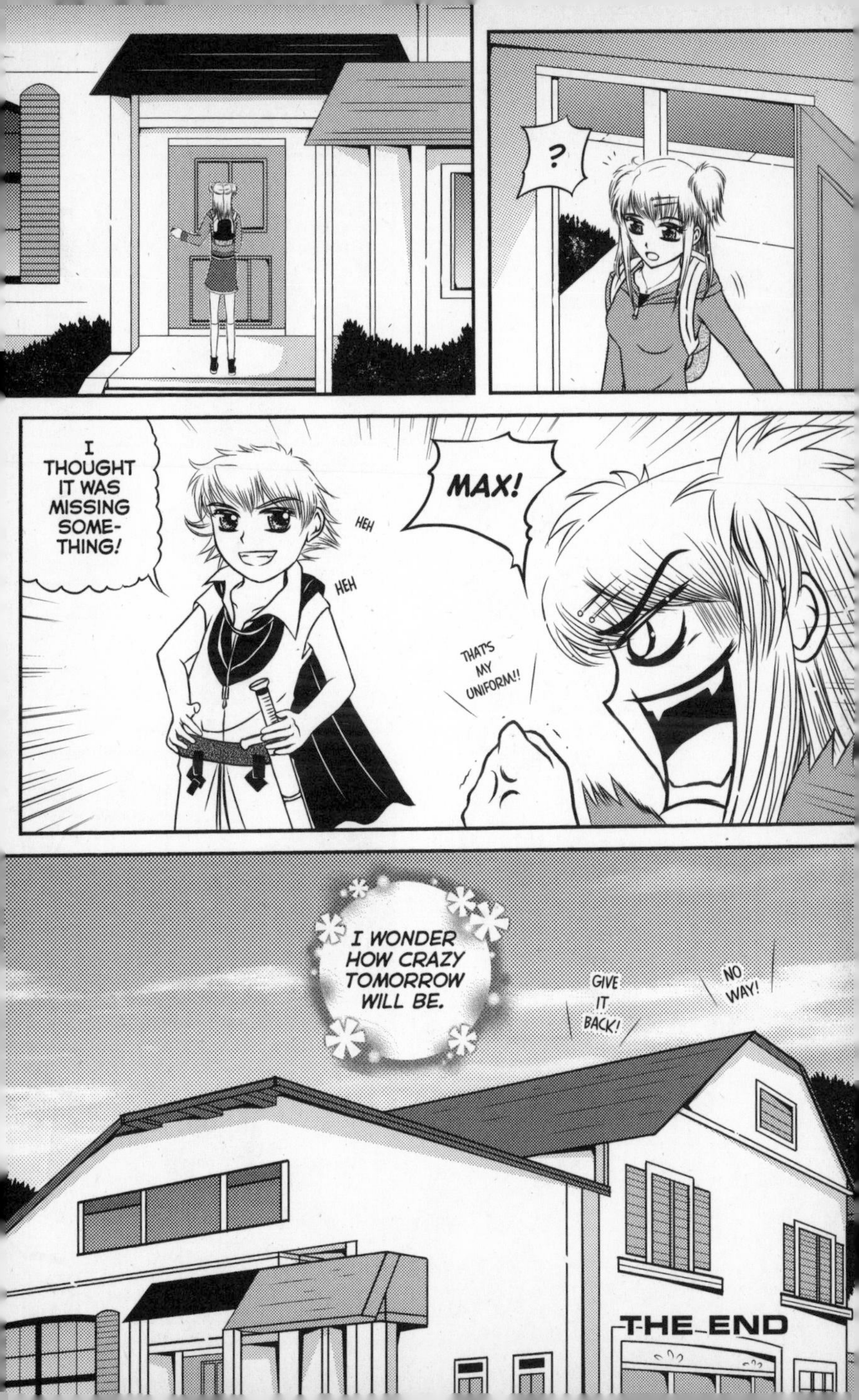
?
I THOUGHT IT WAS MISSING SOME-THING!
HEH
HEH
MAX!
THAT'S MY UNIFORM!!
I WONDER HOW CRAZY TOMORROW WILL BE.
GIVE IT BACK!
NO WAY!
THE END

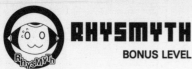

RHYSMYTH

BONUS LEVEL

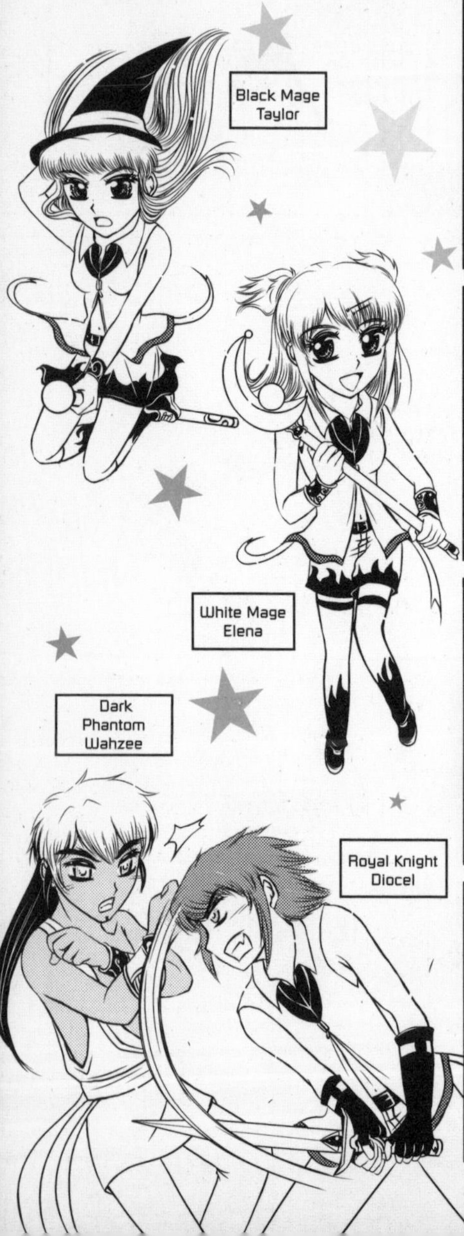

Black Mage Taylor
White Mage Elena
Dark Phantom Wahzee
Royal Knight Diocel

SHORT SHORTS

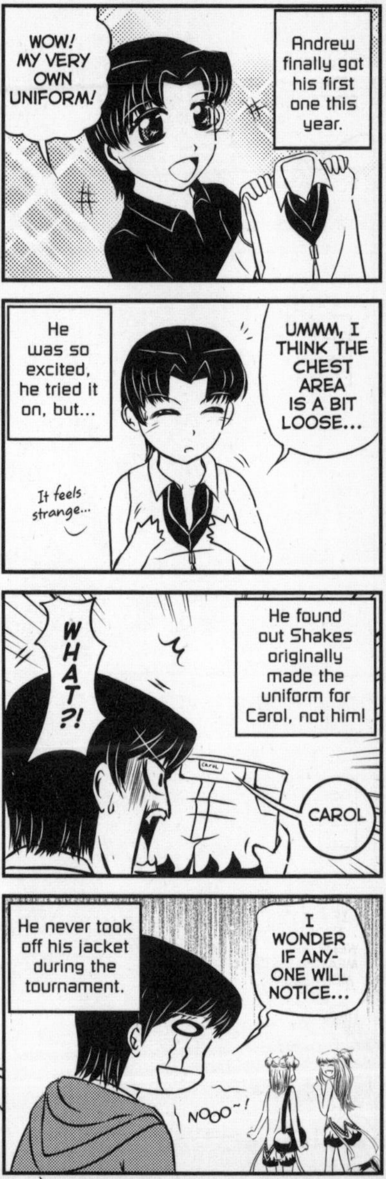

WOW! MY VERY OWN UNIFORM!
Andrew finally got his first one this year.
He was so excited, he tried it on, but...
UMMM, I THINK THE CHEST AREA IS A BIT LOOSE...
It feels strange...
WHAT?!
He found out Shakes originally made the uniform for Carol, not him!
Carol
CAROL
He never took off his jacket during the tournament.
I WONDER IF ANY-ONE WILL NOTICE...
NOOO~!

*Villager NPC, Andrew

LEVEL UP

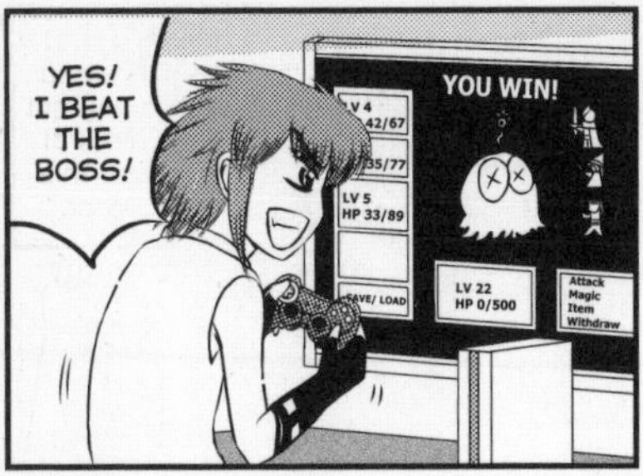
YES! I BEAT THE BOSS!
YOU WIN!
LV 5 HP 33/89
SAVE/ LOAD
LV 22 HP 0/500
Attack Magic Item Withdraw

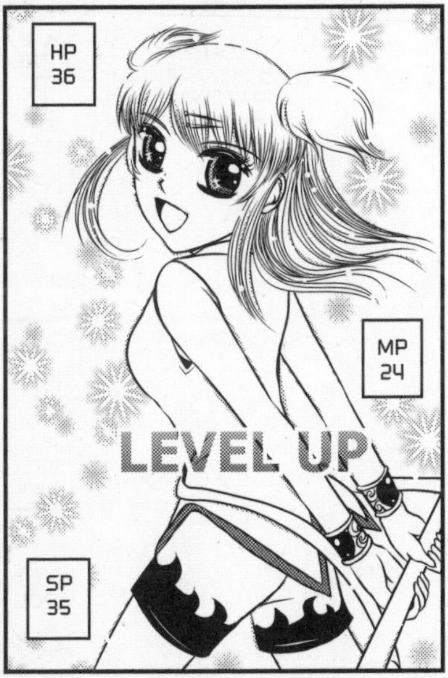
HP 36
MP 24
LEVEL UP
SP 35

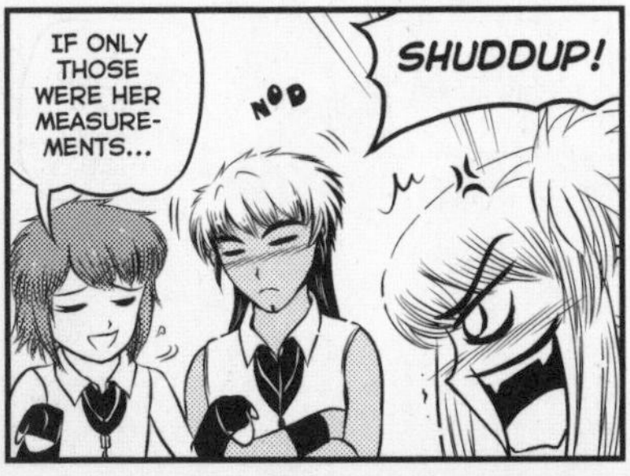
IF ONLY THOSE WERE HER MEASUREMENTS...
NOD
SHUDDUP!

VIDEOTUBE

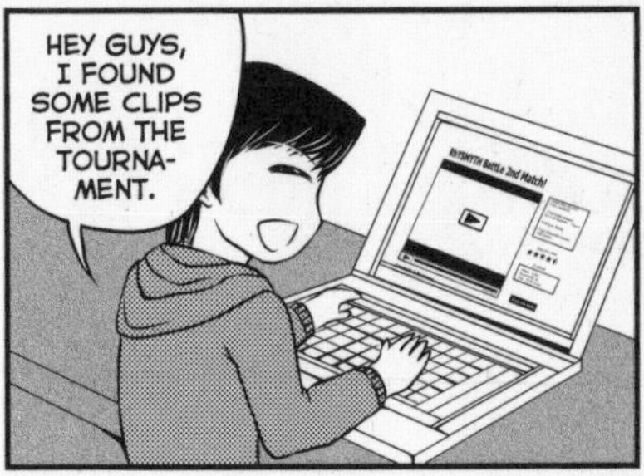
HEY GUYS, I FOUND SOME CLIPS FROM THE TOURNAMENT.

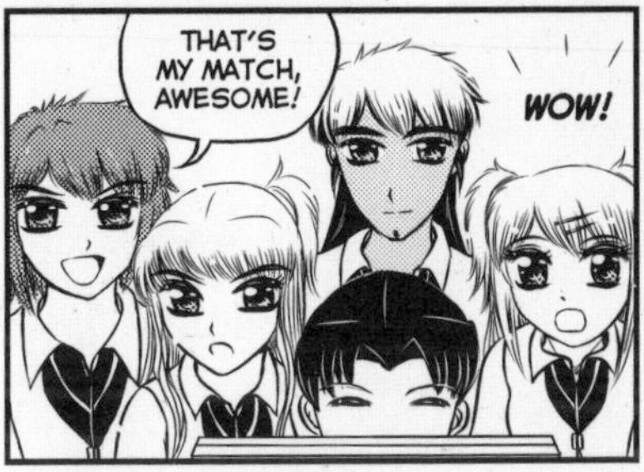
THAT'S MY MATCH, AWESOME!
WOW!

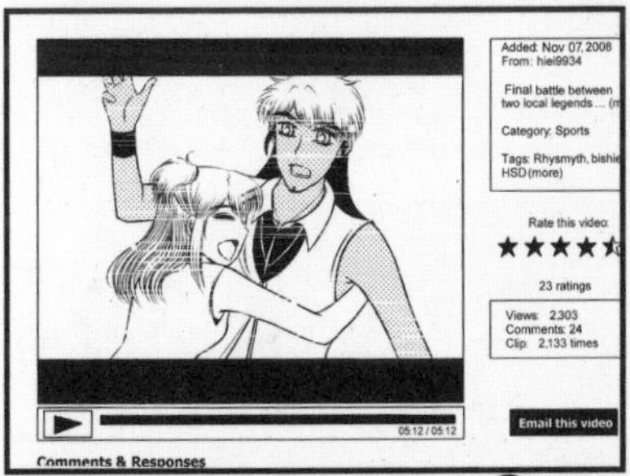
Added: Nov 07, 2008
From: hiei9934
Final battle between two local legends ...
Category: Sports
Rate this video
23 ratings
Views: 2,303
Comments: 24
Clip: 2,133 times
05:12 / 05:12
Email this video
Comments & Responses

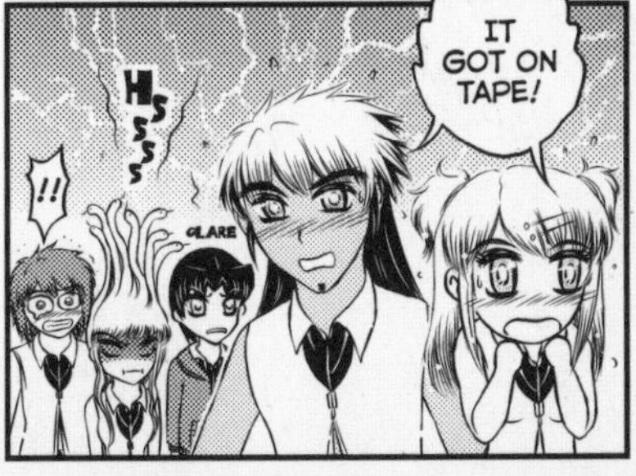
IT GOT ON TAPE!
HISSSS
!!
GLARE

PAIRINGS

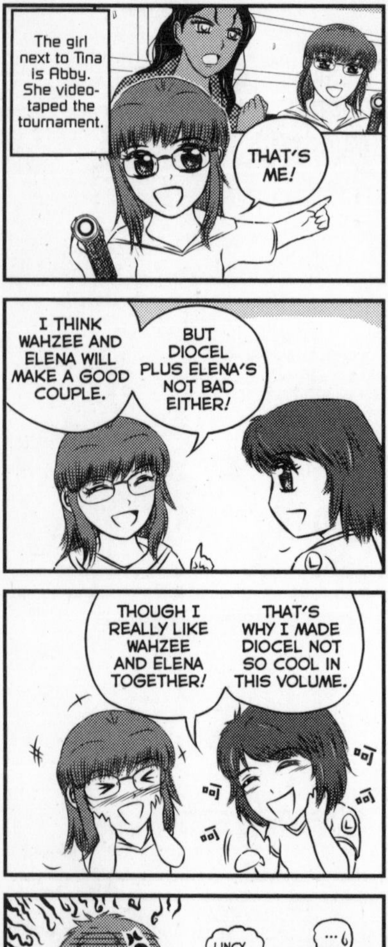

The girl next to Tina is Abby. She video-taped the tournament.
THAT'S ME!
I THINK WAHZEE AND ELENA WILL MAKE A GOOD COUPLE.
BUT DIOCEL PLUS ELENA'S NOT BAD EITHER!
THOUGH I REALLY LIKE WAHZEE AND ELENA TOGETHER!
THAT'S WHY I MADE DIOCEL NOT SO COOL IN THIS VOLUME.
呵
呵
呵
呵
GRRR
LINCY...
...
殺

呵呵 = HO HO　　殺 = KILL

恋のきらめき★ダンシング

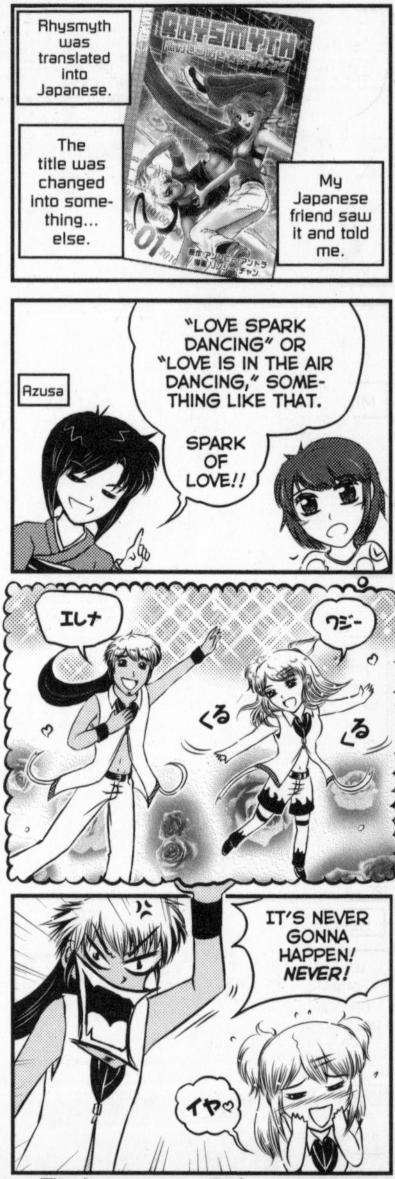

Rhysmyth was translated into Japanese.
RHYSMYTH
01
The title was changed into something... else.
My Japanese friend saw it and told me.
Azusa
"LOVE SPARK DANCING" OR "LOVE IS IN THE AIR DANCING," SOMETHING LIKE THAT.
SPARK OF LOVE!!
エレナ
ワジー
くる
くる
IT'S NEVER GONNA HAPPEN! *NEVER!*
イヤ♡

エレナ = ELENA　　ワジー = WAHZEE

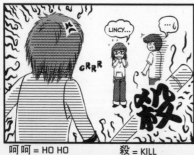

RHYSMYTH CONTEST

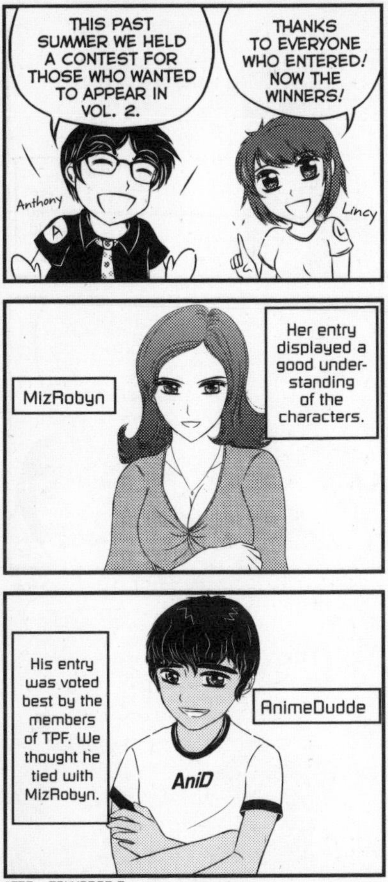
THIS PAST SUMMER WE HELD A CONTEST FOR THOSE WHO WANTED TO APPEAR IN VOL. 2.
THANKS TO EVERYONE WHO ENTERED! NOW THE WINNERS!
Anthony
Lincy
MizRobyn
Her entry displayed a good understanding of the characters.
His entry was voted best by the members of TPF. We thought he tied with MizRobyn.
AnimeDudde
AniD

*TPF = TOKYOPOP Forum

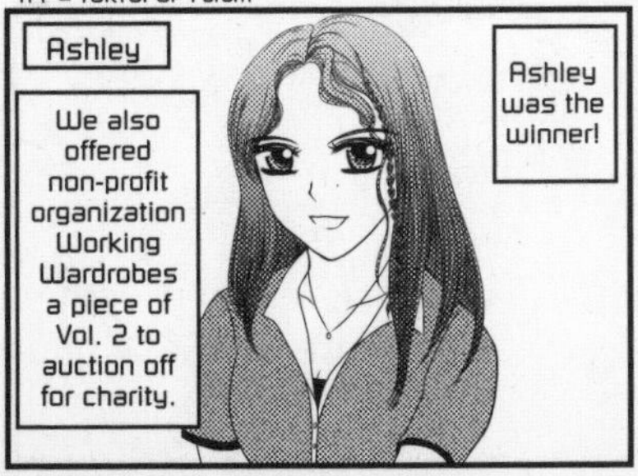
Ashley
We also offered non-profit organization Working Wardrobes a piece of Vol. 2 to auction off for charity.
Ashley was the winner!

Try to find them all in the book!

WATCH OUT! AniD SEXY LASER BEAM ATTACK!

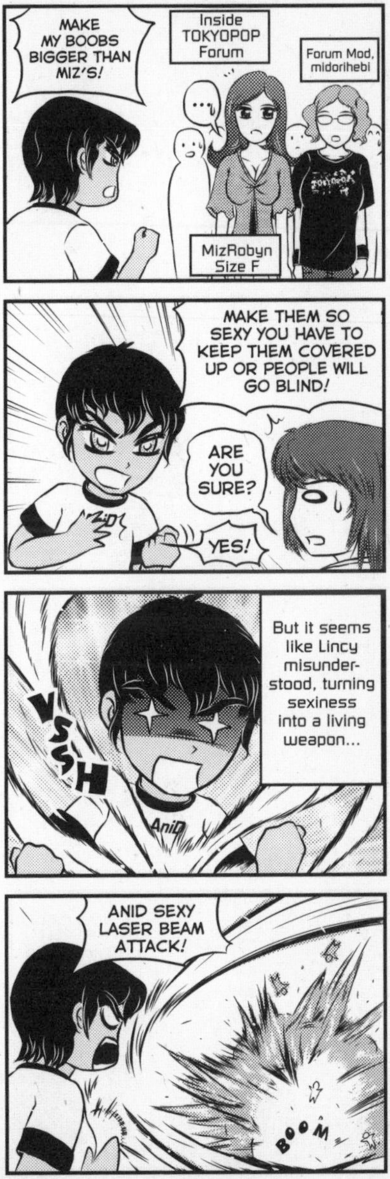
MAKE MY BOOBS BIGGER THAN MIZ'S!
Inside TOKYOPOP Forum
Forum Mod, midorihebi
...
MizRobyn Size F
MAKE THEM SO SEXY YOU HAVE TO KEEP THEM COVERED UP OR PEOPLE WILL GO BLIND!
ARE YOU SURE?
YES!
But it seems like Lincy misunderstood, turning sexiness into a living weapon...
VSSH
AniD
ANID SEXY LASER BEAM ATTACK!
BOOM

Find them in the book, they're huge! :P

A WARM EMBRACE

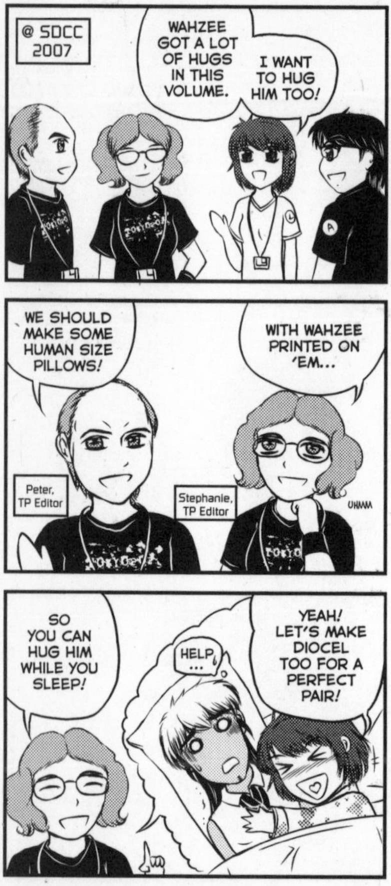
@ SDCC 2007
WAHZEE GOT A LOT OF HUGS IN THIS VOLUME.
I WANT TO HUG HIM TOO!
WE SHOULD MAKE SOME HUMAN SIZE PILLOWS!
WITH WAHZEE PRINTED ON 'EM...
Peter, TP Editor
Stephanie, TP Editor
UHMM
SO YOU CAN HUG HIM WHILE YOU SLEEP!
HELP ...
YEAH! LET'S MAKE DIOCEL TOO FOR A PERFECT PAIR!
......
LET'S MAKE ONE FOR SHAKES AND ANDREW!!

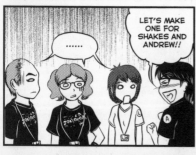

THE ADORABLE MISTER ED

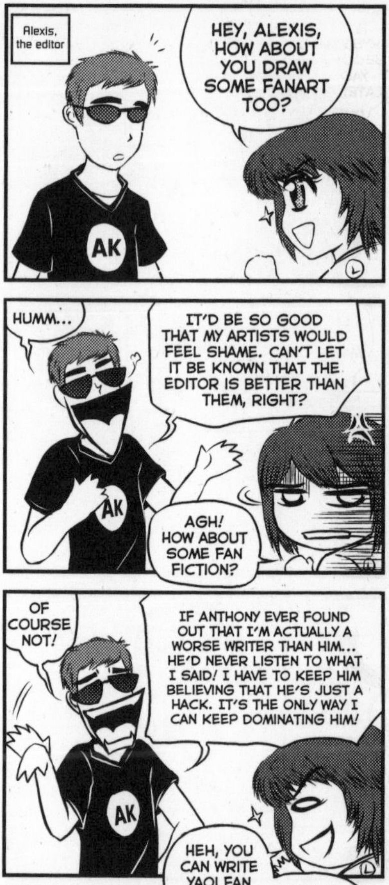
Alexis, the editor
HEY, ALEXIS, HOW ABOUT YOU DRAW SOME FANART TOO?
AK
HUMM...
IT'D BE SO GOOD THAT MY ARTISTS WOULD FEEL SHAME. CAN'T LET IT BE KNOWN THAT THE EDITOR IS BETTER THAN THEM, RIGHT?
AK
AGH! HOW ABOUT SOME FAN FICTION?
OF COURSE NOT!
IF ANTHONY EVER FOUND OUT THAT I'M ACTUALLY A WORSE WRITER THAN HIM... HE'D NEVER LISTEN TO WHAT I SAID! I HAVE TO KEEP HIM BELIEVING THAT HE'S JUST A HACK. IT'S THE ONLY WAY I CAN KEEP DOMINATING HIM!
AK
HEH, YOU CAN WRITE YAOI FAN FICTION--
--WHICH ANTHONY WOULD NEVER DO!
YOU KNOW HE DOES IT IN HIS FREE TIME UNDER A DIFFERENT NAME!
AK
AH-CHOO

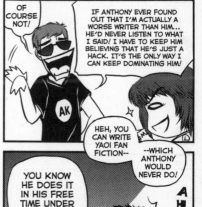

PERFECT COUPLES

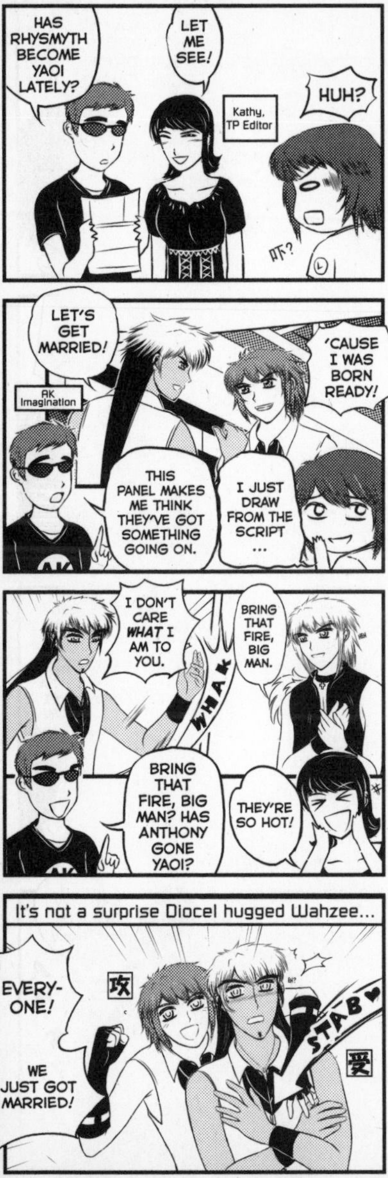
HAS RHYSMYTH BECOME YAOI LATELY?
LET ME SEE!
Kathy, TP Editor
HUH?
吓?
LET'S GET MARRIED!
AK Imagination
'CAUSE I WAS BORN READY!
THIS PANEL MAKES ME THINK THEY'VE GOT SOMETHING GOING ON.
I JUST DRAW FROM THE SCRIPT ...
I DON'T CARE *WHAT* I AM TO YOU.
WHAK
BRING THAT FIRE, BIG MAN.
BRING THAT FIRE, BIG MAN? HAS ANTHONY GONE YAOI?
THEY'RE SO HOT!
It's not a surprise Diocel hugged Wahzee...
EVERY-ONE!
攻
WE JUST GOT MARRIED!
STAB
受

NOTE: He is popular among the boys after all...

A LITTLE TOO MUCH COMPASSION?

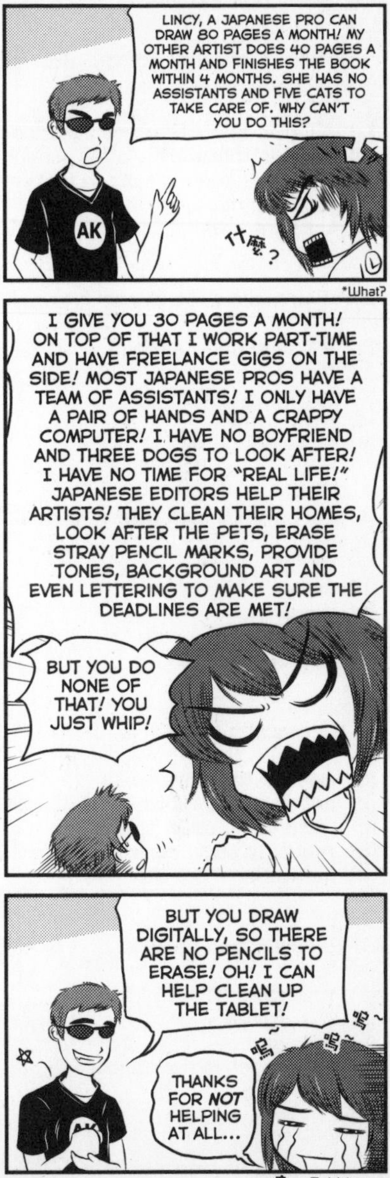
LINCY, A JAPANESE PRO CAN DRAW 80 PAGES A MONTH! MY OTHER ARTIST DOES 40 PAGES A MONTH AND FINISHES THE BOOK WITHIN 4 MONTHS. SHE HAS NO ASSISTANTS AND FIVE CATS TO TAKE CARE OF. WHY CAN'T YOU DO THIS?
什麼?
*What?
I GIVE YOU 30 PAGES A MONTH! ON TOP OF THAT I WORK PART-TIME AND HAVE FREELANCE GIGS ON THE SIDE! MOST JAPANESE PROS HAVE A TEAM OF ASSISTANTS! I ONLY HAVE A PAIR OF HANDS AND A CRAPPY COMPUTER! I HAVE NO BOYFRIEND AND THREE DOGS TO LOOK AFTER! I HAVE NO TIME FOR "REAL LIFE!" JAPANESE EDITORS HELP THEIR ARTISTS! THEY CLEAN THEIR HOMES, LOOK AFTER THE PETS, ERASE STRAY PENCIL MARKS, PROVIDE TONES, BACKGROUND ART AND EVEN LETTERING TO MAKE SURE THE DEADLINES ARE MET!
BUT YOU DO NONE OF THAT! YOU JUST WHIP!
BUT YOU DRAW DIGITALLY, SO THERE ARE NO PENCILS TO ERASE! OH! I CAN HELP CLEAN UP THE TABLET!
嗚~ 嗚~ 嗚~
THANKS FOR *NOT* HELPING AT ALL...

嗚 = Sobbing

Which RhysMyth personality are you?

1. Finally! Friday has arrived after a long, grinding week at school. You plan on...

(a) hanging out with your best friend.
(b) running three miles after school, like you always do.
(c) stocking up on snacks to fuel your 12-hour gaming session.
(d) planning out every single day of next week.
(e) taking a break from having to look good all the time.

2. If you had a superpower, it would be...

(a) extreme multitasking!
(b) flight!
(c) indestructible skin!
(d) mind control!
(e) sonic screams!

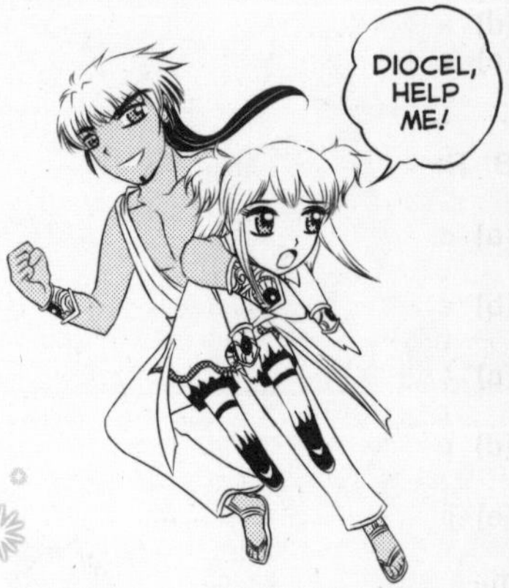
DIOCEL, HELP ME!

3. Your favorite food usually tastes...

(a) tangy
(b) spicy
(c) sweet
(d) mild
(e) extreme

4. Your ideal future job is...

(a) ruler of the world!
(b) nothing that involves gracefulness!
(c) trivia game show champion!
(d) reality tv show personal trainer!
(e) motivational speaker!

5. You most look up to...

(a) yourself–in the mirror.
(b) your friend.
(c) your parents.
(d) your coaches and teachers.
(e) your rival.

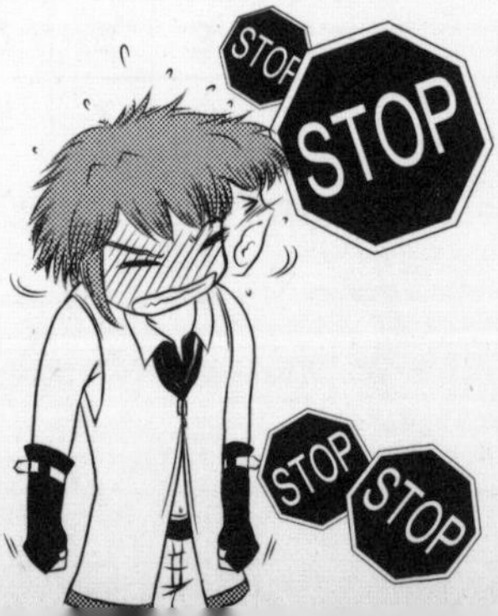
STOP
STOP
STOP
STOP

6. Before you know it, two months have passed and your hair has grown too long. You...

(a) notice it for a second but then concentrate on more important things...thus allowing your hair to continue growing even longer.
(b) KNOW the first sentence must be a joke. You never would have let that happen!
(c) ask your older sister to bring out the rice bowl again (minus rice inside).
(d) cut it right before that next big event in your life.
(e) get the same haircut you've always had at the same place.

7. If you could choose any animal for a pet, whether it be prehistoric, cryptozoological or natural, what would it be?

(a) something cute, safe and low-maintenance, like a goldfish.
(b) a chobobo (large yellow bird, RPG creature).
(c) Cerberus, the three-headed dog.
(d) a unicorn.
(e) a frog princess.

8. The most embarrassing moment of your life involved...

(a) super glue...and lots of it (your eyes never quite worked the same way ever again).
(b) accidentally calling someone by another name—that name really belonged to someone who didn't exist.
(c) a certain younger sibling, an audience of relatives and their constantly rolling home video cameras.
(d) people who no longer remember it or have been coerced into a vow of strict silence!
(e) just one other person...

Turn the book upside down to calculate your score!

	1.	2.	3.	4.	5.	6.	7.	8.
a	1	4	3	5	5	2	1	4
b	2	2	5	1	2	5	3	3
c	3	1	1	4	1	4	2	1
d	4	5	4	2	4	3	1	5
e	5	3	2	3	3	1	4	2

Match up your answer with the point values, add them all up and find out who you are!

To the Answers

WHO YOU ARE!!!

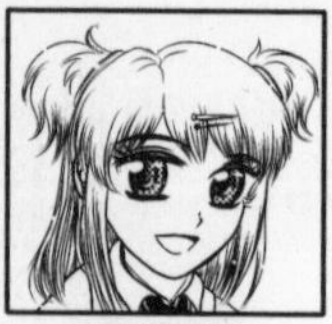

ELENA

8 — 13 points

You are ELENA. Lighthearted and kind, you tend to look for the best in every situation. Self-confidence is not a high as you'd hope; difficult situations make you feel like you're in over your head. You are clumsy, yet sweet and endearing to most people.

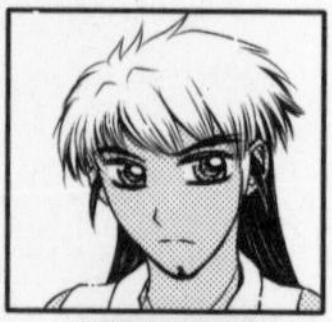

WAHZEE

14 — 20 points

You are WAHZEE. Intense and passionate, you work hard to achieve the goals you set for yourself. You carry a sense of responsibility toward others and constantly feel the pressure to succeed. You find solace in the loyalty of the few friends you have.

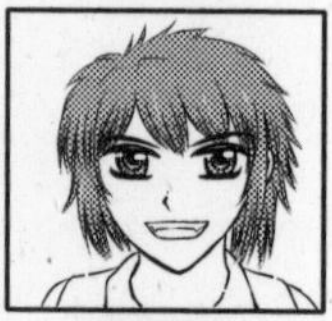

DIOCEL

21 — 28 points

You are DIOCEL. Energetic and talented, you balance your multiple and diverse interests with a practical nature. You are geeky, athletic,smart and handsome–yet you still have trouble when it comes to straightforwardly wooing the ladies.

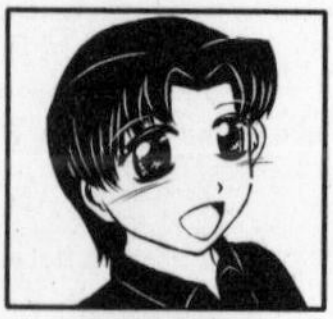

ANDREW

29 — 35 points

You are ANDREW. Reliable and helpful, you do the best you can with your limited abilities. Never the center of attention, you are content to offer assistance from the sidelines. You have trouble expressing your deepest fears and desires.

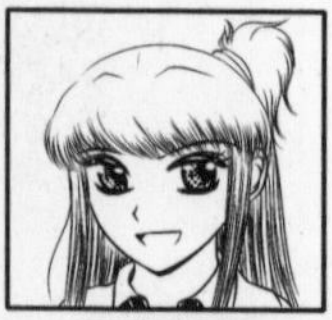

TAYLOR

36 — 40 points

You are TAYLOR. Confident and talented, you command the admiration and attention of others. You never settle for being second best, but run the risk of being considered bossy and pushy. You are a natural leader.

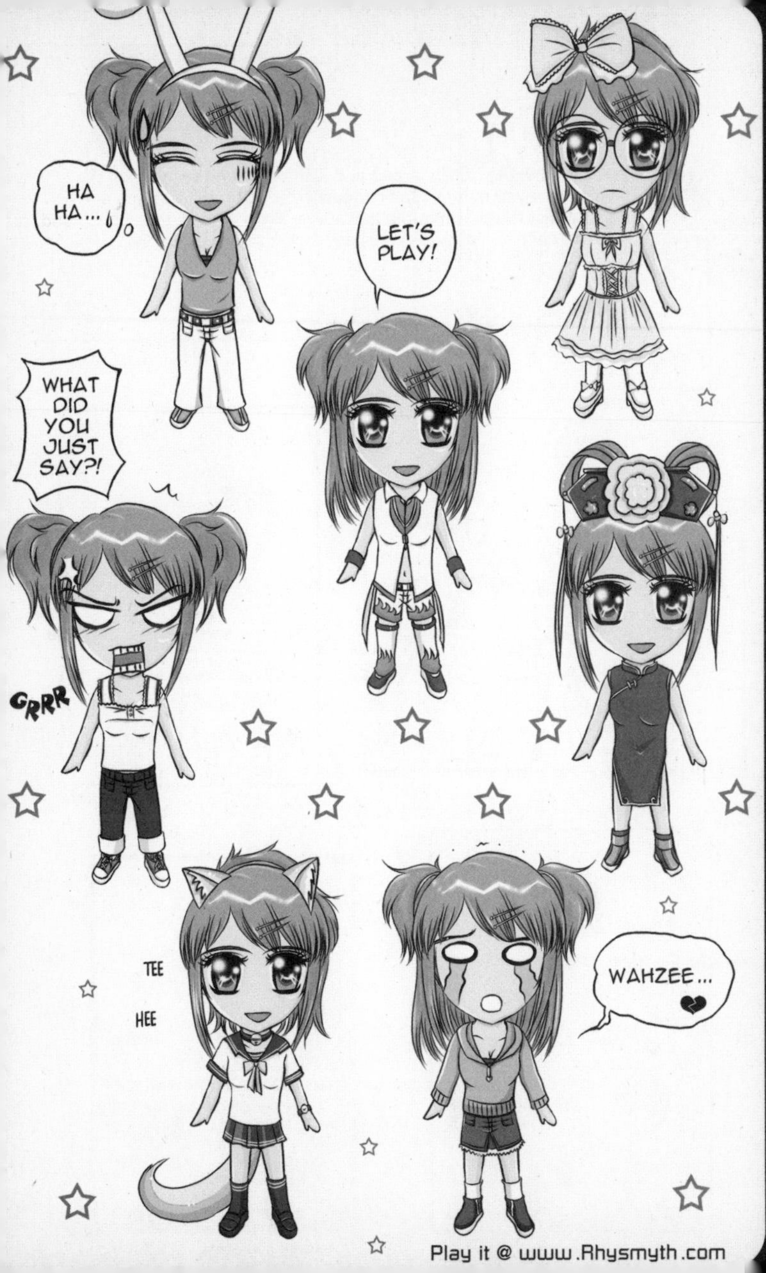
HA HA...
LET'S PLAY!
WHAT DID YOU JUST SAY?!
GRRR
TEE HEE
WAHZEE...
Play it @ www.Rhysmyth.com

Dress Up Elena
Rhysmyth

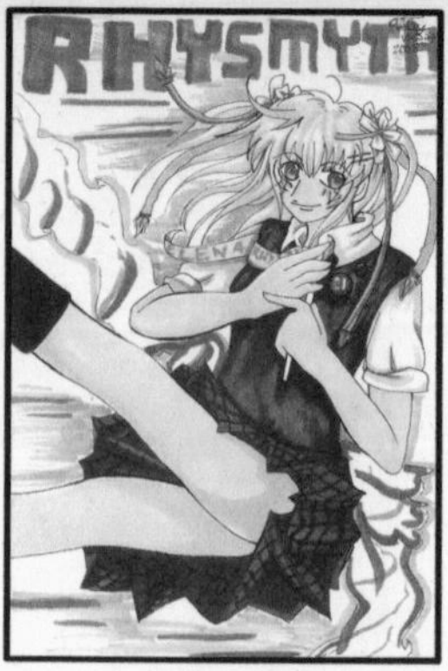
RHYSMYTH

Abby Clemens, CA

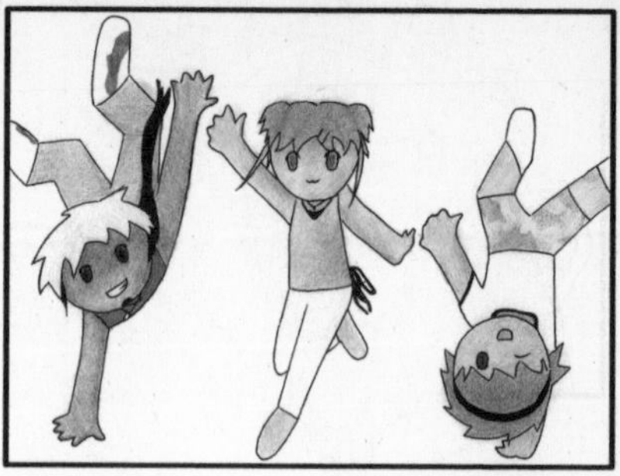

Ahi G. San Diego, CA

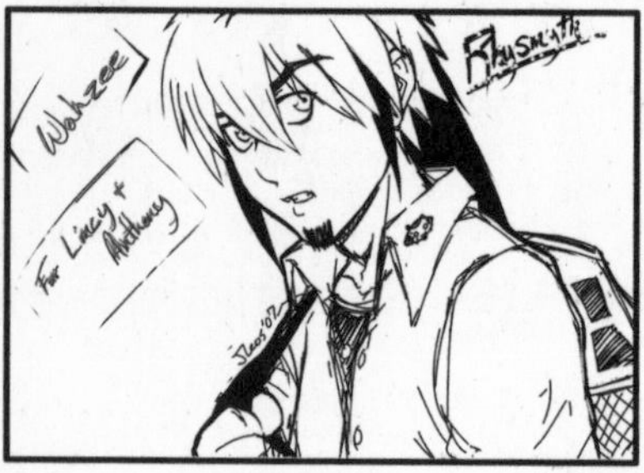
Wahzee
For Lincy + Anthony

Joshua

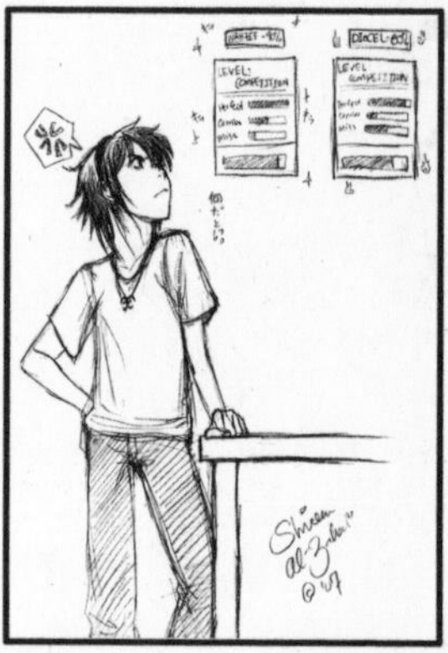

naruru

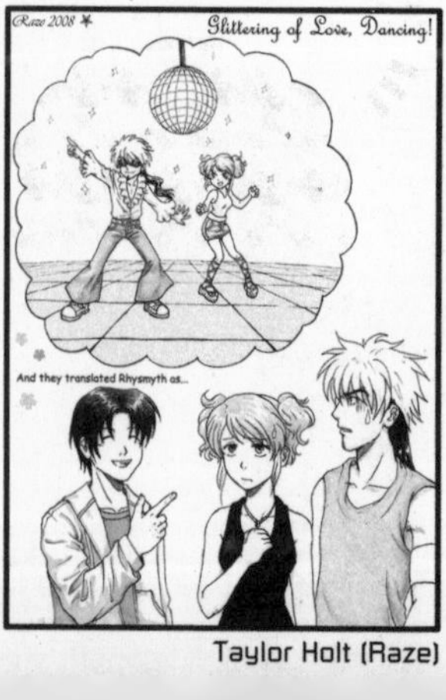
Raze 2008
Glittering of Love, Dancing!
And they translated Rhysmyth as...

Taylor Holt (Raze)

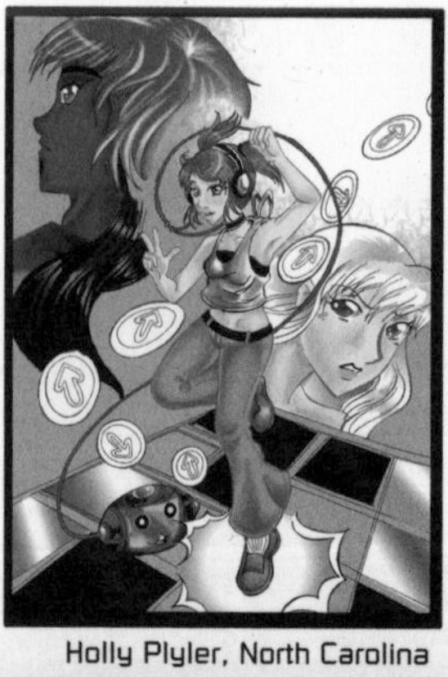

Holly Plyler, North Carolina

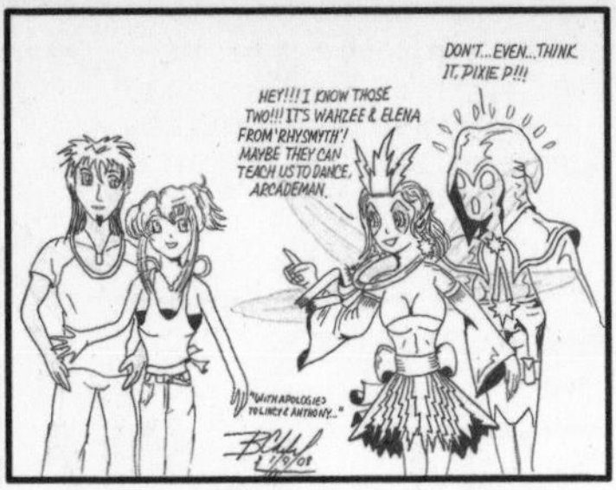
HEY!!! I KNOW THOSE TWO!!! IT'S WAHZEE & ELENA FROM 'RHYSMYTH'! MAYBE THEY CAN TEACH US TO DANCE, ARCADEMAN.
DON'T...EVEN...THINK IT, PIXIE P!!!
"WITH APOLOGIES TO LINCE & ANTHONY..."

Arcademan

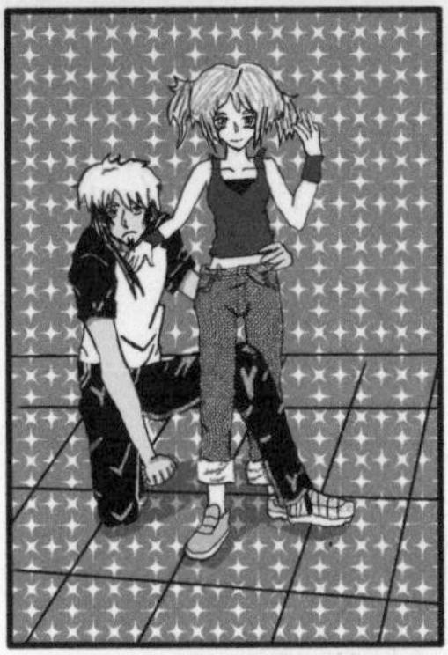

Christine Craft, MI

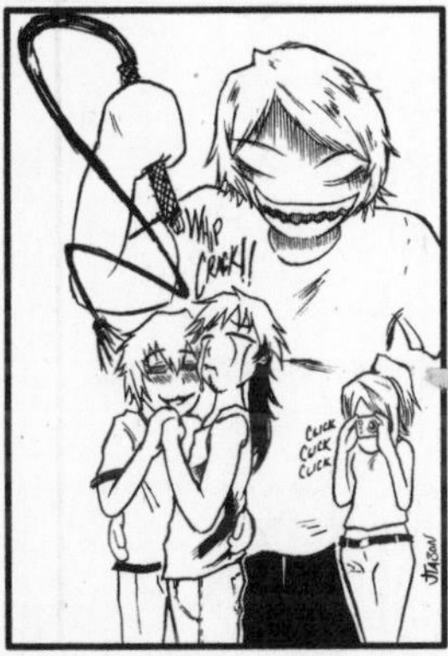
WHIP CRACK!!
CLICK CLICK CLICK

Josh Tabon

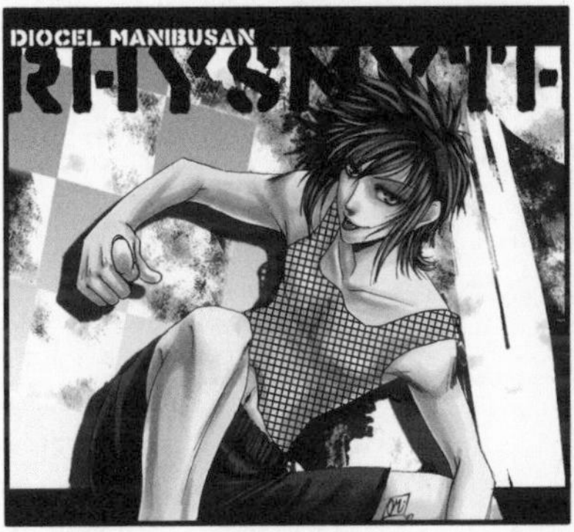
DIOCEL MANIBUSAN
RHYSMYTH

Omi

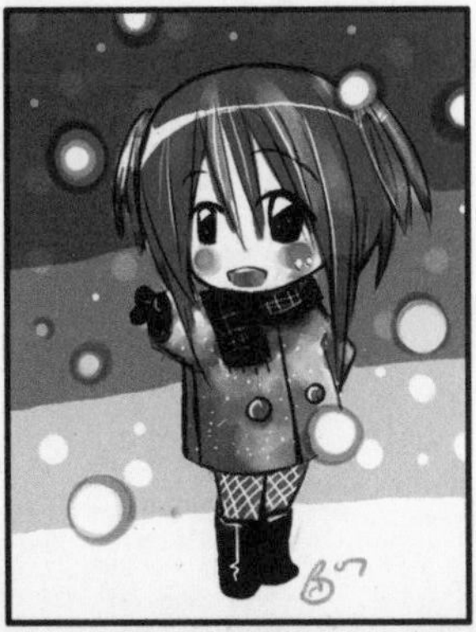

Brynn Handwerker/"Keeta"
Henderson, NV, USA

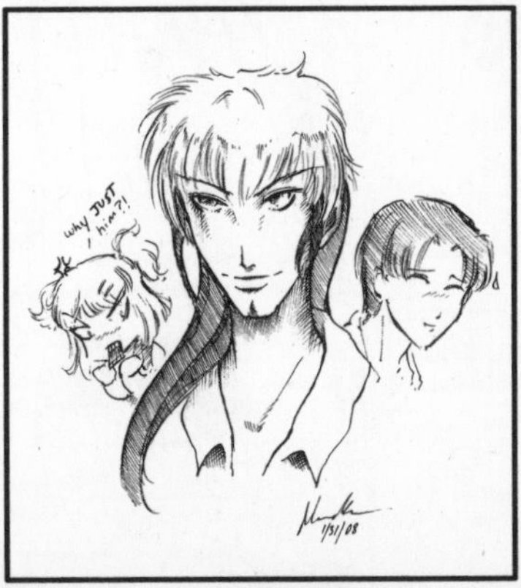
why JUST him?!

Serrifth
Las Vegas, NV, USA

A WORD FROM THE CREATORS:

Lincy and I have grown exponentially in our knowledge and love of the Rhysmyth characters since this all started. We had so much more in store for them! As it stands, Volumes 1 and 2 complete our first act. So we humbly ask you, faithful readers, to help spread the word and put Rhysmyth into as many hands as possible so that we may continue the story in the near future.

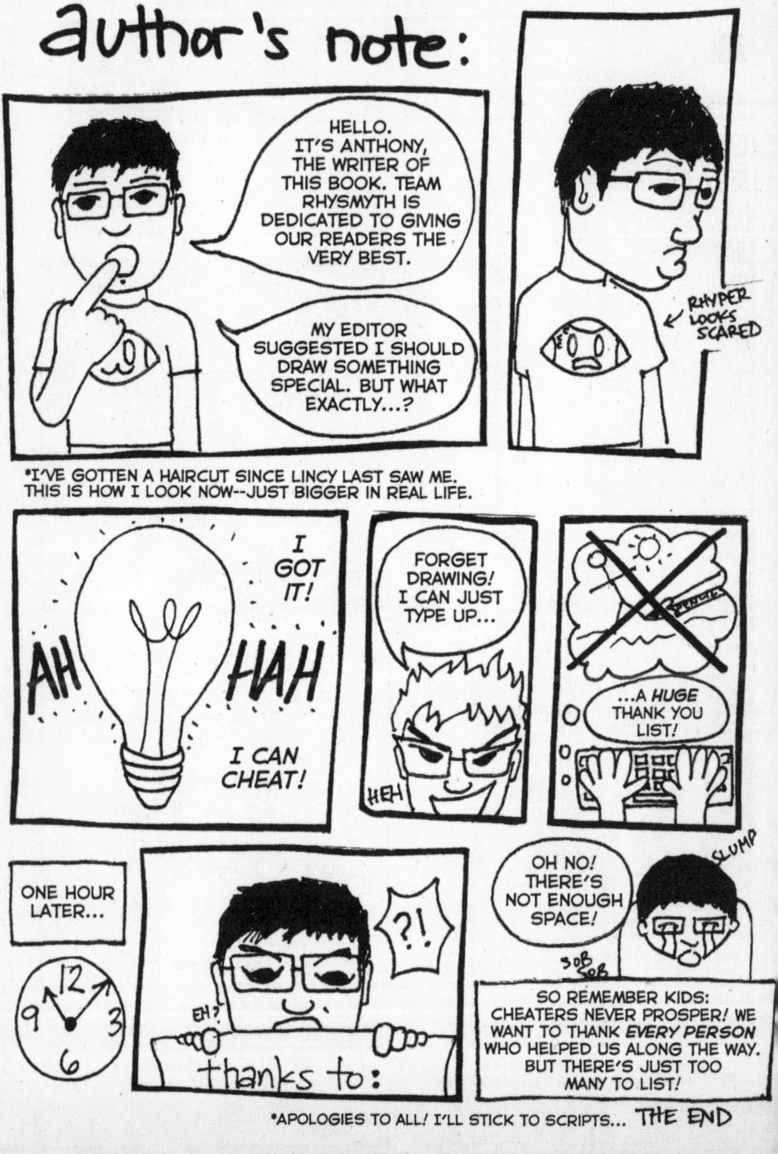
author's note:
HELLO. IT'S ANTHONY, THE WRITER OF THIS BOOK. TEAM RHYSMYTH IS DEDICATED TO GIVING OUR READERS THE VERY BEST.
MY EDITOR SUGGESTED I SHOULD DRAW SOMETHING SPECIAL. BUT WHAT EXACTLY...?
RHYPER LOOKS SCARED
*I'VE GOTTEN A HAIRCUT SINCE LINCY LAST SAW ME. THIS IS HOW I LOOK NOW--JUST BIGGER IN REAL LIFE.
I GOT IT!
AH HAH
I CAN CHEAT!
FORGET DRAWING! I CAN JUST TYPE UP...
HEH
...A *HUGE* THANK YOU LIST!
ONE HOUR LATER...
12
9
3
6
?!
EH?
thanks to:
OH NO! THERE'S NOT ENOUGH SPACE!
SLUMP
SOB SOB
SO REMEMBER KIDS: CHEATERS NEVER PROSPER! WE WANT TO THANK *EVERY PERSON* WHO HELPED US ALONG THE WAY. BUT THERE'S JUST TOO MANY TO LIST!
*APOLOGIES TO ALL! I'LL STICK TO SCRIPTS...
THE END

TOKYOPOP.com

WHERE MANGA LIVES!

JOIN the
TOKYOPOP community:
www.TOKYOPOP.com

**COME AND PREVIEW THE
HOTTEST MANGA AROUND!**

CREATE...
UPLOAD...
DOWNLOAD...
BLOG...
CHAT...
VOTE...
LIVE!!!!

WWW.TOKYOPOP.COM HAS:

- Exclusives
- News
- Contests
- Games
- Rising Stars of Manga
- iManga
- and more...

TOKYOPOP.COM 2.0
NOW LIVE!

© Sang-Sun Park and TOKYOPOP Inc.

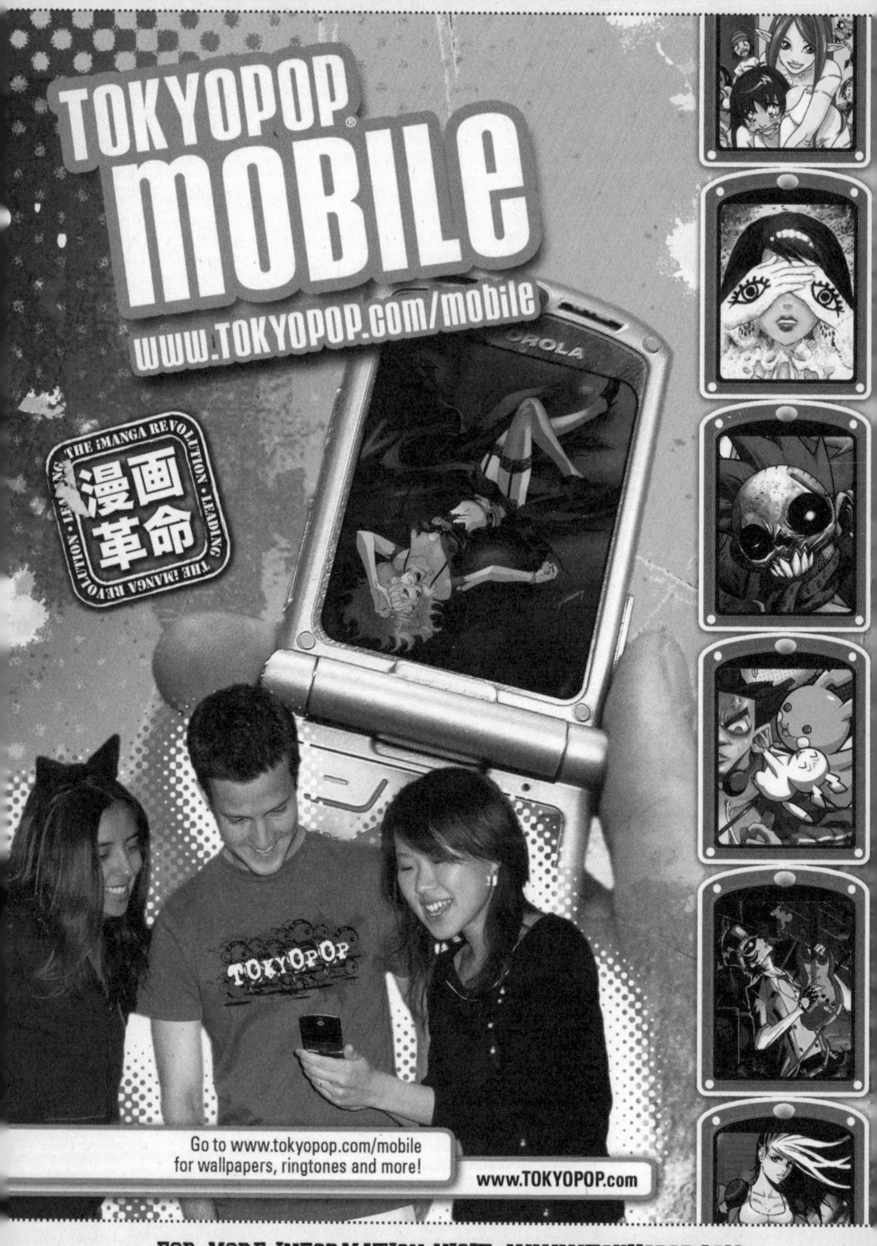
TOKYOPOP
MOBILE
www.TOKYOPOP.com/mobile
THE iMANGA REVOLUTION · LEADING THE iMANGA REVOLUTION · LEADING
漫画革命
Go to www.tokyopop.com/mobile
for wallpapers, ringtones and more!
www.TOKYOPOP.com